THE GARDENER OF EDEN

THE GARDENER OF EDEN

David Downie

PEGASUS CRIME

NEW YORK LONDON

THE GARDENER OF EDEN

Pegasus Crime is an imprint of
Pegasus Books Ltd.
148 W 37th Street, 13th Floor
New York, NY 10018

Copyright © 2019 by David Downie

First Pegasus Books cloth edition March 2019

Interior design by Maria Fernandez

Library of Congress Cataloging-in-Publication Data is available.

ISBN: 978-1-64313-004-0

10 9 8 7 6 5 4 3 2 1

Printed in the United States of America
Distributed by W. W. Norton & Company
www.pegasusbooks.us

In memory of my father,
Charles E. Downie,
the real gardener of Eden.

PART ONE

Homecoming

"She was Eve after the fall, but before the
bitterness of it was felt. She wore life as a
rose in her bosom."
—O. Henry, *Cabbages and Kings*

ONE

Beverley could hear the surf over the wind. Rollers slammed into the totem pole–shaped pinnacles of stone edging the beach, sending up plumes of spray. Looking down from the bluff, she watched the man in the hooded black windbreaker crossing the expanse of wet black sand. Reaching the loose gravel where it showed gray against the blueness of the sky, he slowed, scrambled over broken shale, stooped to scoop up something shiny, then climbed the steep ravine toward the parking lot where Beverley stood, buffeted by intermittent gusts.

The man's stride, strangely sure-footed, was long and determined, his head was bent, and his noticeably large hands were clasped behind his back, as if he were a prisoner cuffed from behind.

"A crow," Beverley said to herself. "No, a monk, in a cowl, with something around his neck." The thought of ecclesiastics took her back to the Convent of Jesus and Mary. It sent a shudder from her fleshy nape to her dimpled knees. As the man crested the bluff, his silhouette's almost supernatural effect on her was spoiled by the close-up vision of bright green-and-yellow hiking boots laced together and dangling over his shoulders.

"I'm so awfully sorry," she said in a loud soprano voice, startling him as he neared the spot where his RV had been parked for the last ten days. "Another foot and it might have done some damage." Beverley touched the pearls at her throat and smiled, pointing at his vehicle.

Unzipping the windbreaker and pulling back his hood, the man Beverley had come to think of as the Mystery Man let his flowing gray hair and bushy beard tumble free.

She took a step back. "I'd swear you were Jesus Christ," she gasped. Then she let out a nervous laugh and added, "Or maybe Rasputin."

With deep-set ice-blue eyes sparkling under cascading eyebrows, the man surveyed her, the fallen tree, its tip curled across the roof of his RV, and the large rumbling patrol car parked at a dramatic angle a few feet away, as if it had skidded sideways to a halt. The engine of the four-wheel-drive sheriff's department Interceptor SUV clacked and shook in time with the swirling lights on its roof. The man's shaggy brows rose and fell as if synced with the engine. Beverley wondered if he would turn on his heels and run back to the beach.

"It broke your fence good, Ms. Beverley," a nasal voice bellowed over the wind. The wild-looking man pivoted as a young, muscular sheriff's deputy came around the back of the RV and waved him into the lee of the wind. "Looks like you were both lucky," the deputy shouted again, cupping his hands. He eyed the stranger with obvious distaste, seeming to smell overripe cheese. "Is this your vehicle?" he asked, letting his hands fall to his sides. The right one rested atop a bulging holster, the other found and felt a set of handcuffs.

The bearded man shaded his eyes from the heatless morning sun, shifting his face out of the glare. He watched the deputy's blunt fingers. "Yes, Officer." His voice rang dry, like boots on gravel, a voice unused for days at a time. "Yes," he repeated, louder, clearing his throat.

"Seen anything unusual on the beach?" the sheriff's deputy barked, glancing past the man at the breakers.

"No, sir."

"No shipwrecks, sea monsters, or cadavers," Beverley interjected, "or other objects and phenomena clearly related to a tree falling on a camper in a parking lot?"

The deputy's shoulders rose toward his earlobes, the nasal tone of his voice tightening. "If you see something unusual," he snapped, "make sure you call us."

"Now that I think of it," said the bearded stranger, his voice warming, "there is a wild pig on the beach right below, dead and outgassing."

"That's what I smell." The deputy grunted. "Just a hog?" he asked. "Nothing else?"

The man thought for a beat. "Nothing," he said, "except for the oil cans and plastic, and something I'd guess was a crushed shopping cart. But it was way out in the surf, so I couldn't see it clearly."

"They must've been shopping for seafood," Beverley said.

Ignoring her, the deputy grunted again. "What about this vehicle? Any damage?"

The bearded man climbed without apparent effort onto the RV's stairs. Reaching with one long arm, he lifted the tree off a folding bicycle strapped to the roof. Again, apparently without effort, he walked the tree's floppy tip to the ground at the deputy's jackbooted feet. "Nothing," he said. "It's soft and fresh." Crushing a fistful of pale green cypress leaves, the man smelled his fingertips. He opened his palm to the plump woman and the deputy. Both stepped back, the sheriff's deputy instinctively unsnapping his holster. *"Macrocarpa,"* the stranger said in a pleasant baritone, making the word operatic while trying to hide his surprise at the deputy's overreaction. "More like lime than lemon at this time of year," he added. "What a shame it came down."

"Macro-carpa?" the deputy asked. "Sounds like some disease."

"It's Latin," said Beverley. "That's deadly, if you don't like the pope."

The deputy laughed convulsively, wiping at his mustachioed mouth with the back of one large hairy hand. "Will you ever let up, Ms. Beverley?" he said, shaking his head. "We have no problem with the pope. He doesn't like us."

Stepping out of earshot back into the wind, the sheriff's deputy cupped his hands, enunciating slowly into his helmet mike. His closely shaved, fully fleshed, noticeably featureless tanned cheeks telegraphed the gist of his report as Beverley and the stranger looked on. "Clean brand-name clothes and high-tech hiking boots," he said. "Clean fingernails and toenails—he's barefoot. Late-model Sockeye recreational vehicle. No rust, new tires, New York plates, no mud or dust on them. Caucasian, male, older, educated, unusually tall and wiry. He came through the checkpoint on Highway 12 a couple weeks ago. He must be in the data bank. An eccentric urban individual, not a vagrant, probably harmless, though he likes trees and talks funny. I might fine him or bring him in for questioning and make him move on."

Fitting a sanitized smile over his face, the deputy walked back to Beverley and the man. *"Macro-carpa?"* he asked again. "I thought it was a plain old cypress tree."

"That depends on what you mean by plain old," the man answered, trying to sound affable.

"Branches come down all the time." Beverley sighed, tossing a strand of bright orange-red hair off her forehead. "But this is the first certified entire cypress tree I've lost in three years. I'm inclined to ask for my money back." She let out a peal of girlish laughter. It did not match her age, girth, or dyed hair. The stranger could not help noticing her pink stretch top with a white, skirt-like frill at the bottom, and her mauve stretch pants. They were patterned with eights and nines of clubs and bloomed beneath her. Remarkably large, her head was joined seamlessly to her collarbone. Around the flesh that passed for a neck was the string of pearls she touched, moving them back and forth like worry beads.

"You been around three years already?" the deputy asked, chuckling despite himself. "It's good the motel's up and running."

"It's not a motel, Tom, it's a resort," she teased. "Now that I know they're *macrocarpa* trees my occupancy rate is sure to rise." Beverley laughed her nervous, high-pitched, girlish laugh again. "No need to fill out a report," she told Tom. "They'll never pay, my deductible is too high."

"That's all right by me," the beachcomber said.

Tom smoothed his apricot mustache and licked his lips. They were thick and split by the wind and sun. The bearded man glanced over and read THOMAS SMITHSON off the name tag pinned to the deputy's military-style khaki uniform. It wiggled when his bulging chest and arms flexed. "Thing is," said Tom, "I'm supposed to file something, it's the regulations. You are occupying two parking spaces when you're only entitled to one. I ought to fine you and make you move." He paused again, weighing whether it was worth the hassle. Beverley would let the whole town know he was bullying an old man again.

"The lot sure is full to bursting," Beverley chimed in. "I'll bet the raccoons are awful mad this vehicle is hogging their space. They'll be wondering what any of this has to do with my tree and his camper. For the life of me, I don't know, but the ways of the law are many and mysterious, amen."

"He's parked where emergency vehicles come in," Tom objected.

"I've seen a few too many of those lately," she said.

"Well," Tom said, "if he can move over there"—he raised a paw toward the garbage cans—"I'll let him off, but he's got to leave soon." He screwed up his lips. "Since the tree is yours, and the fence is yours," he added, "and there's no damage to this vehicle . . ." Scribbling on a narrow pad, he left the sentence to hang unfinished. Then he slipped the pad into a belt made heavy by the holster, Mace canister, truncheon, handcuffs, and radio transceiver. "You've been here about two weeks—"

"Ten days," the man interrupted. "The helpful woman at city hall said I can stay two weeks without a permit."

"Unless an officer of the peace asks you to move on."

"Why might he do that?"

The deputy grinned again, his mustache catching the sunlight, giving him the look of a calico cat, his eyes hidden by wraparound sunglasses. "For instance, if you were causing a public nuisance, or were in danger." Tom glanced at Beverley.

"Oh, he's no nuisance," she said, "you barely know he's here except to see him on the beach before dawn doing some yoga exercise routine, and then sometimes I smell a wood fire and pancakes and bacon." Her smile widened. "Until he got onto the *macrocarpa* trees, I wondered if he was a short-order cook. My guests keep asking me where the restaurant is, and why we don't have one. And he's very neat. He wired up those garbage cans when the wind blew them over last week, after the teenagers set them alight and shot them full of holes. I've seen him picking up litter in the lot, too, running after paper like a scene from that movie."

"What movie?"

"*The Paper Chase,*" Beverley said, then chortled, touching her pearls.

Tom fought off a smile. "I wouldn't mind some of that breakfast right now," he muttered.

"I could brew up some fresh coffee," Beverley offered, "there's a bag of leftover cinnamon rolls. The guests didn't want them, not healthy, they said, not organic."

Tom shook his head. "Can't do it." He grunted. Then he lowered his sunglasses and winked. "Seems you've been watching your new neighbor pretty close?"

"Just doing my patriotic duty," she said. "Isn't that what we're supposed to do?"

"Sure is," said Tom.

"Martial law," Beverley quipped.

"Don't pay attention to Ms. Beverley's jokes," Tom said, turning to the stranger. "It's a county-wide special ordinance. This is a free country."

"Well, you haven't outlawed my sense of humor yet," she said.

"Not yet," Tom echoed, "but we might."

The man turned away from the banter, glancing down the coast. Clearing his throat, he sang out, "No rain today?"

"No rain," Beverley confirmed. "It hardly ever rains, that's why people like it. No rain and no heat. Lots of wind and fog, though, you've got to love them or you're in trouble."

A gust kicked up, blowing sheets of dust across the lot. Pockets of morning fog still hung in the cypress trees and the scrub on the coastal hills. It lay in moist, aromatic tatters across the sloping grounds of the Eden Seaside Resort & Cottages, half hiding the signage. Only the glowing VACANCY sign stood out, its pink neon coils blinking.

"Out of state," the deputy remarked, indicating the license plate. "Like Ms. Beverley here?"

The bearded man raised his brows in mute response.

"On vacation?"

"That's it," he agreed, "and what a beautiful spot."

Unsure whether the man was being ironic, the deputy tipped his helmet back, remembered the built-in camera, and pulled the helmet back down. "You got a gun in that vehicle?"

"No, Officer," the man blurted out. He was about to add something about not liking guns but didn't have time.

"He can have one of mine," Beverley cut in, laughing her strange high-pitched laugh. "I've got a whole roomful of them."

Tom glared at the stranger. "You telling me you didn't hear them shooting off semiautomatics the night before last?"

"Woke the dead," Beverley said, "I should know. I've been in a coma most of my life."

The older man stroked his beard. "Officer, I am a sound sleeper, besides, the surf has been pretty loud."

"It sounds like Armageddon," Beverley put in. "Hellfire and semiautomatics, it's real comforting."

Tom thrust out his chin but could not repress another convulsive guffaw that soiled his mustache. Wiping away the strands of spittle, he looked sideways past the stranger. "Your RV spring a leak?"

"Two," Beverley said, shuffling to the far side of the RV, then walking back with two corks in her pudgy pink hands.

"Don't touch the evidence," Tom blurted.

"What evidence?" Beverley asked. "He hasn't committed a crime, as far as I know." She paused and thrust the corks out.

"This one's from a Napa Valley Cab," she remarked, studying the markings and sniffing the tip. "And this one's from an exotic foreign locale, it's Barolo, so that makes it Italian. Good thing you weren't inside the sardine can when someone decided to perforate it," she said to the stranger, "otherwise I could have added you to my antique colander collection." She clucked as she stuck the corks back in. "That's a kind of sieve, Tom, in case you didn't know."

Tom frowned. "Where'd that happen?"

"I have no idea, Officer, I only noticed yesterday."

"Lucky you like wine," Beverley interposed, "and lucky you don't spook easily. Those are the biggest-caliber semiautomatic holes I've seen. They look more like they came from anti-aircraft or anti-tank weapons. Military-style weapons." She paused for effect, grinning at Tom. "Looks like someone's trying to scare you away, doesn't it? Did you tell Tom about your flat tire?"

"No," the stranger said. He hesitated, scratching his beard. "The air went out of the right front tire, about five days ago."

"Another mysterious leak." Beverley laughed. "Purely coincidental. Because if it had been the result of malfeasance, Tom here or someone else down at the county sheriff's department would've seen the perpetrators at work, right Tom? You are all-seeing and all-knowing." Another sudden fit of laughter made Beverley's upper arms and shoulders quake, revealing white folds usually hidden by sunburned rolls of flesh. "That's why the camera's up," she added, fiddling with her pearls and raising her eyebrows at the streetlight across the Old Coast Highway. Mounted on top, a camera protected by a thick glass shield glinted, reflecting the sun.

"Ms. Beverley feels safer now, don't you?" Tom asked, not expecting an answer. "It's bulletproof."

"Why not take a shot at it," Beverley goaded, waving at the camera, "test the guarantee."

Tom flushed. "We saw the tree come down on your vehicle," he said testily to the stranger. "We called the motel. Ms. Beverley said you were on the beach. You might've been in there, and you might've been hurt. That's another potential danger. This is storm season. When you don't see surfers out, you know we're overdue for some weather."

"Long overdue," Beverley put in. "The Universal Deluge also known as the Flood is right around the corner. With my luck it'll coincide with that tsunami everyone's waiting for. I've already lost half an acre. No wonder we got the property so cheap."

The deputy's radio crackled in his SUV, the speaker-mike clipped to his short-sleeved shirt echoing the dispatcher's voice. Tom Smithson cocked his head, a calico cat, listening to a call and sizing up the odd-bird of a stranger. "Today's Thursday," he said, calculating, a twang slipping in, "so, if no one has harmed you till now, I'm guessing you'll be okay for a couple more days. They know we're watching."

"They?" asked the man. "Who are *they*?"

"If we knew," Tom said, "they'd be behind bars."

"Or Dundee," Beverley quipped, "like that hog on the beach."

Tom studied his outsized wristwatch. "You know how to use that old chainsaw, Ms. Beverley?"

She crossed her meaty arms, rocking her head. "Heck no, I can wait for Taz to show up. Now that this mysterious gentleman has seen there's no damage to his camper, I think it'll be all right. I just hope the deer don't get through and eat my roses."

"Forget the deer," Tom said, swiveling toward his car, "you don't want those feral hogs getting in. They'll eat you and your guests before you can call 911." He brayed out a laugh, pleased with himself. "Does that boy use a saw?" he asked. "I would hardly believe it."

Beverley shook her head. "Taz has an incapacitating allergy to dangerous equipment. I might just get him to drag out one of those old cages and set it up by the breach, catch myself a wild pig, and invite you folks to a barbecue tomorrow."

"I'd help you myself," Tom said, "but we have lots of trees down and more coming." In a hurry now, he dipped his helmeted head at the stranger. "There's a trailer park north of town a couple miles," he said. "Lots of older folks up there. It's real quiet and safe," he added, "and there's one to the south, too."

"Thank you," the man said, "I'll remember that." He and Beverley watched the deputy take several heavy, swinging strides to his SUV, bundle himself in clumsily, still wearing his helmet, and drive off, shrouded by dust.

The sound of the surf returned above the wind. When the dust had settled, Beverley shook her head in astonishment at the deputy's behavior but spoke in a normal voice. "I can't recommend the place down south," she said, "on the other hand, I wouldn't want to go north, either." She offered her hand to the stranger. It was large and felt boneless. "By now you know I'm Beverley," she said. "You can call me Bev or Tater. Everyone calls me Tater the Laughing Potato because I look like a spud and can't keep my mouth shut."

They shook. "James," he said warily.

"Nice to meet you," she replied. "I might just have to call you Jim, the Mystery Man."

"Call me whatever you like," he remarked, patting the sand off his shins. He rolled down his pant legs, pulled a pair of black cotton dress socks from his windbreaker, slid his long bony feet into them, then wrestled on his new bright green-and-yellow boots. "Where's your chainsaw, Beverley," he asked in his reassuring baritone. "Let's get that tree off your fence before the hogs break in."

TWO

In the dusky undergrowth, James paused to nose the air and clear his mind, relieved the nervous, greenhorn deputy had not carded him or asked more questions. The plaintive sounds of foghorns, wind chimes, and whirligigs in need of oil sucked him into a tunnel of time gone by. Beverley had led him down the rutted highway, across a gravel parking lot, through a seven-foot deer fence, past the ranch-style motel, then under a tangle of low branches to a path covered with fragrant wood chips, leading to the bottom of the property. On the way, she had said there were five cottages and ten acres, though half were overgrown, and two of the cottages were closed until further notice. The land was sliding into Greenwood Gulch on the south side.

The farther west they walked, the louder the surf pounded. The beach was only twenty feet below, when they stopped on the edge of a thicket. A foghorn moaned.

"This way," she said. "Watch the gopher holes."

Lying at odd angles inside a large wooden shack, its door open and swinging on a single rusty hinge, were the chainsaw, gardening tools, and a wheelbarrow. The shack and a nearby potting shed edged a clearing that had once been paved but was now puckered and pocked with sea turnip, wild fennel, eucalyptus, and bay laurel seedlings. Piles of lumber and rusting crab pots lay covered by corroded green tarps. A stand of mature blue gum trees rose ghostly and shivering into the mist along an unpaved access road topping the cliffs. Beyond a clump of honey-scented purple buddleia and clotted blue ceanothus, James made out the banisters of a wooden staircase. It was lichen frosted, bleached and sandblasted by the wind. Zigzagging down to the rocks and beach, it ended in knotted clumps of wind-burned, brittle flowering ice plants dangling from the sandy verge. The air smelled of salt and skunk, honey and eucalyptus oil, bay leaf and cypress. James closed his eyes and felt tears welling up.

"The resort's dock used to be down there," Beverley said, raising a pink-tipped finger. "One of the former owners had a boat and fished." Three years ago, a storm had dragged the pier away and washed out the access ramp from the garden. The cliff had collapsed, leaving fence posts suspended by lengths of barbed wire. "There was no point repairing anything," she added. The land wasn't likely to stop sliding. No one came with a boat anymore, either. Slickers up from the city didn't drag boats, and the folks who did didn't stay at the Eden Seaside Resort & Cottages. "Besides," Beverley continued, the flow of words unstoppable, "there are no fish around to catch, not even crabs, not since the big spill last winter."

It was strange how memory played tricks, James reflected. Beverley's running commentary followed him in and out of the shack, killing all thought while he rousted out the tools he would need to saw the tree. The gophers had gone wild, she said, the skunks and raccoons were engaged in civil war with one another and the feral hogs, and the Japanese creeper with whitish-yellow flowers was choking everything, even the cottage behind the main building, where she lived. She ought to drag out those old animal traps, she added, set them up and get rid of the pests and vermin, but who had the time?

Loading the wheelbarrow with the heavy old yellow chainsaw, a gas tank, and a tool kit, James half listened, remembering the slope of the land as steeper, the rocks on the beach as taller, the white, green-trimmed Beachcomber Motel as bigger and longer and closer to the paved highway. Greenwood Creek had seemed a real river then, not a dry gully half filled by landslides, and Mr. Egmont had moored his varnished wooden fishing boat at the dock at its mouth at the end of a long gently sloping ramp. James didn't have a clear recollection of all the cottages, but at least two, built in the 1940s or '50s, must have been around during his adolescent years. One of them, called Sea Breeze, had been here, that was sure. Predictably the trees and shrubs had grown, like the invasive vines cloaking them. Still, he could not have imagined the contours and landscaping changing so much from the days of his youth, subsiding and shrinking like Alice in Wonderland nibbling her magic mushroom. What had it been, thirty-eight years, forty or more?

Beverley insisted he wear goggles and gloves, and would not allow him to start the chainsaw until he had put them on, citing OSHA, the Occupational Safety and Health Administration. As he bucked the downed cypress, the citrus scent mixed with the smell of burning Castrol from the worn-out, leaking saw. The greasy sawdust rained down and sprayed sideways. Beverley moved to a safe distance, clapping her boneless hands and shouting words of encouragement he could not hear. She watched him in turn adjust and lubricate the chain, wield the long blade, refill the tank, and restart the engine by holding the starter cord and dropping the saw like a yo-yo.

"You must have been a woodsman," she enthused, all trace of irony gone, "I have never seen the like of it, you are as good with that saw as my husband was, I swear to god. I sure wouldn't want to cross saw blades with you, Paul Bunyan, you'd make mincemeat out of any murderer."

James did not care for sugar but devoured three sickly sweet cinnamon rolls and drank two mugs of strong black coffee, perching on the thick, scarred trunk of the cypress and staring out to sea, where a silvery glint caught his eye. Was it the shopping cart again, he wondered lazily, or some other stainless-steel relic rocked by the waves?

Prickly with sweat and sawdust, badger eyed from the goggles, his arms and lower back aching as they had not in years, he watched the glinting ocean and waited placidly for Beverley to return from town with more gas and two-stroke oil. The McCulloch was an amazing piece of machinery, he mused, speculating about the object that had caused the saw blade to sparkle and jam as he cut the cypress's roots. Remembering the ghoulish lore about the graveyard that once covered the site where the motel now stood, James fell to thinking about the times he had sat in the shade of the cypress those many years ago, happy to be alone, away from his parents. The foghorn mewling and the whirligigs spinning, he could not help shaking his head and smiling. For the first time in as long as he could remember, he felt something akin to contentment, even happiness.

By mid-morning, James had cut and hauled the top ten feet of the fallen tree out of the seaside parking lot through the gap, and assembled enough fir planks, a hammer, and a box of nails from the shed, to patch the broken section of fence and prop it up.

"That ought to hold for now," he said, surprised to hear the satisfaction in his voice. "What time does your gardener show up? I'll give him a hand with the stump and the fence if you like."

"My what?" Beverley asked. "Taz? He's no gardener." She guffawed. "He doesn't know the difference between a *macrocarpa* and a chinook. You come back over later and meet him, will you," she urged, "show him how to use that saw."

"It's nearly as old as I am," he said, easing the McCulloch, its engine still hot, into the wheelbarrow, then starting downhill past the cottages before she could deflect him. "You ought to take it in and get it rebuilt." He felt his eyes tingling again but refused to believe the discovery of the worn-out chainsaw, and the presence of the Sea Breeze cottage and cypress tree, could move him so deeply when he had rarely wept in adulthood.

"It came with the property," Beverley gasped, catching her breath as she trotted after him. "Like all those darned rusted crab pots and traps and other junk I can't seem to get rid of. Taz will have to take them to the dump one day, when he gets his driver's license."

Taz was her stopgap gofer, she explained as they raced toward the shack. He was a teenager paid by the hour to do the heavy lifting, the grandson of a friend of hers. Taz was a good kid despite his strange looks, she said, a polite kid, but he was all thumbs—thumbs hypertrophied from chronic overuse of handheld electronic devices, and Taz didn't have a license or learner's permit yet, so his usefulness was limited. Luis, the former gardener and handyman, was no longer in her employ, and neither for that matter was Luis's wife, Imelda, the maid, who had also been deported. Despite the unemployment rate in Carverville, Beverley had not found anyone reliable to replace them.

"I called him Mow, and I called her Blow," she said, short of breath, "and man did they work, the lawn was perfect and the rooms neat as a pin. Good people, I'm telling you. Their kids still live in town, in that little pink house near the bypass. They're American citizens."

Muttering something about needing a shower and a shave and maybe a sandwich and a nap, though it was only eleven in the morning, James suddenly felt trapped. He hurriedly followed his footsteps back toward the parking lot with Beverley puffing behind.

"Oh no, sir," she called out, catching up when he took a wrong turn into a grove of flowering maple trees. "Now you're going to have some of my fine home cooking. You can't scamper to your camper and eat a cold lunch."

Despite himself, James laughed at the silly lilt of her words. "I've got to," he began to say.

"You've got to follow me," Beverley interrupted. She held her string of pearls with the fingers of both hands and shook her head with what seemed to James perilous vigor. No one had checked in to the resort that morning, she said, and no one had reserved a room for the night. This was the lowest of the low season. She'd made French beef stew with carrots, and there was steamed rice and a couple bottles of cold beer in the fridge if he wanted, or else a jug of white wine.

Staring at her through his bushy eyebrows, James wondered aloud why she wasn't wary of inviting him in. "Look at me," he blurted out. "I might be a madman or a murderer."

"Yes, and I might be Salome and dance around, then cut off your head." She laughed. "No, I am not afraid of you, Monsieur Bunyan, *au contraire,* as they say in Paris, you might be an asset, especially if armed, and later I will tell you why."

Puzzled, and reeling from the physical workout, the sugary cinnamon rolls, and the overdose of caffeine, a wave of fatigue, curiosity, and loneliness struck him. He did not have the strength to resist, so he followed Beverley out of the woods and across the patchy lawn, past the tuneful wind chimes hanging from the back porch. They entered a small overheated office. It was tiled in pink and white, he noticed. The curtains were mauve and studded with eights and nines of clubs, matching the pattern and color of Beverley's stretch pants.

THREE

G o on in and have a hot shower while I pop lunch in the microwave," Beverley commanded. "How can you take a proper shower in that camper of yours? Maybe that's why you look like Rasputin and smell like a raccoon."

James was getting used to her style. "Thank you, I won't," he objected. "I wouldn't want to put these dirty clothes back on after a shower."

Pursing her lips while pinching her pearls, she appraised him. "You don't have to put anything back on if you don't want to, my good man. I am not being indecent. I can give you a giant gym outfit my husband used to wear. I called him the White Rhino, not for that famous play whose author's name escapes me but for his anatomy, because he was an XXXL, and though you're as skinny as a pike and as furry as a bear, you're awfully tall, so I think you might just fill his clothes out."

She bustled into a laundry room, reappearing with the outfit and a fluffy mauve towel. "Feel free. Use that bathroom down the hall, the door on the left, with the nine of clubs on it. The door on the right with the eight of clubs is the gun room and it's locked up tight, believe me. Sometimes I called the Rhino the Great White Hunter. He liked that. He had seventeen guns, I'll tell you why down the road apiece."

She watched James stoop to untie his boots, muttering again, this time about mud and wood chips and tar from the beach.

"You don't have to take those off," she said, shooing him along, "I'll sweep up afterward, if I need to. Now go on and make yourself presentable."

"You can't sweep up tar," he objected.

"No tar on your boots." She laughed. "They were tied around your neck and they're brand-new. Believe me, I already looked before I spoke."

James knew she was right, yet he hesitated before clomping down the hallway, his boots untied and halfway off. Closing the bathroom door behind him, he shook his head, surprised by Beverley's manner and apparent fearlessness. It was an act of courage or recklessness to be so trusting and outspoken, especially when so many constitutional rights had been suspended across the land.

He was even more surprised to find himself inside the old Beachcomber Motel after nearly forty years. Surely that was a good thing, part of the process of closure? Or was it redemption he sought? He still wasn't sure. Maybe he was flattering himself and intellectualizing. Maybe he was plain old nostalgic and hoping against the odds that he'd find her here, or at least discover where she had gone. Maybe the ugly truth was that guilt had eaten at him for his entire adult life, guilt and wounded pride, ever since the day he'd left Carverville, and left her behind.

When he'd figured out some way to get back into the old house on the bluff, and the old mill grounds, and the old lighthouse, maybe then he would understand why he'd come back.

"Old, old, old," he groaned, chiding himself. Everything in his life was old now, even the adjectives he used.

Stripping naked in the spartan, pink-tiled bathroom, he caught a glimpse of himself in the mirror and was taken aback by his twisted mop of matted hair, his wild-man beard, and the paleness of his flesh. His ribs rose out of what had been a washboard stomach. Though still strong, his muscles had shrunk, and his skin sagged. People had called him Bean Pole when he was young, or Slim, or Bones, but no one other than Beverley had ever called him a pike. He wasn't sure he liked it. Pikes made him think of battle axes and heads on pikes, or bony, aggressive fish, or pikers. He was many things, most of them pernicious, perverse, or downright dangerous if you believed the fake news stories that had circulated about him. But no one, not even the Russian trolls who'd helped bring him down, had ever accused him of being a tightwad and piker.

Opening the hot water tap, he waited until the steam started to rise, then fed in a small stream of cold water, and stepped underneath. Beverley was right. Ever since he had leased the RV in New York, he had limited himself to quick showers, to save water and avoid having to refill the tanks. He knew the drill everywhere in the West was to wet yourself, turn off the shower, scrub then rinse. It was joyless, a reality check. The drought was into its eighth season, they said, though it seemed more like ten or fifteen seasons to him, coinciding with the dawn of the "new" era. It was the "new normal," an expression he had come to loathe. If normality was drought, then drought meant nothing, just as truth, freedom, and the rule of law meant nothing anymore.

But he could not bring himself to turn off the steaming hot stream. He had forgotten what a pleasure a shower could be. Rinsing the sawdust from his hair and beard, he lathered up again using a different bottle of shampoo, realizing too late it was strawberry scented. Like the noise and the smell of the chainsaw, the strawberry scent took him back to the 1970s. He knew why, recalling the Sea Breeze cottage, her scent, and the strawberry-blond color of her hair. "Maggie," he muttered, groaning again, then forced himself to stop thinking of her. It was her fault as much as his, her fault more than his. But what did fault matter after all these years, these decades and lifetimes separating them?

Fishing deeper for happier memories, he came up with the image of a mild, white-haired man in the motel's sloping garden, Mr. Egmont, showing him how to prune the roses. "Count down four knots from the hip and snip clear through at a forty-five-degree angle," Egmont had said, standing behind, his arms around James's adolescent shoulders, guiding James's eyes and fingers. "Remove the cross branches like this, to make a bowl . . ."

Egmont had no son of his own. He had no wife, either. He drove a white Lincoln Continental, and the Beachcomber Motel was painted white with green trim, surrounded by an expanse of white gravel and green lawn, like a golf course, reaching down to the creek and the beach.

James had been fourteen, or had he just turned fifteen, when his family had relocated to Carverville? Richard Nixon was president, a man had walked on the moon, and flags and draft cards were burning in Berkeley, Chicago, Boston, and New York. All four were cities James had seen, albeit briefly as his family migrated west following his cantankerous father's postings. He had soon discovered the only things the locals were likely to set alight in Carverville were backyard barbecues, beach bonfires, and campfires on Big Mountain, where the giant firs reached two hundred feet into the crystalline cloudless sky.

Insisting they stay at the Pink Flamingo Motel on the strip in downtown Carverville, his mother, in a permafrost of sadness, had made a face when his father had chosen the Beachcomber instead, precisely because it was isolated, impractical, and old-fashioned. They had lived in Sea Breeze for three or four weeks, waiting for the painting to be finished and the furniture to arrive at the house they had purchased on Five Mile Creek. That was another thing his mother had resented. The house was too big to heat and too far out of town—exactly five miles north of the Yono River and the town's old fishing harbor—for James to walk to it from Carverville High. But it was convenient to his father's new job at the Wildlife & Fish Department's headquarters.

During those first weeks at the Beachcomber, Mr. Egmont had taught James to prune and graft, transplant trees, and use a chainsaw, the same yellow chainsaw he had found in the shack. It seemed inconceivable. How could it have survived? Egmont had even let him drive the Lincoln around the parking lot and pilot the handsome old wooden powerboat when they went out before dawn to drop crab pots. Egmont had been a hands-on man, a believer in physical proximity. Nowadays he would probably be charged with pedophilia, James reflected, though in truth he had never done anything lewd, limiting himself to the occasional paternal touch or avuncular caress, the only warm gestures or acts of physical closeness James had known in the arctic of his youth. In reality, "old" Mr. Egmont and his white or gray hair had probably been in his fifties, younger than James was now. He could still be alive but if so, where? If dead, where was his grave? James wondered.

Holding on to the word "grave," James recalled what the locals had always said about the scenic, serene site of the Beachcomber Motel—that it was where the Yono tribe had been massacred a century and a half earlier, then buried in a mass grave, and that's why it had become the town's first graveyard, all trace of it gone now, except on certain century-old maps kept in the library at the junior college. *Had Beverley ever dug up bones or gravestones?* he wondered idly. Egmont had. James would have to ask her. Now that he thought of it, hadn't he seen something long and bleached and tibia-like caught in the roots of the cypress, the roots he had sawed through with Egmont's old saw, its blade sparking and bucking?

His thoughts were interrupted by a sharp rapping from the hallway. "Feel free to use the blow-dryer," Beverley shouted, her percussive voice cutting through the closed door. "It's in the drawer on the right. There's a big plastic comb, too."

Dressed in a baggy canary-yellow sweat suit emblazoned with the number three, its elasticized pants slipping off his hips, James carried his boots and shuffled barefoot back to the kitchen, where Beverley had set two places at a small Formica-top table in the corner. His hair, still wet, spread on his shoulders, merging with his long wet beard.

"Couldn't find the dryer?"

"I have never used a blow-dryer in my life and never will," he said, trying but failing to make his words sound lighthearted. "The notion and the noise are an abomination."

"Suit yourself," she said lightly, "I can tell you're a stubborn cuss, same as I am."

James considered for a moment and settled on something neutral. "You're a fine judge of character, Beverley."

"I wasn't head of personnel for nothing," she quipped, steering him into an old wooden chair. "Now they call it human resources or HR, because one good word wasn't good enough, they had to use two weak ones." She paused, catching her breath. He had noticed this lack of breath and wondered if she had the beginnings of emphysema or some other form of lung disease. "Beer or wine or water," she gasped, "or is it milk or more coffee? I have no Barolo or Cabernet Sauvignon, I'm sorry to say. White is my poison, screw-top, jug stuff."

James lifted a gnarled finger and pointed at the beer and the water, thanking her for one of each. "You were right, Beverley, that shower was heavenly. I shouldn't have used so much water. I got carried away."

"Heavenly?" she teased, laughing out loud. "What kind of word is that for a tough old lumberjack like you?" James blushed and though most of his face was hidden by hair, she could see the wave of pink spread across his forehead and neck. "Won't you call me Bev, Jim?" she pleaded. "Call me Bev or Tater, for goodness' sakes."

He shook his head. "I will not."

"Why not?"

"Because," he said, swallowing the entire glassful of water in a gulp then reaching for the beer, "you do not look like a potato." Tempted by an image of a dancing hippo from *Fantasia* dressed in pink and mauve like a fuchsia blossom, he opened his mouth to speak, changed tack, and said instead, "'Beverley' is euphonic. 'Beverley' is your name. Bev, Tom, Dick, Doug, Dave, Tim, Jim—they make me nauseous, I'm afraid to say, with regret, I do not like nicknames, I try not to diminish people."

"No point moving on to last names, then," she said, letting out a percussive guffaw. She beamed with pleasure dishing out the stew. *"Bœuf aux carottes,"* she announced in French. "For your information, I don't know what my last name is. I took my first husband's name and he left me, I don't blame him, though he never complained about the food. I took my second husband's name and I threw him out, the louse, his name was Solomon. I took my third husband's name and he died on me, bless his soul, he was the keeper and we only had ten years together. All I know is, there won't be a number four. Been there, done that." She caught her breath and fiddled with her necklace. "I can see you are thinking I talked Number Three to death, and you may be right. You are in no danger. I'm no cougar, and I'll bet you're at least five years my junior, young man." She drew breath and lifted her fork, wishing him bon appétit with a fine French accent then digging in. "Drink your beer, Jim. Like I was saying, I am no maiden, so I am not going back to that name, either. I'm just Bev or Beverley if you insist."

"And I'm James."

"Cheers, thank you for the tree," she said, silenced momentarily by the necessity of chewing the stew and swallowing the glass of jug Chablis she was clearly enjoying. "By the way, *James,* while we're at it, you aren't from New York City, are you? I didn't think so. I lived in New York and never came across an accent like yours. You speak what my father, the schoolteacher, used to call standard English, very flat, very proper, like my boss when I was at Waste Disposal in West Bernardino, down south, height of my glorious career." She savored another bite, took a sip, took another sip, and waited to see if James would react.

"Delicious," he said, "compliments to the chef."

"That's me," she said, "made from scratch. I do not go in for processed food. I make big batches and freeze them. Imagine, Jim, I own thirty-two cookbooks totaling 3,859 recipes. I counted them at my husband's behest and recounted recently just to be sure. Number Three was very precise. It must've been the engineering background." She reached over and served James another mound of beef stew and rice. "Now, that deputy who was here, Tom Smithson, I call him Tom Cat because he's always licking himself and full of self-love, he might think you're from New York, maybe, but I know better. Tom's a caricature, though he doesn't know it and couldn't spell the word if his life depended on it. He's a certified imbecile. Have you ever seen a deputy wear a helmet inside a police car? Or practically draw his sidearm when someone holds out some crushed cypress leaves to sniff? And why can't he just describe a man's probable height and weight—in your case six-foot five and one-hundred-sixty-five pounds, I'm guessing—instead of going on and on as he did?" Beverley paused and eyed James. "He's never even been down to the city. I know that for a fact from his uncle, the sheriff. But I am not like the local variety of peckerwood, redneck, or hip-neck, as they call the hybrid-type hicks and hayseeds here. I have traveled, I went to Canada and Mexico with husband number two, I lived and worked in Upstate New York and Los Angeles, and you're from neither, am I right?"

"You are right," James said. "Your stew is excellent, Beverley. Do I detect a pinch of allspice or nutmeg? You must have taken cooking classes, or are you a talented autodidact, I mean to say, self-taught?"

"I know what autodidact means, Jim, I mean *James,* and don't go trying to change the subject sounding like a professor. If you think I'm in with the Tom Cat and the Blue Meanies you're wrong, by the way, we all know about play-acting, don't we, so I just play along with them and they don't bother me because, frankly, I'm an old white woman with a business, and I pay my taxes. What they fear are the tree huggers and the dealers and the outsiders like you, and anyone who might blow the whistle on what they're up to in this county, heaven knows what that may be." She drew breath, felt for her pearls, poured herself another glass of wine, and reached toward the fridge to get James a second beer.

"No, I won't," he said, "I've got work to do this afternoon."

"I thought you were retired," she said, handing him the beer over his pro-testations. "A retired professional from the city, I'm guessing, am I right?"

James took his time chewing and swallowing and finished the first bottle of beer. She unscrewed the top on the new bottle for him. He took a swallow. "When did I say I was retired?"

"You don't say much of anything in your opera-singer voice until someone needles it out of you," she quipped. "Now, to get back to what I was driving at before you got me off the track, I did not ask them to put in that surveillance camera or to come over and pester you when the tree fell, and that's why I ran interference, otherwise you'd be eating Spam at the new county jail right now. Everyone in town knows that lot is where the kids come down to indulge in what we used to call necking but now starts at age twelve and involves everything below the neck. They call it snoggling or something appetizing of the kind. Sex and drugs, James, forget the rock and roll. They listen to synthesized drums and jungle music, no offense meant to jungle dwellers, but it does come all the way across the garden and right through the walls, like a bunker-buster artillery shell, or those assault weapons they use for target practice and to scare regular folks away. Yes, I did notice you picking up the shiny brass cartridges on the beach this morning, and I'll bet you still have them in the right-hand pocket of your windbreaker. They make a tinkling and rattling noise when you walk, and I know the difference between seashell noise and gun-shell noise, and so does that deputy, Tom, who also saw you picking them up, just like I did." She came up for air then dove back in. "If you had kids, you'd understand what I mean about the music, but I can tell you don't have them, never mind how, but the black socks you wear are a clue." She finished her glass and refilled it before continuing.

"Because the sheriff is a spoilsport, he figured if everyone knew there was a camera up there, the action would move elsewhere, and he was right. For the drugs, they now drive into my lot right here, and do their deals thinking I can't see them through the deer fence, but if I tell the sheriff, he'll put up another camera, and the next thing you know he'll see the color of my undies, pardon my French. I did take five years of French, but never made it to Paris. Next time around, I will."

James opened his mouth to speak, but she was too quick for him.

"I am no namby-pamby latte liberal," Beverley began again, "and I am glad they got rid of the gangs and growers, even if it was brutal, but I don't like cameras pointed at me, and I never was cozy with law enforcement, especially these rural sheriff types who think the West still has to be won. I'll bet they can see the title of that rare old book you're reading," she added. "What are you reading, if you don't mind me asking? You look very comfortable and satisfied in your deck chair, taking a wind-bath each afternoon." She cackled this time, a variety of laugh he had not heard from her up to now. Her teeth gleamed. "I haven't dared disturb you, so I'm thankful the tree fell."

James shook his head in astonishment and tried but failed to repress a mirthful chuckle. "Well, it's a strange thing you mentioned Rasputin," he said. "I'm reading the autobiography of Prince Kropotkin, my great-grandfather's first edition. Have you read it?"

Beverley brightened, acknowledging that no, she hadn't read his great-grandfather's first edition, if that's what he meant with his dangling modifier of a question, but she knew who he was, Kropotkin, a prince of the tsar's family, and a revolutionary who had an impressive beard and wild hair like his—James's. She remarked that the Tom Cat and Harvey wouldn't know Rasputin from Kropotkin or Stalin and might even be glad to see a Russian name on his book, because Russia was big these days, strategic and commercial partners, we were, and right across the Pacific, with plenty of local investment along the coast, especially in the haulage and petroleum businesses. "I did not finish college, it's true," Beverley admitted, "the children came along, two of them, and then I wasted a few more decades shuffling papers about garbage disposal and sewage treatment, the diapers were good training, I guess, but like you, I am a child of the '60s and '70s. I never went in for the cult of ignorance, unlike the younger generations. Sometimes I wonder how I wound up in this place. It was Number Three's idea, not mine. That darned seventeen, the number, I mean."

A note of seriousness stole into her voice for the first time. "Do you have a favorite number," she asked, "or a favorite suit of cards?" Watching James shake his head, she cleared the dishes and, unbidden, poured two mugs of coffee, her face lighting up again. "There's peach cobbler," she said, "or tiramisu, take your pick or have both. I guess you could say the tiramisu is to die for."

James held up his hands, uniting them in prayer. "Neither, thanks. You've defeated me."

Beverley clucked and crossed her arms. "For a man your size, as active as you are, up before dawn and scurrying like a snipe on the tide line, you don't eat much," she opined. Releasing her arms, she helped herself to the cobbler. "Number Three always wanted two desserts, bless his soul. He keeled over right there, where you're sitting, with the spoon still in his hands. It was tiramisu, his favorite. His people were Italians, way back when, that's why I know Barolo."

"I'm sorry," James said and meant it.

"Oh, don't be, he died happy, I look forward to a similar swift and sweet departure, believe me. It's just he inconveniently didn't think of what old Tater was going to do with the hotel all on her lonesome and pushing seventy. Thank god he finished installing those hot tubs and redoing the plumbing—he was an industrial plumbing engineer, and I guess you could say when he left, he left me flush." She paused to touch her pearls, her cheeks reddening as she laughed. "We are sitting on a plentiful aquifer. That's why I don't mind folks taking long showers, you see. The gray water is recycled, only the black stuff goes into the septic tank, and it isn't wasted, either." She raised a hand and waved toward the ocean. "Those eucalyptus trees down by the access road found the leach lines and have grown about forty feet in two years, I am not kidding, I guess they like the tiramisu." James opened his mouth to express his condolences but felt at a loss, wincing at the image. "How long has it been for you anyway?"

"Since what?" he asked.

"You know what."

He sat back and glanced down at the mug cradled in his hands. "Since she died, you mean?"

"That's it, you win the cigar."

"How did you know?"

Beverley ate in silence for two bites, then could restrain herself no longer. "I read a lot of Sherlock Holmes, Dr. Watson, I have a complete collection of Agatha Christie, and I watched *Murder, She Wrote* a hundred times. Besides, Number Three was the president of the Scarlet Goose, that's the Sherlock Holmes Society of Northumberland, Illinois, where we lived for a spell, and I guess I caught the disease myself." She sighed, put down her fork, and rocked back in her chair. "Even *he* didn't get certain details, though. Men just do not notice things the way we do, and that's why so many people say Sherlock was gay, I mean Conan Doyle. Why that would make him observant I do not know. You are well trained, my good fellow, Holmes might say, not to mention housebroken, as mama used to say of my dear old dad. No bachelor I have ever

26

known is tidy, clean, and quiet, lives like a monk, has a hangdog look all the time, and wears an old wedding ring he's always twisting around, or black cotton dress socks in hiking boots, unless he's a recent widower without off-spring to set him straight." She paused, wheezing and drawing breath. "I also happen to think you are usually short haired and clean shaven and have about as much in common with the Rasputin look as I do with a chinook salmon. I take that back, I feel great kinship to salmon and so do you, I'm guessing. If I were to take another educated guess, I'd say you are a quester pining over something, you're rudderless and full of regrets. Luckily no one has asked for my opinion and I may be off base entirely, I certainly hope so."

James was not sure what startled him most, her unexpurgated perspicacity about the loss of his wife, Amy, to lung cancer twenty months earlier, or his socks and hair and passion for wild fish. "I wish I'd had you as a researcher," he said. "You would have saved me lots of time."

Beverley drummed her boneless fingers on the tabletop and smiled broadly. "I figured as much," she said, triumphant. "I would not only have saved you time, I would have won you plenty of court cases you probably lost." She fin-ished the last bite of cobbler and took a sip of coffee, her fingers sliding the pearls along their string. "Perry Mason, you are, or were, and I'm Paul Drake, or less modestly, Sherlock Holmes reincarnate, though I think Moriarty might be more like it." She guffawed, raising her eyes to a sign on the wall above the sink. It read BAKER STREET. "You hadn't noticed it?"

He shook his head.

"Did you notice the colander collection?" she asked. "Did you happen to count how many I have there?"

James shook his head again.

"Seventeen," she said, "some are a century old." She paused, smiling. "Have you counted the number of steps or treads, if you prefer, in the staircase up the cliff?"

Opening his mouth to ask why he should bother, he shut it when she answered for him. "No, you haven't," she said, "yet you've been climbing that staircase at least twice a day for ten days. If you had counted the treads, you would've known there were seventeen of them, and having seen those colan-ders and that Baker Street sign, you might have understood instantaneously why my Sherlock of a husband Number Three had to buy this place, he just had to, the same way he had to own seventeen guns, not sixteen or eighteen. That conviction would've been bolstered by the knowledge that there are also seventeen treads in the second set of stairs to the beach from the end of the garden. I'm guessing you've also been up and down those stairs many times in your life, though possibly not recently. Now, had you been aware that Number Three and I first came to view this choice piece of property on June 17, exactly seventeen days after we had started searching in this county, and that it was five o'clock in the afternoon when he counted the treads of the stairway, and five P.M. equals seventeen hundred hours in military time, as you know all too well, you would further have understood the absolute necessity of the move. Why Holmes or Doyle was fascinated by the number seventeen is another issue we can discuss some other time. In the meantime, I repeat my offer of loaning you a gun or three. It would have to be an odd lot, out of respect to Number Three."

James went from being stunned to staggered, but he did not have time to speak. "By the way," she said, "you ever want to trim that mane of yours, let me know, I'll be happy to do it. Maybe start by plucking the bridge of your nose, and then do your ears and nostrils? I realize they're part of the disguise, and maybe you aren't aware of it, but you have beards growing out of them, which may be overdoing it just a tad. It's not very attractive and must make it hard for you to hear and breathe. I'm guessing you last shaved when your wife passed away less than two years ago, probably about the same time as my Number Three changed his last washer. I have his ashes over there, in that cookie jar on top of the counter."

James's incredulous gaze followed the fingers of her raised hand and he saw again the Baker Street sign, the cookie jar nearby it.

"That's what he wanted, a chocolate chip cookie jar for an urn, he got the idea from that crazy Italian who invented the espresso machine, if you recall, the pope was not amused. I bought an extra big jar, so they can put my ashes in, too, right on top, if they deign to show up and deal with me once I'm Dundee. They did not take to Number Three, no, no, no. I'm talking about my rotten kids, I'm sure you've guessed by now. They're both pushing fifty, and they resemble their fathers, respectively, numbers one and two."

The landline telephone rang from the office next door just as she was beginning to ask James whether he was an "adept" of Mark Twain and if so, never to speak that demonic name in the presence of the cookie jar. James stood up feeling weak from fatigue and bafflement, but also from unaccustomed laughter. He had been shaken and amused in equal measure by her words. Beverley let the phone ring, then decided to get up and do something about it.

"I know, you have to go back and get to *work*, that's what Number Three called his postprandial snore-fests. But I will see you later, after your afternoon walk to the Yono River, at 2:45 P.M. sharpish, which is when you always get back and write your report, is it not? No need to explain, my good sir, I know you've got to walk and scribble, same way I've got to talk and eat. Do not attempt to object. I have something important to give you. I believe it belongs to you, and you will thank me for my doggedness. Now, don't forget to move that camper or the Tom Cat will be back like a lion after a deer, or a deer after a rosebud, and watch your step on the beach, someone might take a potshot at you for the hell of it, or for reasons I'm not yet aware of, the 'yet' being the operative concept." She opened the kitchen door to let him out, held up her hand in silent salute, and disappeared into the office singing, "Lordy lord, all right, I'm coming, I'm coming, what's the rush?"

FOUR

🍂

Dipping his long prehensile toes in the swirling purple waters of Five Mile Creek, James felt the habitual tingling of his bare feet from an hour-long walk on cold sand. He also felt an unfamiliar ache in his knees, shoulders, and back. That would be the chainsaw, he reminded himself, and lifting those logs.

From the outside, to people like Beverley, he looked strong and solid, James told himself, but inside, where it counted, he felt the years racking up. Checking his watch, he saw it was 1:25 P.M. Clouds had blown in, momentarily blotting out the sun. The lighthouse at the Headlands was already flashing its semaphore messages to phantom ships. He corrected himself. It wasn't "already" flashing. The lighthouse never stopped flashing. Way back when, the first time she'd seen it from the windows of the house, his mother had said it was like his heart. If it stopped, life was over.

Calculating again, he estimated he was twenty-five minutes ahead of schedule if he planned on returning by 2:45 P.M. to see what Beverley wanted, and meet her gofer. It wasn't just the walking and keeping of a diary, as Beverley thought, it was the schedule that kept him sane.

When you have been busy all your life, every day, from before dawn into the night—he told himself in what had become a familiar refrain—your minutes measured by the metronome beat, your sentimental life summed up in your love for your wife of many decades—and your shameful, hidden love for the girl you abandoned all those years ago, before your wife and your career came along—and then one fine day you lose everything, your job and your house and your wife, but not your guilt and remorse, you need something else, a framework, a marching plan, a timetable, to keep you from edging toward self-destruction.

After sawing the cypress and drinking two large bottles of beer over lunch, James had returned to the sterile stuffiness of the RV intending to add a journal entry for the morning. Stretching out, he had fallen into a comatose sleep, a snore-fest, as Beverley described it, waking refreshed just fifteen minutes later, in time for his afternoon walk south to the mouth of the Yono River. Rebelling at the notion of predictability, he decided to walk north again instead, repeating his morning walk. How would Sherlock account for that? he wondered. Moving the RV to the far side of the parking lot, by the garbage cans, to keep the deputy happy, then silently tying Number Three's yellow sweat suit to the motel's office door, he had stolen stealthily back through the parking lot and hit the beach, barefoot, almost running, making record time.

Now, with burgeoning black clouds swirling behind Big Mountain, and the winter sun battling the fog in Five Mile Valley, he could barely make out the gingerbread contours of the towering Victorian mansion poised on the bluff on the creek's north side, rising out of thick river mist. Below it on the beach, three pale crisscrossing concrete buttresses the length of telephone poles had been erected to keep the cliff from crumbling. For how much longer? he wondered. The backyard of the old house was already half gone.

A foghorn moaned. Marine diesels roared in the distance, probably tenders to the oil ships docked offshore, he reasoned, given the lack of local fishing activity, unless he was wrong, and it was a helicopter he was hearing.

Watching as lights snapped on, first in an upstairs bedroom in the fog-wrapped house, then in the main stairwell and the living room, James imagined the unknown occupant navigating in the dusky afternoon twilight of the mansion, flipping other light switches. Counting to five, military-style, as his father had taught him, he watched the silhouette move from one-one-thousand to two-one-thousand, the kitchen and side porch lights coming on in rapid succession.

Was the bench seat still there, fronting the bow window, and did children still thrill when lifting the trapdoor and hiding their toys underneath? Where he and his teenage friends had made out in candlelit secrecy, in the closet under the basement stairs, had new generations also swept aside the mothballs, and killed the black widow spiders, and scattered the floor with their clothes and half-naked bodies?

Closing his eyes and hearing the foghorn's moan, James could smell the mothballs and the loamy, sweet, fresh-caught coho scent of her on his fingers, her adolescent moans merging now with the moans of the sea and surf and foghorn. Madeleine. Damn you, Maggie! Will you never leave me be?

Wrestling himself away from her shadow, his mind's eye focused again on the inside of the mansion. He saw the brass light switches high on the varnished paneling, the round screen of the black-and-white TV set built into a tall wooden cabinet, his parents' overstuffed armchairs, and the heavy carved furniture, the beaten tin ceiling, and baby-blue paint. What color were the walls now, and who were the new owners or renters? Would they let him in to look around, for old time's sake? What would they think when he asked to visit the attic?

Wading farther into Five Mile Creek, he felt the numbing water reach his knees and moisten the rolled tops of his jeans. Years of drought had reduced the flow, but the springs at Narrow Rocks on Big Mountain clearly had not run dry. Could fish still swim up to the hatchery, he asked himself, or had all his father's hard work restoring the riverbed gone to waste? An instinctive understanding of why this had always been sacred territory to the Yono, and why they had been willing to die to protect it, filled him with somber thoughts in the cold, wet silence.

That silence was slivered by the sudden silvery cry of seagulls swirling up from the driftwood and circling overhead.

Hidden by boulders, the swimming hole they had called the rock pool was another hundred feet or so upstream. Legend had it a bear created the pool so a Yono chief's daughter could bathe in it safe from the sea—but not from the white man.

The ford of Five Mile Creek was halfway down to the tide line from where he stood, shivering, at one with the water, sky, and fog. In this season, before the putative winter rains, he could probably still wade across without getting the crotch of his swimsuit wet. But he was no longer that teenager wearing a swimsuit, and he dared not ford Five Mile and knock on the wide oaken door of the old house, not yet.

A trail ran along the creek's meandering south bank inland, mounting slowly like a fish ladder, disappearing under outstretched fir and beech branches as it curved and rose past the hatchery toward Narrow Rocks, he recalled, tempted to boot up and follow it now.

The Yono Headlands, where the mill had been, were another two miles north. Maybe tomorrow or the next day he would feel up to walking there. In the abstract, he was prepared to face reality, to scramble up the cliffs and hang onto the fencing and stare into a dead, ruined world. For years, when he lived in the city and moved around the country climbing the professional ladder, he had quietly followed developments at the Headlands, often as reported by dissident voices whose blogs and websites periodically disappeared. Even before the Internet, he had read in the newspapers about the protests in the woods east of Carverville, and the plant closure at the Headlands, the end, first, of the big-tree mill, then the small-tree mill, then the chipboard and plywood production lines.

The promontory northwest of town had belonged to the mill's owners for over a hundred years. There were no on/off switches there. Everything ran 24/7 and the town prospered. Surrounded by eight-foot fences topped with razor wire, a kingdom with armed guards at the entry and exit gates, this had been the Carvers' Oz. Everyone, in what had long ago become a company town, had feared and respected and sometimes loved and admired the Carver clan since the arrival of Samuel J. Carver Sr., in 1868, and the incorporation and naming of Carverville a few years later. They were stern but fair masters, the local hagiographies claimed. The forests for fifty miles around were carefully if unsentimentally managed, the harvests limited to replacement value. Then Washington-Pacific Corporation had quietly bought out the family, whose bored heirs had migrated to the city, losing interest in the unglamorous, over-mature industry of their forebears. The junk bond collapse had hit, the company's timber resources were clear-cut, and the denuded coastal lots parceled off to real estate developers. That was when the clashes between law enforcement and demonstrators began, when a protest organizer's car had blown up, and the first disappearances were reported. Carverville's death sentence had been pronounced when the Downburst had hit nationwide in the late twenty-teens. It was the worst downturn since the Great Depression, much worse than the Great Recession of 2008. The rest was, as the locals he'd talked to said, not history but mystery, a small-town tragedy few beyond the county would ever hear of or care about. Other parts of the country had rust belts. Here, people said, was the sawdust belt.

Chilled by the rushing water, James turned to leave. He was surprised to see a jogger appear from nowhere, out of the mist on the far bank of Five Mile Creek running north, disappearing again into the fog. It had a sulfurous tang, like rotten boiled eggs. The refinery at the pipeline terminus, twenty miles north, must be coming on tap, he told himself, or they were flaring more gas than usual on the offshore derricks. Maybe that's what would revive Carverville—petrochemicals and gas, the bountiful accursed blessing of what had been, when he was growing up, a pristine wilderness, a "lost" coastline.

Weighed down with leaden reflections, he began the three-mile walk back to the parking lot and Beverley. Chasing dark premonitions away, James forced himself to smile, admiring the way the winter sun turned ribbons of fog into glowworms, and though he hated to admit it to himself, he was glad to have something to do for the rest of the day. After seeing Beverley, he might ride his bike into town, run some errands, and do a load of laundry. He could have a cappuccino and a bear claw at the old diner, a holdover from his youth, and read *The Carverville Lighthouse,* the town's heirloom newspaper. He might even stay out and dine at the old deli down on Bank Street or, god forbid, have a drink at old Mulligan's.

Old, old, heirloom, old . . . Here I go again. He stopped himself and shook his shaggy head. He was getting old not only in body but in spirit, and she would be an old lady if she were alive, if he could find her.

What perplexed him most as he marched along, watching the breakers hitting the beach, was the desire he felt to get back to the garden of the Eden Resort, as Beverley had requested or, rather, had commanded. Disquieting, Beverley, the unlikely Laughing Tater, with dyed orange-red hair, reminded him of someone, but he could not think of whom. James was sure he had not met her before, not in town and not in any of the cities they had shared. Tom, the sheriff's deputy, had said she was an out of towner. Surely in her nonstop recitatives she would have mentioned it if she had grown up or lived in Carverville, as he had decades ago. What was the real backstory on her?

He also could not help wondering how she had guessed so many things about him, right down to his childless marriage, Amy's death, and his professional life as a lawyer and judge. Perry Mason? He wished. Her knowledge seemed uncanny. Nothing on the outside of the RV gave away his identity, and she had not been inside it. Or had she? Sometimes he forgot to lock up the vehicle, or left it unlocked so as not to have to carry keys. He hated carrying things, especially keys. The lease for the RV was in the name of a business partner in New York, not his own. He had always paid in cash in the stores and restaurants in town to avoid anyone noticing his name on a credit card, not that he had anything to hide now that they had defanged him.

Once upon a time, he might have thought himself paranoid for behaving and thinking this way. But he knew he wasn't paranoid. It wasn't him, it was the world that had changed. Certain people, in certain places, had been out to get him, and he knew how far they could reach. Did they know he was here? He remembered the deputy's words: "If we knew, they'd be behind bars . . ."

With the wind kicking up, the waves, already high, slammed down on the long straight beach, flinging flotsam, jetsam, and detritus up the foam-specked sand, sometimes reaching the saw grass, beach bur, and ice plants cloaking the dunes. Avoiding the glistening balls of sticky black tar washed in from the derricks, James picked a swerving path between tangled tentacles of kelp, bone-like driftwood, puckering plastic, and algae-bearded Styrofoam, his usual pace slowed by the loose sand and extra mileage. Logs, some of them twenty or thirty feet long, some with branches and root balls still attached, lolled like dying whales pushed up the beach by successive sets of waves.

Storm season, the deputy had said, that was an additional danger.

Scanning the strand as he went, he noticed the dead feral hog was gone, and so was the crushed shopping cart, both dragged back out to sea.

By the time he came in sight of the trail up the cliffs, he had resolved for the third or fourth time to get whatever it was from Beverley, ride his bike into town, take care of his chores, and then maybe, depending on how he felt, drop by the Eden Resort the next morning to lend a hand with the stump and the fence. He was tired and sore and had had plenty of company for one day.

Stooping to pick up a pile of spent gun cartridges lying in the sand, he dropped them one by one into the right-hand pocket of his windbreaker, hearing them tinkle against the ones he had collected that morning. Why had Beverley been watching him? How did she know so much? And who had shot at his RV? A stray bullet, he told himself, it must have been a bunch of teenagers partying on the beach.

His boots swinging from around his neck, his hands clasped behind his back, he made his way across the final stretch of sand and rock and began to climb the ravine. The experiment was proving inconclusive, he said to himself, trying to frame a logical argument and remain dispassionate. It was nearly always a mistake to go back, anywhere, especially after an absence of so many years, and especially now, with the county under lockdown, one of the worst places in the entire country for law enforcement abuses. Fleeing abroad had made the most sense. But they had made it impossible for him to renew his passport. In a hurry to leave the city, and unsure where to turn, he had flown to New York, then spent eight months meandering state to state in the RV, looking for a place to love, driven by an unknown force farther and farther north by northwest, into his past. He knew he should pull out the blocks again, now, this afternoon, and go somewhere else, before it was too late. Yet he felt compelled to stay, to continue exploring the coast and interior, trying to find what remained, what had become of the places and people of his youth, and what had become of her.

Yes, he confessed to himself for the umpteenth time since his return to Carverville, thinking of the priests and psychologists he'd spoken to over the years. *Yes, I admit it, she is the real reason. She is the magnet drawing my compass needle.*

Counting the seventeen treads of the wooden stairs as he marched up the cliff to the parking lot, James reached out and parted the saw grass masking the edge of the bluff, glancing up as he went. Waiting at the top were a pair of windblown, backlit forms. Had the deputy come back with reinforcements? he wondered. Drawing nearer and shading his eyes, he saw that one of the silhouettes looked like a large mauve-and-pink avocado. It was flanked by a towering bread stick wrapped in a flapping tablecloth. "Strange," he muttered to himself, he had eaten hearty at lunch. "But hunger must be getting the better of me." Recognizing Beverley, he guessed the bread stick in baggy overalls was her helper, Taz.

Slung around the boy's long slender neck were a pair of orange safety ear-muffs, the kind worn by construction workers. Thin wires dangled from his prominent earlobes and a goofy expression animated his coppery, rubberized face. The boy had blue eyes the color of his own, of swimming pools in La La Land on a cloudless summer day. His long eyelashes were the lashes of a camel or a llama.

These arresting features were topped by a green billed cap bearing the logo of a local radio station, whose call letters James recognized from high school days, KRVL 91.1 FM. Out of the cap's ventilated sides and back sprang sprays of curls dyed acid green. James stepped closer, squinting up, the figure no longer inspiring in him a bread stick but a giant stalk of celery topped by a totem pole head.

"Did you spot the shopping cart again," Beverley asked with a toothy smile, fingering her pearl necklace, "and the dead hog?"

"No," James said. "Neither. The tide must have taken them out."

"It must have." Beverley nodded. "Unless it was the 'copter that flew by while you were making sawdust in your RV. We could hear your snores all the way across the parking lot." She let out a guffaw, then prodded the boy standing next to her. "So, we decided to head you off at the pass," she went on, "the top of the staircase is what I mean. Did you count the treads? Of course! Seventeen, just as I said. Now, Taz here has come over specially to meet you and learn to use that saw. I know you have your shopping and laundry to do this afternoon, I'll tell you later how I know that, but I also want you to be aware that you can use my machines if you like, and if you give me your list, I'll be glad to pick up whatever you want at the market, I'm going in with my pickup truck." She wheezed noisily then tugged on the wires in Taz's ears, causing the earbuds to fall out. He caught them with surprising deftness and seemed unperturbed. "Taz, this is James," she shouted into the wind, "the maestro of the chainsaw."

James leaned forward to shake. "Nice to meet you," James said, wondering where the bones in the boy's large sweaty hand had gone. Taz bobbed his head and mumbled.

"James doesn't speak Millennial," Beverley quipped. "Speak up and enun-ciate! Maybe you need to take that spike out of your tongue."

"It's a stud not a spike," Taz said meekly, "and I'm not a Millennial, I'm a Gen Z."

"That may be, but James still cannot understand you."

"I said my real name isn't Taz," the boy repeated softly, grinning while coiling up the earphone cables and stashing them in the pocket of a bright blue hoodie hidden by the overalls. "It's Alexander."

"That's a fine name," James said. "I'll call you Alexander."

"Alexander Z Great," Beverley interjected with a snort.

"You can call me Taz if you want," he said with the same shy grin, "I don't mind."

"If I were you, I'd put on those boots of yours pronto," Beverley told James. "You never know what you might step on in this parking lot, and I don't just mean dog dirt and syringes, I mean horns and tusks and hunks of hide, and human ears and fingers chewed on by hogs." She paused to watch Taz smile a goofy smile. "Now, the coffee is hot, and there are still some cinnamon rolls left. I know you're hungry for a snack, James, so I could also scramble a few eggs if you like, and crumble in some shredded cheddar, if that won't ruin your appetite for dinner. Not that you'll want to drink the gas and that castor oil for the saw, but this afternoon, while you were patrolling the beach, I also bought more of those pestilential fluids. Man does that saw drink fuel!"

Using her banter and arms like a crook, she herded the pair past the RV toward the highway, approving as she went the invigorating strength of the wind and the waves. "A deal's a deal," she said, turning up her palm and looking Taz in the eye. As they crossed the Eden's parking lot, empty except for Beverley's cherry-red pickup, she reached out then pocketed the boy's smartphone and headset. "Ever tried getting any work out of a kid with these earbuds attached, let alone talk to them?" she asked rhetorically, opening the deer fence and stepping through. "It cannot be done. You'll get it back *after* dinner," she told Taz. "If you think this is cruel or unusual punishment," she said, turning to James, "ask his grandmother, she approves. On top of it, a smartphone has five times as many germs as a toilet seat. I heard that on the radio this morning and I will sterilize the thing before he gets it back."

Taz rolled his large eyes skyward and opened his mouth to speak, but she cut him off.

"Generation Z, did he say? Who ever heard of it! They'll all die of septicemia from their cellphones. What's next anyway? We've come to the end of the line, the end of the alphabet. Zzzzzz, as in lay-zee."

James tugged thoughtfully at his beard, following along, unsure what to say. "Since you seem to have a contractual agreement, I recuse myself from commentary," he remarked, trying to sound lighthearted.

"You're a wise man," she said.

"Better a wise man than a wise guy," Taz quipped then seemed to regret it, covering his mouth with his hand to hide his snickering laughter, the way Tom, the deputy, had tried to hide his spittle-flecked mustache.

"Watch your manners, young man." Beverley chuckled, her fingers on her pearls. "I've got a new nickname for you, Z Smart Alex."

"What's an aleck anyway?" Taz asked.

"Another word to google," Beverley said, catching her breath, "once you're home with your darling grandma."

Taz wrinkled his face. "Can someone, like, translate the 'recluse' for me? And why doesn't he have to hand over his?"

James held up empty hands. "I don't have one."

"You don't *have* one?"

"I do have an un-smart cellphone," he explained, "for emergencies."

"You have a burner, like, like a cartel kingpin?"

James laughed out loud. "I keep forgetting to charge it, and the battery runs out or the credit runs out, I don't know which, I only turn it on once in a blue moon."

"A blue moon?"

"Not everyone is an addict," Beverley remarked. "You can look up the verb form later, even though 'recluse' is not what James said just now. But here's a hint. Since you're a natural-born Smart Alex you've hit the nail on the noggin, as my dad used to say. James is generally as tongue-tied and *reclusive* as you are, but he chooses his words with care. I suppose it goes with the territory. All the tall skin-and-bones men I've known have been of few words, I mean mouse-quiet, reticent, retiring, not to say morbidly shy, solemn, secretive, and private, in other words, reclusive." She gasped for breath as they neared the cypress. "On the other hand, lawyers and judges and public or elected officials *recuse* themselves to avoid conflicts of interest, or I suppose I should say they used to. Now it only happens once in a blue moon. You can look that up, too, later."

"That just about covers it," Taz said, his goofy smile reappearing as he tilted his eyes heavenward again. "I recuse myself from, like, more of this crazy talk."

"Well, we know who the wise guy is," Beverley said, launching a final salvo. "By the way, are we going to play the 'like' game today? I've already tallied about ten." She turned to James. "Taz isn't as bad as some of them, believe me. Why they say 'like' all the time I do not know, but it makes me homicidal, so, Taz, you are officially handing over your 'likes' with your smartphone, got it?"

The wheelbarrow laden with the chainsaw, handsaw, and other gardening tools stood waiting by the remnant stump of the fallen cypress. Beverley said she was coming right back with the last of the cinnamon rolls and coffee and could scramble the eggs but didn't want to miss the fun. "Before you do anything, don't forget to put on your safety glasses and gloves," she shouted over her shoulder. "James, please tell him what OSHA stands for."

"I know," Taz shouted back. "Oh Shit—Had an Accident!" He grinned, his blush a deep purple.

They waited until Beverley had disappeared into the motel office. Then in silence they glanced shyly at each other, the stump, the ground, and the sky. James pulled at his beard and cleared his throat. Taz put on the orange ear protectors, took them off, and looked inside his gloves. Finding nothing there, he picked up the handsaw, looked at James again, and batted his eyelashes.

"Tell me something," James said, tinkering with the chainsaw. "If your name is Alexander, why does she call you Taz?"

Taz glanced away, trying to keep his wide smile and shiny teeth out of view. "I'd, like, let her tell you that. She'll tell you whether I do or don't."

James said that seemed all right, they would humor her. "Do you know how to use the saw?"

Taz shook his head no and wagged it yes in a single meaningless gesture. "I mean, it seems dangerous to me," he said. "It, like, makes so much noise and smoke. I've used my grandma's saw, but there are no safety guards on this one and it, like, leaks oil all over the place, I could never get it to work right, and I'm not sure I want to make it work."

"That's judicious of you," James said, "a good reason to go on strike until Beverley gets it rebuilt."

Taz ran an immaculate, manicured hand over his rubberized face and said they had tried that already. The repairmen at the garage in East Carverville had refused to service the saw because it was too old and likely to cause injury.

"They also said it's the best chainsaw ever built, it's, like, forty years old or something."

James felt a pang. Turning toward the ocean, he drew several deep breaths, listening to the wind chimes, foghorn, and surf. "When I was your age, it was new," he said, summoning a sad smile, "and those cottages down there were in perfect condition." Hefting the saw then letting it drop like a high diver, he heard it roar to life, spewing fumes and spraying oil. He revved it, engaged the blade, disengaged it, and turned it off. "The trick," he said, "is to prime it, here, it's not automatic, and if it doesn't start, drip some gas straight into the carburetor, here. You might also have to dry off the spark plug. Now you try it."

Taz set the choke, yanked the starter cord, and seemed startled and terrified when the saw spluttered into life. He revved it, then seeing James waving his hands, let go of the throttle and let it die.

Beverley bustled up, breathless, carrying a tray. "I knew he could do it," she said. "All he needed was a pointer by the maestro." They each took a mug and a roll and sat on the downed cypress in a moment of bonhomie. Noticing what was clearly a jagged white bone lodged in the roots, James slid his boot over to hide it from Beverley. The last thing he wanted was to talk about cemeteries, bones, and death.

"It sure smells good," Beverley enthused. "Not the saw or the coffee, the wood I mean, from the *macrocarpa* tree. I wonder if we could save some of that sawdust and sew it up in bags to scent the rooms."

Taz and James glanced at each other. "Alexander will make some more of it for you in a minute," James said. "But you might want to include some dried foliage, too."

"*Foilage*," Taz said, his camel face perplexed.

"*Foliage*," Beverley corrected.

"*Foliage*," Taz repeated laboriously, as if he were hearing the word pronounced properly for the first time. Then he added, "What's a *macrocarpa* tree? If I had my phone I could look it up."

"Well you don't have your phone, and you're not getting it back," said Beverley.

"*Cupressus macrocarpa*," James said, "the coastal cypress."

"So, it's, like, just a cypress, right?"

"Right."

41

"I'm ready to saw up the *macrocarpa*," Taz said, the coffee clearly giving him a rush. "Can I start the chainsaw?"

"Praise Be!" Beverley exclaimed, raising her arms, "if he turns out to have real razzmatazz, I'll have to find another nickname for him. 'Smart Alex' is pretty good, if I say so myself. But hold your horses until we finish our coffee break, you Tasmanian, you."

Taz spluttered and choked on his coffee, unable to keep from emitting an embarrassed, nervous braying laugh. "You might as well tell him," he said, momentarily mastering his rubberized expression. "I hear it coming."

Beverley caught enough breath to coordinate her talking, chewing, and swallowing. "Well, I'm certain James objects, because he's very serious-minded, but I've got a nickname for everyone, at least one, and often three. He's Taz as in Razzmatazz or the Tasmanian Devil. You remember him, a little whirl-wind of activity that this Taz here definitely is not, unless stung by bees or otherwise stimulated by something electronic. I mean that with no offense, it's a generational plague among Millennials or Gen Zs, as far as I can see, like saying 'like' all the time. My grandchildren are worse, meaning they'd starve to death if they had to do more than lift the lid off liquid yogurt, and they'd rather have a recharge for their telephones than a meal. Now luckily, he's got the happy gene, the serene gene, like Mahatma Gandhi, and that's a good thing, and he also doesn't smoke like everyone else his age, as if enough of us hadn't smoked and croaked in the past so they might learn from our example." She paused long enough to drink down the last of her coffee. "How many 'likes' did he say while I was getting the cinnamon rolls?"

"I didn't notice," James said.

"How many 'likes' did *you* just say?" Taz teased her. "I counted a bunch, like, 'he also doesn't smoke like everyone else.'" Taz grinned, his face a camel-complexioned version of Alfred E. Neuman on the cover of *Mad* magazine, way back when.

Beverley looked at him disapprovingly. "I am an equal opportunity name giver," she segued. "There's Tom Cat, the deputy you met, and his uncle Harvey-Parvey-Sat-on-a-Wall Murphy, a true Humpty Dumpty lookalike you're likely to bump into sooner or later. I'm Tater or Bev as in beverage, and I just might have to call you Henry James you're so literate, or Jimbo because you're a tough, silent guy, or Paul Bunyan for the chainsaw, or maybe Jim Crow, seeing that you look like a crow in your windbreaker, with your hands tucked behind your back, not to mention your beak. The hair and beard do nothing to hide that nose of yours. There are a couple other nicknames I can think of for you, like Gandalf because you're right out of *The Hobbit*, or Ichabod Crane, or Daddy Longlegs, of course, and maybe Dr. Watson or Perry Mason or even Hamilton Burger on a good day, but they'd mean nothing to Taz here."

"You might be surprised," Taz said. "I like reruns."

"Reruns?" Beverley snorted. "We are talking about the icons of classic literature and television! And that is the proper way to use 'like,' by the way. I'm glad you *like* reruns. Congratulations."

James put his goggles and gloves back on. "If you pick up some bacon or links, and some frozen spinach and granola and plain yogurt," he said, "I'll, like, pay you back later. Actually, if you, like, see any fresh local wild salmon, get that, too, I'll, like, do it on the barbecue."

Beverley made a face. "Okay, wise man, I see you two are ganging up on me. It would be just *like* you to take up the cause of the downtrodden, wouldn't it?" She paused for effect, watching James sink back into silent mode. "For your learned information, it'll be frozen Norwegian farmed salmon, there is no local salmon anymore, haven't they told you? Or are they ripping you off at the market because you're a tourist? You haven't bought any of that leathery mess from the folks at Yono Harbor, have you? Besides, you must feel like a cannibal eating salmon, as I started to say after lunch, before that phone call so rudely interrupted us."

James shook his head. It ached with incomprehension. Still puzzling, he picked up the saw, drop-started it, and shouted over the noise, "We don't want to reenact *The Texas Chainsaw Massacre*, so you'd better give us some operating room." He revved up, blowing exhaust and oil fumes in Beverley's direction and watching her retreat.

"I'll be right back," she shouted, cupping her hands. "Dinner will be on the table at 5:30 P.M., precisely."

FIVE

B y the time Beverley had driven out of the parking lot in her cherry-
red pickup, James and Taz had taken turns sawing the cypress trunk
almost to the ground. The older man had carefully removed the bone
fragments lodged in the roots, telling Taz they were probably deer or hog
bones, he thought, and watching to see how the boy reacted. But Taz's face
remained expressionless.

Of more urgent concern was the way James felt, his body a bruise someone
was pressing on with strong fingers. A quarter hour of cutting had been enough
to bring out the aches and bring back the fatigue from that morning. As he
rested on the stump, the whining engine still rang in his ears. His arms and
shoulder blades vibrated, and his fingers and hands shook.

Gingerly picking up sawed sections of branches, Taz stacked them one by
one under a nearby bay laurel tree, clearly interested in aesthetics and economy
of movement. "Cool RV," he commented, glancing into the seaside parking
lot through a knothole in an undamaged section of the fence. "It's just big
enough for one."

"Two would be better," James said, "but she couldn't make the trip, and I
haven't found the other one I'm looking for."

Taz stared at him, then nodded silently. The wind chimes and surf hung between them. A foghorn moaned. "We need one of those grinders to get rid of the small stuff and leaves," Taz ventured.

James roused himself. "I think it's called a chipper," he said, his voice gravelly. He cleared his throat. "It makes a hell of a noise, like that saw. My mother loved to snip everything by hand. She wouldn't own a chipper. I guess I've come around to understanding why." James stretched his spidery legs out across the stump and picked the sawdust and chips out of his flowing beard. Then he began counting the growth rings of the tree. He got to thirty, about a quarter of the way across, and gave up. "Silence is golden," he added, whispering, "it's as worn out an expression as that chainsaw, but it's truer than ever."

"I thought you liked the saw," Taz said, leaning closer. "We could get an electric saw instead."

James pursed his lips. "The cord would get tangled in the shrubbery."

"How about a cordless saw? I've seen them at the hardware store."

Shaking his head, James explained that cordless saws were not powerful enough for the kind of cutting needed in Beverley's garden. "Maybe I'll rebuild that saw myself," he added pensively.

"You know how?"

"Don't you?"

"Why would I?"

"I never met a teenage boy in a place like Carverville who didn't know how to take apart a chainsaw and put it back together again."

Taz thrust his lower lip out and smiled. "Now you have."

"Now I have," James repeated. He closed his eyes and took a deep breath, smelling the iodide in a gust of ocean air. Using his fingers like a caliper, he measured the thirty-year section of the stump he had counted, then moved inward four times until he reached the core of the tree. "I'm guesstimating a hundred twenty or thirty," he said. "It was probably planted in the late 1800s, about the time my grandparents were born. And I was born here, about halfway, and, right about here, I sat under this tree when I was your age."

Taz's camel-eyes grew wide as he stared at the stump, then looked fixedly at James, as if studying himself in a mirror.

"So, Alexander," James asked, suddenly self-conscious, "what say we finish fixing this fence, then take a walk around the property and figure out the next steps?"

"Beverley said you were leaving in a couple days, that the sheriff was going to make you move. Are you going to stay?"

James shrugged. "Maybe."

"She could, like, hire you, like, to run the place, I mean. That would be awesome."

"Watch your 'likes' or Beverley will dock your pay," James joked. "We'll see."

Taz grinned mischievously and felt in his baggy pockets. "If you really want to rebuild that saw," he said, pulling a smartphone from his hoodie and checking to make sure Beverley wasn't back yet, "I can order the parts."

"How?"

"With this, it's my spare. You think I'd let Beverley leave me high and dry?" Taz held up the device and, showing it to James, tapped and stroked it, smiling then frowning then tapping rapidly four times in a row. The entire performance took less than one minute. "So, like, I found the original rebuild kit for the chainsaw, ran a comparison and ordered it from the place with the lowest price, they say it'll be here tomorrow afternoon, by drone."

"By drone?"

"Yeah, drone. They fly along the beach, it's really cool."

"How did you pay for it?"

"I used Grandma's account, it was only $28.99. Beverley can pay her back. See, here's a photo I took of the saw last week, when Beverley and I went to the garage in town to get it fixed. Here's the model name and number, McCulloch SP 125. I found the rebuild and about three thousand reviews, it was first made in 1971, it says." He smiled. "Tomorrow you can show me how to rebuild it."

James blinked and opened his mouth but wasn't sure what to say.

Dispatching Taz to the shack for nippers, pruning shears, and a machete, he walked back to the RV and returned to the stump wearing a daypack, with a pad of graph paper tucked under his arm. Kitted out like explorers, they followed an overgrown footpath south from the lawn toward Greenwood Creek, hacking and snipping as they went. Pausing when they reached an abandoned orchard, with a long row of half-dead plum, apricot, peach, and apple trees,

James made a rough sketch of the property, noting the cardinal directions, adding the beach, creek, highway, and parking lot. Deciding not to include the old burial ground or the locals' unsettling names for the site—Graveyard Creek, Graveyard Beach, and Graveyard Gulch—he counted out fifty squares along the length of the graph paper, and twenty along the width, making dark marks every ten squares, and then he drew in a scale. One acre equaled five squares. The property ran five acres along the highway and two acres to the cliffs but was rhomboid not rectangular. He wrote *Garden Map* across the top of the graph paper and noted with satisfaction that, so far, they had inventoried five fallen cypress or eucalyptus branches blocking paths. They would now know where to come back to buck and saw them.

"We need a weed whacker to get any farther," Taz observed, hesitating in front of an impenetrable wall of vegetation.

"The kind with a metal saw blade," James agreed. Then he remembered the shack. In it he had seen a gas-powered hedge trimmer, also vintage, leaning on the wall behind coils of barbed wire. It might do the trick. "You keep cutting," he said, "I'll be right back."

Crossing the lawn, James detoured following another overgrown path and fought his way west through the undergrowth until he reached the access road and eucalyptus grove. Remembering the staircase to the beach, and Beverley's mysterious injunction, he ducked through the buddleia grove following a second overgrown trail and was soon standing at the top of the stairs, his boots on the warped, buckling boards. Testing each tread with his right foot before putting his weight down, he counted to himself as he descended to the beach. Four steps straight to the first landing, six to the left, eight to the right, then seventeen to the rocks and sand below. "I'll be damned," he said to himself. "There are seventeen."

Trying to recall why seventeen was a significant number for mathematicians and numerologists, and whether he had encountered it in the Sherlock Holmes books he had read when in his teens, he recounted while climbing back up the stairs and was soon burrowing among the discards in the shack.

Clutching the trimmer, a gas tank, and the two-stroke oil, James threaded his way back through the garden to Taz and the trail they were blazing. Another quarter hour slipped by as he tried but failed to start the motor of the antiquated trimming tool.

"What if we wounded a skunk or a raccoon with that?" Taz asked. "It looks like a weapon. Maybe we should warn them . . . we could, like, bang pots and pans."

James set the trimmer down. "Strange, I was thinking the same thing," he said. "Maybe we don't really need to reconquer this part of the property," he added, remembering the old graveyard. "We could map it and leave it alone, a kind of nature reserve with wild native plants."

"Good idea," said Taz, snipping halfheartedly at a blackberry branch. "But aren't these weeds?"

"Weeds are plants you don't want," James said, fiddling again with the trimmer, aware that he was sounding pompous and professorial. "If you want them they aren't weeds. Every plant is beautiful in some way, even that invasive Japanese honeysuckle. It has beautiful white-and-yellow flowers and a beautiful name, *Lonicera japonica*."

"*Lonicera,*" Taz repeated, trying to turn his wavering tenor into a baritone sax and sound like James. "What about beach burs and poison oak?"

James seemed to have a revelation. "*Ambrosia chamissonis* is an amazing survivor species," he said. "That's the beach bur. And poison oak is handsome," he added, "it looks like oak and it turns that oily shade of red in the fall." He scratched his beard. "Have you noticed anything about this property?"

"What? It's full of beach bur?"

"No. That's normal. There's no poison oak anywhere, it's rife everywhere else."

Taz stretched his rubberized face. "I did wonder about that," he said, snipping at the blackberry, "but I don't catch it, I played in it enough when I was young, I guess I developed resistance."

"Strange again," James said, "I don't get it, either." He paused, wrinkling his face. "I have to wonder how it is they don't have it here."

"*Lonicera,*" Taz said again, seemingly mesmerized by the word. "*Ambrosia chamissonis.*" Then he shaped his mouth into a pucker and intoned "foliage," repeating it several times as he struggled to lower the timbre of his voice. Pausing and glancing shyly at the older man he asked, "What about animals, does the weed rule apply to animals?"

Thrusting his bearded chin out, ready to pontificate, James hesitated, wondering again if Taz were making fun of him. "Sure," he said tentatively.

"You call an animal you don't want a pest or a nuisance, or vermin, but they're only pests because we don't want them around, there's nothing inherently bad about them."

"So, the feral hogs aren't bad? People say they're dangerous, they're cannibals, and they'll eat small children or attack you at night if you're alone."

James was startled. "We don't want them around because they're destructive and maybe there are too many in one place, but they're just wild pigs, we eat pigs, don't we, and we even use their organs in surgery, so how can they be bad?"

"So, deer and raccoons and skunks are okay, too?"

"Of course, but you don't want a skunk in your bedroom, or raccoons in your attic, do you?"

"What about rats," Taz asked earnestly, "what if this place was overrun by rats and mice and maybe dangerous animals like . . . like mountain lions and bears?"

James stopped working and stared at the boy. "The same logic applies, if they're a nuisance or dangerous you get rid of them if you must, but they're not by their nature bad, they're just inconvenient or a health risk or they damage your crops and garden, but they're not evil, they're just invasive and unwanted."

"So, what about people?" Taz continued, his face frozen for the first time in a pained expression.

"People are never vermin or pests, and I'm always hesitant to call them bad or evil," James said, surprised by the turn the conversation had taken. "Even the people running our country today. They're misguided and dangerous. But evil? I'm not sure what the word means. You can't put plants and animals and people in the same bag anyway."

"Why not?"

"That's a valid question," James acknowledged, "and the answer depends on many things, including your belief system, but purely for the sake of peace, prosperity, and the survival of the species, we decided in this country, a very long time ago, that human beings deserve special treatment. A hard-core environmentalist or a nihilist might argue otherwise."

"Or a white supremacist," Taz interjected. "So, like, if immigrants are humans and are not inherently bad, maybe just unwanted, then why do we treat them like animals?"

James nodded in somber agreement. "If you can find the answer to that one," he said, impressed by the boy's reasoning, "you will have done humankind a great service, especially if you can somehow ensure that people will not be treated like animals, and animals will be treated humanely. That sounds contradictory but it's not, it's paradoxical."

Nodding thoughtfully, Taz went back to snipping the blackberry, the rubberized goofiness returning to his features.

Getting the graph paper out, James began adding details to the map. He drew in the eucalyptus grove, the buddleia and ceanothus, the flowering maples and the fruit trees, the lawn and the wood chip trails and the overgrown paths, the shack and potting shed. "Speaking of good ideas," James said, trying to sound avuncular and optimistic, "any idea what you'll do when you finish high school?"

Taz stopped snipping and the serious expression returned. "I might go to the Valley."

"Which?"

"There's, like, only one valley where I could find work."

"Got it," James agreed.

"I'm learning to write code for gene-splicing, but social would pay more."

"Social?"

"Media," Taz said. "I might just stay here and take care of Grandma."

James wondered aloud if Taz's grandmother was ailing. Taz smiled. "She's never sick, she's stronger than I am, but she's pretty old, like, maybe your age."

James laughed but followed with a rusty-sounding scoff. "I'm not old," he protested. "You look at me and you see a seedy old guy with gray hair, but inside," he added, tapping his breast, "I'm a little boy, I'm younger than you are."

Taz tried to hide his nervous smile by covering his mouth with one large gloved hand. "That's—that's so weird, it's the kind of thing my grandma says," he stammered. "She's, like, a little girl trapped in an old woman's body, she said it a couple days ago."

"Well your grandma's a wise woman." James tried another tack. "Don't you want to live in your own place and bring your friends over, you know . . ."

Taz seemed not to understand. "I bring my friends over," he reasoned. "There's plenty of room and she doesn't mind, she likes us. She's, like, really mom, really cool."

"That's not what I mean . . ." James scratched his beard, trying to remember how he had felt at age seventeen or eighteen. It seemed to him now that his dream back then was to be independent, to leave home, to go to college, to work, and have a girlfriend and maybe get married, buy a house or travel the world. Clearly Taz was different. "The times are a-changing," he remarked. "I guess the times changed a while ago and I didn't notice. Maybe you're just realists and I'm a dreamer, that's what my wife used to say."

Taz seemed puzzled. "Grandma's going to live another twenty-five or thirty years probably," he calculated aloud, staring blankly. "People live a long time, especially her demographic, and she even runs every day and never smoked, so I don't see the need for me to rush into anything, but I am kind of, like, tempted by the Valley."

"New York, Chicago, the city? What about college?"

Taz shook his head. "They sound kind of scary and besides, I couldn't afford college, I'd, like, wind up with too much debt and what if I couldn't find a job? You went to college, right?"

"Yes," James said. Waiting a beat, he tried to find a diplomatic reply. "Now I'm an old geezer living in my car, so what's the point of college, I see what you're thinking." He paused. "What you don't see is what happened between college and my living in the car, and that was not all bad, believe me. Stuff happens. It's not a reason to skip college, education is important."

Taz nodded sympathetically. "I might go to the community college, I'm already, like, taking some courses there. I like it okay as long as people leave me alone."

"The other kids give you a hard time?"

"Sometimes," Taz said. "They call me the Martian. They call my mother the Squaw. We used to get into fights. But I'm, like, a pretty fast runner now, and I'm taller than most of them and have longer arms, so it's okay, besides I do home schooling as of last year, except for my computer lab courses."

James began to ask about Taz's family, but something told him to hold off. Picking up the pruning shears, he clipped the shrubbery back, widening the path they had made. Turning around and slowly working his way west until he came upon a thick, thorny stump, he pulled up short and shouted, "Eureka!" Taz loped over and stared, his mouth dropping open.

"What is it?"

"Rosebud," James said.

They made fast progress freeing up the survivor roses and watering them with a series of long coupled hoses dragged from the wellhead near the lawn.

Judiciously pruning the overgrown bushes, they resized the cuttings and pressed them into moist soil mixed with sand in a tub rescued from the potting shed. The new moon would favor the formation of roots; they grew faster during a waxing moon, James explained. "Like your hair," he added.

"I'm going to google that," Taz said skeptically. "I think you're pulling my leg."

"Nope, it's the Gospel truth," James said. "We can propagate the buddleia and fuchsias and abutilon, too, as long as you remember to water them regularly because they have to stay moist."

"*Abutilon* . . ." Taz repeated dreamily.

"Flowering maple," James said. "Beverley likes shades of pink, so those are the ones to take cuttings from, though they might not reproduce true."

Shouting and waving her hands, a dismayed Beverley found them breast-deep in what had been Mr. Egmont's rose garden. It was now a graveyard of rose stumps in a forest of raccoon and skunk trails through twining curtains of raspberry bramble, coyote bush, nettle, and climbing crabgrass. James pointed triumphantly to several rosebushes still alive against all odds.

"Count down four from the hip," he repeated to Taz, touching each of the nodules on the stem and unintentionally snagging his finger on a thorn. Drawing back the finger, he sucked the blood off, cursing under his breath. "Snip at a forty-five-degree angle, if you can," he said with his finger in his mouth, "like this. . . . Then remove the cross branches to create a bowl . . ."

"Well I'll be!" Beverley exclaimed. "I guess Number Three ran a leach line under here, too. Or maybe the roots found our aquifer. We have the best water on the coast right here, that's what Number Three said when he found it, here and up on Five Mile, from Narrow Rocks. Now that the word's out, I'm surprised no one wants to buy me out and pump it dry." She turned sideways and shuffled in among the roses to get a closer look. "Any pink ones?" she asked. "No wonder the deer keep trying to jump the fences."

"I count six survivors," James said, pulling out the map and marking the spot with an X. A drop of blood fell from his fingertip onto the paper. He blotted it. "We'll take a few more cuttings and see if we can propagate them."

Beverley tapped her wrist. "Not now you won't," she said, "I've been looking for you, dinner is on the table, I'm as hungry as a hog, and they don't like roses, the deer do."

SIX

Bristling with burs and twigs on their pants and sleeves, Taz and James filed in and out of the washroom, their arms gangling and legs shambling as they bumped into each other along the narrow hall. Crowded at the small table in the corner of the kitchen, James closed his eyes and took a deep breath, nosing the air. The candy scent was divine, he said, wondering aloud what she had made, and amazed to be so hungry again after their copious lunch. As if in answer, the kitchen timer rang, the men set down their empty water glasses, mopped at their brows, and found their knives and forks.

"It's coq au vin night," Beverley announced, "and I baked some soda bread, too. No booze with the kid at the table. You can translate for Taz if you feel like it."

"He'll enjoy it more if I don't."

Taz raised his fork. "Cocoa van?" He poked at the mound on his plate, his nose flaring and eyelashes batting, a suspicious camel. "It's like chicken, in some kind of dark, coconut, or chocolate sauce, right? It smells, like, kind of funny, almost like bubble gum." He dipped his bread in and tasted it.

"Right and wrong," Beverley said. "No bubble gum, and watch the 'likes.'"

"Nothing icky in it, right?"

"Right. Unless you think bacon is icky."

"Icky?" James asked. "Kids still say 'icky'?"

"Bacon's not icky," Taz said, ignoring him.

"And pearl onions?"

"Onions are okay."

"And wine?"

"I don't like wine, it, like, burns my throat."

"That's the alcohol," Beverley said, "when you cook it, the alcohol evaporates, and it doesn't burn your throat."

"Right." Taz paused and ate a forkful. "Pretty good," he said. "Kind of like something we had in the cafeteria once with macaroni. I mean, this is better and all, but it kind of reminds me, that's all. So, why don't people just, like, evaporate the alcohol in wine before they drink it, so it won't burn their throat?"

Beverley and James glanced at each other.

"You've got a million-dollar idea there," Beverley said. "It's called kosher wine, it's pasteurized. My second husband, Solomon, was a lapsed Jew, but he still drank the stuff. Tasted like grape juice. Talk about icky."

"I like grape juice," Taz said.

"So do I," James said, coming to the rescue. "Maybe we're Jewish. My wife was Jewish, lapsed, as Beverley puts it, and ethnically half American and half Japanese. But she didn't go in for kosher wine."

"Well I'll be," Beverley put in, "I thought I'd heard of every possible combo, and that explains your taking off your boots."

"Maybe we are Jewish," Taz agreed. "Grandma says we're all part Jewish anyway."

"She's right at least metaphorically," Beverley cut in. "We're all mixed up, even those of us with pearly complexions or skin as black as that sauce. We're all a coq au vin of genetic material, a real potpourri."

Taz stopped chewing. "Is that another French recipe?"

"Google it," Beverley said, handing him his smartphone. "You've got one minute. That's what your infernal toy is good for, looking up words and learning useful things. Check 'recuse' and 'potpourri' and 'blue moon' while you're at it. I'm counting."

Transformed, Taz batted several text messages back and forth in a matter of seconds, then smiled as he hit the Internet and struck gold. "A mixture of dried petals and spices placed in a bowl to perfume a room," he read aloud, crumpling his face.

"Keep going," Beverley said.

"A mixture or medley of things," Taz added.

"That's it," she said.

"Always check the second meaning," James suggested, "or the third or the fourth. And don't forget to check the etymology."

"The what?"

"The origin."

"Why not say so?"

"Scroll down, Taz," Beverley said. "Go on. Read where it says 'origin.'"

Stroking and tapping, Taz read, "Early seventeenth century, denoting a stew made of different kinds of meat: from French, literally 'rotten pot.'" He twisted his rubbery face. "Rotten pot? That's gross, why do the French eat rotten pots?"

"We're all rotten pots waiting to happen." Beverley laughed.

"I'm already happening," James added. "That saw did me in."

"Old people are gross," Taz said. "Are you always like that, I mean, Grandma says stuff like that, she never swears, she just, like, says weird things I don't get, like, 'enjoy yourself, things'll get worse,' it's so weird."

Beverley thrust out her hand and snapped her fingers, but Taz had already begun tapping and stroking his screen again. "I need to show James something." Seconds later he held up the phone. "With the MapIt app, I just made a map of the property. We can add colors and GPS flags and captions if you want."

Beverley clicked her tongue. From his pocket, James produced a pair of reading glasses, took the phone and admired Taz's handiwork. "That's impressive," he said, handing it back. "But how do you print it out?"

"Why print it out?"

"So that people like us can see it and use it and draw on it and write comments in the margin and get bloodstains on it, you know."

Taz smiled. "Okay, I can download it and send it as an attachment, and Beverley can print it out, and then you can go back to the Stone Age."

"Great," James said. "Then we'll compare."

Taz caressed and tapped his screen, then pretended to hand the phone to Beverley. "I sent it," he said, jerking the phone back. "Just one more minute . . ."

"I'm counting," said Beverley. She and James fell silent and watched Taz tickling his phone. "That's forty-two seconds," she said.

Taz beamed. "I just got a message, the kit will be here tomorrow by drone, at 1:17 P.M., with a margin of seventeen minutes on either side," he said.

"Seventeen?" Beverley gasped.

"Seventeen," Taz confirmed, his face goofier than ever.

"What kit will be here," she demanded, "and what drone?"

James explained without mentioning the backup cellphone hidden in Taz's hoodie.

"Finish your dinner," Beverley commanded, pocketing the phone again, then sticking her hand out a second time. She snapped her fingers and watched Taz dig out and relinquish the secret smartphone. "If you think you can fool the Tater you'd better think again. The chicken is getting cold," she added.

Taz ate one bite then held his fork up like a baton, beating out time. "If you print out the map for James, we can put our plates back in the microwave and the chicken won't be cold."

Beverley glared at him. "Well, just this once," she said, shuffling to the office. On the way back, she slid the plates one by one into the microwave and dealt them back out.

"This is fabulous," James said, studying the map, "but let me be the devil's advocate. What about the pleasure of using a pen or pencil and drawing something with your own hands?" James held the clean, crisp new map in his long, thick, gnarled fingers. "What about the fact that a treasure map on graph paper is unique, it can't be hacked."

"Who would want to hack it?"

James raised his eyebrows. "You never know. What if it really was a treasure map and you didn't want anyone else to have one?"

"My phone is encrypted," Taz said.

"They could torture you," Beverley chortled, chewing and swallowing. "It's back in fashion."

Taz frowned. "They could torture him, too, and make him tell them where he hid the map, and when they got it, they could scan it and then it wouldn't be unique. Nothing is unique and why would you want something unique anyway?"

James and Beverley exchanged glances again. Each took a bite. "You're unique," James said.

"He sure is," Beverley said, "even the stud in his tongue is uniquely awful if you ask me."

"Beverley's unique, I'm unique," James added. "Your grandma's unique, and all the great things in your life are unique, they're unique experiences, they can't be scanned and shared."

Taz pondered, his fork in midair. "But, like, I could be recording and videoing us eating this unique cocoa van, like, and then I could share it with my friends, wouldn't that be all right?"

"You'll do no such thing," Beverley said. "Look at my hair, the wind has made a mess of it, and you two are unmade beds."

"Try keeping it a unique experience," James said, his voice almost a whisper. "Give privacy and uniqueness a try, you might enjoy them."

"Maybe," Taz said.

Back in the garden after dinner, with the daylight fading, and the windless air unusually warm, they compared the maps. Taz said if he added a bloodstain to the printed digital map it would be almost as good as James's inaccurate sketch on graph paper. The way he said it, James was unsure if he was joking.

"My map has a lot more detail," James protested, "the shack and the shed and the shrubs . . . And this digital map shows a paved road to the beach, where it's actually a private access road and a wooden staircase."

Taz studied the digital map and agreed. "If you gave me a few minutes I could, like, fix it and put all that in and more, in scale and color." He smiled. "Let me take a snap, I'll work on something tonight at home."

SEVEN

Wearing a bike helmet with a camera on top and protective pads on his knees and elbows, Taz climbed with his long bony feet onto the projecting pedals of an electric unicycle. Waving goodbye with what looked like hockey gloves, he silently rolled out of the parking lot heading north on the Old Coast Highway. "Watch out for that blind curve," Beverley shouted at him. When he turned to look back, his seven-foot figure wobbled as it receded into the darkening, brittle landscape of coyote bush, gorse, and scrub, then disappeared altogether around the gooseneck bend in the road.

For an awkward, gangling teenager, Taz seemed to James to be remarkably agile at times. That went with his unconventional, changeable looks and flip-flop character, at turns sunny and somber, introverted and outgoing, serious and silly, mature and childish, vulnerable and self-assured. James stopped himself, displeased by the roll call of opposing abstractions in his head. Taz was a human, a kid, not a concept to be defended or described, he told himself.

Realizing just how little contact he had with the young, James wondered if Taz were typical of Millennials or Gen Zs. He understood why someone might call him a Martian, green hair and spiked tongue or not. There was something alien about his manner, something endearing and unsettling.

"He keeps you guessing," Beverley said in her stentorian voice from where she stood by the motel office door, the floodlights on in the parking lot and front garden.

"Nice kid," James commented. She waddled toward him clutching an envelope in one hand and a bottle of water in the other. He removed his gardening gloves and leaned on the shovel he had been using to loosen the soil so he could plant some of the extra cuttings. The sky was a bruised blue, the air cooling rapidly, and the sunset wind picking up.

"It's thanks to his grandmother," Beverley explained, handing James the bottle and watching him chug it down. "She is what we used to call a 'class act.' My handle for her is Glinda the Good, you know, the witch from *The Wizard of Oz*. We play cards together once a week with a bunch of other old bags, that's to say, a group of distinguished seniors like myself. I don't know how she brought up Taz by herself, but that's what happens when your grown son is a louse who marries a whacko druggie, dumps a seven-year-old kid on you when you're struggling to stay afloat solo in your dotage, and then poof, disappears." She paused. "It all comes out when you play cards, believe me, it's as cathartic as gardening. You sure you don't have a favorite suit of cards? No one says you have to like the ace of spades, you are free to prefer the two of clubs, or the eight and nine of that suit. They were Number Three's favorites."

"I'm afraid I don't play cards," he said, baffled again. Finishing the water then wiping his brow, James took the envelope and slid it into his back pocket. "What's the story with his mother? People call her the Squaw."

Beverley said she didn't know, she assumed the mother had been at least part Native American or Mexican, judging by Taz's looks, but maybe not, she could have been Pakistani or Burmese or North African or Jamaican for that matter, no one had seen her in Carverville, not even Taz's grandmother. "It's one of those all-American stories," she cackled, diving in. "I heard she was an Indio and died in Montana at some kind of nutty pipeline protest, froze to death like a fish stick, and the son didn't stick around to thaw her out."

Beverley continued the sad tale. Returning to town one night after an absence of years, Taz's father had left the boy in Glinda's custody, Beverley said, promising he would be back for him one day. Almost a decade had gone by since then and there had been no sign of the louse. "The son had some trouble with the law back when the law was mostly on our side," Beverley said. "I heard tell a tall, dark, mysterious stranger showed up at Mulligan's one night a number of years ago and got to boozing and brawling and then left that reputable establishment in the company of someone's wife. That someone was a long-distance trucker and the wife happened to be the younger sister of someone you met this morning, namely Tom Smithson. A risky business."

"Not a great idea," James agreed.

"When he's not licking himself like a calico tomcat, I call Tom the Smiling Sadist because behind that Doughboy face lies the heart of a vicious moron. It must run in the family, though Tom can't hold a candle to his uncle. Anyway, the sister, her name is Annie, I believe, no longer lives in these precincts, she hightailed it over the hills to Hazelwood once the ruckus was over and her hubby tossed her out."

"And the presumed son was never seen or heard from after that night?"

Beverley shook her head, her pearls rattling. "No guarantee he was the son," she said, "no names attached, and whoever it was he might've hitched a ride out of the county the next morning for all I know. It happened before I got here." She drummed her fingers. "What's worse," she added before James could continue his thought, "is the false rumor that went around a few years back. I will repeat it for your benefit, only because you'll hear it sooner or later if you stick around. It is that the so-called son doesn't exist, Taz isn't her grandson but her son, and that she had him down south with a man of color or a Moslem immigrant when she was already past forty."

Hanging his head, James muttered, "What century are we in?" The mentality clearly had not evolved in Carverville since his youth. But he felt detached from Taz's tale and unwilling to sink himself into the swamp of prejudice. Raising his eyes to the giant blue gum trees waving in the wind, the sunset glow behind them, he focused on the tangled branches and decided they were talking to each other. They sounded like rushing animals, like birds in flight, or salmon thrashing upstream through the shallows ready to spawn and die. Those were the sounds he loved, the sounds he had missed in the cities where he had spent the last thirty-five years.

"No joke," Beverley said, unfazed by his silence. "We're stuck in the nineteenth century." She waited but James continued to gaze as if mesmerized by the eucalyptus grove at the bottom of the garden.

"The sound and scent of those trees is magical, Beverley, but they should be topped," he said at last. "Clearing the rose garden could take a while, too," he added. "Taz can do that now."

"Yes," she said. "Taz could probably do that." She waited with uncharacteristic patience. "What you mean is, if you stick around a few more days, you could help him, and it would all come out better, and he might not cut his legs off or fell a tree on a cottage."

James shrugged. "I suppose I could," he said. "No one is expecting me."

"Well, you'd better stop supposing and pull the blocks out from under your rig. You can park in that lower lot down by my shack." She began organizing the operation. "You wouldn't want to park up here in the lot on the highway in front of the office, it's not private, car doors slamming, people coming and going, drug deals, murder and mayhem, you know." She paused to eye him. "I did get a couple reservations for the weekend, by the way. The first one is arriving this evening, right about now." She waited, watching, but he still said nothing. "First you'll have to get the gates open and clear some brush off the access road. We can run an extension cord from Sea Breeze for now. Even if no one were to shoot you out there in the public lot, in a couple days the sheriff would make you move on anyway, so you might as well get rolling. No surveillance cameras on my property, and you have a private staircase to Graveyard Beach, I don't know why they call it that instead of Greenwood Beach, but they do."

"With seventeen treads on the last flight of that staircase," James said, eager to avoid the topic of the graveyard. "One day you'll have to tell me why Holmes was obsessed with the number seventeen." Taking a deep breath, he stabbed the shovel blade deeper into the ground, relieved not to strike a tombstone, still of two minds about staying. "It won't take long, a few more days, maybe a week."

"Suit yourself," she said. "You're welcome to stay for as long as you want, keep your head low, if you see what I mean, sort out all the private matters that are torturing you. Now, before you say another word, you might want to open that envelope I gave you," she added.

He felt for it in his pocket. "I hope you're not trying to pay me for my hard labor," he joked. "I'd have to pay you for the lunch and dinner and in fact, I owe you money for the shopping."

Beverley scoffed. "Pay you? I'd never think of it, knowing what I know. It would be an insult to offer a pittance to a personage as distinguished as yourself, Your Honor." James gave her a startled, dismayed look. With twinkling eyes, she continued, "Here's a hint, remember *The Paper Chase?*"

James opened the envelope and inside found a dirty, crumpled sheet of embossed letterhead covered with handwriting. Stapled to it was another crumpled sheet of letterhead, this one photocopied, with his own handwritten notes in the margins. "So that's where it went," he muttered. "I thought it blew onto the beach or down the highway. I couldn't find it and went through the garbage . . ."

"Seek and thou shalt find," she said slowly, savoring the words. "Actually I found it in the style of Picasso—'I don't seek, I find,' Pablo said." Her eyes sparkled bright as she fiddled with her pearl necklace. "It was blowing around right here where we're standing freezing to death in near darkness." She flipped a switch and another set of floodlights came on. "Now, I did guess or deduce plenty, but did you really think I had Sherlock's powers? In my defense," she pleaded, "I honestly thought that document had fallen out of the car or luggage of one of my clients. I found it five days ago, when we'd had several guests up from the city. It was a busy week. Which one? None of the names on the letterhead or in the handwriting corresponded to anyone who had stayed. I decided to email everyone who had been here during the week before I found the letter. But I'll be damned if I could locate half their emails, and not everyone answered me. Those who deigned to reply said no, they had not lost any sensitive correspondence with a fancy lawyer from the city." She paused, took the empty plastic bottle from James and waved it. "Come on inside out of this cold breeze," she commanded, not waiting for him to answer.

Inside the kitchen, Beverley poured two glasses of Chablis and set the leftover cobbler and tiramisu on the table. "Now, you did not have any sweets at dinner, you were so busy with Taz and his confounded smartphones, but here it is, you'll need brain food while you listen. And don't forget to take the shopping with you, I spent $39.78, the receipt is in the bag, the salmon is Alaskan, smoked."

James counted out forty dollars, put the cash on the table with thanks, and started to say he was too tired for dessert or talk, and the daylight was just about gone. Seeing Beverley's eyebrows rising high on her pink forehead, he gave up halfway through the sentence. Abashed and curious, he sipped the

Chablis and dug into the tiramisu and could not help declaring it outstanding, the best he had ever tasted, creamy and rich, yet light and fresh tasting.

"You bet it is," Beverley said, beaming. "I'd give you the recipe if I thought you could do more than crack an egg and fry some bacon, but I can tell you're the appreciative non-cooking type, like Number Three, the pancake mix maestro." She dispatched a dishful of the dessert, sipped her wine, and began drumming the tabletop with her boneless fingers. "What would you have done in my place?" she asked rhetorically. "Go to the Tom Cat or Harvey? Call lost and found—there isn't one. Would you have just thrown the letter in the trash? I don't think so. So, I researched the names on Google and boy did I find some interesting stuff." She savored the uncomfortable expression on James's face. "Then I got to thinking, and I put two and two together and got five, so I asked young Taz what he'd do if he were me—I did not show him the documents, don't worry, and I didn't give him any names. Taz said, 'Do an image search with the names, maybe you'll recognize someone.' That was smart. The problem was, I didn't recognize these people from Adam and Eve. They looked very corporate, very liberal-loser type, millionaires from yesterday, if you see what I mean, before the election and the Downburst. Ancien régime if you want to sound sophisticated. One of them was a tall, lean fellow on leave of absence from some court or legal commission or other and, reading between the lines, it sounded permanent. Where was he? That got me thinking again, so I went to the bluff a couple times and stood near the fence and watched you for a while through that knothole. Strange fellow, I said to myself, strange habits, and why is he hanging around here for so long? Is he a bum or a crackpot? Not with a rig like that—and brand-new boots!

"Once I was sure it was you, I did you the honor of not searching too deeply for more information. See, you can fool that facial recognition software with your beard and hair, but you can't fool Tater. I was about to ask you if the letter was yours, and give it back, when the tree came down and that darned Tom Cat showed up and spoiled things. Then you ran off after lunch before I could broach the subject." She paused to gauge his reaction. "I guess you're sore with me, but you ought not to be."

"I'm not sore," he said, "I'm baffled. It's my body that's sore."

"Baffled is all right," she said, smiling at his quip. "I don't know why you're here, or what you're up to, and why you're hiding in all that hair, but

I'm guessing you have pretty good reason, judging by your behavior and background, as reported by about a thousand sources, two or three of them non-Russian and probably reliable. I would have hired you right off at the Waste Disposal District, what with your background and gumption. In my book it's a mark of honor to be drummed out of the corps these days. You must have been on to something big when they set you up and knocked you down."

James shook his head. "That was another life," he protested, "I'm an early retiree and bereaved widower minding my own business."

"And you dearly wish I'd do the same," she said sympathetically. "Believe me, I have no intention of persecuting you or ratting on you. I'm not sure what impressed me more, the varsity football and ROTC stuff from way back, or your career and all the public service. I'll bet the other guys at Carverville High hated you, the valedictorian and scholarship winner and tall, dark, and handsome to boot. It's hard to imagine a boy from this Podunk town doing so well in the city." She saw he was preparing to rise from the table, so she hurried to shoehorn in a few more words. "Sit down a minute. Were you aware that one of your junior-year classmates scanned the yearbook for 1974 and put it on Facebook? When you magnify the images, you can even read the comments, many of them off-color. Whoever heard of a chainsaw race? I sure hadn't. You won that, too. I repeat what I just said. I'll bet you were detested by every other guy in high school. It's startling what you find on the Internet, not to say terrifying."

James cradled his head. "The Internet is like that map Taz made," he said, lifting his face and stiffly getting to his feet. "It's incomplete. It's full of gray areas and inaccurate material, like a staircase or a driveway that's shown as a paved road."

"I get the hint," Beverley said, rising. "To be continued. You'd better get your rig and move it before the yokels start World War Three or the Tom Cat decides he likes your conversational skills." She paused, feeling his discomfort at being outed. "What you do is go south on the highway about a quarter mile, past that billboard, and at the first gravel driveway on the right, turn in. I'll get you the keys to the gates. There's another gate a hundred yards down that private road. Lock them after you, please, otherwise the deer and the hogs and the teenagers get in. I hope the gates are not rusted stiff. Your RV will have to flatten the weeds and seedlings unless you want to do more gardening as you go, in the dark. I will meet you in the lower lot with a flashlight and the extension cord. I rest my case, Your Honor, and forgive me for sounding facetious, I realize you must be hiding something painful, beyond your wife's passing, and I am making light of it for your own benefit. Play cards with me, James, metaphorically I mean, and you will feel better. You were raised a Catholic according to Google. Confess and be absolved. We are both fallen and unlikely to rise, but we can talk and garden and eat ourselves to health and happiness." Looking more like a crocodile than a pink avocado, Beverley smiled and added, "Tomorrow I'm serving veal blanquette."

EIGHT

I *had not noticed the dilapidated billboard when driving north nearly two weeks ago. The poster on it was clearly several years old. It had peeled halfway off and flapped in the wind, catching my high beams. I could barely read the letters* aking carverv reat gain. *Another billboard fifty feet or so farther south, also on the inland side of the highway, was in better condition. It provided a succinct version of the Ten Commandments in antique-looking script, as if Moses had used Old English text when taking dictation. I drove by too fast to read the name of the local church that had sponsored it, but believe it is that white Carpenter's Gothic temple off Pine Street, with the tall wooden belfry and the tinny synthesized bells that peal out of speakers every quarter hour, around the clock.*

As Beverley had mentioned, there was a driveway to the right before the bend and a reasonably recent eight-foot cyclone fence and gate closed with a chain and a case-hardened padlock. She had given me two sets of keys, not knowing which was which, and it was only on the second try with the larger set that the lock opened. I tried to remember which key went with which lock for the next time I would need them, in case I was in a hurry, then realized I was fussing or being manic, the way Amy said I had become toward the end, when she was dying. So, I stopped memorizing details and drove the RV through, locking the gate behind, the rustling leaves and grunts of animals making the hair rise on my arms. All the talk of feral hogs must be getting to me. It's ridiculous. I've never been afraid of animals—or men for that matter.

The terrain seemed familiar yet changed. It was the same feeling I had when I first saw the property with Beverley. The trees were taller and thicker. The slope seemed steeper and the road shorter, but how good is the memory of a teenager when retrieved forty-odd years later and how much had Mr. Egmont and his successors, including "Number Three," done to alter the resort? I am curious to know what happened to Egmont, and who took over after him, if anyone, before Beverley and her husband arrived. Egmont was a good man, conservative but fair, an admirer of Eisenhower. I wonder how he would have reacted to the state of emergency and subsequent events. I suspect Beverley is of a similar mind-set.

Luckily, as a precaution I had taken the pruning shears and the handsaw with me. The road is overgrown, the gravel a notional substance. I had to stop after twenty or thirty feet, get out and cut the eucalyptus saplings to the ground. Some were as thick as my wrist. They are astonishing, growing and spreading like wildfire despite drought, wind, and hostile saline soil. It pained me to cut them. I comforted myself in thinking they would grow back when I was gone. The trees would survive everything, even a tsunami which, if it happens, will certainly inundate and destroy the resort.

The scent of the resinous eucalyptus rose from the shears and the saw blade. I held up the blade and sniffed it. My hearing is not what it used to be, but my sense of smell has become more acute. The untrimmed hair in my nostrils is no impediment. I agree with Beverley that it is highly unaesthetic and should be removed. However, it probably does help confound the facial recognition software. We shall see.

With overhanging branches scraping the sides and top of the RV, I was able to drive another fifty yards before I had to stop and repeat the same kind of radical pruning operation on a large coyote bush. These are even tougher than blue gum. I have always been fond of their peculiar butterscotch scent. At times it is almost as heady as that of Escallonia resinosa, *not the small pink escallonia flowers but the bright, glossy green leaves of the plant. My mother loved both. That struck me as strange when I was young, since she favored the kind of Victorian-era garden she had grown up with near Chicago, a garden full of begonias, daisies, dahlias, and roses. Her instinct should have been to destroy the barbarous native plants in her new garden. To her and Mr. Egmont I ascribe my early passion for plants. That my father was indifferent or hostile to them may also be part of the equation. I am loath to indulge in pop psychology.*

To my father's mind, the excessive fondness for ornamental plants was a sign of effeminacy. Plants were for eating, burning, and turning into furniture or crates, just as animals, especially fish, were for food, leather, or fertilizer. That is why we had no pets. They were verboten. That was the word he used. Verboten. Hunt a deer or a hog, he would say, trap a raccoon before it eats your salmon, that's the most humane thing you can do. It always struck me as paradoxical, doubly so because he was a gentle, kind man in his own gruff way, and well educated in the sciences, a biologist.

My primary concern was to get through the second gate before the night became impenetrably dark. Dusk comes before sunset here because of the thickness of the woods on the property—the trees are being suffocated by invasive honeysuckle. The headlights created a tunnel of light, but around it the blackness erased the filigree of foliage. Thinking about this unintended mental lyricism as I crept along in the RV, I remembered the way Taz had said "foilage" then repeated "foliage" as if he were chewing the word. It is hard to imagine he had never heard it said before, especially since he lives in a rural setting in a house with a garden, and his education, though limited, can't be that bad, or can it? Perhaps he was thinking of someone else saying it differently? I have known people to mispronounce foliage, saying "foilage" instead, but I can't remember who. It is strange how some words take on a life of their own in our minds, often because we associate them with a person or situation, an episode in life that marks us for some reason, usually unknown, hidden in the foliage and filigree.

Luckily the second lock opened easily despite the rust, and I was able to drive as far as several piles of lumber, crab pots, and rusty old animal traps, all of them half covered by shredded tarps and tangled in that Japanese creeper. The eucalyptus seedlings and a few saplings I encountered as I drove forward gave way, bending and scraping the underside of the RV. The scratching sound made me queasy, evoking images of caged animals trying to escape, probably raccoons, as I heard so many times at the salmon hatchery, when my father let me go with him early in the morning before school.

The complete designation of the hatchery was NSHRC, the Native Salmon Habitat Rehabilitation Center. Since both the Wildlife & Fish Department and the hatchery were defunded and abolished several years ago because of pressure from the federal government, I don't mind exercising my memory, unearthing that impossible dead acronym, an indigestible mouthful.

I suppose I might as well admit right here that my secret dream, my "dear diary" confession, is that I would love more than almost anything to revive that hatchery and fill the rivers and ocean with salmon again. Maybe I will. Maybe that's why I came back, and I just don't know it yet. Maybe it's because I had no children and have militated since adolescence for birth control and family planning because there are too many of us, no matter how you spin it. Yes, I was brought up a Catholic, but my mother was a WASP and a religious skeptic, and she inculcated doubt and nature worship in me. Silent Spring *was her Bible. Maybe the explanation is simpler. I'd just like to give back, not only to self-obsessed, anthropocentric humankind, but to the world, the Earth, in the larger sense.*

I wonder how many trapped raccoons father shot for the good of the fish and the community, meaning the human consumers of the fish? The sight gave me nightmares. Shooting into a wire mesh cage at close range seemed especially cruel and made an ungodly mess his subordinates had to clean up. That did not help buoy his popularity, which was waterlogged from the day we arrived—we, the educated city folk with attitude.

His attitude extended to his family. More than once he forced me to stand there with him and take the raccoon or hog executions like a man. The war must have done that to him. Had he fired at close range on Germans and Japanese? *I asked myself.* In what ways had he been tortured when he was a POW? *But that kind of information was verboten. He never talked about the war, and everything I learned about his experiences in Europe and Japan, and the torture that made him suffer for the rest of his life, came from my mother.*

Mostly because of the massacring of raccoons and other wildlife, I took no pleasure in target practice and I refused whenever I could to go hunting with him, especially when it came time for the cull. The wild pigs were the hardest of all to trap and kill—they have human eyes and whimper and cry like children. But he was a stubborn cuss, to borrow from Beverley, and dragged me along too many times to count. He did not appreciate rebelliousness in his son, saying I had better know how to handle myself and a firearm, because man was a violent species and sooner or later another war would break out, maybe this time on American soil. Giving me Sinclair Lewis's It Can't Happen Here *when I was fifteen, he made me read and summarize it to him. There was no Wikipedia back then, and no edition of crib notes on that book. Sadly, not only could it happen here. It did happen here. Except for my time in ROTC, I have not picked up a firearm since leaving high school in Carverville.*

I hope to the god I no longer believe in that I never pick one up again, and never have to meet another man who has been tortured.

At the same time as I was remembering the dead raccoons and deer and feral hogs, and rolling along at two or three miles an hour in the RV on the access road, it struck me as courageous of Beverley to run the Eden Resort on her own at her age, when she clearly has limited energy and little practical knowledge of the business. The spot is as isolated and potentially full of dangers as ever. She is armed with her late husband's pistols and rifles, as my father was, as other residents of Carverville surely are today, judging from the signs on houses and in yards everywhere. We Shoot to Kill. *That ought to be the town's motto. Does she live in fear as they do? Does she shoot the raccoons in the garden, as her third husband did, with alacrity? It seems unlikely. I detect little anger and no fear in her.*

My impression is that, after a life of three marriages, two resulting in children, now estranged, and having held jobs in many cities, Beverley has come to the end of the line. The Eden is her Last Roundup Trailer Park. I borrow the name from the establishment the sheriff's deputy recommended, south of town, which I spotted on the way in and made a note of because it seemed so insensitive a name. The place did not exist in the 1970s, to the best of my recollection. As the product of a peripatetic military family, with no real home, and having kicked around the country for the last three decades, I certainly empathize with Beverley. She has no last name. I have no home and no family.

Beverley apparently enjoys life in Carverville enough to stay, even if the cottages collapse and the garden goes to pot or slides into the ocean. I surmise that her pension as a civil servant, and her social security benefits, survived the economic collapse and the blanket privatizations, at least in part. From what she says of her third husband, the plumbing engineer, he prospered and presumably left her enough cash and securities to keep her afloat now, even if the vacancy rate at the motel is high. Beverley interests me on more than one level. She is blessed with the gift of the gab wedded to a sharp intellect. But I fear she may be suffering from a pathological need to talk, some form of logorrhea. In coming days, I am sure to find out more from her about her biography.

Beverley had agreed to meet me in the lower parking area, and she kept her word, dragging an outdoor extension cord from one of the abandoned cottages. Unfortunately, it was not long enough. I assured her that was all right, like her, I had a generator. We could, I told her, buy a longer extension cord tomorrow, or plug in another one to cover the last ten feet. I wanted to go to the hardware store anyway. When I was growing up, Alioto's was my favorite store in town. Does it still exist?

She was also concerned about my water supply and began a long-winded explanation of how she knew how much water I had remaining in my tanks, and how that in turn had led her to make serendipitous discoveries in town about my need to do laundry, and so on. She is exhaustingly garrulous and a magpie for details. I admit she has first-rate powers of observation. I was being truthful when I said I would have been glad to have her as a researcher.

This comment of mine was, I gather, the real reason she said this afternoon that she would have hired me despite the bogus "revelations" about my misdeeds, which were not misdeeds and never occurred, in any case. My judgment may have been deficient. I reacted emotionally and was not coolheaded enough to cover my tracks. So, my good deeds were uncovered, and I was identified as the author. No good deed goes unpunished, they say. Moral turpitude has become the norm. The unclean are tarring the cleanup crew. Who could have imagined the extent and depth of the changes that were on the way? Once upon a time we spoke of mob rule, meaning a form of populism and the tyranny of the majority. Now what we have is the Mob that rules, as in mobsters.

With luck, Beverley will not broadcast my presence or mention my name to her guests or the locals. I wonder how she can resist the temptation, especially when she plays cards with the "old bags" as she calls her friends. This is not the first time I have heard of talking or card playing as therapy. They're right up there with laughter therapy. I prefer not to be the subject of discussion, that's all. She has assured me she is equally capable of being "a tomb." I like this expression and wonder where she got it.

By the time I drove the RV onto the blocks, the garden was pitch-black. Perhaps I should attempt poetry and say "buddleia black." The blossoms of the bush so beloved of butterflies are, in the case of those on the Eden property, such a deep purple they appear black the moment the gloaming arrives. I purposely parked as close to the buddleias and ceanothus as I could, to drink in the honey scent during the night and as soon as I awaken before dawn.

Is this because we had buddleia in our garden on Five Mile Creek? It grew outside my bedroom window, a bow window with a view over the creek through panes of glass turned wavy and purplish with age. The buddleia blocked much of the sunlight, but I begged my parents not to cut it. I remember lying in bed watching the butterflies dance and twirl and spin, buffeted by the breeze. They were like the notes from a color organ, yellow and orange and blue notes, blown in the air. How could I not be happy watching the butterflies, and how could I not want to fly with them, and be as free as they were? These were secrets I could only commit to my scrapbook, not share with my parents, especially my father. The garden was my mother's preserve, my father had no say, but there was always the risk she might reveal something about my unmanly love of butterflies. The patter of their wings on the windows when they were trapped was a torment for me until I released them, opening the window wide. That part of the garden facing my old room is no longer, from the looks of it. I think it collapsed onto the beach several years ago. I must return to the bluffs in full daylight and have a closer look.

Since I myself have never possessed a copy of my high school yearbook, and since I would never have thought of googling myself, let alone searching for such a thing, Beverley's revelation this afternoon took me very much by surprise. Should I attempt to locate the yearbook? With Taz's help I'm sure it can be found. But I am not sure I want to see it, or anything else about my former life here. I do not miss a computer or smartphone. It has been hygienic to live without them. I never particularly enjoyed watching television. Giving it up was not a sacrifice.

It is true that the Internet, when you are wagging it and not the other way around, can be both useful and a source of pleasure. For instance, I had forgotten about those chainsaw races. I did not remember that I had won any of them. I must have participated in several. Whoever made the comment in the yearbook might have been recalling the one I won. Was it against Harvey Murphy? I think so, another nail in the coffin of our friendship. He was a good athlete and average in most other things, but I did not take to his sadistic, vindictive side, and he was envious of me. I always thought he, too, was in love with Maggie, and her rejection of him made him even more envious. It alarms me to think he is the county sheriff now. But it doesn't surprise me. Sooner or later I will encounter him, as Beverley says, unless I pull up stakes in the next few days. I might. It would be smart.

Tomorrow I must ask Taz to google "chainsaw races." Do people still do them? Competing to see who could cut fastest and straightest through a foot-wide tree trunk reveals a great deal about the world I spent my formative years inhabiting, often as an outsider, a kind of Martian of those days, though my hair was never green like Taz's, and I would never have worn a stud in my tongue. I was a reluctant conformist. Did I use my father's Husqvarna or the Stihl, or might I have borrowed Mr. Egmont's McCulloch? All three were powerful. Think of the noise, the stench, the destruction for no good purpose. We didn't cut trees for firewood the way I cut them on my summer job, during my senior year. We raced, using pine logs dragged down from Big Mountain, logs left over from the first big clear-cuts on the reservation. Sometimes we used blue gum. They were too sappy to burn in a stove, but we burned them in campfires or barbecues, though I don't remember the details.

It had not occurred to me until now, but in some ways those good old days were as destructive, mindless, and macho as today. The contrast comes from comparison with the halcyon days of the early twenty-teens. That kind of behavior was no longer thinkable. Since then, we have reverted to the 1970s if not the 1950s or the 1850s. But that is not right. Those pre-digital days, though anything but golden or innocent, were incomparably different in spirit, immeasurably freer in comparison. The first gilded age of the 1800s was an orgy of greed and violence, but it was not a police state. Coincidentally, that is when Beverley's cypress tree was planted. It survived until this morning, shortly after dawn.

At the beginning of today's notes, I mentioned Amy. Over lunch I spoke of her for the first time in months. Now this is the first time I have written her name in these yellow pads. Is that good or bad?

There have only been two true loves in my life, Amy and Maggie, the last and the first, with several dozen between of varying intensity. I did inventory them, and made a note of the tally, not as a boast before old age claims me but as an exercise in memory, as suggested by a smart, sensitive male therapist friend whose name I will not mention. The connection between sex and love is tenuous, that much is clear. I would need an entire yellow pad to begin exploring the topic.

Speaking of names, Amy Adams was a fine one. Even when you added her maiden name, Sasaki, between the two, it was still euphonic. There must have been some heroic, self-effacing Japanese substrate in her, though on most levels she was more than 100 percent American and did not even speak Japanese or like Japanese food.

Amy instructed me to do two things when she was gone. It feels like a betrayal to write of them here. I will do so as part of the cleansing process. "Do what you always dreamed of doing but never dared" was the first. It sounds cliché. It was simple wisdom and sincerity, two things we have great trouble dealing with as adults. The second I tried to keep her from saying, shushing her as she spoke, with tears in her eyes, and her shorn head on the pillow. "Find someone to spend your life with," she urged, "let yourself fall in love again, and be happy."

I have blotted this legal pad more than once. Ballpoint pens do not run, but the paper warps when it absorbs tears. Be happy? Who's to say how you define happiness? In my own way, I am happy now. The prospect of seeking love is daunting after nearly three decades with the same partner, and with an aging, shriveling body and half-dead spirit. My hormones are on the wane, my fantasies and recollections waxing nostalgic. I admit, I would like to know what happened to Maggie. We would not recognize each other, almost certainly. Two years younger than I but only one year behind because she was smart and skipped a grade, she was an ethereal, translucent being with ridiculously long strawberry-blond hair and the soul of Beauty seeking the Beast. Her physical delicacy and robust appetites seemed incompatible and alarming to me at that age. It has been nearly forty years since I last saw her. The mention of that cottage, Sea Breeze, is all it took to revive her again, though in truth she has never entirely disappeared, and needs no reviving. Was it on the creaking, sagging, worn-out old mattress in Sea Breeze that we made love that first time? I think so. Mr. Egmont knew. He gave me the keys but said nothing and did not wink, only smiled to himself.

How to find her? I admit, I did search a year ago in a haphazard way, but I had no success. If Maggie is alive, she has changed her birth name, doubtless adopting her husband's name or perhaps husbands' names, as Beverley and Amy did. She was here during my first return from college, over Christmas, in 1977, and she was here the following summer, the summer of '78, our summer of love. But ours was more than a summer romance. We dated for nearly three years, until college, and then life got in the way. Her parents moved at some unknown time, my parents divorced and moved in opposite directions, so that I had nowhere to land except on borrowed couches. She disappeared without leaving a forwarding address. Why?

I remember the shock I felt upon hearing that she had married the man she had taken up with after I returned to college that last summer we spent together. Professor Johnson. What was his first name? I should know it. He was our editor and friend, at least I thought he was a friend, a grown-up ten or twelve years older than we were, smart, good-looking, a spirited role model. With a search engine, I might find him. "Teacher of English at Carverville High in the mid-to-late 1970s, created the school newspaper, The Voice of Big Mountain, *reportedly married one of his students, Madeleine Simpson alias Maggie, Maddie to some . . ."*

Then what? Find them and their three or four children and dozen grandchildren in some suburb of Little Rock, Arkansas? That was where Professor Johnson came from, and where, I heard, he had returned when he left Carverville with Maggie.

Perhaps they made it to New York City as she always said she wanted to, and perhaps they are still married. I doubt it. I'm not sure why.

It's still hurtful to think she might have been two-timing me, carrying on with him when she and I were inseparable that summer, in August, when I knew I was incurably in love with her, and I promised to come back when I graduated so we could marry. She said I wouldn't, and she was right, for the wrong reasons. I would have but had nothing to return to once I found out.

Maggie, Maggie, Maggie, why did you forsake me? It was no juvenile infatuation but rather the divine chemistry of body and soul. Maggie was my first love. I certainly was not hers. She was too self-assured. We were too young. She was too wild. She scared me. If Maggie is alive today, she has gray or white or dyed hair and is a grandmother or a great-grandmother, unless she, like me, decided not to have children. It seems improbable. She might be a pink avocado or a giant purple pear like Beverley. If she's healthy, what does it matter? But it's hard to imagine those bird bones of hers buried in flesh stretched by maternity and rich food.

She probably doesn't even remember me. If she does, she remembers a clumsy, earnest, gawky boy she initiated in a cottage or a Victorian house overlooking the sea. For her it must have meant little, but I never forgot her despite the others, and despite being in love with Amy and blissfully married to Amy forever and ever, hallelujah. Except "forever" came early, too early.

This is a betrayal. I must stop. Writing this is too painful. I am still ashamed, though I never acted upon my feelings and fantasies and never betrayed Amy. How can you be in love with two people at the same time, one of them not a person but a memory, a ghost?

Rereading his hastily written entry, James made several corrections and let the deeply scored pages of the legal pad fall back into place. They curled like the leaves of a medieval parchment. He would have to stop pressing down so hard when writing, he told himself. It gave him a cramp and made his already crabbed script harder to read.

Twisting and turning his wedding band around his finger for what he decided would be the last time, he worked it off with difficulty, weighed it in his right hand, and then taped it down to the legal pad with an adhesive. "A scrapbook," he murmured to himself, "another one."

Stowing the pad inside a large ziplock bag sandwiched between baking pans in the cooker, atop a stack of other scored legal pads, he stretched his aching arms and shoulders, and listened to the wind and the branches of the buddleias brushing against the RV. He had overeaten again at dinner. Air is what he needed.

Following the beam of his flashlight, James crossed the poorly lit garden uphill along the scented path leading to the lawn and office. Beverley should install night-lights and motion sensors, he told himself. How did her guests find their way in the dark once they had left the floodlit parking area? That could be another project for Taz. Then again, was it really such a good idea? Darkness did not scare him, darkness and silence were restful, the portals of enchantment, he reminded himself, and something to get used to before the final big sleep.

The mist had curled into the vegetation. The air was moist, droplets clinging to leafy tree branches and the convolutions of the creepers. In the night, he knew, the drops would swell and fall in silence to the parched soil, where surface roots would drink them in before daybreak and the first drying winds. That is how the plants survived in this rainless part of the world.

The lights in the office were on. Beverley stood by the threshold in conversation with a guest whose car idled on the far side of the deer fence. James signaled to them and then, excusing himself for interrupting, said good night, he would see Beverley in the morning. He let himself through the deer fence into the wind-lashed darkness before she could call him back.

NINE

Awake even earlier than usual, James did his ROTC stretching and muscle-building routine in deep darkness, amid the honey-sweet buddleias, listening to the surf and the animals scurrying through the underbrush. The garden's residents were unused to his company, he told himself. The skunk was displeased. Though he had not sprayed the RV, he had made his presence known.

Red circular reflectors flared as James clicked on his flashlight and recognized the eyes of not one but three raccoons, two standing erect with paws in the air, as if ready to shake hands. Unafraid yet blinded by the light's beam, they observed him for a full minute before sauntering away. Were these the raccoons he had heard on the RV's roof each night in the public parking lot next door? Or had the noise come from prankster teenagers?

The bleached bonelike banisters of the staircase seemed to glow in the predawn darkness. The foghorn moaned and mooed, "mooing sea cows," his mother had always said, hearing "cows, and wounded mermaids, and drowned sailors." The mist hung above him in the tops of the cypress and eucalyptus trees. A new moon shone bright enough that he did not need his flashlight as he descended to the beach, the surf pounding. Breaking with habit again, on the spur of the moment, he began walking south toward the mouth of the Yono River. It was usually his afternoon route.

The beach and bluffs looked different in the shrouded darkness. The breakers were even higher than they had been the previous day. He was forced to stay close to the cliffs and meander through the forest of totem pole pinnacles of stone calved from the steep escarpments, his feet alternately sinking into loose sand or sliding on decomposed shale.

Since meeting Beverley, he had failed to take his afternoon walk, a four-mile round-trip indistinguishable along most of its straight length from the beach that continued north as far as the Headlands. When added to the six-mile round-trip he did each morning, it brought him to his daily ten-mile total. Though segmented in a different order, it was the same route he had run every morning before dawn when a student at Carverville High, five miles up, five back. Forty years later, he could no longer run that far or that fast, but he *had* to walk. It was a psycho-physical necessity. Anything shorter than ten miles meant unsound sleep.

After resigning from the legal partnership, stepping down from the bench, then leaving the boards and, finally, roving the country in an RV, he had become a stickler about walking. Gardening at the Eden Resort also provided plenty of good exercise. He anticipated another session with Beverley and Taz later. Nonetheless, when he neared the end of the beach and saw the navigational channel and the concrete walls of the Yono embankment ahead, he did not turn back. Lacing up his uncomfortable new boots and feeling himself pushed inland with the crying seagulls by a powerful wind, he followed the paved bike path upstream a mile or more along the estuary, passing under a towering wooden trestle bridge, until he reached Yono Harbor. Until now, he had not possessed the psychological strength to revisit the harbor, afraid to see what had become of it.

Infrastructure projects had transformed South Carverville, but the estuary still curled like a giant question mark in the Yono River Valley. From the 1800s until the late twentieth century, this had been the historic nucleus of Carverville's fishing industry. One of a dozen fisherman's shacks, and a single warehouse, had been preserved, James observed, at least their facades had. Rising out of the windblown river mist, the bleached gray clapboard exteriors were now false fronts on postmodern glass and steel structures, surrounded by parking lots, empty at this hour except for the gulls and resident crows. The remnant shack housed a café–restaurant, The Yono Coho, its terrace spilling along the old pier. The inevitable chocolate factory, candle works, and souvenir shops filled the shell of the old warehouse.

Jostled forward by salty gusts and cheered on by the birds' cries, James cupped his hands around his eyes and moved along the windows peering in, trying to remember the coils of rope, the crab pots and floats in the fisherman's shack, and the timber and crates of canned fish in the warehouse. One summer, when he had worked as a timber-faller and firewood cutter, he had driven a tractor, delivering truckloads of wood to this warehouse. Or had it been one of the other warehouses demolished by developers?

Two reconverted trawlers and a purpose-built ferry moored by a jetty advertised whale-watching tours and sports fishing excursions. Across their gangways dangled guano-spattered signs declaring CLOSED FOR THE SEASON. Splashing in the oily, slow-moving, brackish water between the boats was a family of sea otters. They dipped in and out of the dark river, pausing to glide on their sides or backs, barking and watching as James walked upstream, his hands clasped behind him, his windbreaker flapping like a flag.

Farther inland on Yono estuary, at the eastern end of the parking lot, the old cannery built of red brick, with a kiln and chimney on one end, and a receiving and shipping dock on the other, was now a multilevel mini-mall emblazoned with the predictable name The Old Cannery. James spotted a sign on the ground-floor boutique closest to the main entrance. YE OLDE SMOKEHOUSE, it announced, PURVEYOR OF THE AUTHENTIC CARVERVILLE SMOKED SALMON AND POTTED CRAB. From Norway, he wondered, or Alaska?

Spiderwebs on the doors and windows hinted at slow business. When James peered into the dusty panes he could see nothing but his own ghostlike reflection. More than ready for coffee and some breakfast, checking his watch as he went, he wondered aloud why not a soul was in the harbor. The tourists might show up later. Where were the locals?

Climbing the coiling two-lane road from the parking lot to the bluff, and from there to downtown Carverville, James looked back toward the ocean. He could see now that the old abandoned trestle bridge had been flanked on one side by a concrete overpass, and on the other by a freeway bypass four-lanes wide. A few cars and several trucks rumbled along, disappearing and reappearing as the river mist and ocean fog thinned then thickened along their route. He could barely hear them over the gusting wind and crying or crowing birds. Gas stations, the Seaside Mall, and a series of big-box outlets were ranged on the rough denuded hills to the south. Ahead and to the east, an amphitheater of glassy condos with decks overlooking Yono Harbor had been built, probably in the 1990s or early 2000s, by the look of them, obliterating the switchback hiking trails that he and his high school friends had ridden their bicycles on, the balloon tires keeping them from sinking into the sandy loam. Counting the FOR SALE signs and shuttered windows, he guessed half the condos were unoccupied.

The grid blocks of late-nineteenth-century streets on the windswept Plateau appeared little changed. Only a few cars and one comical pickup truck seemingly on stilts passed him as he marched along an alphabet of tree species. Starting with Aspen and Birch, and ending prematurely with Oak and Pine, the streets running from the treeless hills in the east to the ocean bluffs in the west were lined by modest one- or two-story houses and cottages, some of them a century old or more, built when Carverville had been a company town. Flanking them were single-car garages and oil-stained driveways. Most of the hard-driven structures were insulated from their neighbors and the street by tall cyclone fences topped with barbed wire surrounding untended yards where the crabgrass and raspberry bramble suffocated the tatty privet hedges. Counting on his fingers but soon running out of digits, he surveyed the abandoned houses, remembering how so-and-so lived here, and such-and-such lived there. Several places were burned out and boarded up, and one had a gaping hole in its tar-paper roof.

The same small windblown houses and ticky-tacky cottages with peeling white or pink or green paint lined the numbered streets running north to south. The exception to this rule was the crossroads in the center of town, where Main and Bank streets met. Here, facing each other across an asphalt expanse, stood the post office, a bank, the old county sheriff's office, and city hall. All were housed in surprisingly small wooden buildings from the nineteenth century, with false columns and slumping wooden porches. All were painted white, flanked by large modern or postmodern additions, and wrapped by parking lots.

Alleyways led from the parking lots to a seedy unseen section of town. Here the front yards of tiny semidetached cottages stood behind tall wooden fences. The entrances to several abandoned flea-bag motels faced the back doors, receiving docks, and garbage can areas of the town's remaining Main Street businesses. The entire downtown area was several streets deep and wide.

Detouring west down Redbud Alley for half a block, James paused in front of the single small window of Mulligan's Saloon. It was still too dark to see the architectural details above the porch, where the gambling den and cathouse had been way back when. But from the smell of bile, and the mounds of cigarette butts on the pitted asphalt, James guessed the town's favorite hangout and pool hall had not changed a great deal since his youth. There was only the one window, about half a yard square, curtained off with thick brown material to a height of six feet, so no one, especially the ladies, meaning the wives of clients, could see in from the alleyway. Back in the 1970s, old-timers claimed the place got its look during Prohibition, when Mulligan's became the town's very own House of the Rising Sun, run by the notorious Kitten Caboodle. At some point after World War II, the gambling room had migrated upstairs from the back, Kitten and her hookers had moved off campus into the Redbud Motel next door, and the saloon's owners had been required to take down the prominent sign inviting people of color and anyone wearing improper clothing to seek elsewhere for companionship and entertainment. The sign was gone, the spirit, no doubt, remained.

Recalling now how he and his sometimes-pal Gus Gustafson had threatened to pay a professional from the motel to service young Clem Kelley, a dwarfish, effeminate boy always luckless in love, James smiled wryly and chuckled. Still shaking his head, laughing and muttering to himself, lost in the past, he made his way farther west to Fir Street, then north on Second, passing the whitewashed picture windows of Ocean View Realtors, the FOR SALE sign tacked to the door weathered and warped.

Blown westward by powerful gusting winds, he stumbled on the sidewalk then lifted his eyes, finding himself in front of a new place he did not recognize. The name Cappuccino Milano was traced in gold filigree across the café's shop front. Peering into the big picture windows as he passed, he studied as if at a zoo the clutch of frosty-haired retirees, all of them wearing bright elasticized sportswear, dipping long spoons into whipped cream atop a variety of hot drinks. Two of the café's patrons listlessly or fearfully returned his gaze, keeping their eyes on him as they might watch a skunk, until he had marched out of sight. Outsiders, he grumbled to himself. Members of the ghetto of house-rich nearly-deads who had crowded onto the coast before the bubble burst. "And now they are stuck with unsellable albatrosses," he said to himself, chortling with wicked satisfaction, unsure why. The town was not his, he reminded himself; on the contrary, he was the original outsider.

On First and Heather, James pushed through the revolving door of The Logjam Breakfast Diner Deli, picking up a copy of *The Carverville Lighthouse* on the counter, and sitting in his habitual place, the last booth on the right, his back to the wall, facing the door. This had always been his spot, with his parents, his high school friends, and Maggie. Outwardly little had changed, except perhaps the color scheme of the tuck and roll upholstery, and the walls, though in truth he could not remember. The menu was a gem of hillbilly humor, except it wasn't a joke. "Proud to Serve Gluten-Rich White Bread" it declared at the top. "No Buckwheat and Nothing Organic" it continued halfway down. Across the bottom it ended with a salvo "Support American Farmers: They Love the Land in God's Country."

The newspaper was three days old and heavily creased. James did not care whether it was fresh and, for a moment, felt a surge of warmth and nostalgia, hoping irrationally an old pal might sit across from him and shoot the breeze. Searching his pockets for his reading glasses, he cursed under his breath, realizing he had left them in the RV.

Leaning back, James observed his fellow patrons. The middle-aged men at the counter bending over their scrambled eggs and bacon did not look familiar and would have been children when he was in high school. Neither did the pair of blue-rinse ladies, at least his age, in a booth at the other end of the diner. Though he had gone to high school in Carverville, he had never been accepted; he was too old when his family arrived, and his father, a civil servant, and mother, a historian, were rejected as part of the "urban elite," the persnickety city folks sent in to civilize the hicks. The hayseeds and rednecks, the KKK members and John Birchers, even the so-called hip-neck refugees born of hippies and the unionized millworkers who voted for "commies" and other Democrats, had not welcomed them. Worse still, he was an only child when every other family in town seemed to run from four on up.

A similar fate had befallen Maggie, another only child, and her overeducated parents. Her father had been dispatched from the University of Virginia to create a series of junior colleges in this and adjacent rural counties. His brand of top-down liberal enlightenment was even less desirable than James's father's state-sponsored "environmentalism." Social science, psychology, history, environmental studies, family planning, and public health—what were they? People needed real jobs and the freedom to create businesses. They needed vocational training, not higher education. And what was wrong with a big family? There was plenty of room. The government had no business telling folks what to do in their own homes and bedrooms.

As to the Wildlife & Fish Department, the fish would come back of their own accord, the locals said. Why keep timbermen from doing what they needed, just to protect some lousy salmon for the Indians? If the trees didn't grow back then so be it, the grasslands would replace the forests, and cattle ranching might stand a chance. Beef was better than fish, wasn't it, and what did the Indians know?

Righteous wrath was giving James a stomachache, so he was glad when the sleepy waitress poured him a cup of black coffee. Thinking of Beverley, he ordered a cinnamon roll. He was not sure why. He never ate cinnamon rolls or sugary breakfasts. Deconstructing the pastry with his fork, and then using his fingers, he fed its convolutions through his unkempt mustache and beard, disgusted at the memory of his reflection in The Old Cannery's windows. He was not a ghost, he told himself. He was not Jesus J. Christ or even a troll from *The Hobbit*. He was the Grim Reaper.

Facebook had been developed from the yearbook concept, he recalled now, remembering Beverley's revelations from last night. Scanning the faces in the diner and the handful of people passing on the sidewalk, he still did not recognize a soul. Did Harvey Murphy and his brawny nephew, the deputy, hang out here, like true-blue locals? Almost certainly they did. Then might it not be better to get things over with, be done with the charade, show his hand and face and shave off his beard and long hair? Had he decided to stay? But how could he stay and why?

James awoke to the realization that he was shaking his head and muttering out loud, drawing baleful looks from other customers. With a gesture of grumpy displeasure, he snapped open the newspaper and held it before him until the others turned away. *If this is home, then I have no home*, he said to himself. *It's too small, too incestuous, too narrow, a bastion of ignorance and prejudice as it always has been, made worse by the new politics and the new white flight. I might as well leave today.*

Preparing to fold the newspaper up and finish his breakfast, his eye fell upon the masthead. Thrusting the page out almost to arm's length until he could focus on the small print, he read the name of the editor, reread it to be sure, smiled wryly, and called the waitress over, asking to pay. She arrived as he was pecking the newspaper's phone number into his old throwaway cellphone and muttering, "That little jerk . . ." He hit the send button, but the phone squawked repeatedly as he squinted, trying to read the tiny screen, unsure why it was not working. *The damn thing never worked when you needed it,* he groused, thrusting it into his pocket and getting to his feet.

Paying his check in cash and leaving a ridiculously large tip, James devoured the last of the cinnamon roll while standing by his table, tucked the newspaper under his arm, clasped his hands behind his back, and strode out of the café, heading west by northwest toward Alioto's Hardware. "If anyone knows, Clem knows," he said to himself, thinking of the newspaper's editor, "to hell with the phone, I'll drop by later in person and ask him."

His long shambling stride was accompanied by the tinny ringing of synthesized church bells. Surprised, he noticed the parking lot of All Souls Parish Evangelical Temple was full. Glancing up at the marquee, he wondered if it wouldn't be more accurate to correct the third word in the name, replacing the "a" with an "e."

James was gratified to find Alioto's still in business, one block beyond the new elevated highway and the abandoned freight railway yards. They had cut off the low-rent neighborhoods from central Carverville and the coastal strip since the town's inception. The big-box stores and Internet had not killed off the venerable hardware store, possibly because, like the Eden Resort, it did not need to turn a profit. On the other hand, maybe it was still a cash cow. How practical would it be to order heavy building materials and bulky wood products online? Drones would have difficulty delivering them.

As it had been decades earlier, the lumber was piled and stacked high in a wide yard and under an old ironwork hangar. James paused, watching a forklift scuttle like a giant crab between the stacks, lifting or lowering pallets. The store area abutting the skeletal hangar still covered an entire city block, offering aisle upon aisle of merchandise, from chainsaws and cement mixers, to coatracks and electrical appliances, plus screws and hinges and calipers. Feeling like a boy in Aladdin's cave, James wandered up and down the aisles, an irrepressible smile on his face, occasionally picking up and examining screwdrivers, wire cutters, or bottle brushes, until he noticed he was being followed by a young employee.

"The outdoor extension cords," he barked, turning on the boy, unused to being taken for a shoplifter, "and whatever tools I need to rebuild a chainsaw."

Standing at the information desk, he asked if by chance they had a replacement chain and a rebuild kit for a vintage McCulloch. The employee swung a screen around, pulled out a keyboard, typed in the model number and said, "The chain we have—it's standard. The rebuild we do not, we don't stock that item anymore, no one does, but I could order it for you."

"How much would that be?"

"Let's see . . . $29.99, plus tax," he said. "Want it?"

"How long would it take?"

The salesman searched again. "You could have it tomorrow afternoon," he said. "You want me to order it?"

"That won't be necessary," James said, "next time, thank you for checking."

Paying again in cash, he folded away the receipt, slipped his arm through the coiled extension cord, and stowed the chain and tools in his large pockets, along with the newspaper. Then unconsciously adopting his habitual handcuffed gait, he strode out of the store, eager to get back to the Eden Resort.

Heading west by northwest, James veered away from city streets, taking a dirt alley out of a defunct freight yard and then an overgrown shortcut he remembered from high school days, reaching the Old Coast Highway a mile or so north of the resort. As he strode south down the ocean-side shoulder of the road, a cutting wind from the west struck an uppercut to his nose. Bending forward, he plowed into it, his eyes tearing up.

There was no beach access on this stretch of highway, and nowhere to go but into the poison oak if a lumber truck came by. He was surprised and relieved to count only two cars and one delivery van going north on the opposite side of the curving, two-lane road. No vehicles so far were headed south. Then he recalled what Beverley had told him. Recurrent landslides and a broken bridge had downgraded the old highway to a residential street, she'd said, calling it "the original roadkill." There were only a few scattered houses in the vicinity, isolated down dusty dirt roads. The downgrade was good for sleep, but not for business, she had commented wryly. Fittingly, the old Road Kill Grill and the Spotted Owl Café two miles south of the resort had both gone belly up.

The same narcoleptic state seemed to apply to nearly everything in Carverville. It had been sleepy thirty-five or forty years earlier, in his youth, a place that turned the young into dried fruit, as Mark Twain might have put it, but now seemed utterly comatose, on the point of death, a ghost town in the making.

Like the billboards he'd spotted just south of the Eden Resort, a pair of rusty outdoor advertising panels on the inland shoulder of the highway were shrouded by tattered paper flapping in the wind. The first was unreadable. The second quoted from Gospel. "We know that we have come to know Him," James read aloud, pausing and looking up, "if we obey his commands. 1 John 2:3–11."

Shaking a fist in sudden anger, he glanced from the words to the sky, thought of the Grim Reaper and Jesus J. Christ, fresh off the cross, and began walking again, faster than before. Were these the same people who generated fake news reports, he demanded of the sky. The pious crusaders, Bible in hand, ready to kill to preserve life, and eager to take down any opponent by any means? Obey his commands? Whose commands?

The question seemed topical. The conflicts of interest and ethics issues he had wrestled with and interpreted for decades on the public's behalf were unsolvable if the law of the land was not respected, and if those like him, entrusted with its application, were driven to resign to avoid incarceration from trumped up allegations. Good Christians, were they? As his wife lay dying, and he had begun stepping away from the bench, they, whoever they were, began their campaign of mudslinging and disinformation, accusing him, denigrating him and his colleagues. The IRS inspectors had shown up, following tip-offs, they said. The planning commission had suddenly found the ten-year-old remodel of his house to be in violation of building codes. Burglars had broken in and trashed the place when he and Amy were at the hospital one afternoon. And then he had discovered, thanks to a tech-savvy friend, that his bedroom, office, and car were bugged, that his private world had been violated from top to bottom and sideways. As the weeks turned into months, and the hate mail and death threats piled up, several of his colleagues were jailed while most voluntarily resigned, took early retirement, or became rhinos, collaborating with the regime. For James, there had been too many factors to process at once. His resilience and nerve had failed when Amy had died in the midst of the ruins of his career. Clearly the time had come to pull back and rethink. It was a strategic retreat, a reset, not a defeat. He would make his return when the time was right.

As he rounded the blind gooseneck curve just north of the Eden Resort, the roar of an approaching vehicle shredded the silence. James turned in time to see a jacked-up SUV careening down the road, two of its oversize tires churning up dust along the shoulder. Jumping to safety, he tumbled down through a tangle of glowing crimson-colored poison oak. Catching his breath then feeling his pockets to make sure nothing had fallen out, he counted to ten, military-style, and began hauling himself back up to the highway. Pausing there to reconnoiter, he dusted himself off then continued south, swiveling his head every few seconds as he covered the remaining quarter mile to the Eden Resort in a matter of minutes.

Noticing several unfamiliar cars in the lot, James remembered the newly arriving guests Beverley had mentioned. He hurried down to the RV, eager to empty his pockets, splash water on his face and clean up, then write a diary entry and rest in silence—and think through this latest shot across his bow. Was it the usual reckless driving of a Carverville hick, he asked himself, or a deliberate attempt to run him down? Before he could unlock the rear door and climb inside his RV, he heard a familiar wheezing and shuffling.

"Ready for a second breakfast" Beverley asked brightly. "No, I am not the Wizard of Oz, they told me at Alioto's Hardware, but even if they hadn't told me, I could have guessed you'd already eaten at the diner."

Glancing around like a trapped animal, James did not understand what she was talking about. "Alioto's?" he asked. "What were you doing at the hardware store?"

"Getting supplies," she said, catching her breath and extending something to him in her hand. "Here are your reading glasses. You left them behind, on the steps of your vehicle, when you skedaddled before dawn." She savored his surprise. "So, here's the scoop, Dr. Watson. The salesman who was sitting at the counter of the diner wearing an orange Alioto's Hardware cap was finishing his breakfast when you came in, and he noticed you right away, but

I'll bet you didn't notice or remember him, not even when you saw him again fifteen minutes later at Alioto's Hardware, where he served you? He was right there at the diner when you picked up the newspaper, and then you showed up at Alioto's flushed and flustered and acting suspiciously, like a shoplifter who'd made off with the goods. You also have not noticed there's a piece of cinnamon roll stuck in your beard, and I happen to know the only place in town with a cinnamon roll like that is The Logjam Breakfast Diner Deli."

James batted the half-inch morsel of pastry out of his beard, mortified to think he had been shopping at the hardware store and then walked through town looking like a hobo. "Good thing I just happened to go to Alioto's to get that extension cord we talked about," Beverley added with a crocodilian smile. "The Tom Cat was already looking for you, the lights swirling on his Blue Meanie-mobile."

"Looking for me?"

"It seems you pocketed a precious document at the diner," she ironized, touching her pearl necklace. "Now, I'm sure you didn't steal that newspaper on purpose, any more than you left your reading glasses behind on purpose, and that's what I told Tom, you're distracted, a kind of mad-professor type. I told a fib and said I'd asked you to get me a copy of *The Lighthouse* plus that electrical cord because you were going to help me in the garden today, so young Tom backed off when I also told him I'd go up to the diner and explain and pay for the paper if that's what they really wanted."

James searched for words. "But it's—it's three days old," he stammered, waving it in front of her, "it's creased and greasy, and I left the waitress a $3.00 tip on a bill of $8.00, and the paper only costs $1.50."

Beverley shook her head, commiserating. "I'm not sure where you've been the last few years, Your Honor," she said. "In Carverville, that waitress has no say, the owner watched it all in real time on a screen in the back room, and the Tom Cat just happened to be coming in right then for breakfast and wanted to see the paper. Good thing Harvey wasn't with him. Harvey is always down at the new HQ in South Carverville. He is not known for leniency. Just so you know, the newspaper only comes out once a week these days, not much call for it anymore, so a three-day-old copy is coveted by the local intellectuals. The editor also happens to be the mayor of Carverville."

"Clem Kelley?"

"That's right, Napoleon Kelley we call him. A mean little cuss if ever there was one. You know him?"

James subsided onto the stairs of the RV and shut his eyes. The vision of the hurtling SUV on stilts that had nearly run him over on the highway filled his consciousness, but he dared not bring it up with her. "Thank you, Beverley," he said in a hollow voice, swamped by a wave of exhaustion. He took several deep breaths and tried to put the morning's incidents out of mind.

"Don't mention it," she said. "Just watch your step. We're in an unincorporated area here, but there's a camera on every light pole in town, and in all the businesses and offices, and believe me, you are noticed in your Gandalf disguise when you walk like a madman from the harbor across town and down alleys and dirt roads only local teenagers use, as the Tom Cat put it. They may not know *who* you are yet, but they sure have you on the radar, everyone in town does. You know what the Tom Cat said to me? He said, 'We saw the RV was gone, we saw it go down the highway south last night, so we thought he'd left Carverville. Is he a guest of yours?' And I said, 'Why, yes, he is, he's a kind soul who likes gardening so he's helping me out for a while, he did ROTC, and he was a great hog hunter and fisherman when young, he's one of us, don't worry.' And you know what that Tom Cat did? He winked his eye like a dirty old man, the way he did yesterday in the parking lot, lowering his sunglasses." She paused and sucked her lower lip. "If you stay much longer you're going to have to register with the authorities, you know that, that's federal law, it's everywhere, the thirty-day limit. You can pack your pistol anywhere and kill just about anyone you please, but you can't stay put without telling the man."

James got to his feet and began pulling out the tools he had bought at the hardware store. "Where's Taz," he snapped, regretting the impatience in his voice. "We should get going." Wandering from the RV across the overgrown parking area into the shack, he cleared a space on a rough wooden bench, tossed the newspaper into a corner, laid out the tools, and picked up the chainsaw, carrying it like a wounded animal.

A bloodhound with the scent, Beverley tracked his every step. "He's late, that little scooter contraption of his ran out of juice." she laughed. "We had another blackout last night all over town, I'm sure you didn't notice down here with your generator, so his scooter didn't get charged up. His grandmother is dropping him off right about now. Like I said yesterday, he does not have a car or a license, he claims the DMV discriminates against him, and he may be right, in fact I know he's right. On the other hand, he is so clumsy . . ."

She cocked her head then dipped it with satisfaction, hearing the distant slamming of car doors. Grabbing James by the sleeve and pulling him into the garden, she shouted into the wind toward the parking lot. "Come on down here, both of you! We're in the shack." She turned to James and grinned. "Something tells me Grandma Glinda would like to meet you," she said, "Taz has been telling her about you, I guess. I'll find out soon enough over cards."

James stood rigid and silent until Beverley let go of his sleeve. He tried to back away but she reached out and snagged him again. At the top of the hill, half masked by the vegetation, stood Taz, his grandmother by his side. She was a slight woman, bundled up in winter clothes. Peering down at Beverley, she glanced at James, waved and walked swiftly back to her car.

"Think of that," Beverley clucked, "she's as shy as you are. Who would've guessed?"

Taz stepped up on cue, his recurrent goofiness stretching his rubbery face, his eyes bulging and glued to the screen of his two smartphones. Sub-base drum music thumped out of the buds stuck into his large ears.

"I just got a message," he shouted as if deaf, "the drone is arriving early, at 12:34 P.M. and fifteen seconds, with an average error of within thirty seconds. Cool!"

"Bad timing," Beverley observed, "that's right in the middle of our lunch."

"Great," James grunted, removing his windbreaker and rolling up the sleeves of his gray cotton sweatshirt. He paused to look it over, realizing he was about to sacrifice the garment to engine oil and grime. Stepping back into the shack, he was followed by Taz and Beverley. "Did you know we could have phoned Alioto's or gone in yesterday and had the rebuild kit today for the same price you paid?" he asked.

"Alioto's?" Taz shook his head and plucked out the earbuds. "Why do that?"

James and Beverley exchanged looks. "Use it or lose it," she said.

"One day you might understand," James added, "but it will be too late, you might miss having an actual real-life store like Alioto's."

Taz shrugged. "I don't think so," he said, "the drone doesn't call me names behind my back."

Beverley raised her eyebrows. "The drone shows up at lunch," she grumbled, "and that's possibly worse. You two want some breakfast?"

"Let's skip it," James said. "How about a break at ten o'clock instead? Once we've achieved something and stopped the palaver?"

Stung to the quick, Beverley said she would be leaving them, she had to put coffee, orange juice, and rolls out for the guests, and straighten up the rooms for their second night's stay. After a quick round of negotiations, she let Taz keep his favorite smartphone, the one with the dragon motif on the black housing, in case a message about the drone delivery came in, or if they needed tech assistance. "Can't you tell that darned drone to come a little later," she shouted back at them, turning around partway up the slope. "I made *tarte aux pommes* for dessert . . ." Receiving no answer, she wheezed her way out of view.

His mind was a cloud of gnats or butterflies swarming on buddleias. Buzzing, James felt he was in ten places at once, thinking about the newspaper, its editor, Clem, the incident at the hardware store, the reckless SUV, Maggie, the drone, the engine of the vintage McCulloch, and getting the hell out of Carverville before it was too late. Arranging the tools on the bench like the scalpels, forceps, and scissors in an operating room, he wiped the saw body clean, eased out the screws from the housing, and removed the old chain. Taz held up his phone and announced he was making a video, in case they forgot how to put it together again.

Probing the guts of the hard-driven machine, James unplugged, unscrewed, loosened, wiped, and slid parts in and out of place, stopping several times to remove oil from his hands, put on then take off his reading glasses, and continue the procedure.

"Now, would you like to help me remove the piston?" he asked with a sigh of relief.

Taz seemed surprised. Lashing his head back and forth in something like horror, he held the smartphone up, an amulet. "I don't see why we should both get, like, dirty," he reasoned, "besides once you pull that out, and dismantle it, everything is done, right? Then we need the kit. That's what it said online . . ."

James pursed his lips until they formed the stemless top of a bell pepper. "Ever heard the expression 'hands-on'?" Returning to the engine, he tinkered then fumbled, dropping the piston pin and watching helplessly as the main bearing fell and rolled across the dirty floor, lodging under a coil of rusty barbed wire. About to curse, he restrained himself by counting to three, military-style. "Okay, now we need some solvent, and you're going to have to lay that phone down and get dirty helping me put those parts back on the bench."

Unable to see in the dark recesses of the shack, James snagged a finger on the barbed wire and jerked his hand back in pain, smashing his funny bone on a leg of the bench. He was about to suck the finger clean until he saw how filthy it was. As he and Taz crawled around on hands and knees, bumping into each other, Beverley bustled in with a tray calling, "Coffee break." She watched them and began to cackle. Standing up, Taz beat the dust and dirt off his overalls and observed James filling a cracked blue plastic bucket with gasoline, then lowering the engine parts into it to soak. "That took you just over an hour," Beverley remarked, "oh, and you're bleeding like a stuck pig." She cackled again and handed James a clean paper towel. "Will you ever get it back together?"

Shrugging, James squeezed blood out of the cut on his finger and washed his hands in the gasoline, wincing involuntarily. "Will the parts actually arrive?"

"We can track the drone," Taz said, stroking and tapping as he backed away to the door of the shack for better connectivity.

"It's a crazy waste of energy, if you ask me," James grumbled.

"There's no driving into town to buy the parts," Taz countered. "So, you don't burn gas or waste time."

"But you'd be going into town sooner or later anyway, and you could always walk or use your electric scooter or a bike, you know, one of those two-wheeled contraptions that you power with your own little legs."

Taz considered this and seemed unperturbed, holding up his smartphone and pointing to the screen. "I downloaded the owner's manual for the saw and it says we should be able to break down the engine and rebuild it in about an hour."

"Right," said James with an ironic snort. "Except that it's been over forty years since *we* touched one and *our* fingers and eyes are not what they used to be."

"And your assistant is a voyeur and electronic onanist, allergic to sweat," Beverley added. "I've never met a Gen Z–Millennial hybrid type who wasn't. Google it, Taz, since you have that blasted thing in your hand anyway. 'V-o-y-e-u-r' and 'o-n-a-n-i-s-m.'"

Taz tapped then blushed. "I'm not a voyeur, I mean, I, like, don't watch . . . and I, I don't do that, either . . ."

"Check the definition of 'figurative,'" James snapped, "or look up 'irony' or 'tease' instead, and if you still don't get it try 'sense of humor.'"

"We don't get the same jokes." Beverley sighed, pouring the coffee and taking a slug. "It's like the music. We don't know the same songs."

"That's not true," Taz objected, swiping at his screen. He held up an earbud for Beverley but she recoiled with disgust, so he unplugged the cable and turned up the volume. *"Come on . . ."* roared out of the tiny speaker. James and Beverley's faces lit up. She began shaking her shoulders and singing. Taz joined in, dancing and wiggling like no teenage boy James had ever known.

"Vive la différence," Beverley shouted, wheezing and out of breath.

"It was Grandma's LP," Taz said when the song was over. "I transferred all her vinyl LPs to my phone, it's, like, really cool. She's still got an awesome stereo from, like, I don't know, 1980 or something."

"Prehistory," Beverley quipped.

James smiled despite himself and shrugged the tension out of his shoulders. "Who on Earth could have imagined," he muttered, walking out of the shack back into the garden and burying his face in the buddleia's blossoms. "Let's make some cuttings before lunch."

TEN

❧

S he had prepared the *blanquette de veau* using "the authentic and original" Paris recipe, she said, meaning the tiniest pinch of flour and no cream, slow-cooking the hunks of tender veal with plenty of homemade veal broth. Taz was still licking his lips as they hurried downhill across the garden and filed onto the wooden landing atop the stairs to the beach. Leaning with one hand each on the rickety banister, Beverley and James shaded their eyes, staring south over the sand and surf while Taz, stroking the screen of his phone, announced excitedly that the drone was 2.8 miles south and about to fly over the Yono River. Holding the phone at arm's length, he turned his back to the beach and began talking like a reporter. "Selfie video with drone," he intoned, speaking loudly and clearly at the smartphone while sweeping it to get a panoramic view, "with Beverley and James."

"Don't put me in it," Beverley scolded, fingering her pearls and trying to shield her face. "My hair is a mess."

"I'll send it to Grandma and she can show it at your bridge club." Taz snickered.

"You'll do no such thing!" Beverley exclaimed, holding up her hands. "It isn't a bridge club anyway, we play cribbage and poker. Turn that thing off, will you?"

James, continuing to stare south down the beach, rolled up his sleeves to catch the warm rays of sunshine slanting through the fog. The scene made him think of the baroque paintings he had seen in church, votive offerings showing the Virgin in clouds shot through by the Holy Spirit's shafts of light. The surf sparkled now, alternately crashing and roaring then growing calm. The wind had dropped. The warmth of the afternoon sun and the sound of the waves were mesmerizing, the water twinkling and glinting then dark and dull. Through this dreamy haze something metallic on the tide line flickered and lolled in the waves, catching his eye. Pointing to it, James asked Beverley what she thought it might be.

Staring hard, she shook her head. "Too far, I'm not sure . . ." She hesitated, uneasy. "It looks like that shopping cart from the supermarket again."

"That's what I thought," James said. "But it isn't, there are no wheels and no handlebar in the back. There's something white inside."

Taz lowered the phone, and turned to glance at the beach. "It's a big crab pot," he said. Pointing the phone, he clicked then zoomed and scanned the screen. "Definitely some kind of steel crab or lobster pot or an animal trap maybe," he said, "with something white inside . . . but it's all wrapped up in rusty wire . . . with a broken rope attached." Suddenly remembering the drone, he tapped and tickled the screen and started the video again. "It's coming," he shouted, "there it is . . ."

They saw what at first looked like a large bird merged with an octopus, a daddy longlegs, and a helicopter, its multiple rotors a blur of motion. The drone flew straight along the beach, slowed as if slamming on the air brakes, then veered directly overhead, whirring across the garden, its payload secured underneath, like a helicopter carrying construction material to an isolated site.

"Quick," Taz shouted, "let's run up to the parking lot."

"Run?" Beverley asked. "I don't run. You go on up there and deal with it. Bring the delivery down," she added as an afterthought, shouting after him, "so James can finish the saw."

James leaned on the banister, watching the glinting object rocking on the beach, hit by waves. "It's too big to be a crab pot," he said. "I'm going down to see."

"Now, isn't this just wonderful!" Beverley exclaimed, watching as Taz ran uphill and James, putting on his gardening gloves, descended the stairs like Peg-Leg Pete. "Boys will be boys, and boy, am I glad I never had one . . ."

The drone was back in the air and on its way north before Taz could reach the parking lot. It whizzed overhead as James crossed the shale and loose sand and marched to the tide line. From her lookout atop the stairs, Beverley saw him approach the object, get one hand on it, then rush back as the rollers came in. He followed the waves out, grabbed the wires around what looked increasingly to Beverley like an animal trap, wrestling but giving up again as a new set of breakers crashed down, chasing him up the beach. He was on his third attempt when Taz returned clutching a padded envelope, glowing with triumph. Before he could gloat, Beverley pointed and said, "Go on down and give him a hand, will you? He's going to get drowned if he's not careful. Tell him to leave that darn thing alone and come back up, my French apple pie is waiting and I'm hungry for it."

Beverley thrust a pair of gardening gloves at Taz. He took them, handed her the envelope and his smartphone and timidly obeyed, climbing down the stairs like a cat crossing a puddle, then bounding like a baby camel across the sand to the water's edge. Beverley shook her head, muttering, watching them wrestle the basket, or whatever it was, up to their knees in water, knocked down by waves, then up again and dragging the object across the beach above the high-tide line. A sudden sense of déjà vu, of a nightmare reenacting itself, seized her. How could she have not recognized that cage? Cupping her hands, she began to shout into the wind, then gave up, realizing it was pointless. Panicky and breathless, she clambered down the staircase and waddled over the beach to where they stood gasping, splayed out on the sand. Both were soaked, cut on their arms and legs and bleeding, their clothes torn by the rusty razor wire coiled around what was unquestionably a large, battered, steel animal trap encrusted with barnacles.

"Oh my god," Beverley said, sucking in her breath and covering her mouth. "What in god's name is it?" She peered into the cage, screamed and fainted, dropping the envelope and phone and falling heavily on top of them.

Taz leaped up, rolled her over, and hoisted her back onto her feet, while James, still out of breath, stared at the skull and bones in the trap, and the rusty saw blade jutting out of the galvanized mesh coiled in razor wire and trailing seaweed. "We've got to call the police," he said, fumbling onto his hands and knees and crawling to get closer. He tried to reach through the mesh to touch the bones and determine if they were real. One was clearly a thighbone. "They might be plastic," he said, tugging the severed rope attached to the cage. "It might be some sick hoax, I can't tell unless we get the trap open."

"Don't touch it!" Beverley screamed. "For god's sake don't."

Taz stared dumbly, then scooped up the phone off the sand and began taking pictures.

"What are you doing?" she said. "Don't do that, don't call the police, are you out of your minds? Let's get out of here, let someone else find it and report it. Let's go before any of the guests look down and see us."

Taz and James glanced at each other, hesitating. "We've got to call," James said, "it would be unethical not to. That could be what's left of a human being."

Bending with difficulty and snatching up the envelope, Beverley regained her sangfroid. "I will call the police," she said, "from the office. If it is a real skull, that person has been dead a long time and can wait." She burrowed her hand in a pocket of her stretch pants, retrieving a set of car keys. "James, you drive my pickup to the emergency room before you both wake up and realize just how cut up you are. Now, don't argue with me, you're in shock. Taz knows the way, and he's got GPS if he screws up, so go on, get going!"

James moved ponderously away from the cage, pausing to do damage control up and down his body. A gash on his upper left forearm, where the razor wire had torn a small flap of skin away, looked like a raw filet. It was bleeding, but he could tell by feeling around that the wound was superficial. "Show me your leg," he commanded, pulling up Taz's overalls. "Not good," he remarked. "That's an artery."

"Damnation, he needs stitches, then," Beverley wept. "I'll be damned," she added, "his first and only war wound."

"Stitches?" Taz asked, looking down and awakening to the reality of the situation, the blood trickling down his leg and pooling inside his sneakers. His cappuccino complexion went ashen. "I don't have insurance . . ."

"Go on," Beverley ordered, pushing them toward the staircase, "before he keels over like I did, it's either emergency or your family doctor's office, Taz, you decide on the way."

"What'll I tell him?" he blubbered.

"Oh, hell's bells," she said, "tell them you got hurt in the garden, I've got insurance, it's not a big deal. Say you were putting up a fence with James and got snagged in that barbed wire." She paused as they reached the staircase, then snatched at the ripped leg of Taz's overalls drenched in blood. Then she went for James's bloody sweatshirt, but he backed away.

"What are you doing?"

"Never mind," she barked, "go on, take him to the emergency room, they probably won't ask questions."

Beverley waited until the two of them had lumbered up the stairs and into the garden. She beetled back across the beach and, using the rope, tried to drag the cage to where the surf might wash it back out to sea . But she could not budge it. Cursing, she marched around the trap, raking with a piece of driftwood to wipe out footprints and the signs Taz and James had made where they had rested on the sand.

Back at the shack, she dragged the coil of barbed wire out of the corner, dropped it in the garden near the door, and draped the snippet of Taz's torn overalls on it. Then she found the blood-dotted paper towel James had used and left it on the workbench. "Out to sea and dropped by helicopter," she whispered to herself, breaking a sweat. "Damn, damn, damn it!"

Walking as fast as her thick legs would carry her, out of breath and coughing, Beverley banged violently on the door of her guests in the Honeysuckle Cottage and rousted them out in their bathrobes, saying she had been in the garden looking at the beach and had spotted a suspicious object, would they please come with her to see what it was? Her apoplectic expression and wheezing alarmed them, and after a moment of muttered complaint while they got dressed they followed her back to the beach.

ELEVEN

*T*he most extraordinary event of the last thirty-six hours was not the discovery of the feral hog trap but Beverley's shocking revelation. It is why
I have decided to bury this and my other legal pads and compromising
documents, in case the RV is searched. The bloodstain on the hand-drawn garden
map, now displayed in clear view in Beverley's office, marks the approximate
location of the plastic container filled with sealed ziplock bags holding these pads. I
had been digging there earlier, on the edge of the rose garden and the old graveyard,
worried I might unearth a tombstone or skeleton, and though lugubrious, it seemed
the least suspicious spot. But it is pointless noting these details: Anyone reading this
entry will have found the pads and documents, god knows when, how, or why.

    Let me try to arrange things in chronological order before I begin to forget. It will
be essential to remember and justify every action going forward and backward in
time. Sooner or later, an accounting will be demanded.

    Driving Beverley's pickup with Taz in the front passenger seat, I had no trouble
finding the hospital—it was in the same gloomy 1960s breeze-block and curtain-
wall buildings in East Carverville, though glassy annexes and a new bungalow-style
wing have been added, reflecting the relative prosperity or penury of the periods in
which they were built. Taz was coming out of shock and realizing he was in pain.
He and I entered the emergency room together. While we must have looked thoroughly

bloodied, torn, and pale, no one seemed to take notice, neither the staff nor the others waiting their turn for attention.

For a dying, half-abandoned timber town miles from the nearest city or interstate, the emergency room struck me as unnaturally busy. What I guessed were several road accident victims lay on gurneys screaming and writhing, their disfigured bodies and faces covered with gore, their flesh torn and, in one case, badly burned. Why were they parked in the entrance, surrounded by armed guards, and not inside operating rooms being treated? I did not know at the time. I found out only later that a bus filled with a reforestation crew had collided on Highway 12 with a truck carrying farmworkers. The emergency services were overwhelmed.

Arrayed on wooden benches in the hallway was a Court of Miracles out of Victor Hugo's Les Misérables. *But why be coy? Hugo would not have recognized them. These were desperate, poor, bedraggled men, women, and children, their skin various shades of brown, black, yellow, or red. I surmised they were uninsured illegal immigrants, farmhands, pipeline workers, and drifters, with a few reservation residents among them. Native Americans once ran fishing boats out of Yono Harbor. I knew a few of them way back when, but beyond them I never saw a person of color on the streets of Carverville in my youth, and had not seen anything but Caucasians during this, my current visit. So, I was taken by surprise. Where had they come from?*

Whether they were obtuse and malevolent or merely overwhelmed and exhausted I couldn't say, but the nurses, doctors, and orderlies on duty made it clear we would have to wait, triage was ongoing and noncritical patients were non-priorities, even one with a partially severed artery. Someone pushed a pile of papers at me and told me to fill them in. Another asked if we were insured and where we lived and who we were. I purposely allowed the blood to trickle from my arm onto the counter, and I tried but failed to get some gauze from a nurse to bind up Taz's gashed leg. Snatching out several tissues from a dispenser, I mopped at his blood and dumped the tissues on the counter to make my point. The staff reacted with hostility and said they would call security if I persisted. A pair of them glanced up at a camera and nodded, signaling someone behind the scenes. Angry and worried, I led Taz out of the hospital back to the pickup and drove off.

"Where's the doctor's office?" I asked, not meaning to sound so harsh.

Taz mumbled an address I could not understand and then fainted, falling forward and hitting his head on the windshield. I shook him by the shoulder and made him repeat what he'd said. "I don't have insurance," he added in a pathetic voice.

"If you bleed to death you won't need it," I said, again too harshly, but my arm was throbbing, and I, too, was in pain. "We're going to your family doctor and I need his name and address." This seemed to wake the boy up. Using his smartphone, he guided us to a new section of town southeast of the bypass, to a complex of modern shingle-sided buildings near the Seaside Mall, where Dr. Dewey, a gerontologist, has his office.

To say we entered like a pair of bank robbers playing paintball may be overstating it, but we did unintentionally burst through the doors and stagger into the reception area, with Taz in a faint. That explains why the receptionist jumped up screaming. Naturally I apologized to her and the half-dozen elderly patients who, in dead silence, had been quietly reading out-of-date magazines. I couldn't help noticing that one of them was Seventeen, *an unlikely publication given the doctor's specialty. Taz and I were sound and fury, and I understand why several of the nearly dead, despite reduced mobility, managed to struggle to their feet and back out toward the exit, one of them using a walker.*

"He's had an accident," I explained, "we tried the emergency room, but they're swamped . . ."

Luckily, the receptionist recognized Taz—he's hard not to recognize. She reassured everyone, then led us into an examining room down a hallway, putting on disposable gloves, then tying a tourniquet around Taz's thigh before trotting silently away to get the doctor.

"Dewey" was a name I vaguely recognized, but he had not been in my class at Carverville High and seemed a lot younger than I in appearance. It turns out Dr. Jake Dewey, gerontologist, graduated three years after I did, so while technically we might have known each other when I was a senior and he was a freshman, I had no recollection of him and he clearly did not recognize me. His older brother, Jonathan, was a year ahead of me, I realized later, and I did remember him slightly. Apparently, Jonathan found a custodial job at the junior college and was still there, nearing retirement, with the high-sounding title of property manager. I also learned both brothers had known Taz's grandmother for a number of years, and Jake had been her GP before he specialized, so she and Taz were "grandfathered" into his practice. Jake's wife belongs to the club where Beverley and Taz's grandmother play cards once a week.

Imagine a tall, heavyset, benign, bespectacled man in his late fifties, with a ruddy complexion, small hairy hands, an unusually reedy, upbeat tenor voice, and that piebald look of thick salt-and-pepper hair so many people view as distinguished in a medical man or lawyer, yet suspicious on the head of an indigent.

Above I used the word "technically" for a reason. It leads me into our somewhat stilted, telegraphic conversation, following quick handshakes and further apologies on my part for bursting in without an appointment. There were video cameras in the reception area and examining room, and security cameras outside in the parking lot. I have no way of accessing the data they recorded. But I do have the exact words spoken during the consultation, thanks to Taz. He had the presence of mind to record the episode with his smartphone. Given what I learned later, this might prove a godsend: It demonstrates we were not trying to hide anything. There is no video footage. The smartphone was in the pocket of his hoodie. I reproduce part of the dialogue here as follows. Presumably the rest can be found on the server Taz used in the days following the incident to store photos, videos, texts, and telephone conversations related to it.

"What has happened to you, Alexander?"

"I—I guess I cut myself . . ."

"Evidently, let's take a look at that. . . . Hmmm, a nice laceration you have there, Alex. Let's see, let me clean it up a little and see how deep it is . . . this might hurt a little . . . hmmm, yes, this might smart a little more, so make fists and grit your teeth and it'll be over in a second. . . . Yes, it's not that bad, but you did graze the anterior tibial artery, so I'm going to need to put in a few stitches. Ever had stitches, Alex?"

"No, I never . . ."

"Now, I'm calling my assistant, Nurse Jones, you know Jeanne, Alex, and we'll take care of this in a minute."

Dewey left the room and returned with the nurse, who appeared with a tray on which a syringe, disinfectants, cotton fluff, and gauze flanked what looked to me like the kind of needles and thread used to sew up a turkey at Thanksgiving. She smiled at Taz and said hello and how sorry she was to see he'd had an accident. It was clear Taz was about to faint again, so I stood by him and patted his shoulder and said everything would be okay. I did not realize my arm wound was dripping blood. A few drops splashed on Taz's shoulder and one hit the doctor's hand. Meanwhile, at calf level, he and the nurse busied themselves with Taz.

"Ah, it looks like you're wounded, too," Dewey said, wiping away the blood, and seeming to notice me for the first time, "mister, mister . . ."

"James," I said, "everyone calls me James."

"Nurse, once we're through with Alex, let's take a look at Mr. James's arm there. He might be able to explain what happened. Some domestic accident perhaps, Alex, are you going to be all right?"

"I'll be all right, I think."

"Hmmm . . . was it a blade or a wire of some kind? Nurse, let's give Alex a little lidocaine right here?"

"Yes, doctor . . ."

"It was a wire," Taz said, wincing, "barbed wire, in the garden, I guess, I mean, we were, like, gardening and watering and, like, James was rebuilding an engine, and we made some cuttings from the roses and . . ."

"Was the wire rusty?"

"I think so," Taz said.

"Perhaps Mr. James knows?"

"It was rusted, Doctor, very rusted, we'll both need tetanus boosters, unless Taz has had one recently, and by the way, I am not seropositive, and I do apologize for dripping blood on your hand."

Dr. Dewey smiled and did not recoil—that surprised me.

"You call him Taz?" he said. "You must be a friend of Beverley's."

"That's right, I'm passing through. I've been helping Beverley in the garden, like Taz, I mean Alexander."

"I see," said the doctor brightly. "Well, unless Taz has been to another doctor in the interim, he hasn't had a tetanus booster since his grandmother brought him in for the first time, what was it, nine years ago, Alex? You were eight then and now you're seventeen. Nine and eight make seventeen, wouldn't you say?"

"I guess so," Taz said.

"You guess so? I know so! So, the two of you were gardening and managed to get in a fight with the barbed wire at Beverley's motel?" The doctor winked benignly and looked at me for confirmation. I nodded. "What's she doing, putting in a sand pit for children? Or building a clubhouse for card players?"

"Everything Taz has said is technically accurate," I explained, "we were gardening, watering the cuttings we'd made, working on a rebuild of Beverley's old chainsaw, and tangling with barbed wire in the shack, where I also got these bruises by bumping into the bench."

"Technically accurate?"

"Yes, it's a question of unintended omission," I said. "Taz has fainted a few times and I'm not sure how accurately he remembers things. We also went down to the beach, briefly, when waiting for the drone, and we got tangled up in some flotsam and jetsam with lots of rusty wire."

"Waiting for the drone?"

"Yes, the drone that delivered the rebuild kit for the chainsaw."

"For the chainsaw," the doctor repeated. "I see. So, you're saying the cuts may have occurred on the beach, not in the garden, is that it?"

"Yes, Doctor, I just want to be precise."

"Thank you, Mr. James, that explains the sand and seaweed. . . . So, how was it, Alex? Didn't feel a thing, did you?"

Taz shook and wagged his head, no and yes, in the meaningless way I had seen before. "Are you done? I'm, like, feeling kind of queasy."

"Just about, now we need to give you both tetanus boosters and patch up Mr. James's arm, unless he has other wounds we don't know about."

"Just scratches," I said.

Dewey raised his piebald eyebrows and had us both strip off our shirts and pull up our pant legs. He painted the scratches and small cuts with disinfectant, and the nurse applied several adhesive bandages to each of us, at first staring at, then actively turning her eyes away from, the tattoos of skulls and bones on Taz's knees and thighs. It was the first time I'd noticed them, and I, too, must have winced in disgust.

"Now," I said, "I understand Taz has no health insurance. Beverley said to send the bill to her. I will pay her back for my share . . ."

"Hmmm . . ." the doctor began, checking his watch and smiling evasively. "I think you'll survive your injuries," he added. "I know Alex has no insurance, and I'm guessing you don't, either, and that makes for lots of paperwork. Let's chalk it up to experience, you can buy me a drink one day, Mr. James. Now scoot," he said, addressing Taz, "I have a bunch of ornery folks who've been waiting a long time to see me. Say hi to your mom, Alex, I mean your grandma. She'll have to bring you back next week so we can take out the stitches. Lucky for you, I didn't need to put one in for each of your seventeen years! Tell her to phone and make an appointment this time, okay?"

TWELVE

I t was nearly three in the afternoon. James had decided to drop Taz off before returning to the Eden Resort. There was no need to further involve the boy in what was sure to be a complicated aftermath. As they pulled out of the doctor's parking lot, Taz sent a text to his grandmother, who was still at work, informing her he would be home early, so not to bother to pick him up at the resort. Then, at James's request, he phoned Beverley. She did not pick up. Eventually the answering machine kicked in.

"He's taking me straight home," Taz said into his phone, "everything's okay, we went to the doctor, I'll, like, be in touch tomorrow, I guess. If you see Grandma tell her I'm going home now. I'm too dizzy to talk to anyone else."

"Where to?" James asked as he merged onto city streets from the Seaside Mall.

"The Old Coast Highway, on Five Mile Creek, I'll show you," Taz said, shivering. "I'm cold . . ."

James's heart pounded. "Which house is it?"

"You can see it from the beach, that big old wooden house on the creek. Some people call it the mansion. Can you turn up the heat? I'm really cold."

James swallowed hard, his throat narrowing, the word "mansion" reprising itself in his head. What were the chances? In fiction it would seem unbelievable, a clumsy coincidence, but he knew real life was not only stranger than fiction, it fueled and infused fiction, it set the mind and the world in constant, uncontrollable motion.

Driving in silence due west across the defunct narrow-gauge railroad tracks, he continued west under the bypass, then headed north on the coast road, passing what his father had always called the "rural slum." It was a shantytown populated once upon a time by those who had not found work at the mill, the drifters, the grifters, and the drunkards, and those who had worn themselves out with monotonous, dangerous work, then fallen by the wayside. James was surprised it hadn't been cleared in the boom years. But no, here were the shacks with tin and tar roofs set among groves of scruffy blue gum trees and scrub brush; the chickens pecking in the dust between the carcasses of abandoned cars; the rusted box springs and woven rusty rebar transformed into fences and gates; and the resilient, un-killable crabgrass and Japanese creeper engulfing stumps, broken uprights, and piles of firewood, manure or discarded sheet metal. A tire biter rushed at them and ran alongside the pickup, barking and snarling. Some things never change, James told himself, accelerating away. Poverty preserves.

"You think they were real?" Taz asked, staring vacantly out of the window.

James clenched his jaw involuntarily then relaxed, shrugging the tension out of his face and shoulders. "Maybe not," he ventured, trying to sound nonchalant, "it's probably some stupid prank. When I was in high school, and even in college, I knew a few guys capable of doing that kind of thing. I'd forget it for now, if I were you."

With his lips grayish blue and pursed in silence, Taz appeared to James like an ailing young camel again. Did Taz have the resilience of a dromedary, James wondered. Crossing the deserts of the coming decades was going to be challenging for everyone, especially someone who looked like Taz, above all in a place like Carverville.

The mansion had always appeared different when viewed from the level highway, seeming less tall, less grand, less a mansion than a ramshackle old Victorian house. Back in the day, some higher-up from the mill probably lived there. In the 1970s no one had wanted to rent or buy it—except his pigheaded father. James noted how neat the three-car graveled parking area and small front yard were now, bounded by the same low hedge of flowering *Escallonia resinosa* alternated with abelia that his mother had planted forty years before. The house was still painted white, the trim still brown, and both were reasonably fresh. In normal circumstances, even Taz might have noticed how naturally and smoothly James pulled in across the gravel, parking Beverley's pickup truck where he had always parked his own secondhand car, a clapped-out Mustang convertible from 1966 he had bought with the proceeds from summer jobs.

Getting out of the pickup, James inhaled the butterscotch scent of escallonia, his nostrils flaring. He glanced around but did not see the giant buddleia bush under his former bedroom window. Helping Taz up the wide wooden staircase, with its painted gray treads, and then across the porch, James sought the porch swing his parents had installed but saw it was gone, replaced by wooden benches facing terra-cotta planters brimming with white pelargoniums and trailing blue lobelia.

"I'll settle you in then get going—Beverley must be wondering," James felt he had to say. "And she might need her pickup truck back." Pausing by the bow window, he tipped his head at the trapdoor hidden under the cushion of the bench seat and asked, "Ever open that?"

Taz nodded and brightened. "Yeah, it's where I used to keep my toys, isn't it cool?"

"Very cool," James agreed. Steering Taz to an armchair in the living room, helping him out of the gardening overalls, and draping a plaid blanket over him, he waited until the boy had propped his injured leg on an ottoman, and pulled out his smartphone. James couldn't help thinking of a pacifier, but he banished the thought and tried to sound unworried. "Shouldn't you change out of those wet, sandy clothes? Maybe put on a pair of long pants or sweats?"

"I will later," Taz said dreamily. "With the blanket I'm okay."

"I could build a fire in the fireplace," James said, "or the wood-burning stove."

Taz seemed suddenly to have an idea and asked James to go into the rumpus room and bring back a "controller." James asked what that was. "The console with two little joysticks," he said, surprised at the older man's ignorance. James did as Taz had requested.

"How about some water or juice before I leave," James asked.

"Juice would be good," Taz said, pointing toward the kitchen without raising his eyes off the phone's screen. He had plugged the controller into his smartphone and was tapping and fiddling with the joysticks.

James knew his way to the kitchen. He paused in the semidarkness to see if the old sliding pocket doors built into the walls of the house were still there. Having always loved their beveled glass and carved wooden panels, he had never understood why his mother had hated them with such a passion. Feeling along the edge of the threshold, he could not resist flipping up the inset brass pulls hidden inside the width of the doors. They were still there. That meant the doors were, too. But if he pulled them out on their overhead slides he would give himself away and then be forced to explain everything to Taz.

In a corner of the room stood an upright piano. On it was a windup metronome in a pyramidal wooden case, surrounded by family photos. Peering at them as he passed through the gloomy room, he could not make out the faces and profiles of the woman, man, and child standing formally side by side, looking prim, proper, and very white, a perfect Norman Rockwell. Without his reading glasses and better light, he would not be able to identify them. Who were these people? he couldn't help asking himself. Upright WASPs with an adopted camel-colored grandchild?

The icebox of old was gone, as he'd expected, replaced by a high-tech refrigerator whose wide double doors offered crushed ice, whole cubes, and hot or cold running water. On one door, held down with a magnet, was a childish drawing of a rhinoceros with a diagonal line drawn through it and the rainbow signature "Alex." No rhinos allowed, or don't kill the rhinos, James wondered, a partial, dismembered adolescent memory of a play staged at his high school floating to mind, then sinking again into darkness.

A kitchen island with a stainless-steel sink and six-burner stove rose in the center of the room where the old kitchen table had been. James found a water glass in a cupboard, filled it with orange juice, and stopped to stare out of the windows at the view of the beach and ocean. The fog was coming in, the sun already lost in an apricot haze. The waves pounded. Between sets, he could hear the rush of Five Mile Creek.

"Pretty special," he said, returning to the living room and handing Taz the glass.

"What?"

"The view, the house, everything—it's very special here."

"I guess so," Taz remarked, unconvinced. "It's always cold and damp, and the fog stinks like rotten eggs some of the time, but Grandma says she liked it a long time ago and wants to die here, like it's something she looks forward to. She was living here already when I moved in, but I don't think she was, like, born here or anything."

"I understand," said James. "It's very peaceful."

"Peaceful?" Taz asked. "Sometimes I can't sleep at night thinking we might, like, slide into the creek. I went to bed for a while wearing a life jacket. Part of the yard slipped a couple years ago, so they, like, put up those concrete pilings on the beach. The tsunami is coming anyway, everyone says so, even the deniers."

Sighing, James said he'd better get going, the dusk was thickening, and the day was far from over. "Your grandma text back?" he asked. Taz nodded and drank his juice, staring at the smartphone and using one hand, fingers splayed wide, to move both joysticks, clearly on another planet. "See you," James said. As he walked to the front door, he heard a whirring sound and turned as a small drone appeared from the rumpus room carrying fireplace kindling in a claw. It followed him across the front hall. Laughing, he remembered the toy-tethered helicopter he had played with as a boy.

"Once I get a real robot arm installed," Taz said in his goofy voice, "I'll, like, never get out of this armchair, I'll be able to pick up the bag of potato chips and fly it over here, but right now I'm, like, building fires with kindling . . ."

Letting himself out of the heavy oaken door with a bemused smile lingering on his lips, James paused by the mailbox and struggled in the low light to read the name "Hansen." Then he sat for several minutes in the pickup truck with the heat blasting and the window down, breathing deeply, batting his eyelashes, trying to clear his vision and make sense of things. The butterscotch escallonia scent blowing in with the misty wind merged with the smell of the nearly new cherry-red pickup's interior, making him light-headed and slightly nauseated. So, too, did the fatigue and stress and cold. "I must replant that buddleia," he said to himself, feeling drowsy and disconnected, "over by the propane tank." He closed his eyes, nodded off for a few seconds, and jerked his head up, glancing around as if inebriated. Noticing for the first time the eight and nine of clubs dangling from the rearview mirror, he stared blankly at the cards and felt his teeth chattering. Shivering and itching all over, he realized with rude suddenness that he was soaked to the skin and covered with scratchy sand and beach burs. His own state of shock was wearing off.

Turning on the headlights and pulling carefully onto the Old Coast Highway heading south, he saw the same late-model compact he'd seen that morning, the one that had dropped Taz at the resort, and watched it now approaching, saw its turn signal come on, and stared intently, drunkenly, as a woman at the wheel, silvery hair piled atop her head, drove slowly past him, glanced his way, leaned into the turn, and swung her vehicle into the mansion's parking lot with remarkable imprecision. Braking then crawling along, James checked his side mirror. Framed by it was the woman shutting the car door, using rubbery body English. Then she crossed the lot to the house as if she were dancing the swing, arms and legs flung wide. She was medium height, thin, and wore what looked like warm, sensible clothes of fawn, brown, and white, the same ones she had worn that morning. But it was hard to tell anything more about Grandma Hansen in the dim light and from an awkward angle, and his mind was not tracking normally. What was it about her driving and gait, glimpsed in the gloaming, that seemed somehow familiar? And how had a WASPy-looking elderly woman wound up the guardian and presumed grandparent of an adolescent camel? Recalling Beverley's gossip, he smiled wryly.

"Grandma Glinda," James said under his breath, amused yet instinctively, unaccountably annoyed by the way the woman had unnecessarily leaned into the turn before pulling into the parking lot. He'd known people who drove that way, most of them hopelessly bad drivers who also couldn't dance or ski. *Good thing she's back,* he added silently. *Taz doesn't realize how traumatized he is, not by the stitches but by the skull and bones, and the scene at the hospital.*

Remembering the trap and the rusted wires and saw blade, James squirmed in his seat and accelerated around the curves in the highway. *Were they real?* he asked himself. But he already knew the answer. During his stint as an underpaid assistant district attorney fresh out of law school, a twenty-six-year-old tossed into a rough precinct in the rotten core of the city, James had seen real bones, lots of real bones, usually with blood and sinews and cartilage attached, but sometimes bleached or clotted with dirt, and, once, a tibia and fibula still intact and sticking out of a half-rotten sneaker. Even when soaked in seawater, brined and battered by waves, in a steel cage thrown against rocks, ground by sand, and gnawed by fish and worms, you could tell real bones from fake bones. These were real, very real.

Dusk galloped headlong at him, riding sidesaddle on the fog, a translucent white angel of glowing darkness. Covering the three miles to the Eden Resort in a matter of minutes, James felt rushed, chilled, and uneasy. Rounding the blind, gooseneck curve, he slammed on the brakes, only half surprised to see the deputy's Interceptor SUV, its roof lights flashing and swirling, in the public lot where earlier he had spent ten days parked in the RV. Near the SUV were a long heavy-duty van from the local TV affiliate, a big flatbed truck, a tow truck with blindingly bright lights, another police cruiser, and the cars, SUVs, and pickups of a dozen or more onlookers.

Parking in front of the resort, he heard the distant throb of rotors and the growling, growing roar of a helicopter's engine. Where would Beverley be? he asked himself, not waiting to look indoors but crossing the garden at a trot toward the ocean. Distraught, her dyed red hair tousled, Beverley was leaning heavily on the banister at the top of the staircase, watching a group of men in wet suits on the beach below attach tackle to the cage, the tide smashing in around them and the fog now a hungry orange-white jellyfish sucking the dying sun from the sky.

On three sides, the beach was roped off with phosphorescent yellow tape twisting and flapping in the wind. James could make out the words POLICE AREA: DO NOT ENTER. The surf formed the fourth side and, with the waves pounding, was complicating the task of the flailing police crew. Deputy Smithson and several other law enforcement officers stood back above the tide line, waving and shouting, keeping the onlookers at bay. Other officers posted in the parking lot seemed to be doing the same, judging by the commotion. James could hear them barking into their transceivers. One was using a bull-horn to beat back the crowds. The TV crew rushed backward and forward. Floodlights were on, and the satellite dish stood erect as they filmed scenes of the beach, parking lot, and flatbed truck.

"Did you get our message?" James asked, striding up behind Beverley. She did not respond. He repeated his question, shouting this time over the increasing noise of the helicopter's rotors.

Beverley started, clutching her pearls and blanching. "My god, you scared me," she blurted. "There you are . . ." She took his hands. He could feel her trembling and told her concisely what had happened. But Beverley seemed to only half listen, her face averted, turned toward the beach, her eyes fixed on the helicopter approaching slowly from the south, as the drone had earlier. Within seconds the noise was deafening. The sucking vacuum effect of the rotors as the 'copter slowed, dipping then rising, pulled at their clothes and hair with unexpected force. The skids hung no more than fifteen feet above them. Then the 'copter moved forward like a dragonfly, positioning itself over the cage, and dropped a thick steel cable with a hook on the end. The three divers in wet suits leaped in turns out of the waves, one finally catching the hook. Scrambling to slip it through the tackle on the cage, they signaled with a thumbs-up and retreated to safety.

Rising with a ferocious roar, the helicopter yanked the steel hog trap out of the water, hoisting it until it swung free, directly in front of the staircase where James and Beverley stood. She began to swoon, but he propped her up. Reviving, she stiffened with embarrassment, then apologized with a silent sweep of her hand, clearly angry at herself for showing weakness. He could not hear what she said because of the roar of the rotors. They watched the helicopter rise, repositioning itself a hundred feet north this time, above the flatbed truck. Then the cage began to sink and dropped out of view behind the trees.

Trotting uphill along garden paths plunged in darkness, James and Beverley saw the scene illuminated from the side by the floodlights of the TV van and the headlights of the trucks and police cars. Breaking into a run across the resort's parking lot, along the highway and into the beach parking lot, James realized Beverley was no longer by his side. As he swiveled to look for her, he tripped, falling forward and blundering into Tom, the deputy, and a tall man standing near him wearing blue overalls.

"Watch your step, for chrissakes," Tom snarled, heaving him away like a medicine ball. James felt himself lifted and flying, and when he landed he saw the glowing yellow police tape on the edge of the highway. "This area is off-limits," the deputy shouted at him. "Get back behind the tape."

The man in blue overalls climbed into the driver's seat of the flatbed truck, started it and revved the engine until clouds of black diesel exhaust filled the air.

Backing off, his beard and hair blown wild by the rotors, James retreated into the twilit garden and found Beverley leaning against the fence, peering through the knothole, panting and wheezing. She shushed him before he could speak. Just tall enough to see over the fence, James shuffled through the sawdust of the sawed cypress trunk and stood under the thick foliage of a bay tree, a branch across his face, hoping not to be spotted.

By now the cage had been lowered onto the flatbed and was being roped down and cinched tight with movers' belts. The TV cameraman followed the procedure from various angles, scrambling onto the bed of the truck then sweeping the parking lot as the crew moved toward the sheriff's deputy in charge. The helicopter lifted higher, circled once and roared south following the line of the beach.

"The department is not making statements at this time," Tom Smithson said into a bullhorn when the noise had subsided, facing the camera and lights and holding up his left hand aggressively. "You know from social media that guests staying at the resort here saw the object this afternoon and reported it. The sheriff's office responded immediately. We are now able to confirm that it is a feral hog trap. A forensic team will examine the items in the trap in due course and we will provide information to the media when appropriate," he shouted, his left hand still in motion. "The consensus at this time is that this is a hoax. Its perpetrators will be tracked down and prosecuted to the full extent of the law. I have nothing further to say at this time. Now go on home, there's nothing to see and I don't want to have to tighten the curfew or round you up."

Clustered a few feet from the fence where James stood, the TV crew cast rapidly around, the reporter calling for eyewitnesses. Someone started talking loudly about Graveyard Beach, saying the spot had always been cursed and full of bones. James felt fingers tugging at his beard and looked down to see Beverley, terror in her eyes, motioning for him to pull his head down. She led him painfully by the beard, bent in a crouch, away from the fence, then let go and beckoned him through the garden down to the RV.

Whispering and pointing, she hurried him to open the door and climb in. "We don't have much time," she said hoarsely, her words barely audible. "They've been through the garden and the shack once and came into the resort office and poked around. I think they're suspicious. I watched, they didn't get inside your camper but they will. If you've got anything to hide you'd better get it out quick before they come back in daylight. If I were you, I'd change out of those wet, smelly, bloody rags, take a long walk and come back after nightfall, unless you want to see the inside of the new county jail." She handed him a fistful of keys. "At the end of the access road you can climb down into the ravine and take the beach to the harbor. Then come back on the beach. Rap three times on the kitchen window once you see the cars and trucks are gone and I'll let you in. And stay out of range of that damn spy camera on the highway. Now get while the getting's good! I'll explain why later."

THIRTEEN

T here's no need to synchronize watches, but let's get our stories straight," Beverley whispered, leading me through the moonlit darkness into the center of the lawn. "Tell me exactly what happened and what you said at the hospital and doctor's office."

Shushing her in my turn, I cupped my penlight in my hands and switched it on, pointing the beam down so only we could see it, then I found the path Taz and I had cut through the orchard into the abandoned rose garden. Crabbing sideways, Beverley followed me and once we'd found a flat spot among the rose stumps, I switched off the light and in a low, even voice gave her the blow-by-blow account.

Eventually my eyes adjusted to the moonlight, but it was too dark for me to see her expressions. I could tell from the negative energy vibrating through the clammy air that she was frowning, and I could hear her huffing and wheezing like an asthma sufferer. The last thing anyone needed was for her to keel over now. I'd have to take her to the hospital, and then what?

"First," she said, sounding exasperated and impatient, "I turned away a bunch of rubbernecker types who swamped me with requests to stay tonight. They'd seen everything on social media and the TV news. People are strange, and I am not feeling great warmth toward mankind just now, and furthermore, I'm also getting cold standing in the fog in the middle of winter in this wind. So, let me shift into *high gear and get to the second and more important point. Why in god's name did you make such a scene in the emergency room? I know, I know, you were trying to get their attention so they'd call Taz faster, but it wasn't smart, it was not smart, they may already have reported you."*

"What for?" I demanded, unable to hide the incredulity in my voice.

Beverley scoffed. "What for? What for? *They report everyone for anything these days, and bleeding all over the desk and throwing dirty tissues around and just looking the way you two did in those wet, filthy, bloody clothes, and talking like an educated person and being from out of town is plenty, plenty I'm telling you. I'm hoping they were too busy, what with that bus accident." She paused, raising a finger, the pink nail catching the moonlight. Then she added, "Maybe Harvey-Parvey won't make the connection."*

I told Beverley that I frankly didn't see what the worry was and couldn't make the connection myself. We hadn't done anything wrong, we'd just seen the cage and pulled it onto the beach because it seemed the right thing to do, and she'd called the authorities, end of story. Why the cloak and dagger routine?

Again, I couldn't see her face, but I could tell she was glowering at me. I felt a cold sweat break out all over and bundled my windbreaker tight.

"End of story? Try again, Your Honor, it's more like the beginning of the story." She paused and I heard the click of a safety catch being lifted, then I saw the glint of a revolver in her hand. "Forget Perry Mason, maybe I should be calling you Hamilton Burger on a bad day? I'm glad you've made me so mad, I'm no longer scared to death. And I've got a gun and know how to use it. Quiet! What was that?"

"What was what?"

"That noise . . . someone's coming, walking down the trail, it sounds like Harvey, limping, using his stick. We'd better duck and hightail it. I can't shoot Harvey, not yet anyway."

Gripping her by the arm so she could not bolt, I cocked my ears like a spaniel or a cat stalking a bird. Then I saw the red rings of the raccoons' eyes, breathed freely and wiped the sweat off my brow. "It's the raccoons, never mind them, they won't bother us. Now put that gun away."

"Just what we need," she said, gulping, "getting bitten by rabid coons, and back to the hospital we go."

"Exactly what I was thinking. You shoot that pistol or have a heart attack and back to the hospital we go. Please hand over that gun," I said firmly.

"I will not," she said. "Now how do you like that? You're always saying 'I will not.'"

I held my hand out the same way she held hers out for Taz's smartphone. She huffed and muttered. The pistol's safety clicked back on. She opened her palm. I pocketed the handgun. It was a small-bore pocket pistol, a kind of derringer.

Suddenly Beverley stooped and scrabbled in the darkness, found a rock and hurled it at the family of raccoons, hissing at them. "Now get!" she cried in a suffocated voice. I turned the penlight back on for a few seconds and watched the startled animals moving deliberately away from us, a pair of strange, dangerous beasts known as human beings. Then whispering and wheezing and coughing to clear her throat, she told me her side of the story, working backward in time.

"They wanted to know how the cage got so far up the beach, above the tide line," she said, "and I told them I had no idea. Then they asked me where that scruffy-looking guest of mine was, the old man with the beard, and did he see anything? And had he dragged that cage around? And why hadn't I or he called the authorities immediately? I said you'd borrowed the truck and went into town with Taz, but I didn't say why, and they didn't ask. I said you didn't drag any cage from my property to the beach—that's what they were claiming—and that you couldn't have called them if you'd wanted to, because you don't have a phone, as far as I know, and besides, Taz needed immediate attention, he'd cut himself on the coil of barbed wire, at least I thought it was there he'd done it, but I couldn't be sure. I showed them the wire from the shack and the shred of his pant leg I'd draped over it, so they gave up and went away, thank god."

"Why did you do that?" I asked. "Beverley, this is making no sense to me. Why are they asking all these questions, and why did you try to make it look like we got cut in the garden instead of on the beach?"

"Hold your hogs," she snapped, "and don't be obtuse. They might pretend *to think you dragged that cage from here down to the beach in order to incriminate you."*

"Pretend?"

"Yes, pretend. Don't you see?" She paused to underscore her exasperation. "I also showed them the rebuild kit and that poor old chainsaw all taken to pieces."

"Did you mention the drone and that we'd wrestled with the cage?"

"Quit interrupting me. No, I didn't, why would I?"

"Why wouldn't you?"

"Well, stay quiet a minute, Mr. Hamilton Burger, let me talk and maybe you'll understand," she snapped. "Rewind a couple years, to when Number Three died, that's when this nightmare started, at least for me."

Then Beverley told me what I still find to be an inconceivable and absurd tale of cruelty and horror. If true, we are all in danger now, Beverley, Taz, and I. I am not known for obtuseness or naïveté, but I suppose I'm capable of both, or guilty of both. I will try to give a close rendering of what she said but, having reread my words just now before hiding this pad, I still can't credit most of it.

There were the disappearances, Beverley said. People just up and disappearing. Poof! She likes that word, "poof," and has used it in conversation before. They had started a few years before her arrival, from the evidence she pieced together, but Beverley did not learn of the disappearances until much later, when her husband died. Tramps and hobos and druggies and gangland dealers and tree huggers and troublemakers—whatever that means—suddenly vanished from the streets of Carverville and the county, the crime rate falling by half overnight. Had they been rounded up and dumped in another county? No one knew. Worse, no one cared. Transients, vagrants, and other drifters by their nature disappear from towns and cities by the hundred every day, everywhere in the country, as they move from place to place. But some of the people snatched from Carverville left things and connections behind, including friends or traveling and drinking companions, and then some of the friends and companions disappeared after reporting the disappearances. Why the FBI wasn't called in Beverley did not know, but she suspected it was Sheriff Harvey Murphy's influence: He is the bureau's liaison for the county.

So, the missing persons were drug dealers, addicts, and other felons? That's what the grapevine said, plus maybe a couple gangland types from south of the border trying to stir things up and move the action north, and maybe a few of the violent pipeline protesters, too—they were all druggies and troublemakers anyway. The sooner such people decamped, the better.

"How did they purportedly disappear *them?" I asked.*

"Easy, they were dropped from boats or helicopters in old cages Wildlife and Fish used for trapping feral hogs and raccoons and whatnot. When they shut down operations in the county, there was a mess of traps left behind. That's where we figured the ones on the property came from."

"No," I protested, "those cages were here, they were Mr. Egmont's, I saw them nearly forty years ago."

"You knew Egmont and you never told me?"

I nodded and explained about my family's stay at the old Beachcomber Motel, and how I used to jog from home to here every morning and say "hi" to Egmont when I was in high school. "Besides," I added, "the traps at Wildlife and Fish didn't look like that, my dad worked for them. I saw a million of their traps. They weren't welded together as shoddily as this one was."

"That was decades ago," she snapped. "Maybe they changed the traps, or the way they made the traps, had you thought of that?"

I scoffed and lowered my voice. It sounded preposterous, I started to say, but stopped myself. I thought of the cage and the skull and I shook my head in disbelief and confusion. "Who was in charge?"

"You don't want to know," she whispered.

"How did you find out?"

She hesitated. "I saw it happen through the knothole," she said at last, jabbing her finger toward the fence. "I heard a kerfuffle in the public lot and came over from the resort because I was turning on the alarm and about to leave—I was late and was going to have to drive in the dark all the way to the city for a meeting the next morning. I saw two men arguing with each other. Then some guys who must've been waiting in the dark nabbed them from behind, right there in the lot where you parked your RV. They were cuffed and dragged away and put in a car, except they didn't go far, they circled right back and whoever it was driving the car had a gun on them when they stepped out. A long flatbed truck drove up, and the men with guns made the others crawl into a big cage on the back of it." She paused, gulping air and grabbing my wrist for support. "There was a giant hog in that cage, and it tore into the men, and the screaming and shouting and crying was horrible, it was just too horrible to describe even now. The next thing I knew, a helicopter was overhead with searchlights on and people were shouting and the cage was in the air right above me, and blood was raining down onto the trees and dripping on my hair. I could hear screams and wild laughter and swearing and someone shouting, 'Scream all you want, assholes, ain't no one gonna hear you,' and then the 'copter flew west out to sea." Beverley paused, her body shaking with uncontrollable sobs. I waited, letting her regain composure. My hair was standing on end. I, too, could barely breathe.

"See, they thought I was gone," she began again, "and there was no surveillance camera back then. I'd parked my old blue pickup behind the garage where no one could see it, not to hide it but because I was loading it up with my suitcases and laptop and I'd put up a 'closed for the season' sign but I was late, it took me way longer to close the place than I expected. I had to deal with Number Three's estate and was going

down to the city to see the lawyers, and I'd told Harvey and Tom and asked them to check on the property now and again . . ."

When she finished, almost expiring from breathlessness, I realized I'd been gritting my teeth, and my neck and jaw were sore. I'd broken a sweat and felt dizzy. It was all so outrageous, something from some South American dictatorship forty or fifty years ago, except it wasn't. I'd seen the cage and the bones myself. I'd been cut into ribbon pasta by razor wire. "Who were they?" I blurted out. "Rival drug gangs?"

"I don't know," she whimpered. "I couldn't tell. It was dark. I didn't hear everything they said. I couldn't swear on the Bible that I saw two sheriff's vehicles in front of the resort in the lot, or that the license plate of that flatbed truck and the registration number of that helicopter were the same as today."

"They were?"

Beverley nodded. "These guys were pretty sloppy," she said, "sloppy or very confident. They left the running lights on, thinking no one was around to see them." I could hear her gasping for breath. It sounded like she might pass out. "Those helicopters aren't operated by the good old Coast Guard we knew, James, you realize they privatized and outsource? If you look up those registration numbers the way I did, they'll lead you to two local Carverville businesses. One of them is a garage, the other a helicopter services company. You know what they do?" I shook my head, fearful yet fascinated by Beverley's story. "They take people like our sheriff hunting for feral hogs and deer. They are so damn lazy or obese they can't even walk anymore when they hunt, they just lean out of the 'copter and shoot. Plus, they're always transporting stuff and personnel out to the offshore installations. You want more? I have more."

"Okay," I said, "let's stay calm. Let's assume I believe you and that what you've told me is accurate." My mind raced. I couldn't think straight. "How come there's only one skull in the cage, a thighbone, and no hog bones—these pigs have huge heads and the hog head wouldn't have fallen out if the human skull hasn't?"

She stared at me and coughed with something like rage. "I never said it was that cage, who knows how many they dropped. I heard it was dozens. That cage wouldn't have been big enough for two grown men anyhow. Maybe that's why they sawed up the people in it, why else is that blade stuck in the wires? Anyway, there are only a few big bones and part of the skull left inside. The others must've fallen out, unless the body parts were never put in."

I winced remembering the rusty handsaw blade. "Why would they bother?" I asked, trying to figure out the motives for the crime. "Why not just drop them from the helicopter into the ocean, and why put them in a cage with a live hog, that's got to be hard to pull off."

Beverley nodded gravely. "To scare people," she said, "because they know word will get out that this is what happens when you come to this county. Why do those damn terrorists and mafiosi do what they do? To terrify people!"

I unclenched my jaw again. "You said you heard about dozens, from whom?"

"Yes, I heard, and if you think I'm going to tell you who told me you're wrong, I never will, not even under torture."

"Now wait a minute," I protested, "we're on the same side. I'm just trying to digest all this."

She waited two long beats then laughed a sardonic laugh in a hoarse, guttural voice. "Speaking of digestion," she continued in another tone, trying to sound normal, "I'm starving, we should have some dinner, that wouldn't be suspicious, they'd expect that. Just don't say anything in the house, in case they bugged it this afternoon." She released her grip on my wrist. "No one else knows that I know, believe me, I'm a tomb. But I am not ready to wind up in a tomb yet, especially if it's a cage, it's just too awful to contemplate. Imagine being trapped inside with a live hog, it would tear you to shreds before the cage even sank."

"Beverley," I started to say, "you're going too far—"

"Too far?" she cut me off. "I should have left when I could. I should have warned you off the minute I saw you, but how was I to know? And I thought, well, it's over now, they got rid of the undesirables, they built their damn pipeline and dumped their waste in the woods, and now the political climate is changing, best to let it slide, best to forget it and bump along, and I always wondered if I'd imagined the whole thing. But now, seeing that cage . . ."

On the way back up the hill to the Eden Resort's kitchen, Beverley asked me if I'd ever heard of "midnight dumping," and I said it sounded vaguely familiar, something to do with illegal dumping of polluted water from fracking, happened in Pennsylvania during the first natural gas boom. She said, "Yes, and it happens at three or four A.M., not at midnight, believe me, I know from being in the waste disposal business. It isn't just toxic water from fracking that people dump. It's also heavy metals and leftover PCBs and radioactive hospital waste, a hell of a lot of stuff from hospitals. And if you were looking for a quiet, remote, unpopulated place to do your dumping, Sherlock, where might you find that? I'll tell you where. Drive inland toward Narrow Rocks, or drive up north twenty miles on the highway, and poke around the woods where they laid the pipeline. People up there watching the territory have itchy fingers, they're trigger happy, as we used to say. There's a special posse of vigilantes and if you mess with them you wind up looking like one of my colanders, full of holes, in a hog cage at the bottom of the ocean." She waved her pudgy hand and gasped for breath.

"You should write detective novels," I said. Neither of us laughed.

"I might just do that," she retorted, finding her footing, "and put you in one, but I'm not sure about the happy ending."

Gulping visibly because my throat was so dry, I wondered aloud how long it takes for a body to decompose entirely, leaving only bones behind. Remembering my long-ago experiences working with the district attorney, I wondered if any genetic material would be left on the bones, in the marrow, for instance, or around the teeth, and whether the forensic team would try to identify the person, possibly using the dental records as a means, or merely pretend to and purposely fail, if Beverley's conspiracy theory was right.

She kept muttering, "I don't know, I don't know, I don't want to know."

When I floated the idea that maybe I should knock out the blocks and leave tonight, she grabbed my arm again and gave it a yank. "If you do that, they'll come right after you and arrest you," she said in an urgent, outraged whisper. "That's the perfect pretext. They'll say they wonder why you left all of a sudden, and wonder what you know and who spilled the beans and spooked you, don't you see? We'll all wind up in cages somewhere."

I did see, and had no intention of leaving, but I had to float the idea to get her reaction. "All right," I said, "I figured as much. Don't fret, I won't go."

"Pretend like nothing has happened," she wheezed, "keep taking your walks and working in the garden. For god's sake, don't go up north to the pipeline, maybe it'll all blow over, and then you can go, and I might go, too, not with you, but I'm not sure I can stick it out to the bitter end after this."

Beverley drank little with dinner and the conversation was stilted. She forgot to serve dessert. Everywhere she turned as she reheated the veal stew and then washed the dishes, she lifted objects, looking for microphones, bugs, and other listening devices. She pointed to the landline telephone and the old switchboard and made a face. She even checked behind the colanders and Baker Street sign and under the cookie jar. At one point she put the AM radio on and picked up the local news and whispered a few words to me, but I had trouble hearing what she said—something about a big *plastic container and ziplock bags, if I needed them, to hide my things. Before I left the resort office, she handed these to me in silence.*

Looking back on the events of this and the days that followed, it may have been rash of me to write this entry. On the other hand, if anyone is looking for my buried treasure, the game is up already. I will be more than tired by the time I dig the hole and bury these pads. With them I will include my final report to the state ethics com-mittee, annotated with sources, in cipher. Even here in these pages I cannot reveal the kind of cipher or the key. If my suspicions are correct, the committee has been infiltrated, so it is worse than pointless to contact them. The fate of whistleblowers and leakers today is well known. Hence this report will almost certainly never be sent, but I might, using an alias and a secure server, post it one day on the Internet, if I can find some way to get it and me safely out of the country first.

FOURTEEN

Wound up like a whirligig, James slept fitfully for a few hours then gave up at three in the morning when the raccoons began dancing on the RV's roof. Showering military-style, he dressed in a set of clean clothes, brought some instant coffee to life, and hesitated in the moonlit, shadowy garden before following the orange extension cord uphill to Sea Breeze. The old clapboard cottage had not been used in a long time, he guessed, by the state of the weathered white paint and the cobwebs, and the sand and tree litter accumulated on the narrow porch. Trying the door and finding it locked, he shined his penlight through the window, tracing a path into the past, a Milky Way of dust motes raised by his furtive activity. Dazed by lack of sleep, he imagined Maggie moving toward the cottage, floating across the summer sky, the sunlight in her hair. A reprise from a rock classic started up and played relentlessly in his head. *Sunlight in her hair . . .*

Heading north on the beach, the earworm devouring his brain, James tried to drive it out by counting the plastic bottles, floats, broken surfboards, lengths of rope, and other detritus appearing in his flashlight beam. *Would he find another animal trap?* he wondered. How long would it be before the Tom Cat and Harvey Parvey showed up to question and possibly arrest him?

The wind and tide were as ferocious as they had been the day before. His path wandered from the tide line to the top of the beach, and a few times into the stable sand dunes clotted with saw grass and ice plants and choked by skeletal driftwood from super storms.

Having had the presence of mind to charge his cellphone during the night, he switched it on now and watched the screen glow as the antiquated, disposable "burner" came to life. He had only one bar of connectivity and, checking the time, realized it was far too early to send Taz a text message.

The beam fading, James's penlight died as he approached Five Mile Creek a little before six A.M. Standing knee-deep halfway across, he stared up at the ghostly silhouette of the mansion, glad to see all was quiet and dark. An owl hooted, fluttering overhead. The creek rushed into the rock pool where he had skinny-dipped with her that summer, when the sunlight had shone in her hair, when blood had run in the streets of the city, and he had decided the best way to save the world would be the law, and not a career in journalism or the military.

Bustling along, the creek once beloved of the Yono spilled itself out of the rock pool and down between the sand banks to the beach, disappearing into the infinitely bigger, noisier, wilder waves. They beat with a rhythmic roar. James felt strangely elated. Squinting into the void stretching between him and Japan, far out to sea, he could see the glow of the white and red lights on the oil rigs, a string of luminous beads floating on the inky darkness, and, for each rig, the garish orange-yellow flares of burning gas. They transformed the scene into a watery infernal funeral procession. The distant thrumming rumble of a helicopter came and went with the wind, its running lights a migratory constellation. *Were they looking for traps*, he wondered, *or for him?*

Hitching up his pants as high as they would go, he forded the rest of Five Mile Creek, then walked swiftly north, the semaphore winking and foghorns moaning ahead. "To the lighthouse," he said to himself. The words made him think of Clem Kelley, mayor of Carverville and editor of the newspaper, and of finding Maggie. Both could wait. He would have to lie low and leave when the opportunity arose, the sooner the better, then circle back when the coast was clear—"Meaning, in another thirty years," he said to himself, scoffing aloud.

Maggie, Maggie, Maggie, three times blessed, the name made his heart race. The last time he had been inside the old mill compound was with Maggie those many years ago. Back then, when things ran 24/7, there had been no surveillance cameras, and no smartphones or Internet. Employees and security guards watched over the precious timber and equipment. Maggie had dared him, he had said no, it wasn't right, and what if they got caught, and she had said, we won't get caught, and if we do, we'll make up something silly, we'll say we saw a stray cat trapped inside, a *pussy pussy pussy*, and we wanted to save it. She had tugged and laughed in that wild woman-child way of hers, provocative, lusty, her tendril arms and long strawberry hair lashing as she ran toward the fence, tossing her head and beckoning. "Goody Two-shoes," she had sung, her wet bathing suit clinging to her pale, shivering body, "you're such a *goody*-goody-two-shoes, JP. Will you ever do anything fun?"

Before the scene had finished playing in his head, James found himself standing below the escarpment at the Headlands, staring up at the perimeter of the mill property. The razor wire glinted. There were no overhead lights anywhere until you reached the highway, a half mile inland and blanketed now by yellowish, sulfur-scented fog blowing in from the offshore flares. The place had been abandoned not years but decades ago, James knew. He put on his boots and laced them tight. Patrolling the edge of the fence atop the escarpment looking for an entry point, he tripped over the saw grass, then tripped again, and then a third time, his boots catching in the long cutting leaves of grass. The sky was already liquefying into melting layers of pink and orange topped by scoops of pale blue. The fog blowing in from the ocean amplified the light, blurred and muted it into a swirling kaleidoscope sunrise. Looking west to the ocean, he watched a solitary figure heading north in the distance by the tide line, a runner in jogging clothes with a hood drawn up. "Crowded place," James said to himself, "especially at dawn."

About to return to the beach, he caught sight of a sag in the chain-link fence under a faded signboard warning KEEP OUT: POSTED, NO TRESPASSING, VIOLATORS WILL BE PROSECUTED. Another sign wired to the fence shouted TRESPASSERS WILL BE SHOT. SURVIVORS WILL BE SHOT AGAIN. Shuffling and sliding toward it, he found the fence had been undermined, and wondered if humans or dogs or feral hogs and raccoons were responsible. The ground dimpled. Testing the terrain with his boot, he felt the loam cave in, forming a funnel spilling sand and dust and dead leaves down a narrow ravine hidden by the saw grass.

Why go in? The question seemed rhetorical, pointless. "Maggie isn't here," he said to himself. "No one is here but me. There's nothing to see. There's no reason to risk it. There might be cameras. There might be guard dogs. What if they catch me? With what's going on it's not just stupid, it's idiotic even to contemplate." *Goody Two-shoes* . . . the refrain rang in his head, Maggie's haunting, taunting smile hovering in the fog.

Before he had finished thinking himself in a circle, the earworm had started up again, and the words "lashing" and "lighthouse" had joined in with "sunlight" and "hair" to form new lyrics. On remote control, James crouched down and began wriggling on his elbows and stomach up the narrow ravine through the saw grass and under the sagging fence. Panting and sweating, his head and shoulders sticking out like a gopher's, he placed his hands flat on the weedy asphalt and pushed himself up and out of the hole on the other side, remembering the horse and the rings and the torturous floor exercises he'd done in high school, and the wriggling and rolling and wrestling in ROTC, and how Maggie had teased him about that, too, saying he would wind up a muscle head like Harvey Murphy, good for curls and push-ups and bullying but nothing else.

Dusting himself off, then moving in a crouch, he followed what looked like a path through the weeds toward a set of ramshackle Quonset huts, the cubist jumble of half-ruined mill buildings in the glowing east, swathed in morning mist.

"Maggie," he whispered, "Maggie?"

Had he taken her, or had she given herself, or had *she* taken *him*, here, he struggled to remember, here behind the last hut, in the sheltered, hidden secret spot cut off from the beach by the top of a tall, tufted sand dune? *Yes,* he'd said, *yes.* Lifting her gently he had curled her, his hands cupped under her buttocks, until her sweet, salty lips had met his. Heels locked in the crooks behind his knees, her breasts crushed against his chest, her nipples erect, she had found him, had pulled the crotch of her swimsuit to one side and taken him in, raising and lowering her lithe young, wet salty body slowly, rhythmically, squeezing and releasing, her breath catching, her eyes half closed, her whispered words a *yes, yes, yes* merging with the moaning of the foghorn.

Rustling saw grass and a gust of wind brought James back to the present. He opened his eyes now to find himself standing behind the Quonset hut, lost in thick fog, listening to the foghorn, waiting for Maggie's words. Peering up at the rusted, helter-skelter light poles and dangling insulated wires, he tried to work out whether the yard was still electrified and if it was monitored by security cameras. Why would they bother? If his theory was correct, it might backfire on them one day.

Crouching again, he moved swiftly along the edge of the yard where the biggest raw logs had always been stacked, until he came to a dilapidated hangar, like the one at Alioto's Hardware. Strewn around were broken wooden crates and rusted machinery untouched for years. "Why am I here?" he asked himself, his mind suddenly blank, the vision of Maggie coming back to him. "What am I looking for?" Then he knew, and he crouched and moved forward to another hangar hovering in the mist a hundred yards away.

This one had been used more recently, he guessed. There were smudged tire marks and half-filled ruts and flattened weeds outside, and black sticky pools of spilled engine oil from months or years ago. Inside, James found the burned-down nubs of welding rods, lengths of baling wire, and hunks of rotten leather belts, the castoffs of warehousing activity, he guessed, or the making and binding of something metallic, a cage or trap for instance. He picked up a nub and slipped it into his pocket. In one corner stood coils of razor wire, the same weft of wire that topped the fence. Was this where they stored it? They would need plenty to maintain miles of fence around the promontory.

Inspecting the glinting jagged edges and the vicious twist of the bladelike metal, his reading glasses perched on his nose, James was reasonably sure the type was identical to the wire that had shredded his skin and punctured Taz's artery. He wished for the first time in years that he had a camera or a smartphone, a phone like the one he had used when an active member of society, not a powerless recluse. *Better still*, he thought to himself, stooping and scooping up a snippet of the wire glinting in the dust, then thrusting it into his pocket with the nub, *better still than an image was a sample.*

Pocketing his glasses, he surveyed the yard, trying to trace out the most direct way back to the hole under the fence. The light was brightening dangerously, but the fog had grown thicker. He stole into it, heading toward the ocean and the roaring surf, trying to retrace his steps, listening for the thrumming growl of a helicopter, remembering Beverley's description of the fat, lazy sharpshooters hunting feral hogs from the sky.

Pausing to orient himself, as if in a waking nightmare, James heard and felt something, the same vibration and roar he had heard and felt in the parking lot. Now he knew what it was. The 'copter had followed the line of the beach, picking up his footsteps in the sand, and was closing in for the kill, its search-lights making the fog throb and glow but also, James knew, blinding the pilot and crew, like the high beams of a car driving through a snowstorm. Racing toward a skeletal shape nearby, he threw himself underneath the chassis of a broken-down lumber wagon. Closing, closing, then hovering overhead, prowling, then moving again, this time slowly, very slowly, inching inland, the blinding glow of the hellish eggbeater helicopter lit up a rusting hangar a football field away from where he hid. James stood and ran.

Stumbling on the tall, tenacious weeds filling the lot around him, he fell forward, landing on his palms. Breathless, as he pushed himself upright he heard another noise, a different noise, the distant tinkling and panting and scrambling of paws. So, there were guard dogs after all, he said to himself, primed, ready to fight, but with what weapon he did not know. Would they be German shepherds or mastiffs or Dobermans, their teeth as sharp and deadly as razor wire, or would they be bloodhounds, the kind the sheriff used to track men or hogs on the run?

Gunfire rang out as the helicopter spun around, its beams searching for prey.

Bent double and sprinting toward the fence, James turned and stumbled again, falling hard on his side. Up again, drenched in sweat, aching and dizzy, he rushed forward, hearing the growling and snarling noises closing in from behind, and the deafening rat-a-tat-tat of semiautomatics tearing through the air, fired from the glowing gunship thrumming above. The path he had first taken through the weeds appeared before him and he charged along it, his windbreaker flapping, no longer bothering to stoop or hide. Tripping, stumbling, gasping, he glimpsed the breach below the fence. About to dive in, he swiveled and saw not three feet behind him a mastiff-sized wild pig, its spittle-flecked tusks jutting on both sides from a massive, wagging, piebald head. Seeing James in that same instant, the hog let out a keening oinking snarl, butted him out of the away, and slipped as if greased into the hole under the fence, followed by six squealing piglets.

"Holy god," James gasped, seeing them disappear down the ravine to the beach, "my freaking god, what have I done to deserve this?" He sank to his knees by the fence, slipped underneath it into the saw grass, and, lying in the ravine with his arms covering his face laughed out loud, the laughter mixed with sobs of anxiety and exhaustion as the helicopter sped away overheard, gunfire strafing the sand around him and the fleeing, terrified hogs.

FIFTEEN

✿

*S*trange, after months of writing by hand, typing on this borrowed laptop
seems strange. The keys are unfamiliar, the screen is too bright, the letters
too small, the typeface unreadable. Times New Roman? Where will my
words wind up, in a cloud or in the cloud?

Stranger still, Taz told me that since just about anything with a Wi-Fi chip in
it can be used as a mike, and any camera including the one built into the housing
of this laptop can be hacked and used for spying, I have disabled all such devices,
disconnected the Wi-Fi, and covered the lens and mike with sticky putty, the belt
below the suspenders. The next step in terms of security, Taz said, is to put everyone's
smartphone and tablet device in the microwave oven. Only in there can the signals
of hackers be completely cut off.

Strangest of all, for me at least, on my return journey from the mill, was the sight
of Taz leaning out of the mansion's top-floor bedroom window, his bedroom it turns
out. Feeling a hundred years old and looking like a dead man, I stood on the beach
below the concrete buttresses and read his reply to the text message I had sent him
a quarter hour earlier. "Come up, Grandma went into town so it's safe." The time
stamp was 8:07 A.M.

Pointing to the mouth of the creek, Taz flapped his paddle-like hand then shouted,
"Over there!"

Thinking of Beverley and her obsession with the number seventeen, for the first time in my life I counted the treads of the stairway, the same "stairway to heaven" I used a thousand times in adolescence, repaired here and rebuilt there, yet essentially the same as in the 1970s and early '80s. It turns out to have thirty-nine cracked, half-rotten steps from the sand to the first landing. The coincidence seemed unlikely, straight out of Hitchcock or Buchan, so I was about to climb down and count again, but Taz came out on the deck, unlocked the head-high security gate, and waved me up the last flight. He was wearing his usual blue hoodie, this time paired with Hawaiian shorts and flip-flops. I couldn't help staring. The tattoos I'd partially seen in the doctor's office for the first time actually covered both his legs, starting just above the knees then spreading up his thighs. They showed coiled snakes, not just bones and skulls.

"I thought your grandmother was retired," I remarked, out of breath, as I crossed the porch and followed him around to the front door, unsure whether to say something about the tattoos and the obvious danger of the authorities linking the skulls to the cage and bones.

"Hut-uh," he said, "she, like, works part-time at city hall, so we can get insurance."

"You said you didn't have insurance."

"I don't but I will if, like, she hangs on another year, I think. She usually goes in two or three days a week and on Saturday mornings."

I asked him how his leg was and he seemed surprised, he seemed to have forgotten the wound. Looking down he said he was fine, he guessed.

Luckily, he didn't ask me how I was, because after my tour of the mill's grounds, complete with apocalyptic helicopter accompaniment, I felt as weak and jittery as ever I have. Clearly, it was time to leave town. But I wanted to say a proper goodbye, and I needed to get into the mansion one last time.

The oaken door swung open with a strangely familiar creaking sound. Inside, the house felt overheated and damp. But Taz said it was always cold and clammy, especially in winter, when the beach fog and the river mist formed dense cloud banks. I was about to say, "I remember them well," but I hadn't decided yet whether to tell all.

I felt I should tell him the whole truth, especially if I was leaving. I might not see him again. So, I bought time and said, "Maybe if you put on warmer clothes the house wouldn't seem so cold."

"Maybe," he answered in his default noncommittal way. "This is the only place I can wear shorts. I always wear long pants outside, so no one sees the tattoos," he added.

"Then what's the point?"

"The point?"

"Yes, why have tattoos?"

Shrugging, nodding, and wagging his head, he said, "Some people see them, I see them, they're, like, reserved for a private audience." He smiled his disarming goofy smile and instead of looking like a thug seemed a little kid again.

Taz said he didn't usually drink coffee, unless he was at Beverley's, but he'd have some with me now if I made it. He wasn't sure how the machine worked, he claimed. How a seventeen-year-old could not know how to make drip coffee I cannot explain.

On the way to the kitchen, I glanced at the portraits on the piano and my heart skipped a beat. "Is that your grandmother?" I asked. His dyed acid-green curls whipped around when he said yes, it was, at least he thought it was his grandmother when she was two or three years old, with her parents, his great-grandparents, but it might be his grandmother's mother, he wasn't sure. He'd never met any of them. Had I met my great-grandparents? he wondered out loud. I said no, I barely knew my grandparents—people didn't live as long back then.

I went over and picked up the portrait and fumbled to get my glasses on. Could it be? I asked myself, recognizing something in the great-grandparents, and in the face of the blond toddler. "They look nice," I said. "What did they do in life?"

Taz seemed surprised and searched for an answer, admitting he wasn't sure. "I think he was, like, a teacher or professor," he said, "and she was just a housewife, the way it used to be, you know."

Sitting unceremoniously on the piano stool, he unexpectedly started playing. Chopin. I'm not sure which piece, a polonaise, I think. He played from memory, beautifully, missing a beat now and then but still, it was impressive and I said so. Taz blushed and claimed he was out of practice, that he loved the romantics and wished he had more time to study and practice. His grandmother was much better than he would ever be, he added. I asked if he'd performed in public. Shaking and wagging his head faster than usual, he folded the cover over the keyboard and walked wordlessly into the kitchen. I stared a moment longer at the photo, picked it up and checked the back. A date in the early 1960s was inscribed in pencil, nothing else. A fluke, I said to myself, it couldn't be.

The other photos on the piano showed Taz, aged probably five or six, alone against a sunlit scabrous stone wall somewhere, perhaps Mexico or Brazil. There was a relatively recent photo of him holding a pole in one hand and a trophy in the other and wearing a sports team outfit. I'd noticed the trophy on a shelf nearby. It had his name on it and a date from five years ago. "You're a champion pole-vaulter," I shouted in a jocular way. "Very cool . . ."

"I guess so," Taz said from the kitchen. "It was when I was, like, young, I don't do it anymore."

"When you were young?"

"I mean, like, when I was younger. And I ran a half marathon two years ago . . ."

Drumming my fingers—the way Beverley does, an irritating habit I don't want to pick up—I said as casually as I could, "No portraits of your grandparents?"

"Grandma doesn't like having her picture taken, and I never met my grandfather," he said, again in a matter-of-fact way. "She says, one day, Grandpa might come back, he's not dead." I could hear him opening the fridge and rummaging around.

I called out, "What about your parents?"

"Fuck my parents," he shouted back, his words a vicious snarl, as violent and unexpected as the snarling feral sow at the mill. Something dropped to the kitchen floor and exploded. Taz cursed and muttered.

"Strong words," I said, stepping into the kitchen. "I shouldn't have asked."

Taz nodded and shook his head in a by-now familiar gesture as he mopped up a splash of spilled milk and put a broken, leaking pickle jar into the sink. "I don't remember my mom, and my dad left me here and never came back."

The anger and bitterness in his voice came through, but they disappeared a moment later and his puppy-camel look returned. "Are you hungry?" he asked. Feeling my stomach growl, I nodded. Fear and tension, once gone, are the best stimulants to appetite.

The kitchen was noticeably clean, spotless, in fact, and I suddenly remembered that I hadn't removed my boots and had probably tracked in sand or tar. "Don't bother," Taz said, "Grandma likes cleaning the house, she does it all the time."

I asked if he helped her and he seemed puzzled. "Nah," he said, "it's, like, a hobby for her, I guess, and I'm no good at it."

"Practice makes perfect," I quipped, "like playing the piano."

"I'd rather play the piano," he said. "Or work on algorithms or fly my drone. We're doing some cool stuff in my computer lab, it's awesome. I have to go later this morning. If you had a smartphone, I could, like, patch you in and you could watch through my helmet camera when I ride down the highway and when we fly the police drone on the playing field."

"That would be great," I said, "but I'm not equipped."

Smiling triumphantly, Taz said he could get me a smartphone cheap, a reconditioned unit, that's what he did in his spare time. It was lucrative, he added, and they were easy to sell online, in fact, he had one upstairs if I wanted to see it, or he could put a different chip in the extra one he always carried around and sell it to me. I thanked him and said I'd kicked that habit. I really didn't want another smartphone. Life was good enough without one.

Telling him that making drip coffee was no harder than fixing a phone or pruning roses, I showed him how to fill the tank with water, put in a paper filter and add coffee grounds, close the hatches, place the pot under the spout, and press the button. But he wasn't really interested. He had been sending and answering text messages on both phones, I noticed, and grinning, smirking, and chuckling with a goofy laugh, our conversation of a few minutes ago already ancient history. Out of the blue, he declared that he had texted Beverley, telling her I was with him, and she had texted back with the all clear. Now I understood what she had meant about Taz, and why she had imposed her smartphone confiscation order.

"Have you eaten breakfast?" *I asked, my stomach roaring by now.*

"Nah," *he said, yawning.* "I just got up. Your message woke me. I, like, do stuff at night, a lot."

I checked the cupboard and fridge and looked for a mixing bowl and a whisk and a frying pan, and told him I was going to make fried eggs and pancakes, I couldn't imagine his grandmother would mind. Taz's eyes grew large, the lashes beating.

"Now, if you hand over those phones, I'll teach you and then we can eat together," *I said. I could see him hesitate, calculating whether it was worth digital deprivation to eat. Silently, cautiously, he gave me the first phone, then handed over the backup unit.* "Great," *I said,* "now help me find an apron."

"I'm going to put some music on first," *he said,* "one of Grandma's LPs. Got any requests?"

Without thinking I said, "I'll bet she doesn't have Pink Floyd, The Dark Side of the Moon."

Taz grinned his patented Alfred E. Neuman grin and raced away to the living room. A few seconds later, I heard the LP drop onto the turntable and the music booming on the stereo. "Cool," *he said, coming back in,* "that's, like, one of our favorites."

We ate in the kitchen at a big old wooden table in the corner by the back door, The Dark Side of the Moon playing for a second time as the sun broke through the fog and mist. The table had been repainted a glossy canary yellow, but I think it was the same one we'd had forty years ago, a leftover from the previous owners back then. I was happy and proud that the eggs over easy came out perfectly, the whites firm and cooked, the yolks nice and runny but not raw. The pancakes were on the heavy side, but with the eggs and the maple syrup and butter it seemed like a pretty square meal. It certainly helped chase away any remaining anxiety I felt about the helicopter and the mill. They'd been out hunting hogs, I decided, they'd never even seen me.

Taz drank a whole mug of coffee, eating and singing along with the album. He knew the lyrics to every tune. Again, I was impressed. The coffee had the same effect on him as at Beverley's. He became increasingly effusive, extroverted, talkative, agitated, and ready to vault with a pole. Getting up and clearing the table, he didn't wash the plates or put them in the dishwasher but dumped them in the sink alongside the broken pickle jar, then ran back to the living room. The second the Pink Floyd album finished, he began playing the piano again, Rachmaninov this time. I recognized the piece but, again, not by name. The notes thundered and roared through the house, proof that an acoustic instrument can be a powerhouse.

Still wearing the apron, I stood by the piano and watched him play. His finger-spread was as wide as mine, the only obvious advantage of having such big paddle-like hands. Making the piano shake, he leaned into it, closing his eyes, transported by the instrument and the sound, the way the smartphone transported him. But I couldn't take my eyes off the old black-and-white portrait of his great-grandparents and his infant grandmother.

"Was their name Simpson," I asked during a lull. Taz wasn't listening. He finished the piece and shrugged and said that sounded right, but he didn't know for sure, they were dead when he got to Carverville. He'd ask his grandma if I wanted, he added nonchalantly. He could send her a text message right now if I gave him back one of his phones.

"It's not important," I said, recognizing a ploy. Tapping the piano with my fingertips, I struggled, deciding what to do—tell him or leave things as they were and hit the road. "Aren't you curious about what happened last night, with the cage and the bones," I asked, surprised he hadn't brought up the incident.

Taz shook and wagged his head meaninglessly. I told him how the helicopter had lifted the cage off the beach and put it on a truck and he said, "We hear helicopters all the time, day and night, I think it's the Coast Guard, but there's some kind of charter service out to the oil rigs, too. Grandma says they take food out when the ocean's too rough for boats." Pointing to the breakers beyond the windows, he slumped into the big old armchair in the front room and put his leg up on the ottoman. The skin around the stitches was purple and puckered. "I guess it does, like, hurt sometimes, I feel kind of tired and bruised," he said. Then, in what seemed a non sequitur, he added, "I watched the whole thing anyway, from, like, five different angles."

"What thing?"

"The helicopter and the cage, last night," he said. "It was on social media, didn't you look?"

"I was there in person," I said, "why would I?"

Taz didn't seem to have an answer, and he made his goofy face and asked for his black phone back. He said he could show me an angle I couldn't possibly have seen from the ground. I said I didn't want to see it again from another angle and that I'd seen enough. He said this was particularly "cool" and "awesome" and it wouldn't take a second and then he'd give the phone back to me. I surrendered. Beaming, he tapped and stroked and held up the screen. I recognized the scene but as he had said, it had been filmed from an unusual angle somewhere along the highway. "Very cool," I admitted, "who posted this?"

Taz said it hadn't been posted, it was footage from the 24/7 surveillance camera on the Old Coast Highway. I said I wasn't aware that was viewable by the public, and then he really surprised me.

"It isn't," he said, "I hacked in, I do it all the time, it's, like, so easy you wouldn't believe it, I could teach you how to do it, like, like making coffee or pancakes or pruning roses."

"You hacked into the sheriff's video system?"

Nodding firmly and smiling without wagging his head, he said, "I found a back door, we can watch the cameras anywhere in town." He brought up a multiple split-screen view with a dozen or more thumbnail images.

I asked if his grandmother knew he was doing this. He did his trademark yes-no meaningless nodding wag. So, I asked if the authorities could tell he had hacked the system. "If they were any good they could," he said, smiling in a way I hadn't seen yet, a satisfied, wicked or malicious way, for lack of a better description. "They're hopeless, they're, like, pitiful." He began toggling from one camera in town to the next, until I asked him to stop and held out my hand for the phone.

"Here's the parking lot next to Beverley's place," he said, "and here's Main and Bank from one, two, three, four different angles." He added, "Grandma works right *there, in that office, through that window . . . and here's the last camera on the highway, on the way up to the house, by those shacks on the edge of town we drove past yesterday."*

Curiosity getting the better of me, I asked if there were any cameras up at the old mill site. He shook his head. "No, except for one at the front gate where the trucks used to go in and out years ago. See what I mean, they're pretty dumb, like, they should have cameras inside or in other places, not at the main gate no one uses anymore." Tickling the screen then tapping it as if it were a piano, he showed me live video from the helmet camera of a deputy pulling over a motorist on Highway 12. He hiked the volume. It was the Tom Cat.

"That's more than enough," I said, opening and closing my palm in front of his face. "Do you realize what they could do to you if they discover you're doing this?" I asked, debating whether or not to tell him about penalties for hacking into law enforcement systems. He could be charged with treason and put to death. "What if they get ahold of this phone and make you unlock it?"

He fiddled and said they wouldn't and he wouldn't, it just wouldn't happen, they were too stupid. Handing over the phone reluctantly, he made a goofy face, avoiding further questions and asking if I wanted to see his drone or hear another album. "I can stack three," he said.

Waiting until my frown softened, I asked, "All right, does she have Earth, Wind and Fire, no one has that?"

Taz wriggled with delight and started singing, "Child is born with a heart of gold . . ." as he skipped over to the stereo.

"Don't let it grow hard and cold," I segued, misremembering, watching him dance, blissful. On top of that LP, he stacked a Led Zeppelin and The Doors and said we'd be climbing the stairway to heaven soon.

It's not clear to me what clicked, maybe it was the talk of hacking, and that phrase, but I knew I would tell him, tell him everything I could, quickly, and then get back to the Eden Resort and clear out of town. "What are your favorite books?" I asked, shouting over the music, trying to find a back door or a side door into my tale. Then I realized that was the wrong question.

"They're on my phone," he shouted back brightly, "I download them all the time. I can show you . . ."

Shaking my head, I said, "How about the favorite books you have in the house?"

"You mean old-fashioned books?" he asked, shouting back. "Like printed books, you mean?"

The stereo filled the rooms with soda pop soul as Taz led me to the library and pointed to shelf upon shelf of Harvard Classics, plus the collected works of Twain, O. Henry, Stevenson, Thackeray, Turgenev, Tolstoy, and others, arranged floor to ceiling on oaken shelving. "I've read most of them," he said, then smiled enigmatically so that I wasn't sure if he was joking. They turned out to have been his great-grandparents' books. I could see there were others, hundreds of others, Orwell and Huxley and Hemingway and Golding, Sinclair Lewis and Ray Bradbury, Graham Greene and John Le Carré, Dashiell Hammett and Raymond Chandler, most of them in paperback editions. An adjoining office area was where his grandmother worked, he said, and she had lots of books on childhood education, psychology, and art therapy.

Selecting and taking down a handful of incendiary works, including Eugène Ionesco's plays, I asked Taz if he'd really read them. A few, he said. His grandma had made him study Rhinoceros.

"We put that on in high school," I remarked, snapping my fingers and recognizing the same 1970s edition we'd used at Carverville High—I'd kept it all these years, until I left the city and sold or gave away everything. "Is that why you did that drawing on the fridge?" I asked. Shaking his head, Taz said it was the other way around. He'd done the rhino drawing in a geography class at school and later his grandmother had told him to read the play and watch out for rhinos. That's when he drew the slash through it. "Never collaborate," he said, as if reciting, "unless it's a way to become a mole and undermine the system."

This seemed promising, very promising. It indicated his grandmother was progressive and smart and he was cognizant of collaborationism—the pith of the play. But like the tattoos and hacking, it also raised another red flag. I told him that, given what had happened with the cage and the bones, and the way the authorities had reacted, according to Beverley, and the fact that he was a hacker, and I wasn't necessarily a great person to know for too many reasons to list, it might be good if we removed some of these books and his drawing and hid them for a while, just in case.

"In case of what?" Taz asked, his eyes widening.

"In case the sheriff wants to make trouble and comes over looking for things to incriminate you with."

"Does that mean you're a rhino?" he asked.

Taken aback I said, "The opposite." I reflected for a moment then added, "Will you trust me? I think we should start by hiding these books and your drawing in a place no one will ever find. I'll show you, and it will be your secret place, in case you want to put anything else in it. Rhinos don't do that kind of thing. Members of the resistance do."

Surprised but clearly not alarmed, Taz seemed ready to humor me. The contrast between our intense conversation and the saccharine 1970s soul music in the background could not have been starker, at least for me. Taz didn't seem to notice. He said hiding things was all right by him, but how did I know where to hide something in this house? "Come with me," I said, handing him a stack of books that were now officially "un-recommended"—the word "banned" hadn't been used yet. I unstuck the rhino drawing from the fridge door and climbed upstairs with it and into what had been a spare bedroom in my day but was now Taz's room.

"Bear with me," I said, opening the door to the big walk-in closet and getting the long wooden stepladder that had always been there leaning against the side of the built-in highboy chest of drawers. Taz watched me, his eyebrows raised and head cocked, like Tom Smithson, the deputy.

"How did you know about that ladder?" he started to ask. But now it was I who wasn't listening. I climbed six steps, pushed up the trapdoor, waited for the worst of the dust to settle, and crawled into the attic. "Bring those up," I said, turning around and coughing, "then come on up yourself. I'll explain."

There was no need for a flashlight. A small dormer window, designed to give access to the roof, let in enough light that you could see across the long, low, wide room with slanting ceilings. The dust was prodigious, swirling and choking both of us. Taz coughed and sneezed and hesitated on the ladder, peering in, clearly unwilling to get dirty. I opened the window, took a deep breath and reached down, taking the books out of his arms. Then I signaled him up, offering him my hand.

The attic was almost empty. A few hanging closets made of cardboard, the kind used by moving companies, stood against one wall. I couldn't remember if they had been ours or had always been there, even when we moved in. The floor was covered as it had been with unfinished, loosely aligned rough wooden planks laid on the crossbeams between the joists.

"Watch your head," I said, stooping and making my way to the far corner, batting away the cobwebs. "Watch out for black widows, too," I said. That was a mistake. I must have been thinking of the closet under the basement stairs. Taz paled and

I heard him say, "Black widows?" But by then I was lifting the floorboards in the corner, flipping them one by one out of the way. I stepped to the side to let the light shine in and smiled when I saw the scrapbook was still there, where I had hidden it nearly forty years earlier when I left for college. Lifting it out, blowing and beating the dust off, I set the heavy leather-bound volume on the floor and caught a faded pink envelope that was about to fall out. Slipping it back in, I said, "Hand me those books and the drawing." I took them one by one and laid them between the joists. "When this blows over, you can get them out. You can do the same trick with the floorboards in the big closet in the basement." I turned to see Taz's large camel eyes open wide, his jaw hanging slack. Then I remembered the snippet of razor wire and the burned-out end of the welding rod in my pocket, and I nested them underneath a volume of Fahrenheit 451. *I flipped the planks back over and aligned them as they had been, then used the soles of my boots to smooth away the footprints in the dust. "Now let's go downstairs," I said, blowing my nose and taking up the scrapbook. "Storytelling time has come." It sounded more ominous than I'd intended.*

Taz was down the ladder in a shot. I paused by the window and opened the scrapbook. My mind reeled back in time. "A diary is not manly," my father had told me, my mother standing by my side. It was not masculine. But a scrapbook, that was good. "The boy can put in baseball cards and photos of race cars and suchlike," he'd added. "One day he'll be happy to have it."

Now I was happy to have it. Flipping the dusty pages, I came to the faded pink envelope and stared at the postmark, reading off a date from the start of our summer of love. I lifted the flap and extracted the card. Welcome home, *she had written,* I've missed you. XOXO M. *My hands trembling, I slipped the letter into my breast pocket, closed the window, and climbed down to where Taz was waiting.*

"Go on up and close the trapdoor, would you?" I asked, trying to buy time and get my emotions under control. Taz hesitated before obeying and returned beating his hands and clothes and making faces as he coughed exaggeratedly. The hard rock music booming from downstairs filled the void for the seconds I stood motionless, my eyes blurred. "Let's sit down," I said, pointing to his bed. "This might take a while."

A visual aid, the scrapbook helped me illustrate what life at the house had looked like forty years ago. I started by showing him the title page. It read Property of J. Paul Adams, 27,900 Old Coast Highway, Carverville. *"The 'J.' is for James,"* *I said. I showed him views of the house and beach, taken with my first Kodak Brownie camera, and color snapshots of my Mustang convertible. There was even a photo my father must have taken of me with Harvey Murphy, each of us holding a chainsaw. Because it was black-and-white film, I couldn't tell immediately whether it was Egmont's yellow McCulloch or some other saw.*

At first Taz refused to believe me and thought it was a prank, that I was making things up, but then, seeing more and more photos, he came around and had a thousand questions—was it cold and misty then, too, most of the year, with yellow fog banks creeping down from the north? Were there as many deer, raccoons, and wild pigs, and tar on the beach? Were the kids cruel and racist bullies, the sheriff and deputies scary and dangerous? Why hadn't my parents let me keep a diary, and why had I hidden the scrapbook and left it there, instead of taking it with me? What job had I done when I grew up, where had I gone to university and law school, and on and on and on.

I explained about my father and the hatchery job, and how the salmon were endangered even then, and how my mother had always hated Carverville for some of the same reasons he mentioned. My parents didn't get along but had waited until I was grown up and in college, starting my junior year, and then they separated, sold the house, packed up, and moved away from each other before I could come home and interfere. I no longer had a home in Carverville, they said, we were never welcome here anyway. I could take turns staying with each of them, if I wanted, they'd added, following with a "but." The "but" was, I was all grown up now anyway, wasn't I, and would be going to law school, if I kept my grades up and did well enough on the LSAT exams.

During that same semester, the girl I loved had left town, and I'd never been able to find her, I told Taz, adding that I'd always wanted to come back, if for no other reason than to find closure. But I should not have come back, and now I must go. I stood up, wondering whether to take the scrapbook with me or hide it again upstairs. The music boomed below, The Doors lighting fires in LA, fires that had spread across the world all those years ago but had now gone out. I wiped my dusty hands on the apron, gave Taz back his smartphones, and turned toward the stairs to the entrance hall.

"See you," Taz said as if in a trance, the glowing screens already his new master. "At Beverley's," he added, "tomorrow. I've, like, got to go to my computer lab now. I'm late already. You can let yourself out, right?"

"I know the way," I said. But when I reached the landing, I froze. The music had gone off.

"Who is that up there," asked a thin, frail-looking woman, staring up from the bottom of the stairs, her hands clutching defensively at the throat of her overcoat, her voice breaking with fear.

"It's James from Beverley's," shouted Taz from the bedroom. "The garden guy," he added, "he's, like, totally cool, Grandma, and I'm late for class."

She released the grip on her coat and stepped back with relief, her anxious eyes still on me.

"Maggie?" I asked as I reached the bottom of the staircase, barely able to speak, my mind racing and hands beginning to shake. "Maggie, is it you?"

I must have looked like a madman. She stared at me with pained incomprehension, scrutinizing my face, my hair, my beard, my clothes, the color draining out of her as the realization dawned. She grabbed the banister and swayed. "I don't understand," she began to say, "how could it—"

"It's me," I said, stepping up to her, "it's JP, I'm back, I've been looking for you everywhere."

Maggie sobbed and gasped, wagging and nodding her head yes and no, then falling into my arms, then pushing and brushing my hair and beard away from my face. "What took you so long," she moaned, drawing a deep breath, "I've waited so long, JP, it's been so long."

SIXTEEN

W here do we start," James asked Maggie, watching Taz limp down the front steps of the house dressed like a space-age warrior in rubber armor carrying his wheeled steed. Mounting his unicycle, he waved to them, then rolled south on the Old Coast Highway toward his computer lab session.

"How about cutting your hair," Maggie said with a laugh as light as a butterfly. "Your hair and your beard." She stood with her arms wrapped around her body, brimming with contradictory emotions.

James uncrossed her arms gently, held her close for what seemed a lifetime but was only a few seconds, then took both her small hands in one of his. "Yes," he said, pulling the pink envelope from his shirt pocket and giving it to her. "I guess there's no point wearing the disguise now." Pausing to watch her read the letter she had written a lifetime ago, he opened his mouth to speak but she finished his thought for him.

"Now?" she asked, stifling her emotions. "You mean, now that you've come home?"

"Am I home?"

She pulled him close again and hugged as hard as she could until his kidneys ached. "You are home, JP, and you're never going to leave again, unless you want to." She released him, pushed him back and looked up, unable to hide her revulsion. "But we've got to get rid of that hair and beard. They're horrible. They're downright repulsive, and your b.o. is pretty bad, too."

Leading him into the echoing old tiled bathroom-cum-laundry room, she dragged out an antique folding stepladder and sat him down on the top tread. "Take off your shirt," she commanded, sounding like a nurse. She dropped it in the washing machine in the corner of the vast room then draped a bath towel over his shoulders and pinned it together with a clothespin. "What are all the bandages for," she asked, "and this patch?"

"Didn't you hear about the cage and wire?"

She made a face and nodded and sucked at the air in empathy. "First things first," she said, the slight southern twang he loved coming into her voice. "We shear you then we soap you up and do the fine trimming," she added, a mothering note entering her pleasant soprano lilt. "Then we catch up on four decades, right up to the cage and wire. I watched the report on TV last night, and Alex filled me in." James leaned forward, laying his head on her bosom, then reached up and gently cupped her breasts. "Whoa cowboy," she said, gently pushing him back, "let's get to know each other again."

"Yes, ma'am," James said. "We are virtual strangers." But it felt to him as if he had seen her yesterday, as if she had always been with him over the years. He wondered if she felt the same. Could such things happen?

As the tufts rained down, James looked up surreptitiously to make sure he wasn't imagining the scene, but Maggie scolded him and said he'd be sorry, he'd get hair in his eyes and regret it. "Cut it off, please," he murmured, "cut it down the way I used to wear it in summer."

Maggie stood back and frowned. "This is winter and you're pale and as skinny as a scarecrow," she said. "With all these scratches and cuts you'll look like you had a car accident."

"Cut," he said, making a snipping motion with his fingers. "My life has been a series of car accidents. Finally, here's a happy one."

"You're as pigheaded as ever." She laughed.

"And you're as beautiful as ever," he said, staring into her eyes.

"You must be dreaming," she teased, but her voice quaked.

"I must be dreaming," he agreed, nuzzling. He pulled her close and kissed her neck and ear.

"Stop," she said but meant the opposite, her defenses falling, "or I'll never finish." She flushed and seemed a woman-child again, wielding the scissors for play in a kindergarten classroom, alternately cutting his hair and sliding his hands away whenever they reached out and touched her. After what seemed an eternity, his shorn hair stood up like gray and black boar bristles atop a white scalp. "You must be freezing," she said.

"I'm numb," he answered. "You could put me on ice or in a fire and I wouldn't know it." His arms encircled Maggie's hips. This time she did not retreat. Reaching down, she pulled his beard taut and snipped, gray clots of fur raining to the floor again. "Let me loose," she said, "just for a minute more." Bending forward and whispering in his ear, she said, "I'm getting the electric clipper and the razor and then we'll be done."

"The small-animal clipper," he remarked, watching her cross the bathroom to a wicker chest and go through the drawers. "Is it the one your dad used on the dog? What was the name of that horny old dog of yours anyway?"

"Frisky," she said, her face lit with joyful nostalgia. "Don't you remember? You frisky dog . . ."

James blushed now recalling how she called him the frisky dog, a dog with a bone. "Maybe you can teach this old dog some new tricks," he said.

"Can I, now," she asked, trimming with the clipper until his remaining head and facial hair were as neat as a croquet lawn. She ran her hand over it and laughed. "It tickles," she said.

Speculating that she must have become a professional hairdresser since he last saw her, James let Maggie finish trimming his sideburns and eyebrows then lather his face and neck and shave him. She used one, then a second, then a third curved pink throwaway razor designed for legs and underarms, she said, but equally good on an old turkey's neck. Still encircled by his arms, she produced a pair of round-tipped scissors and snipped the hair out of his ears and nostrils. Then she wielded tweezers and plucked the ridge and tip of his nose, hair by hair, clearing away the gnomish thicket that had grown there in the last year. James did not flinch, not even when she nicked him or yanked at the long curling tenacious white hairs on the ridge of his nose that refused to be uprooted.

Pointing to the shower, Maggie wriggled free and said she'd wait outside, in the kitchen, if he was feeling shy. She was starving anyway, they must eat.

Then she would check for messy patches of hair she might have missed and finish the job.

"Why leave," James asked, dropping his pants and drawers and stepping unself-consciously under the stream of water.

"Watch that bandage," Maggie said, her eyes appraising him as she snatched up his dirty clothes and threw them in the washer. "I'll get you a fresh one."

The water stung the wounds on his arms and legs, but it also reinvigorated him and removed the fallen hair that had started to prickle his neck and back.

When he stepped out, Maggie said, "Why, you frisky old dog! You look fifteen years younger."

Drying off and wrapping the towel around his waist, James said he felt forty years younger. Before she could move or speak or stick the new bandage on his wound, he stooped to scoop her up but halted halfway, wincing. Hearing his back click, Maggie put her arms around his neck and took the weight off by slowly climbing halfway up the stepladder. "That easier?" she asked, lowering and cradling herself in his arms as he swung her up and walked toward the door. With the towel slipping off and dragging on the floor, he could feel Maggie unpinning her hair and shaking it loose, feel her mane falling free and brushing his belly and loins.

"Across the threshold," he murmured, making for the master bedroom.

"In there," Maggie waved shyly. "I don't know, JP, maybe we should wait, it's been so long . . ."

Setting her lightly on the bed, then watching her hesitate before tugging down the coverlet, he saw how the sunshine poured through the windows and filled her hair with golden light. It was silvery grayish hair now, only a hint of strawberry and yellow remaining, and it was as thin and fine as silk. He felt it with his fingertips and on his freshly shaved, pale, sensitive cheeks. Unbuttoning, unzipping, and unhooking her clothes, he nibbled and brushed her skin with his lips as he moved up and down. "You know," she said, putting her finger to his lips and blushing. "It won't be the way it used to, it can't be, JP."

"I know," he said, "the heroic age is over. I'm not twenty, either."

Pensively, with a shyness he had never seen in her before, Maggie pulled the blinds and drew the curtains closed, until the room swam in dust-speckled semidarkness. "I'll be back," she whispered. "We old ladies have our tricks."

They made love with slow and gentle kindness, caressing, exploring the creases and wrinkles, tracing patterns on scars and stretch marks, grateful to be alive, overwhelmed with joy to have found each other, to hold each other again, to lose themselves again in carnal embrace.

Waking up an hour later, James could hear the clock ticking and the waves crashing on the beach. Then Maggie sat upright. "Alex," she said, fumbling and finding the alarm clock. "He's back early. Someone's at the door." She started to dress, throwing on a gown and twisting her hair up and out of the way. "I'll check his helmet camera," she added, flipping open her tablet.

James slipped off the bed and lifted a corner of the blinds. Looking diagonally across the porch past the front door to the parking lot, expecting to see the sheriff's SUV idling there, he chuckled and pulled Maggie back to bed. "It's the raccoons," he said, nuzzling, "a whole family of raccoons."

PART TWO
Family Reunion

Humpty Dumpty sat on a wall,
Humpty Dumpty had a great fall . . .

SEVENTEEN

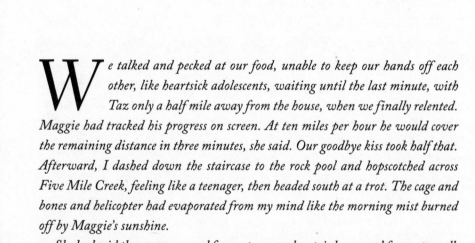

We talked and pecked at our food, unable to keep our hands off each other, like heartsick adolescents, waiting until the last minute, with Taz only a half mile away from the house, when we finally relented. Maggie had tracked his progress on screen. At ten miles per hour he would cover the remaining distance in three minutes, she said. Our goodbye kiss took half that. Afterward, I dashed down the staircase to the rock pool and hopscotched across Five Mile Creek, feeling like a teenager, then headed south at a trot. The cage and bones and helicopter had evaporated from my mind like the morning mist burned off by Maggie's sunshine.

She had said there was no need for me to go, and certainly no need for me to walk to Beverley's. She could run with me down there, or run me down there, meaning give me a ride, I wasn't sure which she meant, but I thought it best to let her talk to Taz alone, and tell him more about me and us, before breaking the news that I would soon be a permanent fixture.

How will he take it—his adoring servant-grandmother sharing her until-now undivided love and attention, and her house, with another male? Who would be the prince and who the king? Maggie said she thought he'd be fine, that he was an unusual boy and seemed unfazed by things that bothered other teens. Also, he liked me and had said so. I was "cool" and "crazy" and he loved my hair and beard and *thought I should dye them pink and green and learn to ride a unicycle, it would be "awesome." "He'll be disappointed to see you clean shaven," she'd said. Then she added the real October surprise.*

"I've been preparing him," she told me without further explanation. Questioned on this, she smiled and said, "I knew you'd come home, sooner or later. I hoped it'd be sooner, but later is better than never. Here you are. It's a real family reunion."

So the mansion had been a trap? I joked. She started to answer, but with Taz rolling down the highway closing in, we had no time to explore the subject, let alone finish catching up on basics. Repeating what she'd already said, that she knew I would come home one of these years, and she knew I'd come to the old house because she knew me better than I knew myself, she assured me she had no sentimental attachments now and had not dated anyone in a long time. Taz was the pretext, she explained, the perfect excuse to keep suitors at bay. The real reasons ran deeper, and she would tell me about them in due course.

The basics were fairly straightforward, it seemed to me. Maggie still worked half-time at city hall in the Office of the County Clerk, mostly for the benefits and to get health insurance for Taz, down the road, I learned. Her parents, who had been well off, had died about fifteen years ago, leaving her enough to buy the derelict mansion outright, remodel it, and invest a nest egg. Like me and a hundred million others, she had lost most of her savings in the economic Downburst. But the deflation and devaluation of the U.S. dollar mitigated the effects, and as long as she didn't buy a foreign car or travel abroad, she was all right, she said, as was I.

Canada had always been an expensive destination, she had added, I'm not sure why. But to think Mexico would become prohibitive was beyond her wildest imaginings. Had I been to Mexico? she asked. Alex might have been born there, she thought, there or somewhere even farther south, she didn't know, no one knew where Alex's mother had been from, other than her son, meaning Alex's father. We ran out of time before she could tell me Alex's father's name or anything about him.

How could she have known I would come home one day when I didn't know it myself? The question keeps playing in my head, even now, as I write this. Had she really bought the old house and waited for me these last ten years? Ten years in Carverville? If so, she was a Penelope of the twenty-first century, a martyr for love. Why she didn't search for me on the Web and write me an email or a letter I can't yet explain—ten years ago I was a minor public figure, so would have been easy to trace. I couldn't believe it any more than I could believe Beverley's cockeyed story about the cages and bones and helicopters. Yet there was Maggie in the house, expecting me, having moved back here from the East Coast, she said, and there were Beverley and the cage and the bones and the helicopters. I do not have the powers of imagination to conjure them. Knock on wood they don't spell the end of me and Maggie just when we've found each other again.

To believe or not to believe, that was and is the question. I learned soon enough there was good reason to be apprehensive about what seemed at first a ludicrous series of banal coincidences leading to our reunion.

Covering the three miles south on foot to the Eden Resort in record time, my mind buzzing as never before with questions, anxieties, hopes, and plans, I thought about climbing up to the public parking lot to see what, if anything, was happening, but I reconsidered and decided to use the staircase to Beverley's property instead. I needed time to put my things in order, and I was determined—rashly—to finish rebuilding that chainsaw, god knows why. Maggie had said she would call Beverley and let her know I was coming, so I anticipated she would be on the lookout, and swoop down like a drone before I could get off the stairs from the beach. I was surprised and relieved when I made it to the RV without encountering her, and had time to clean up the interior, pack my toothbrush and some clean things in a duffel bag, and get ready for takeoff.

Maggie and I had not discussed the logistics yet. It was so sudden, so new. I needed to figure things out and regain my balance. Should I drive the RV to the mansion right away, and park it there, or leave it at the resort for the time being, or move it somewhere else entirely and then terminate the lease and get rid of it? We had both said spontaneously that, for many reasons, I should con-tinue spending time in the garden with Beverley and Taz. That was the safest, smoothest way to start the relationship. "Besides," Maggie had added, "you've got to keep the foilage under control at Beverley's or it will become a jungle and catch fire."

"Foliage," I corrected.

"Foilage," she said again, unable to hear the error. The proverbial penny dropped—that's where Taz had gotten it.

Also playing in my mind was a scratched LP repeating "The cage and the bones are a hoax." The words picked up an old Sly & the Family Stone melody, and I started mumbling out of tune, "The bigger the hoax, the more it fools the folks," or something idiotic like that. But I knew that in reality, the likelihood was near nil the episode was a farce or a prank and would blow over. Beverley had to be right. Something sinister was going on.

I was in the shack, halfway through the rebuild of the chainsaw engine, when I heard the kind of panting and shuffling in the garden I'd heard earlier at the mill. So, naturally, the first thing I thought of was the feral hogs. I wondered if they'd come in under the barbed wire, climbing up the escarpment from Graveyard Beach where the ramp to the dock used to be. Snatching the reading glasses off my nose and looking for a weapon of some kind, I turned and found Beverley leaning breathless on the doorjamb, half hidden by the shadows of the trees. Her face was a ghastly gray, but she managed to raise her eyebrows and speak with them like Groucho Marx. Catching her drift, I brushed the sawdust and dirt off the top of a wooden crate and pulled it out of a dark corner so she could sit.

"We don't have much time," Beverley whispered, hoarse. "I see you outed Glinda the Good, alias Maddie the Baddie, the bewitching Dame of Carverville. Cherchez la femme, *they say. I thought it must've been the sainted Madeleine you pined for, but there was nothing in that high school yearbook or on the Internet about her, there still isn't, as you probably realize, and no, she never said a thing to me about you. If she had, I would not have revealed it." Beverley paused and shushed me by gasping for breath. "Let's not go into the gush stuff just now. By the way, I knew you were a handsome devil under all that hair," she added, looking me over, "in a kind of craggy Stonehenge way. It won't do you any good, not with Harvey Parvey, no sir, it might make him even madder and more jealous once he gets over the shock of seeing you. And when he finds out you've found Maggie. . . . You know what he calls her sometimes, when it's not Maddie the Baddie?" She paused for emphasis, studying my face for a before-and-after reaction. "He calls her Kitten Caboodle." Grinning like a jack-o'-lantern, Beverley pulled a smartphone from the pocket of her stretch pants and glanced at it. "Taz texted a few minutes ago, saying Harv and the Tom Cat were on their way out in the patrol car, he's tracking them on the cameras."*

"You knew he was hacking the cameras?"

"Of course I knew," she wheezed. "Listen, there's no time for explanations. This is what you need to remember. They don't know that I know about the murders. That means they have no reason to think you know or Taz knows or anyone else for that matter. What they want is a scapegoat for what they're going to call a hoax, and by god do they have a pair of scapegoats in you and that tattooed Tasmanian devil. But it won't add up, and that cage won't hold water, not even in Carverville, where justice

is a colander, and Harv knows it, believe me. He may be as ignorant as a fish, and a vindictive cuss, too, but he's not stupid, and he's damn hard to fool, so he's equally good at spotting a flaw in his own plans."

"How do you know?" I started to ask.

Beverley cut me off, waving her pudgy, boneless hand again. This time I noticed it looked even more bloated and pink than usual, the hand of a future heart-attack victim, the clock ticking. "Never you mind how I know, the important thing is, they don't know we are in the know, got it? You don't even know he's the sheriff, do you? Whatever happens, don't ever let on that you think it's anything other than a hoax or some freakish murder, maybe perpetrated by a lunatic with a handsaw or a chainsaw, whatever." She paused and listened. "They're coming. Get back to that engine and we'll pretend everything is hunky-dory. And for god's sake, don't correct him when he says 'perpetuated' instead of 'perpetrated.'"

Taking a deep breath again and diving into her act, Beverley began talking in a stentorian, bantering way, almost shouting at me, her voice higher than usual, the way it had been that first time I met her in the parking lot. "Now, for dinner, I'm making an Italian specialty Number Three loved," she brayed as the sheriff and deputy approached the shack, "spaghetti carbonara. The White Rhino just went wild for carbonara. I make it with bacon and butter and egg yolks, no whites. I used to add a dollop of cream for him but—" She stopped the stream and feigned surprise. "Hello, Harvey," she sang out brightly in her little-girl voice. "Hello, Tom," she added, seeing the Tom Cat stride into view. "What's new in Dodge?"

Too heavyset to easily pass the threshold, they each peered into the chiaroscuro interior and tipped their Stetson and helmet, respectively, like a pair of stand-up comics. Did Harvey Murphy really wear a central casting cowboy hat? The acrid stench of chewing tobacco and ingrained nicotine wafted in.

"Nice to see you, Bev," said Harvey in his strangulated nasal tenor, his voice unchanged from high school days. Looking past her at me, he squinted the way he always had and wrinkled his nose. Then raising his bentwood cane for emphasis, he added, "Everything all right?"

"Everything's great," she said, beaming. Only her heavy wheezing gave her anxiety away. "Meet Mr. James, my guest," she added, "I guess I could fry up some extra bacon and beat a couple more egg yolks and we could all have dinner together." She got to her feet. "Oh, how could I be forgetting the parmesan? Lots of that in the *carbonara mix, and none of that sheep stuff, pecorino, it's called. The White Rhino loved it, but I don't. James is almost finished with the rebuild, right?"*

"Right," I said, wiping my hands and standing, then joining in the act. "Is that Harvey?" I asked, extending my right hand, full of astonishment, "Harvey Murphy?"

"One and the same," said the sheriff, peering at me with his brown, bulging, slightly walleyes. He had not aged well and, like Beverley, seemed the proverbial candidate for a heart attack, the road map of burst capillaries on his cheeks and his bulbous nose a purplish red. I could see his greasy scalp through his thinning hair. It was dyed jet-black. Cocking his head in the style of his nephew, he took a step forward to get a better look at me. I saw genuine, honest-to-god astonishment transform his fat, sulky face into a fleshy-lipped smile button.

Pumping my hand and turning to Beverley and Tom he barked, "It's JP, I can't believe it, what in the heck are you doing here? You're not the guest I was expecting." He let go of my hand and swiveled, growling at Tom, "This is the guy you saw?"

Tom made a face and looked me up and down as if he had real doubts. "Yeah, I guess so, but he's looking different now, he's shaved off his beard and cut his hair, that's it."

"That's me," I said, "good to see you again, Deputy, that was very kind of you to come out and make sure my vehicle wasn't damaged by the tree." I paused and laid it on thick. "I've been traveling cross-country for months, Harvey, and I guess the time had come to shed all that hair. Now that I'm home and can shave regularly with warm water, I think I'll keep the beard off."

"Well I'll be darned," Harvey said, the reality setting in, "who could've believed it? So, you are the mystery man, the eccentric urban individual with the RV. I didn't know you were a gardener, JP. Old man Egmont did that, I guess, I'll be darned." He glowered at his nephew again and said, "Why didn't you tell me it was JP Adams, I would've come right down?" But Harvey wasn't expecting an answer and rolled on, his cane raised higher now. "What say you go on up to the house with Tom?" he suggested to Beverley with false bonhomie, "and maybe make us some coffee. You'll be more comfortable up there while me and JP have a little heart to heart. It's been a long time and this is a hell of a surprise, isn't it, JP?"

"It sure is, for both of us," I lied.

"Make that three," Beverley tossed in. "Now I can call him JP instead of James—"

"You can't imagine how glad I am to see you, Harvey," I said before she could add anything.

Grinning, he winked and quipped, "No, I can't imagine it, but the feeling's mutual, I'm sure."

"Come on," Beverley said to Tom, leaning on his muscular forearm and navigating through the straights of the doorjamb. "I guess it's not dinnertime yet, so maybe I'll brew up some java and we can have a little snack before deciding on the carbonara. You like cobbler, if I remember," she added, hobbling alongside him out of view, "and I was going to make a banana cream pie . . ."

When Harvey and I were alone we paddled each other on the shoulder like seals at the zoo and I confirmed I was indeed the stranger with the bushy beard, on vacation, a retiree and refugee from the city, I said, got tired of the politics and wanted some fresh air. Pretending not to have known Harvey was the sheriff, I took his badge in my fingers with more feigned feeling, then clapped him on the shoulder even harder and shook his hand again, giving him my heartfelt congratulations and saying it was terrific, had he been elected a long time ago, or was it a recent honor?

I may have overdone it and wound up sounding like a character out of the Adventures of Huckleberry Finn. Swinging his massive head like the turret on a tank, Harvey said no, no election, he'd been appointed almost three years ago, it had been a real challenge, but the county was doing fine now and had come out of the troubled times stronger than ever, thank god.

Harvey perched on the edge of the crate where Beverley had been sitting and leaned on his cane. He looked up at me and rotated his head back and forth, back and forth, as if it were stiff and sore, while saying, "I can't believe it, I just can't credit it, JP, back in Carverville. So, what's the story, my friend? Why did you come back? I know you went to law school and became a lawyer and a judge somewhere, noticed that some years ago, and I heard you'd caught flak for something, but I don't know what." The tone of his voice was already changing. I saw him glance at the chainsaw, his expression morphing from curiosity to mild annoyance. "Don't tell me that's Egmont's old McCulloch!" he exclaimed, standing up and shuffling over to the bench. "Did you know it was here?"

I told him I was as surprised as he was to find it, and find the Beachcomber Motel still standing, though changed in appearance and atmosphere.

"Haven't we all changed?" he asked, looking me up and down, a scowl coming over his features. I recognized it from way back. It was that face he'd made when I beat him at tennis or in the chainsaw races, the scowl he'd made, probably without realizing it, whenever he'd seen me and Maggie together.

Harvey may have aged badly, but he had clearly prospered in his own way. His western-style boots looked handmade from caiman skin, I guessed. His tan-colored military-type sheriff's outfit was expensively tailored. The heavy gold and large diamond rings on his fingers were not meant to replace brass knuckles. I doubted he'd bloodied them of late. He caught my glance and I could tell he knew I was sizing him up in return.

"Maybe I should take that back," he said, "you don't look much different, just older, but you're not fat and crippled and half bald, so I guess you've had a pretty good life. Married?" Nodding, I told him I was a fairly recent widower and he commiserated, though it sounded hollow. He jerked his forefinger at the engine. "Go on and finish putting it together if you want," he said, trying to sound indulgent, "I'll be curious to see if it works."

"Oh, it'll work," I said, then regretted it. "I used it to cut up that fallen cypress," I added.

Harvey thrust his thick lips out and smacked them. "I heard all about it and watched on the video," he said, "Mr. Macrocarpa, I'll be damned if I knew it was you."

"Well, likewise, I had no idea you were still here," I said.

Harvey smiled wryly before answering, still rotating his head. "Where else would I be, JP? I'll bet you had no idea I was here, why would you care about folks in a place like Carverville when you'd gone off to the city all those years ago and become so successful and famous? We heard about you every once in a while, and I even saw you on the TV news a couple times." He paused and I could hear it coming. "Some of us stayed," he added, "some of us love this place and are struggling every day to keep it great. We've got the lowest crime rate in the state, the lowest opioid addiction rate, the lowest number of growers and dealers, and the lowest percentage of illegals." The way he pronounced "struggling" made it sound like the word had an "h" in it, "shtruggling," reminding me that he, too, had come to Carverville from outside, dragged here by his father from a rust-belt town in the Alleghenies in the early 1970s.

Telling Harvey how marvelous it was that he had stayed and become sheriff and made good, and how appreciative everyone in town must be, I said it was true, I'd left a long time ago and had never come back. He knew I had nothing to come back to, I added, but my heart had always been here.

"Your heart," he said and let out a bitter, snorting laugh. "Yeah, I think you're speaking true now," he added, "your heart and your privates. I guess you've seen Maddie, you knew she was here?"

Swinging my head in imitation of his own body language, and smiling my dumbest golly-gosh smile, I said, "I swear I had no idea until this morning that Maggie Simpson was here." It sounded convincing because it was true. "Believe me, this is a day of revelations."

"I'll say it is," Harvey scoffed. "She goes by the name Hansen, must've been her first or second husband," he added, "or maybe the third one. I heard he was a buck or at least half and half, and probably Islamic." Harvey grinned maliciously. "They all dropped dead on her I heard, her children, too. She's been around the block a few times she has, old Maddie. Remember that Elvis song? Walks like an angel, talks like an angel? But she really is the devil in disguise." He paused to let it sink in. "So, you came on vacation and bingo, here you are, you found Maddie the Baddie, and now you're going to stay and keep your beard off, do some fishing? That's the story?"

Before being drawn into his adolescent web of envy, I said, "Actually without knowing it, I think I came back to start up the old salmon hatchery. It sounds crazy, but I've always wanted to do that, and now I realize I came out here for that reason, so, you're right, I'm going to do some fishing—fish raising."

Harvey was temporarily disarmed. "Nothing to do with old Kitten Caboodle, then? I can hardly believe it." Snorting and revolving his head, he added, "If only I'd known, I'd have arranged a welcome committee."

"I'll bet you would have," I said, trying not to sound sarcastic. "What about you, did you marry?"

Nodding with apparent difficulty, he said, "Peggy Bryson. Remember Pegs?"

"Peggy," I repeated, trying to remember, "I'm not sure . . ."

"Why, of course you aren't, she wasn't as pretty or smart or as fast as Maddie." He let the phrase hang. "You never screwed her, JP, she must've been the only girl you didn't." He let out a braying tenor laugh and clapped me on the shoulder, as if we were still best buddies. "Come on, Your Honor, it's just locker-room talk, we still like locker-room talk around here, don't you?"

I didn't rise to the bait and asked instead, "Any children?"

Grunting, Harvey said, "Two, both girls, got married, left town, hardly see them or the grandkids. Lousy deal, I'll tell you, parenthood isn't what it's cracked up to be."

Who could blame them, *I felt like saying, but held my tongue.* "Not much work in town still, I guess, youngsters have to move elsewhere?" *I realized as the words came out that I'd put my foot in it again.*

"Well it ain't the big city," *he said, swiveling his head and jabbing his stubby, nicotine-stained forefinger at the chainsaw engine.* "But it has its advantages, it's a hell of a lot cheaper here for one thing, and we like the monotonous cool weather and the monotone, monochrome, if you get what I mean." *Letting out a guffaw now, he waggled his fingers like a magician and said,* "Go on and finish the rebuild, JP, then we can go out and cut some trees the way we used to. I see you even bought a new chain, it'll be nice and sharp." *He brayed again like a horse's ass and rearranged his broad backside on the edge of the crate. I was starting to feel jangled as I turned back to the bench.*

Putting on my reading glasses and taking up the dismantled carburetor, I heard Harvey sigh with an exaggerated, theatrical flourish. "Yeah, I am very glad the mystery man turned out to be you," *he began,* "and I'll tell you why. Just think if it'd been some honest-to-God hairy tramp who'd roped Maddie's jackass grandson and his green hair into perpetuating that hoax, figuring out how to open an old trap and put those bones in from the graveyard." *Pausing to gauge the effect his words were having, he watched my fingers, waiting for me to fumble.* "With the current legislation, that kind of thing is punishable by imprisonment, for distracting law enforcement and deputized Coast Guard crews from their urgent duties, and for spreading panic in the general population. And, you know, incarceration these days isn't much fun, JP, you meet the strangest customers in jail, people who do things to you that you wish they hadn't done. I hate to think what might happen in the county jail to that cappuccino kid, with his curly green hair and stud in the tongue and all those tattoos. No transgender bathrooms in our nice new jail. You ought to come down and see it, see my new office—"

"I need more light," *I said, interrupting, but did not falter.* "It's too late to work by natural light. I'll finish this tomorrow."

"Uh-huh," *Harvey said, rocking backward and forward, leaning on his cane.* "Yeah, I get what you mean, too dark to see your private parts, though maybe not for you." *He slapped his thigh.* "See, what we can't figure is, why anyone would want to drag an old hog cage out from under those tarps and stick some old bones in it dug up from the old graveyard on the property, or stolen from somewhere, and that rusty saw blade, too. It doesn't figure, does it? It's some kind of hazing thing, maybe, a *prank. We figured we'd ask the mystery man, but since he's you, I know you wouldn't have done such a thing, and you wouldn't have known about those skeletons stolen by some jackass kids about fifteen, eighteen years ago from the JC science lab, I think it was, to be confirmed, and all this is absolutely off the record, JP, we're just having a friendly conversation."*

"Interesting," I said, buying time. Pondering whether I should argue that clearly the cage hadn't been dragged from Beverley's property, that the old traps under the tarps were coiled in Japanese honeysuckle, and there were no traces of the creeper being cut back or of the traps being moved, and no readily available skeletons on the property, either, as far as I could tell, I decided to play along instead. "It certainly does seem like some kind of silly thing college kids would do," I agreed as amiably as I could. "But it must have been a long time ago, judging by the barnacles I saw on that cage. It was rusted shut and impossible to open." I paused long enough to see Harvey squint and run his fingers through his thatch of thinning hair. It looked like a bad toupee. "I sure wouldn't want to try to haul those traps around, either," I added for good measure. "Remember how heavy they were? Remember when we helped my dad move them that summer?"

Screwing up his face and puckering his lips, Harvey said, "Oh man, do I, who could forget. That was when we sawed all those logs up on Big Mountain and drug them down to the warehouse at Yono Harbor. Your dad still alive?" I shook my head but he hardly noticed. "All of mine are gone too," he said, "parents, aunts, uncles, even my older brother, Jack. Remember Jack?"

I nodded. Who could forget Jack? He'd fought in Vietnam and had been taken prisoner. God only knew what they'd done to him—worse than the Germans or Japanese did to my father. Something about a bamboo cage in a river in the Mekong Delta, with water up to Jack's chin, and fish biting him for days on end.

"I learned a lot from Jack," Harvey added wistfully, shaking his head. He got to his feet and, before I could give my condolences, said, "Let's go on up to the motel and get some of that pie Bev was talking about. On the way up, you can tell me why the mystery man behaved like he did at the hospital, throwing dirty tissues around and bleeding all over the place, when those first responders and orderlies were dealing with a major road accident. Doesn't that strike you as suspicious behavior?"

"Suspicious?" I asked, and laughed. "That's not the word I'd choose. Taz was bleeding like a stuck pig," I said, instantly angry with myself for lapsing into

Carverville-speak and mentioning hogs. "I couldn't just let him bleed to death, his artery was severed."

"Uh-huh," Harvey said, creeping uphill on the uneven path covered with wood chips, his head revolving as he hunted out a cigarette in a nearly empty pack. "I've got to have my knees and my hips replaced," he said and added a memorable non sequitur, asking if I still went to church and believed in the Lord. I told him I hadn't in decades, that I'd lost my faith way back, when we were in high school. He lit up and grunted a few times, said I'd be welcome at their services, then said Beverley's property was an overgrown firetrap. All it would take is a butt to set things alight, and she ought to get that lazy jackass mulatto kid to pull down the dried-up infesting vines, or maybe she could have those ragbag hippies down the coast herd the goats in, goats will eat anything and turn it into cheese . . .

Then he swerved back and picked up his earlier thought. "That scene in the emergency room, it seems like real strange behavior for a distinguished circuit court judge, doesn't it?" He exhaled and coughed, sounding like Beverley. "But let's let it go, JP, we reviewed the hospital tapes this morning, and I got hold of the ones from Dr. Dewey's office, and that's where we confirmed what we already knew, that you and the cappuccino kid went out and wrestled that trap and that's where you got cut up."

"Correct," I said. "We saw it from the top of the staircase, Taz, Beverley, and I, when we were waiting for the drone."

"The drone that delivered the rebuild kit," he said, "I know, I heard it all, JP. It sounds just, what's the word? Outlandish? Doesn't it? Like some fake news story that a blogger would invent for some damnable reason, to discredit the authorities, for instance. Good thing a blogger didn't get hold of it, can you imagine? 'Bones and Skull on Graveyard Beach' . . . a great title. But there's so much speculation out there, online and on the street, we couldn't prevent any jackass sitting on his sofa from spinning a whole damnable yarn and tarring Carverville and you and me, too. So, let's see, you and the cappuccino kid rush down and drag the thing out of the water, God knows why, and you get sliced like salami, and you go in for medical assistance, but the hospital is swamped and it's as simple as that, right?"

"Right," I said, smiling. "The cage was totally wrapped in wire and rusted shut, as I say. It was impossible to open it and check if the bones were real. Luckily lots of photos were taken, and we have a number of eyewitness reports from guests, and of course you have the bones, so everything should be easy to clarify."

"Uh-huh." He grunted skeptically and swiveled his head to spit into the bushes. We were approaching the motel. I could smell the coffee and said so, that it was late for me to drink coffee, but man, did it smell good. *"Like that coffee, do you?"* he asked. *"Doesn't look like you eat much pie, JP, you're as skinny as you ever were."*

"Not my fault," I said, *"I have nothing to do with it. You can't blame me for being skinny."*

Harvey chuckled and seemed to be mellowing now that he'd fired a few warning shots. *"Blame you for lots of other things, but not for being Mr. Bones, wasn't that it, or just Bone? Like I say, it's all awfully suspicious, the bushy guy from New York with a throwaway cellphone shows up and parks in the lot for nearly two weeks."*

"It was ten days," I cut in, *"I asked at city hall."*

"Oh, I know you asked at city hall. So, you stay there for ten days doing what? Walking up and down the beach collecting shells, riding around town on your little folding bicycle, making barbecues and living it up with Bev? Maybe you're looking for Maddie, maybe you're fishing for salmon, what the hell? Then all of a sudden, there's this cage and you and the cappuccino kid are cut up, and you aren't from New York, you're a judge who fell off the bench and came crawling home." He paused and flicked the butt into the shrubbery. *"Good thing the fake news people didn't get ahold of it, that's all I can say, JP."*

"Well," I remarked, pausing and unconsciously mimicking his speech patterns, *"I guess Beverley's guests took lots of nice pictures and made some videos. I saw them earlier that day making videos on the property, by those ragged tarps with the flowering creeper growing out of the old crab pots and traps that look like they haven't been touched in years. So, maybe their footage will come in handy at some point, to prove that cage wasn't on Beverley's property, it just could not have been."*

"Maybe," he said and gave me a baleful look. We had reached the motel. *"I'll keep you posted,"* he added, *"the forensic people are checking on everything now, and they went through the shack and the garden and the motel, too, with that fine-toothed comb of theirs."* His smile revealed his dark, purplish gums and large yellowish tobacco-stained teeth. *"Now, you wouldn't mind if we did some checking in the RV, would you? Seeing that you're absolutely innocent and eager to cooperate with law enforcement? Or do I have to go to the kangaroos and get a warrant?"*

We stepped into the motel and Beverley and Tom fell silent. *"Of course,"* I said to Harvey, *"come on over, I'll make us some instant coffee and we can bring in the cinnamon rolls from the diner or get some of Beverley's pie."*

Harvey grunted, took off his Stetson and found a perch at the small table. "Oh, so much to catch up on," he said mockingly, taking a slug of coffee and helping himself to the cobbler on his plate. "Why, thank you, Bev. I think we're going to have to put in a few more cameras along this stretch of the highway, maybe one real tall one overlooking your lot, too, just to make sure nothing like this happens again," he added, digging in and grunting with pleasure. "Mm-mmm, man that is good." He looked up again, a wicked smile contorting his face. "There's so much to talk about, JP, this could take days or weeks or maybe even months or years. Not planning on leaving anytime soon, I hope? I want you to come and see our headquarters. We have a new jail with twice the room as the old one, and a new courthouse right next door, and a facility for illegals we're going to send right out of the country. Come to lunch or come to dinner one night, Pegs will be thrilled to see you, and so will Gus and Clem and Pete, they're still around. Clem's the mayor for goodness' sakes. Now that I think of it, we could throw a little pool party—we have an indoor-outdoor heated pool. Pete helped Gus install it. Did you know Pete Smithson married Sally, my little sister? That's her son right there, Tom, my top deputy."

"You don't say," I blurted out, trying to remember names and faces and failing across the board except for goofy Pete and pimply Sally, a roly-poly girl a few years younger than we were. I remembered her for more than one reason. "Your dad and I were great friends," I told Tom, shaking his hand. "Say hi to Pete and your mom for me."

"Yes, sir," Tom said with a tone of deference that had been missing up to then. "I'll do that this evening."

"Pete owns the garage now," Harvey remarked, "you remember the place, he worked there as a grease monkey back in the day."

I nodded and made congratulatory noises, saying I'd clean forgotten his last name was Smithson.

"Sally has been known to play cards with us," Beverley chipped in after an unnaturally long silence. "I detect a family resemblance," she added wryly. "You show no allergy to cobbler."

"No, ma'am," Harvey and the Tom Cat said seemingly on cue, one after the other. Harvey laughed at this for some reason—a private joke. "So, you'll be around if we need you?" he asked me again, swiveling his head and spraying crumbs on the table from his overfilled mouth.

I glanced at Tom, then Beverley, and forced a sheepish grin. "I have no reason to leave," I answered, "and plenty of reasons to stay. Someone has to water all those cuttings we've made." I paused for the comic effect, which was probably a mistake because Harvey's expression went sour again. His bullshit detector could pick up irony a mile away. "Beverley, I'd love some of that cobbler," I added in my most homespun voice, "Harvey says I need to fatten up."

EIGHTEEN

W e were lying in bed the next morning, holding each other and watching the dawn light come into the house from Five Mile Valley, when Maggie said, "Tell me about Amy."

I felt a stab. But, after all, it was only fair and normal. She had told me a great deal about herself and I had said almost nothing. "Let's see," I began, buying time. "Except for her icicle toes, she was essentially your opposite, physically and temperamentally, though I'm sure you would have had a great deal in common and would've liked each other."

"That's not much of a description."

"I'm getting there," I said, trying but failing to keep things lighthearted. "This is the first time I've spoken of Amy to anyone."

"Do you miss her?"

"Of course, how could I not?"

"Did you love her?"

"Of course, very much."

Maggie sucked her bottom lip, then said, "I wanted to ask you, do you miss her the way you missed me, and do you love her the way you loved me, but the psychologist in me and the adult in me told me to rephrase my questions."

"So you did, but now you're asking them anyway?"

"That's right, and it's thanks to you, to you being here."

"Honesty," I began to say then stopped myself. "Actually, it turns out not always to be the best policy. That's why we invented diplomacy, the art of honest or honorable dissimulation, as opposed to lying or the propounding of falsehoods." I paused, feeling pompous and foolish. Was this the way I had spoken in court, or talked to my clients and students? "Amy was your height," I began again. "You had that in common, about five foot seven. She had short, straight black hair that was as thick as the hair on a coconut, and in fact, I sometimes called her Coco, even though, as you know, I hate nicknames."

Maggie nodded and shook her head in the patented, incomprehensible yes-no way that Taz had picked up. Then she said with false gravity, "Yes, you have always called me Madeleine, haven't you, and I notice you're calling Taz by his proper name, Alexander."

"Mm," I agreed, the irony striking me for the first time. "It's strange, I hadn't thought of that. And it never bothered me when you called me JP. Do you think my hatred of nicknames is an adult phenomenon, some form of defensiveness, or a simple desire to be taken seriously?"

"Could be, what do you think?"

"I think you're starting to analyze me, and you're telling me I'm just an old, pretentious ass, or a stick in the mud." I paused, hoping she would rescue me, but she didn't. "Be that as it may," I began again, "Amy had black hair and black almond eyes and a porcelain complexion, one of those tiny nonexistent noses and tiny ears and a tiny mouth and tiny hands and tiny feet. She looked like a china doll. I suppose that's where the cliché originates, though in her case she was genetically half Japanese. She seemed much more Japanese than American in appearance. In character I suppose it was the other way around, though I hate to think in terms of identity politics, and I am not proud to admit that I have never been to Japan and couldn't generalize if I wanted to."

"She was outspoken, demanding, decisive?"

"That's it, along those lines," I agreed. "I've always liked strong women." Pausing and eyeing her, I waited for Maggie to hit the bait but she resisted. "We met in court," I added, "we were actually adversaries and she won the case, I don't remember what it was about, something bureaucratic and innocuous by today's standards. She said she'd take me out and buy me dinner as a token of peace. She knew she owed it to me, because by all rights she should have lost. My client was in the right and she knew it, but she argued her case more effectively than I and the jury was convinced."

"That's all it takes, isn't it?"

"That's all it takes," I repeated, adding, "Amy brooked no nonsense as the expression goes. She was tough, feisty, even ferocious at times, a born trial lawyer. She stayed on that side of the bar until the end. Something in me pushed me to the other side, and then out of the courtroom. The adversarial element is wearing."

"And you never wanted children?"

I took a deep breath and plunged in. "I've always thought the world had enough people in it, and I also thought, given my father, especially, but also my mother, who was pretty chilly as you'll recall, that I wouldn't make a great father."

"That's probably not true. You seem to be doing pretty well with Taz."

"Well, he's not my son. Don't get me wrong. I like kids, and he's your grandson, so how could I not like him?"

"What about Amy, how did she feel?"

Wincing involuntarily at the continued questioning, I answered as fairly as I thought possible. "I think she had similar feelings. Small family, difficult, spoiled, coldhearted intellectual parents who espoused liberalism but in daily life seemed to me to behave like princelings and were profoundly conservative when it came to protecting their status. She had a sister who produced two children, both of them self-absorbed, so Amy seemed to think that was enough."

"And you still think the world would be better off without the human race?"

"Is that what I used to say?"

Maggie nodded. "I always tried to talk you around but . . ."

"But now you're not sure?"

"You might feel different if you had children. You might be more optimistic or fatalistic. The world wasn't perfect when we were born, either."

We got up one after the other in a silence broken only by seagull cries and the thundering surf.

"JP, why did you come back?" She slipped in the question as she slipped on her dressing gown. "Tell me the truth. Were you looking for me?"

Again, I felt at a loss, largely because I was still not entirely sure why I had come back. "I was looking for you without looking for you," I said, feeling inarticulate. "Because I never lost you, in a way. I was looking for a salmon, for the past, for my youth, for answers to questions, for a place to settle down, for all kinds of things, but most of all, for you."

She eyed me and smiled that old saucy smile from our summer of love. "Aren't you supposed to tell the truth and nothing but the truth?"

"That's the whole truth, ma'am, except there's more," I said. "I had thirty years of suits and ties and pressed shirts," I started. "Three decades of serious discourse, of impeccable, upstanding behavior and speech, of positioning papers and rulings and judgments and dissenting opinions and stays and moral indignation and righteous wrath and cocktail parties with donors and fund-raisers for the dubious guardians of our democratic institutions."

"And you burned out," she said, "you had a breakdown."

Disagreeing vigorously, I said, "No, no, I didn't burn out, I was burned out of house and home. I was broken down from the outside in, not the inside out. Maggie, let's let it go. I want to fish and build campfires and walk on the beach. I want to be happy again. I want to figure out another way to live and contribute and help turn this ship of fools around."

"How about finding your own well-being first?"

"Precisely," I said, taking her in my arms, "Our well-being. There's not much time left for us. We have a lot of catching up to do."

This time, when I bent to lift her, my back did not give out. With the litheness of a teenager she wrapped her legs around mine and hooked her heels . . .

James stopped typing mid-sentence, startled by the appearance of two familiar silhouettes. Standing at the threshold dressed as if ready to go out, Maggie and Taz said everything was ready. Had James forgotten? "Forgotten what?" he asked, perplexed. Clicking the save icon, he shut the laptop and stood, removing his reading glasses.

"We're going out for pizza and then doing some shopping," Maggie said. "Are you all right?"

"Fine," James said, "I'll come right along."

Taz shouted excitedly as he ran down the stairs to the car, then ran halfway back up again like an overeager dog late for his walk. Maggie gave James a knowing look. "I'm glad you're keeping a journal," she said. "You always wanted to write."

"Did I?"

Smiling indulgently, she said, "You were going to be an investigative reporter, so was I, and write novels on the side."

James assented distractedly and said yes, now he remembered. That seemed to him another life, another person altogether.

Taz reappeared at the threshold, smartphone in hand, announcing he had already chosen his pizza and could order theirs online if they wanted. "That way they'll be ready when we arrive," he said brightly.

"And be stone cold," said Maggie.

"Why not have the pizzas delivered by drone?" James asked. "The shopping, too. We could subside into the couch like pearls in an oyster and never leave the house."

"Cool," said Taz. "Let's do that!"

NINETEEN

*T**he longer I stay, the more I find myself slipping back into Carverville-*
speak. Improper word choice is bad enough. Even my cadences and pro-
nunciation are changing. Telling half-truths and playacting does not sit
well with my constitution, either. Telling the truth, the whole truth, and nothing
but the truth, is what this journal must continue to be about. I am a camera, but
I am also deciding what to frame, when, and how. Is the subjective objective, or
the objective subjective? I'm not sure. Have I been holding back? Yes, of course I
have, but not knowingly. I may not realize, even now as I write this, what it is
I'm not telling. But certainly, there is more to tell. If only I can resist the temptation
to subside into the mindlessness of the Carverville sump.

Beverley, too, has been infected: Her father was a schoolteacher. She is capable of
speaking excellent, unaccented, standard English, and speaking her mind truthfully
with sincerity. But circumstances have transformed her into a consummate actress
and fabulist.

So, I find it all the more surprising that neither Taz nor Maggie has adopted the
prevailing rural twang, circumlocutions, wanton falsity, and depleted vocabulary,
not to mention the gleeful vulgarity, of so many of the locals, the people who constitute
"the base" of the current state of nongovernment. What a psychologist or linguist

might say about my state of mind right now I do not know, but I am determined to stop being folksy, mendacious, and facetious, before it becomes a habit.

The drawback with truthfulness and clarity is that I am trying to reintegrate into the community and lie low, if only to buy time, until we decide to stay or leave. The first thing locals notice is an earnest attitude and a persnickety out-of-town manner of speech. For instance, at the diner yesterday with Maggie, simply by speaking properly, without gesticulating or shouting and using slang or being jokey, we felt like fresh-off-the-boat immigrants or unwelcome refugees faced by scowling native sons and daughters. When Taz joined us, the needle on the hostility meter shot to the right. But that's racism and prejudice, plain and simple. No matter, we are an autonomous, if unusual, threesome. As long as no one attempts to do us physical harm, we'll be fine.

I never believed in conjuring tricks. Yet as I write this, a helicopter is hovering exactly at the level of the mansion, a hundred yards away, over the beach. The noise is deafening. I have stood up and stared back defiantly, and pulled down the roller blinds in case they are watching me. If they think this is a clever way to keep tabs on us they are delusional. Intimidation won't work, either. I'm not sure who "they" are or what they want, but I'm determined to find out. Something tells me this is Clem's ham-fisted way of saying he knows I'm here. There. You see? The chopper is gone now. Driven away by a roller blind and my unfriendly thoughts? I have raised the blind again and can see the wild, pounding surf.

It has been four days since Maggie and I were reunited, and five days since the cage incident, with no news from Harvey, and no visits by his deputies or the forensic squad, unless they came while I was away and let themselves into the RV. On at least two occasions, I failed to lock it. There is nothing to steal. The likelihood of any thieves venturing onto Beverley's property these days is near nil—county workers have been there all day, every day, erecting new security cameras. But, as she has pointed out, what if someone wants to plant something? They wouldn't be stealing, they would be leaving a poisoned, incriminating gift behind.

The only odd things I noticed while cleaning the shack after finishing the rebuild of the McCulloch is that the handsaw and the old chain for the chainsaw had disappeared. Searching nearby, I found a cigarette butt and compared it with the one Harvey flicked into the bushes the other night, when he almost set the garden on fire. Accidentally? I wonder. It was the same brand, but millions of tobacco addicts smoke that brand, and dozens of them unwittingly start wildfires by tossing lit butts out of their car windows or dropping them when hiking or camping.

Taz probably has the limb saw folded up in the pocket of his new overalls, bought for him by Beverley. I'll have to ask. We've been pruning trees for the last few days. Why anyone would want the worn, filthy old chain from the McCulloch, however, I can't imagine. It was too greasy for Taz to dream of touching it. Harvey or the Tom Cat and the forensic experts? That makes no sense. My guess is, Beverley threw it away with the other derelict items and trash when she whisked through the shack a few days ago. Again, I must remember to ask.

Little by little we are finding our footing. Maggie and I have adopted a piece-meal approach to catching up. We hold our parlays on the beach, at dawn, as she jogs slowly and I walk as fast as I can to stay by her side. She was the solitary runner, it turns out, the only other human form on the sand, the one I spotted several times. Now she's my companion as I hike to Beverley's in the morning. Then she doubles back and goes to city hall, afterward driving to the Beachcomber in time for lunch. I must stop calling it by that name. It's now an upscale resort, with the most plentiful aquifer in the county, as Beverley has often reminded me. The water is sweet and good-tasting, better than anywhere around except up at Narrow Rocks. If she really wants to sell and get out, she should have no trouble.

So far, we have managed to organize three lunches together, two of them including Taz, and each more delicious and life enhancing than the preceding one. Beverley also excels at making fried artichokes in the Jewish style of the former ghetto of Rome, she says, and steak and kidney pie. Luckily, we did not tell Taz about the kidneys. He ate hearty. Watching the three of them interact is a joy. For some unknown reason, in Maggie's presence, Beverley quiets down and sometimes hardly says a word. They are confidantes. That is clear. Sometimes I wonder if Beverley is in awe of her elegant, younger friend. Taz, too, behaves differently around Maggie, he's less introverted and erratic, and he laughs from the heart. I'm beginning to think she has a similar, beneficial effect on me. The magical Glinda the Good?

The explanation may be simpler: We are happy in each other's company. Happiness is a much-abused concept. The more you seek it, the more it evades you. That has been my experience. "For as long as it lasts," were the famous words spoken by Napoleon Bonaparte's mother, a realist, who happened to be Corsican, not French. "After us, the flood," said Madame de Pompadour, half a century before her, expressing similar sentiments. Both were right. I'm not sure which phrase is more apt or topical, but, given the persistent drought here, I'd rather plump for Pompadour.

My diligence in keeping this journal has not been laudable. In plain English, I have been too busy and too ecstatic and too worried and too worn out emotionally and physically to sit down and write. Perhaps happiness is not conducive to good poetry, journal writing, or gumshoeing.

Finally, after having moved the RV to the mansion's parking area, and also gotten beyond the sham of sleeping in the extra bedroom when Taz knew very well I was sleeping with his grandmother, and having opened a new bank account and paid for my own post office box, I am feeling the keel beginning to right itself.

Unbeknownst to others, I've also indulged in some amateur sleuthing. Yes, I am being facetious and must stop it: As an assistant DA, then lawyer and then judge who worked with professional investigators for three decades, I don't have the luxury of pretending I'm a dilettante. Rather, I am a gelded, proscribed pariah. Anyone who helps me risks a backlash if discovered. Yet, in both San Antonio and Missoula, my old network appears to be coming through. That is the beauty of the great confraternity of women and men who believe in the law over all else: They are willing to put their lives in peril to uphold it, and assist their fellows. Those old enough to remember Operation Stay Behind during the Cold War will understand: The best way to resist is to stay behind, blend in and bide your time. I will say no more, other than to note that my research is ongoing.

On a hunch, thinking of what Beverley said when talking about Maggie and her elusive son, I went through the ABA directory online and found a colleague I vaguely knew decades ago, based in Montana. As discreetly as possible, I asked about recorded deaths of non-Caucasians on Native American lands during the various protest gatherings of recent decades—the kind of information that should be but isn't readily available online.

In San Antonio, the question was, what chance is there of a record somewhere in the country or south of the border of an Indio woman presumably marrying a Caucasian American, though they may not actually have formalized their relationship, giving birth to a boy named Alexander, last name, like the father's, presumably Hansen or Johnson, then dying suddenly, presumably fourteen to seventeen years ago, when the boy was too young to remember her, the death probably occurring in Montana during a pipeline protest? It's a tall order, I realize, especially given the tensions in our official relations with so many foreign governments.

I will provide information to the investigators as it crops up, and they will report back through safe channels I cannot reveal, not even here. Neither Maggie nor Taz nor Beverley knows of this research. They think I am focused entirely on the garden of the Eden Resort, and my harebrained scheme to revive the salmon hatchery.

Taz and I planted several dozen buddleia cuttings around the house and in front of the big, old, ugly, white propane tank. It leaks and looks like an accident waiting to happen. I must get it replaced. To create the screen of shrubs, we moved the spare sandbags out of the way—Maggie got in a truckload of them when the house was propped up a few years back, and they're all over the place, in the way. Overeager, Taz has been watering the cuttings several times a day, to the point that I am beginning to fear they will get root rot.

On another front, though it is probably a pipe dream of mine, Maggie is trying to find out, through city hall, whether the hatchery and surrounding land can be purchased from the county or state authorities—the current title is not clear. Soon we will hike to it and have a picnic there, even though Beverley says that's not a good idea.

So, is my boat really righting?

What trouble me most are the cage and the bones, the razor wire and the helicopter, Beverley's unlikely thesis, and Harvey's near-psychotic behavior that afternoon at the motel. Before leaving, he took me aside and asked what Amy had died of, then he grunted and nodded and said, "Maddie probably cast a spell on her, she knew where you were, we all did, we just never thought you'd come back."

Does he really think she's some kind of witch? And why has he gone quiet? Where are Gus and Clem and Pete? In their position, I would have reached out a welcoming hand, not hovered in front of the house in a helicopter. Are they waiting to hear from me? Maggie has warned me off all three of them as part of "Harvey's gang."

TWENTY

Too curious to heed warnings, the other day I decided to seek out my old friends separately, and play the bumbling, distracted old fool. At the least I wanted to see them with my own eyes and judge for myself. At best, I hoped to consult the archives of the The Carverville Lighthouse *and try to determine whether in fact skeletons had been stolen years ago from the junior college, as Harvey suggested. The newspaper isn't online. Beverley thinks I'm wasting my time, that it's obvious Harvey made up the skeleton story on the spur of the moment. But I'm not entirely sure of that. What if they pilfered skeletons years ago as part of a future cover-up strategy?*

Starting with Clem, I waited until Maggie had gone to work in the morning and, sending Taz ahead to Beverley's garden, I said I had errands to run. Instead of walking on the beach to the Eden Resort, I rode my bike into town and chained it to a pole on Second and Acacia. I could have gone to city hall to see Clem during his office hours—as Harvey said, he's also Carverville's part-time mayor—but I knew Maggie would be in the building. So, I preferred seeing him for the first time at the premises of the newspaper, the second-oldest continuously published paper in the West, after the Mountain Messenger *in Downieville, California, where Mark Twain briefly cut his teeth, painfully, it's said.*

The offices of The Carverville Lighthouse *are a few blocks away from down-town, in a vintage clapboard bungalow, down a one-way alley a hundred yards from Mulligan's. I walked quickly by the entrance, circled the block, and walked past again in the opposite direction, conscious of being observed by the security cameras.*

The day was cold and windy, and as usual I saw no one on the sidewalks. Only a few cars passed. Glancing at the building, I noticed the old ten-foot wooden model lighthouse on the roof looking forlorn, rattling in the wind, held upright by guy wires. Loitering on a corner and pretending to check my cellphone, I waited a few more minutes until Clem drove up. I recognized him right away. Barely five-foot-four, Clem had always been an ornery, vain, high-strung stump of a boy among the towering lumberjack giants of Carverville. His gingery hair is still thick and wavy but going gray now, and he wears thick black-rimmed glasses that hide his small darting blue eyes and the girlish features of his leprechaun face.

Hopping out of his outsized pickup truck, he bustled down the alley with a bundle of papers tucked under one arm and a smartphone clutched in his free hand. He wore a bright yellow reflective vest emblazoned with the words EMERGENCY CREW. *I couldn't help noticing that, like Beverley's, his sporty pickup was bright cherry red. Hadn't Clem wanted to be a professional fireman? No department would hire him—he was too short and too mean to get past the HR interviews. I also couldn't help wondering what horsepower hid under the hood of that monstrous vehicle, and how many miles per gallon it got. But Clem wasn't the kind to worry about climate change hoaxes. He had never given a damn about anyone or anything other than himself, except, maybe, his strange friendship with Harvey. Clem was the puppeteer who made Humpty Dumpty dance. I wondered if that was still the case, or if the roles had been reversed.*

Staring at his truck, unable to make up my mind, I suddenly knew I'd seen it before—close up. The vanity license plate read GOCLEM76, and now the penny dropped. On my second day in town, before the tree came down on the RV, I'd ridden my bike around and that customized SUV had forced me into a ditch, the driver flipping me off to add insult to injury. I'd meant to report his reckless driving but thought better of it, wanting to avoid the authorities. Irate now, I was about to follow Clem down the alley and give him a piece of my mind, when Maggie's words came back to me. "Clem is the worst of the pack," she said. "He's got little-man syndrome. If you think he was ever a friend of yours, you'd better think again." So, heeding Maggie's words, I thought again, shrugged involuntarily, and walked back to my bike, deciding to take a rain check. There would be other ways to find out about the skeleton theft, if such a thing had occurred, and I'd no doubt meet Clem sooner than was healthy for either of us.

Gus and Pete turned out to be a twofer. When I rode up, they were standing in a wide shared driveway shooting the breeze, surrounded by outsized tow trucks and industrial equipment, country music blaring from the open doors of a yawning, greasy garage with four lift bays, all occupied. Tipping back their red billed caps one then the other, as if doing the same comic routine as Harvey and Tom, they didn't recognize me at first. They probably knew from Harvey about the silly little fold-up bicycle, though, and eventually they put two and two together and got five, to borrow another expression from Beverley. We shook hands and paddled at each other and they seemed sincerely glad to see me, so much so that I began to wonder if Maggie and Beverley weren't exaggerating when describing their potential for nastiness. If Pete was so bad, how could Sally still be married to him, I found myself wondering. Gus? He'd always been mild mannered, polite by Carverville standards, and respectful of his second-generation Swedish parents and kin, the Gustafson clan.

Looking like a prosperous patriarch from hillbilly heaven, Pete led me in, telling me he now owned the Carverville Garage, where he had worked back in high school, as Harvey had mentioned. Gus Gustafson had set up business next door. Renting out trailers, trucks, mini-dozers, and other earth-moving and tree-trimming equipment, dumpsters, cement mixers, and industrial chippers, Gus also sold and serviced chainsaws, blowers, lawn mowers, weed whackers, quads, dune buggies, and similar useful, noisy, polluting, destructive devices for the garage, garden, forest, and beach. Both men had done well in a small-town way, and both looked remarkably unchanged, like Clem, though they were thicker and graying. As Pete and I took a tour through the garage and into Gus's store, I spotted half a dozen paying customers—about the most animation I'd experienced in town so far, outside the old diner. In Carverville, cars and machinery and food are the be-all, end-all, after all.

Watching the two of them interact, I remembered wondering if Gus and Pete weren't cousins or secret half brothers. Pink complexioned, big boned, and burly, they had the same sunstruck, vacuous look in their gray eyes, the same grease in the deep creases on their outsized mitts, the same slow, vaguely Scandinavian rural drawl, and they even wore the same make of blue industrial overalls. On one set, Carverville Garage was picked out in large yellow letters stretched over Pete's broad back and *shoulders, with his name in cursive on his left breast. Similarly, Gus's outfit said Carverville Equipment Rentals and, on his breast, you could read the name "Gus." Both also wore small official-looking badges that identified them as first responders, deputized by the county sheriff's department. Then another penny dropped, and I recalled seeing the overalls on one of them, the driver of the flatbed truck, the evening of the cage incident, but it had been too dark to make a positive ID of who it was. They were part of the problem, not the answer.*

What other details about my old "friends" might Beverley demand of an investigator, or Maggie of a budding psychologist? Sadly, I couldn't identify the twanging country rock on the sound system in the garage. I did notice Pete's hair. He had a head of thick black hair once upon a time, but, like Harvey, had lost much of it, and what was left contained more salt and slate than pepper. He reeked of cheap aftershave, and the smell brought back to mind his peculiar body odor problem, a torment and a cross to bear through high school. Gus's blond mane had receded like his pinkish-black gums, which I saw when he smiled at me, but he was tall enough so that most people wouldn't notice the bald spot and turtle dove coloration. They both still chain-smoked and chewed and spat, like Harvey, and within a few minutes I think we all realized we had less than zero in common, and nothing much to say to one another, a deep past, a shallow present, and no future. But we pretended otherwise and agreed to get together soon for a "high school reunion" at Harvey's, a pool party in winter, since Harvey now had an indoor-outdoor heated swimming pool and gas-fired barbecue and was living the high life.

"Or we could do some hog hunting from Sam's 'copter," Pete said with his roller-coaster diction, his head bobbing in time.

"Sam's my son," Gus explained affably. "He's a pilot, he's got lots of work doing deliveries to the rigs and taking folks hunting," he added with evident pride. "Harvey loves it, you would, too."

"Sounds great," I said with inexplicable enthusiasm, and immediately regretted it. Pete and Gus smiled approvingly and flapped me on the shoulders again, glad to have me back. Why, they said, I could join the volunteer fire department, and they needed a new man for the Patriot Posse, too, since Casey had left town for good. Did I remember Casey Hallard? No, I said, I did not.

"Posse?" I asked, an afterthought. "I never could ride a horse," I said, joking, but they didn't get the joke. "We'll work something out," I added, clapping them both on the shoulders.

What came through during our brief encounter were not Harvey's sadistic vindictiveness and Clem's celebrated Napoleonic nastiness, but rather plain old stupidity, ignorance, and dullness covering an abyss of horrors from the past, with others waiting to happen. They were the kind of good old boys who obeyed orders, never asked questions, and deeply believed whatever they did was right and proper.

After a long parlay with an AAA dispatcher, Gus asked, "Which way you headed?" I told him I wanted to take a peek at the old junior college, I was on a roots rediscovery journey, and Maggie's father had founded the place. They glanced at each other vacuously.

"I never saw the point of going to college," said Pete defensively.

"Me neither," said Gus. "I'll drive you over," he added cheerfully, explaining that he had to drag away a stalled car down on Highway 12. "I'm going your way."

Before I could object, he and Pete were lifting the bike onto the back of the tow truck and strapping it down with movers' belts. I paused, glancing at the belts, not sure where I'd seen them before, then shook my head and let it go. We climbed into the cab. Turning on the truck's swirling lights, Gus laid scratch as he pulled out. "Got 425 HP under there," he said, pointing at the hood, "and more torque than you've ever felt."

My head snapped back as he accelerated, and I worried about whiplash. But I had to admire the simplicity and naturalness of Gus's pleasure. Glancing back through the cloud of black diesel exhaust Gus had produced, I saw Pete smiling broadly, waving. "Heard you rebuilt the McCulloch," Gus remarked as we tore south on the frontage road, "you be careful, you haven't been doing much cutting lately I'll bet, and that old saw is a killer, go right through wood and plastic and bone and metal, too—no safety guards. We turned it away, wouldn't touch it. Like I said to that colored boy, Maggie's boy, that saw should be in a museum or a junkyard."

When Gus laughed he whooped and hiccupped, and suddenly I remembered how I always thought of him as Carverville's leading Dumbo, not a bad guy, just plain dumb.

The truck's dispatching radio fizzed and crackled, and Gus smiled and shifted into fourth gear. Thinking of Beverley, I noticed the furry dice and miniature bowling pin dangling from the rearview mirror, and a three- or four-inch plastic Bible lying open with the words "Let Jesus into Your Life" glued to the top of the dashboard. Gus was wearing a shiny gold crucifix on a gold chain around his neck, just peeping out of his undershirt and chest hair. Then I focused on the golden band on his ring finger and, pointing at it, asked whom he'd married.

"Which time?" Gus quipped, "the first or second or third or the fourth time?" He laughed loudly from a deep place in his big, cavernous body. "Married Sheila back in 1981," he added. "You remember Sheila Svensson? Didn't last. Anyways, we had two kids, Sam and Jenna, he's the pilot and she does the checkout at Farmstead Market at the Seaside Mall. Then I married Sue, remember Sue Lamont, the tall gal, stacked, blonde, bad teeth?" I made reassuring noises and let him go on. "We had another one, Gus Jr., she got him and moved away . . ."

By the time Gus pulled over near the driveway to the junior college campus, he'd run through four wives and six children of his own, a catalogue of soap opera names, adding that the latest was only three years old, a boy named Taylor. "His mother is Hannah," he said, "she's Annie's best friend, or she was Annie's best friend until a couple years ago, so I guess that makes Hannah seventeen years younger than we are."

"Seventeen?" I asked. "Beverley must be glad to know that," I remarked. Gus didn't get it, so I let it go. "Who is Annie anyway?" I added. "I've been gone a long time, I don't know any of these people."

"She's Pete's youngest, Tom's little sister. Moved up and over the hills after some trouble with her husband, Granger. You heard of Granger yet? He was Sheila's son by Bill Jones, the varsity football player, so anyways I guess that makes Granger my ex-stepson. Remember that big, old yellow house on the road to Lakeside, just over the county line, in the outskirts of Hazelwood? We used to go hunting up there sometimes, in high school, that's where Harvey wrecked his trail bike, that old Honda job. Don't tell me you don't remember? Little Annie lives in that house we used to go to sometimes for fun, remember? Some of Kitten Caboodle's gals were up there back then . . ." Gus paused and I saw him blush.

"Is that where we took Clem to get him laid?" I asked. "I thought it was the motel behind Mulligan's?"

Gus shook his head. "It was the big, old yellow house in Hazelwood. So, Annie hooked up again with someone, runs the Hazelwood Hops & Hog now, but don't mention her name to Tom or Harvey, they never forgave her, and I don't blame them."

"For what?"

"For taking up with that long-haired hippie troublemaker from out of town, and dumping Granger like that, and just being friends with all the wrong people."

Feeling slightly dizzy, I swung my head a few times to clear it, then said I didn't really remember much about the yellow house or know the Hazelwood Hops & Hog, but I guessed it was a bar or restaurant. "Microbrewery," Gus said. "Good stuff. Too bad about the people who go there."

I shook his thick, rough hand after he unstrapped my bike and lifted it down. "Gotta get you something better to ride." He grinned, his gums showing. "I have a whole range of off-road vehicles you can buy or lease, might come in handy on the beach up there, if you're staying at Five Mile with Maddie."

"We have lots to catch up on," I said as affably as I could. "I might drop by and rent one of those quads," I added, "take a ride in the woods, for old times' sake."

Gus thought that was a great idea. Hunt some hogs the old-fashioned way, he said.

This time it was my turn to stand in the cloud of diesel exhaust and wave at the receding tow truck. Pushing my bike up the long drive toward the campus, avoiding the pair of jacked-up hot rods that roared by with teenagers at the wheel, I reviewed what Gus had said. When might he have used the McCulloch to know it was so dangerous? And why all the talk about this Annie woman? Also to my surprise, he'd corrected me when I called the school a junior college, saying it was now a community college, as in commies and left wingers, but that was about to change, soon it would be just a plain old vocational school, with training in computer science, drone technology, and accountancy, on the high end, and mechanics, woodworking, and forestry on the other.

The thought of having to bring up a three-year-old at our age filled me with something like dread. I wished Gus well and started to put him out of my mind, when the thought of Annie returned—Annie and the missing young brawler of Mulligan's. Maggie's son? Those were yet more dots to join. I might want to try some of that microbrewery's beer after all.

Compared to what it had looked like back in the 1970s, the college was unrecognizable. It had doubled in size since Professor Simpson's tenure and, like certain other parts of Carverville, showed periods of clumsy growth or corrosive decline in its glassy postmodern carbuncles and current decrepit infrastructure—pitted parking lots, unfinished traffic islands where the landscaping had dried up and died, beaten earth instead of lawns, a half-built sports complex, and so on. "Third world" is the term that sprang to mind, another new normal.

Asking directions from a handful of hurried students, I eventually found the library and was not surprised to see it closed until further notice. Maggie had told me the librarian had retired and not been replaced due to budget cuts and political choices. The facility was being transformed into a digital learning lab,

Taz had noted approvingly. Everything was being scanned and uploaded, and the obsolete paper documents were being transferred to a storage facility some-where or recycled. Partway through the move, funding had run out. It was a familiar story.

Further inquiries led me to the basement office of the property manager, where I found an older, heavyset man, presumably Jonathan Dewey, the doctor's brother by the looks of him, seated on a broken-down swivel chair at a gunmetal desk in a low-ceilinged room with fluorescent strip lights. Talking on an old camel-colored landline telephone with a knotted cord hanging from the handset, the man nodded me to a folding chair and when his conversation was finished asked me in a friendly tone what he could do to help me. I offered my hand and, confirming to me that he was Dewey, the elder, he joked, saying he was in no way as distinguished or successful as his younger brother. I told him who I was, how we must have known each other at Carverville High, and how I'd seen his brother recently, and was living with Maggie.

Dewey brightened as he led me upstairs into the sunshine. Standing on the vast, unfinished concrete esplanade with a view over barren hills to the highway and the ocean, he said he had the keys to everything, and we could go to the library if we wanted, but he doubted if we'd find anything of interest, since so much had been removed already.

"It's the old maps I'm looking for," I said. "Somehow, way back, I remember seeing a book about local history, with maps of the county from a century or more ago."

"You may be in luck, then," he said, opening the door to the library and flipping switches as we progressed into the half-dismantled stacks. "We haven't got to the local history room yet." Clearing a spot at a long study table, he said, "Help yourself, call me when you're done." Jonathan gave me his cellphone number and started back out as I pecked it into my disposable phone.

"One other thing," I said as an afterthought. "Did you ever hear of skeletons being stolen from the science lab here? It would've been a few years back, maybe a decade or more."

Dewey paused and for a moment looked astonishingly like his plumper, shorter brother, the piebald hair, wrinkled brow, and smiling eyes identical. He shook his head. "No skeletons stolen from here," he remarked. "We have a skeleton staff, if that's what you mean." He laughed. "No one else has lasted as long as I have, all the smart people moved out a long time ago. Been here since 1980 and believe me, I would know. Where'd you hear that?"

Shaking my head and looking down at my feet as if puzzled, I said, "I can't remember. Maybe I read it somewhere? The Lighthouse, *for instance?"*

Dewey shook his head again. "I've read every issue of that rag since the day I could read." He chuckled. "Plenty of stuff about the weather, who got married or divorced, who sold or bought a house or a boat, or died or gave birth, the hunting and hogs, the deer and raccoons, the fact that it just isn't true there's tar on the beach and not a stick of wood in the hills, and no jobs in town, and then of course, there's all the local advertising for hardware and rental equipment, helicopter trips and whale watching without whales getting in the way, and stuff at the Seaside Mall on sale because no one wants to buy it, plus a survey of the best retirement homes, real estate deals, secondhand baby clothes, you name it, but never anything as exciting as stolen skeletons."

TWENTY-ONE

✤

As I rode from the campus across Carverville to Beverley's, I thought about the book of maps I had found in the local history room, published in 1890, guaranteed accurate and based on the land registry. I was genuinely happy my memory wasn't wrong. I had seen that book forty years ago but remembered it because of the graveyard on Egmont's property. It turns out the burial grounds corresponded to the area now occupied by the public parking lot, where I had spent ten days in the RV, and the stretch of land bounded by the fallen cypress and the lower parking area at the bottom of Beverley's property, as far as I could tell. Another old town map of the same kind, from the 1940s, showed the graveyard had been cleared, the current beach access created, with that seventeen-step staircase, and the Beachcomber Motel built. Borrowing Dewey's smartphone, I got him to take photos of the two maps and email them to me, Taz, Beverley, and Maggie.

So, I was pleased with the research I'd managed to accomplish, the graveyard and skeleton questions no longer hanging over my head, so to speak, and those curious tidbits from Gus about the McCulloch and Annie to keep my mind turning over as I pedaled the undersized bike down an unpaved shortcut to the Old Coast Highway. I was also pleased I'd seen Gus and Pete and defused any potential hostility from that quarter. I decided that, what the hell, I would go hog hunting with them in the helicopter. Maybe I would discover something I might not see otherwise.

Yet it troubled me that I'd made some strategic blunder without realizing it. This feeling persisted and grew over the next few days, following my conversations with Beverley and Maggie. "Harvey's gangsters" were "trouble" they each said, over and over, in different ways.

When, that same afternoon following my visit to the college, I mentioned to Beverley what Gus had said about Annie falling out with her family, living in Hazelwood and working at the Hops & Hog, and how I might rent a quad or borrow Maggie's car and drive up there without telling Maggie, of course, Beverley looked me up and down with a gimlet eye as if I'd said something obscene. We were working in the garden toward sunset—I was trimming the escallonia bushes on the south side of her parking lot while she shuffled around me, talking nonstop.

"What do you take me for, JP?" she asked with an indignation that did not seem feigned or jokey, then answered herself before I could open my mouth. "Can you really imagine I would not have betaken myself over yonder to Hazelwood long ago and talked shop with little Annie, the lush with long thighs? She and I weren't exchanging recipes for cakes and ale, Your Honor. Do you think I wasn't as curious as you, if not more curious than you, about the tall, dark, mysterious troublemaker who passed through town four years ago and then, poof, disappeared?"

I started to object that when the subject had come up before, she hadn't seemed to know much about either Annie or the unknown visitor. She cut me off with a sweep of her pudgy hand.

"First, Mr. Hamilton Burger, Annie has been thoroughly debriefed by yours truly and Maggie, who is no mean interrogator, believe me, as you may one day find out. Second, Annie will not talk to you or anyone else about the incident, she is scared witless, and she doesn't have many wits to spare or to scare, whatever portion she started out with having been properly pickled. She says she never knew the man's real name or anything about him other than he was good-looking, a companionable bedtime partner, and friendlier and politer than the local charmers who haunt Mulligan's. In fact, she wondered why John Doe had brought her there at all—he told her to call him by that name if anyone asked. And she especially wondered why he was talking to her so freely in front of the locals, as if to provoke them. She and Mr. Doe did not meet in the sawdust and spills, by the way, they went to Mulligan's on day two of their brief romance. He was hitching a ride because his car broke down on Highway 12, he said, and she picked him up. They went to Mulligan's following their nocturnal tryst, if I may describe it in such terms. The gentleman said he had

*relatives in town and was up to see them. He joked he was busy saving the world,
asked if she would like to join him, and, if not, how about a moonlit stroll by the
beach in the meantime, up toward the mansion on Five Mile?*

"That's when Granger's old buddy Sam tapped the stranger on the shoulder and
punched him in the nose when he turned around," Beverley added. "Annie tried to
stop the brawl, but when the Tom Cat showed up with the handcuffs it was too
late. They said they were taking him to dry out overnight in the county jail and she,
Annie, ought to skedaddle and be ashamed of herself, and pack her bags, too, before
Granger got back." Beverley drew breath, pulled out her car keys and dangled them
in front of me.

"If you can do better, Hamilton, please borrow my truck and drive on over to that
brewery or the old whorehouse, feel free. Before you go, I would add that Sam and
everyone else at Mulligan's denied they'd ever seen anything, and there is no record
of any of this on the books at the sheriff's department, no record of a tow truck or
breakdown on Highway 12, either. Maggie found ways of checking, believe me. So,
if you were planning to undertake your secret mission without telling Glinda and
Alexander Z Great, then, as I just said, feel free, take my pickup, the tank's full, and
I'm sure the GPS tracking devices imbedded all over the truck by the sheriff and his
posse are in perfect order. Go in for a lube job, come out with enough spy hardware
to thrill a Russian.

"They would also have built those pesky bugs into the quad, if it comes from Gus,
and I'll lay you a bet they planted a few on your little old bicycle there while they
were at it, not to mention the RV." She shook her head, clearly disappointed in me,
and rattled her pearls. I started to object, then recalled how Gus had taken the bike
from me with great solicitousness when Pete and I toured the garage and shop. "Go
on, instead of grumbling, take a look under the fenders and the seat," she insisted,
jabbing a pink-tipped finger at the folding bicycle.

Blushing the cherry red of her pickup as I disengaged two GPS tracking devices
with sticky adhesive bases embedded under the seat and front fender, I slipped them
into my pocket and muttered something about needing to sharpen the pruning shears
and then calling it a day. Slinking off to the shed before she could stop me, and
pushing the bike alongside, I stuck the devices to a sawed-off section of two-by-four,
walked down the rickety staircase to the beach, and threw the wood into the waves.
Afterward, bypassing the motel office, I left the resort grounds carrying the bike up
through the undergrowth to the stump of the cypress. My face was still burning from

embarrassment and anger. Beverley was right on all counts. Who was I to come along and compromise their efforts? Kicking sulkily and digging with my heel, I found another bone fragment, wiggled it free from the roots of the tree that had fed on it, and slipped it into the pocket of my windbreaker. One day I'd figure out if it was a human or an animal bone.

What if, I said to myself, confused and flushed, making my way home on my ridiculous little bicycle, what if Beverley and Number Three had somehow been complicit with the authorities early on, and she had been spooked and now wanted out? That might explain a number of things. I started to list them, beginning with the McCulloch and ending with Beverley's supernatural ability to know exactly what I was doing, thinking, hoping, and planning.

The disconcerting thought persisted as I rode home on the Old Coast Highway, my head swiveling back and forth as I scanned the road ahead and behind for speeding jacked-up SUVs or Clem's cherry-red fire engine. Out to sea, right about where I'd thrown the two-by-four in the water, a helicopter hovered and circled. Then the pilot swerved away and flew slowly parallel to me over the beach for at least a mile before spinning around and zipping south out of view. He must have spotted me on the highway. Clem or Gus?

Also in the category of troubling discoveries, I noticed after I got home, when I was searching for the keys to the RV, that Maggie carries a handgun in her purse. Why? It's so out of character. Then again, how well do I know the new Maggie?

Like panic, paranoia is contagious. As a precaution after my encounters with Harvey, Gus, and Pete, and my conversations with Beverley and Maggie, I hid my copy of Kropotkin's Memoirs of a Revolutionist *under the floorboards in the attic, along with the new bone fragment, and that compromising photo of Taz as a child, in front of a wall somewhere south of the border. I also encouraged Taz to make sure his photos and videos of the cage incident were posted anonymously on social media and shared widely on pages already hosting images of the incident.*

Saying he could set up multiple accounts for the purpose, he circulated the material, at my behest, to members of the legal and scientific community out of state, asking questions and leaving comments from his multiple "fake" accounts or aliases. I put the word in quotation marks because it has lost all meaning in recent years and stands for "anonymous" in this case. Feedback from coroners and marine biologists, about everything from the time it takes for bones in seawater to be stripped of all flesh and genetic material, to the growth rate of barnacles on stainless steel, will be welcome.

Safety in numbers, I said, then followed with another cliché, the best defense is a good offense. I can't help wondering if it is the concept of legal precedent that leads me to use so many shopworn phrases.

Maggie and Taz and I have instinctively avoided talking about these issues when we are together. For instance, I have not yet shared with them my speculations about Beverley's outlier theories, or my own possibly fantastical worries that the old mill property was a site used in the recent past and possibly still used today by the disappearance squads, if such squads ever existed.

But they continue as the main topic of conversation each morning, when I go to Beverley's to work in the garden. Often neglecting her duties, she tags along, a step behind me wherever I go, whispering and croaking and wheezing. I almost snipped off one of her fingers by mistake the other day when she grabbed the slender branch I was trimming off the flowering maple, the one leaning over the wood chip path to the lawn. It was only because the sun struck her pearl necklace at that moment and reflected into my eyes that I saw the imminent danger. Now, in another troubling twist, she says she hears voices, and that Harvey is waiting to spring something, she knows it in her bones.

Reminding her about the old graveyard and skeletons, I told her I thought the expression "knows it in her bones" seemed too close to the bone, and she ought not to use it. That got her coughing, wheezing, laughing, and shivering worse than ever—with a mixture of hilarity and fear. She won't stop insisting that the motel's premises, especially the cottages, were a staging ground for extrajudicial disappearances from the pier by boat, and are haunted, that the raccoons and skunks and hogs are reincarnations of the victims, and that the White Rhino has been urging her from his cookie jar to sell up and move out.

"I hear him in the night," she croaked at one point, clutching her necklace and glancing side to side. I realize she is constantly joking in her morbid, sardonic way, unless this time around she really is having aural hallucinations or believes in ghosts. She may be on the edge of some kind of nervous breakdown or pulmonary crisis. She seems to be suffering from intermittent fevers. I think she should see Dr. Dewey. She and Maggie describe him as an "ally." But she says there's no use, that she sees plenty of him, if I only knew. "I've seen him seventeen times in the last year," she quipped. I was about to question her further but sensed the tombstone firmly in place so backed off.

Speaking of tombstones, with access to the Internet at the mansion, I have been able to find, among other things, that there is no proof of the massacre of the Yono, now considered fake news from centuries past, or the existence of a pioneer grave-yard on the property. So, either those maps are wrong and my memory is flawed, or someone has been actively scrubbing files and editing Wikipedia, purging the record and rewriting history.

As to the stolen skeletons from the college lab, there were no reports of that in any county or state publication of any kind that I could access. I went back eighteen years. Beverley says it's worse than a farce, it's a ruse or a lure. Harvey is still trying to find some way to trap me and Taz. I fear she's right. Something tells me we'll soon find out. ·

I have also been able to confirm that the abandoned Beachcomber Motel had been confiscated by the county for unpaid property taxes immediately after Mr. Egmont died. He left no heirs and no will. Apparently, the place eventually sold for a song at auction just over three years ago to Beverley and the White Rhino—his real name was Ronald Rossi. How the buildings managed to survive the vandals and firebugs in this remote location I cannot imagine—unless Beverley is right and the property was a staging ground. I'm guessing Harvey and his friends were surprised and dismayed when Number Three, the waterworks engineer, found the underground stream, all that is left of Greenwood Creek, meaning the land is very valuable.

Since Beverley also dropped a few hints about "skeletons in closets," then left them hanging, this may be the place to note my fuzzy recollections of the pubescent Sally Murphy. Her name came up in conversation last week. She is Harvey's younger sister, Tom's mother, an old if dull friend of Maggie's and the same age as she, two years younger than Harvey and I. When we were growing up, Sally seemed the typical kid sister. I never gave her a thought, other than to class her among the obtuse and pimply. As brother and sister, she and Harvey were very close, too close, some alleged. I knew those allegations to be well grounded because, not long after I arrived and befriended Harvey, he shared an unspeakable secret with me.

Pudgy, prickly, and spoiled, the young Harvey loved to hunt squirrels and gophers back then and wasn't averse to trapping rats, either. He demonstrated great ingeniousness in figuring out how to lure and kill them, usually with his pellet gun. We were only fifteen or sixteen and he didn't have a real gun yet, unlike his older brother, Jack. But a pellet gun of the right kind can kill, maim, and stun small animals, and Harvey, probably influenced by some movie he'd seen and egged on by his brutish father and brother, had strung up a large collection of the unlucky creatures, some wounded and unable to escape. They dangled, wriggling and hyperventilating upside down on fishing line or twine, dying or already dead, under a big fir tree in his backyard. They made a godawful noise and stench. It was a great privilege to be shown this gallery of horrors, I learned, so I pretended to be enthusiastic, telling him how my father hunted a great deal, mainly deer, raccoons, and hogs. Harvey said he wished my dad were his dad. That surprised me. I figured it was because my father had been a major in the army and was decorated with a Purple Heart. Then he said, "'Cause if he were, then Sally wouldn't be my sister."

I recall being puzzled by this and the logic it suggested. I told him I didn't understand. Instead of revealing what he meant, he took me through the side door into the house and we climbed up the rickety servants' stairs to his bedroom. It was a big old dark brown wooden house with a shingle roof and giant dormers and built-in closets and servants' passageways behind the walls, like our miniature Victorian mansion on the cliff. The servants were long gone, but the whispers and secrets remained. Harvey showed me the closet in his bedroom, and how he'd laid an air mattress in a corner on the floor, under the hanging rod and coats. "That's where we do it," he boasted. "Now, don't you tell anyone," he added, pushing me out of the closet and across the room. I pushed back and we fell and began wrestling. It was the first time we'd fought and he bested me, largely because my heart wasn't in it.

Harvey was always heavyset and powerful. But he never bested me again, I made sure of that. Somehow, for years afterward, I blotted out the memory of the air mattress and Sally. The truth is, I wasn't sure what he was doing with her, I had no experience with girls and had no brothers or sisters to ask. My parents certainly never mentioned anything about sex. In fact, I was not initiated into the mysteries until late, when Maggie took me under her wing, so to speak. I never understood Harvey's obsessive claims about me and girls when we were in high school. He was off the mark. Naturally I preferred to let him think what he wanted and never denied being a Don Juan, even if the significance of the term escaped me.

Harvey's mentioning of Pete and Sally is what jogged my mind. This morning Beverley said something about Sally's first child, the Tom Cat's older sister, and how she was mentally retarded, and for some reason this awoke in me these unsavory and unpleasant recollections. They got me thinking.

I might as well admit here and now that Pete wasn't really a friend of mine. He was Harvey's stooge and sidekick, like Gus, and all three were in the thrall of Clem. Pete and I played tennis and baseball together once in a while, and that was fine, but he always struck me as weak willed and slow-witted and, as I mentioned earlier, plagued by a nauseating fishy kind of body odor. I believe his family subsisted off seafood, which was very cheap at the time.

The more I recall the past, the more I realize that, beyond my friendship with Mr. Egmont and my love of gardens and butterflies, my life in Carverville was pretty miserable until Maggie came along. Our time on the high school newspaper with Professor Johnson was certainly one of the highlights of my adolescence. Exposing injustice and finding facts seemed like the most important of all jobs, and as current events prove, I wasn't half wrong. I seriously considered taking a degree in journalism, but something held me back, perhaps, I now realize, it was the knowledge that Johnson had betrayed me.

I can now give a more detailed account of Maggie's life during the lapse of four decades, when we lost sight of each other. She admitted to me several days ago that she left town with Professor Johnson shortly after I departed at the end of semester break. She had argued with her parents, she said. Though progressives, they were practicing Lutherans and disapproved of her behavior "with the boys," threatening to cut her off and send her to live with her aunt in Philadelphia. But she was eighteen by then and strong willed. So, Maggie packed a suitcase and left with Professor Johnson, who was planning to leave town anyway, it seems. Her parents followed suit, moving away one semester later, saying Carverville was cursed, a place guaranteed to wreck families and render normal humans imbecilic. The truth is, Mr. Simpson had accomplished his job, the junior college was up and running after something like six years of monumental effort, and he and his wife were eager to get home to Virginia.

Finding herself in Little Rock with Professor Johnson, Maggie enrolled in a community college but dropped out soon after because she was pregnant—with twins. She gave birth to a stillborn boy, choked by his brother's umbilical cord, and to her surviving son, Paul. It was a difficult, traumatic birth and she almost died. A last-minute caesarean saved her. That explained the foot-long scars on her abdomen I noticed when we made love again for the first time. Maggie named Paul for me. Professor Johnson knew it but she says he didn't mind—he was easygoing, mature, and had "advanced tastes," she added, whatever that meant. It's worth recalling that, at the time, I went by the name J. Paul Adams, but most people called me Paul not James. Only a few friends like Maggie or Harvey used the acronym "JP."

So, Paul Johnson, son of our former professor of English, was the father of Taz, or Alexander if you prefer. I must stop calling him Taz. But the nickname fits him, somehow, whereas Alexander and Alex do not.

Let me go back to Maggie for the time being, before moving to the tall, gangling, rawboned malcontent Paul and his unusual-looking son, Taz. Since I have limited time to show her life in Technicolor in this journal, I will have to content myself with telling what I can in a concise, telegraphic style. Maggie and Professor Johnson were married in Little Rock, moved into a big wooden house near the college campus where he had landed a professorship, and stayed married for about five years. But his "advanced tastes" turned out to be bisexuality. Eventually it matured into homosexuality, or perhaps it allowed him to discover his true homosexual self. While she had nothing against it, she wasn't prepared to lead a celibate life while he carried on, sometimes bringing home his lovers, who were mostly students and fellow teachers.

She and the infant Paul wound up living separately from him under the same roof. But the relationship was untenable, and the weather in Arkansas was even harder to take than the climate she'd grown up with in Charlottesville, where she was born. With her parents' help, she moved back home, enrolled at UVA and eventually took degrees in English, then psychology. That's where she met Zack Hansen, professor number two, another father figure many years her senior, who adopted Paul and brought him up for the next several years. That's why I'm not clear about what Paul's last name is or was. Why can't I bring myself to ask Maggie?

Their luck didn't last. "It's not that Paul was a bad seed," she told me the other morning as we moved swiftly south on the deserted beach among the mounds of rotting seaweed, dead snipes, garbage bags, and driftwood, heading to Beverley's. It turns out Zack Hansen had two children of his own from a previous marriage, a boy and a girl. No one got along. Zack never felt affection for Paul, who was a disturbed, needy, hyperactive, and disconcertingly intelligent child. Because Maggie was desperate for the new marriage to work, she unwittingly neglected Paul in favor of Zack and his children. This was the psychologist speaking. She told her tale in a detached way, almost as if the events had not happened to her but to someone else she knew.

By the time this second marriage failed, Paul was an awkward, gawky teenager, and that's when he had started to smoke and drink and experiment with soft drugs, and then hit the road, running away, the archetypal rebel without a cause. "You can imagine what happened," she said. Yes, I could imagine, having judged many cases in juvenile court and heard incontrovertible proof of the progression from cigarettes and marijuana to hash, crack, and opioids, with associated chronic delinquency. He fell under the influence of various gurus and preachers, was in and out of jail on misdemeanor and felony charges, but remembered to send Maggie postcards twice a year, on her birthday and Christmas—from distant places such as Afghanistan, Morocco, or El Salvador, plus Mexico, Alaska, and Montana. Then he disappeared altogether for a decade, only to return one day out of the blue, to leave Taz behind, and go underground again.

"If he's still alive," Maggie said in her quiet, detached way, "Paul is now almost forty, a confused, lost soul with a criminal record and little education." She paused. "Some people speculate he came back four years ago, planning to get Taz, but if it was Paul, they ran him out of town before we saw him. Last year I talked to the woman who gave him a ride and shared his bed, and I showed her photos of him when he was a child and then a boy of sixteen, before he ran away, but she wasn't sure, she's not exactly a reliable witness, and the man she met had a beard and long hair." Maggie paused and swallowed. "Part of me hopes he never comes back, for Alex's sake."

It was heartbreaking, another reason to resettle elsewhere and cover our tracks, we agreed, the sooner the better.

The list of incentives to leave is growing longer by the day. In practical terms, the choice might not be ours. One more record-breaking storm and the house might wind up on the beach. Maggie has already spent tens of thousands of dollars installing concrete buttresses and storm drains and anchoring the foundations with steel rods and cables—an "act of faith" she calls it. But if the land underneath gives way, what good would any of that do? Propping the house up from below with additional concrete trelliswork would cost more than the place is worth. Besides, if the economy ever recovers, and the refinery and northern bypass are completed, and if the Old Coast Highway is repaired, straightened and widened as planned, this last lost stretch of underdeveloped paradise will lose its magic. It feels like the time has come to roll out of Carverville forever.

Yet, for an equally long roster of reasons, we agree that it is impossible to leave for the time being. Maggie has professional commitments, for one thing. "If you only knew what goes on behind closed doors in this town," she added, dropping her guard, lowering her voice and taking me by the hand as we stopped below Beverley's staircase on Graveyard Beach.

Opening a practice as a child psychologist when she first returned to town ten years ago, she was confronted with the town's impoverished economic reality combined with the hostility of the locals to mental health treatment, which had forced her to give it up and get a regular job. She still has a few clients and does pro bono consulting for the beleaguered social services administration, so she cannot simply pick up and leave.

"The stories I hear," she said, but declined to provide details. They were too upsetting, she added, and professional ethics forbade her telling me more.

One sticky item on that roster of reasons for staying regards Taz's nationality and birth certificate, or lack thereof. It's the reason he has not been able to get a learner's permit to drive. It's also the main reason I am in touch with my counterparts in Missoula and San Antonio—their initial findings are starting to come in, but I am hesitant to share the unsettling news with Maggie until we have the whole picture.

Other than the postcards he sent his mother, for years no trace of Paul surfaced despite research by private investigators and police departments. Not even the FBI—at the time of his disappearance still a benign, law-based enforcement agency—had been able to find him. They speculated he had assumed one or more aliases, and that he might have been and still be linked to international drug trafficking or terrorism. How else had he, a felon, managed to get a passport and find the funds to travel all over the world?

None of this was surprising to me. The number of young men and women who vanish every year boggles the imagination. There are not dozens or hundreds but hundreds of thousands of them, and tens of thousands of unidentified remains stored in morgues around the country. I was about to ask Maggie if she ever wondered whether Paul had wound up in a feral hog trap, but, again, I decided against it. I will bring up that supposition once the reports come in from my colleagues, not that I have much hope in that direction.

"Harvey knows," Maggie said out of left field, driving the nail into the coffin.

I pressed her. The only reason Taz hasn't been deported, she explained, is he's a minor in her custody, has committed no known crime, and might reasonably be supposed to have been born in America to a U.S. citizen, i.e., Paul, her son, whose birth certificate she obtained from the authorities in Little Rock. Maggie has sworn an affidavit to the effect that she is the grandmother and Taz is American. Technically, Taz is an alien from an unknown land, and therefore an illegal immigrant. Technically, Maggie is also liable to prosecution for harboring him and making false statements. Since there is no proof of the boy's parents' identity, or anything about the child's origins, the case has stalled.

Given the political climate nationwide, and especially in the county, I remarked, and especially given the boy's obvious ethnic genetic component, they were lucky he hadn't been placed in a juvenile detention center pending a decision by ICE.

Shaking her head, Maggie whispered under her breath, "I haven't told you the most important thing." She paused to glance around and up at the bluffs along Grave-yard Beach as if someone above were listening. "We're being sheltered."

"Sheltered?"

She squeezed my hands and dipped and wagged her head in that strange, singular, meaningless movement she had imparted to Taz. "Yes," she whispered in confirmation, "by Harvey."

"Harvey?" I blurted out, a sudden fury turning my cheeks crimson. "What does he have on you?"

"On me, nothing, it's what I have on him."

TWENTY-TWO

❦

From the beach inland for about half a mile, the banks of Five Mile Creek meandered through lush undergrowth. Atop them, a hiking trail paralleling the course of the creek had once been part of the coastal parks network. Now it was a mad botanist's medley of raspberry bramble, nettle, and poison oak, unpassable to all but the intrepid. Wearing long-sleeved leather gloves and thick overalls tucked into waders, and armed with machetes, handsaws, and clippers, James and Taz began hacking and snipping their way along the abandoned trail, pausing every ten to fifteen feet to check the condition of the creek's banks and bed. Could salmon still swim upstream? That was the question.

Related sub-queries revolved around the amount of shade and branch cover, the temperature, depth, flow-rate, clarity and purity of the creek, and the existence of potential manmade or natural obstacles. Without a laboratory to test the water James could only begin, for the time being, with a visual inspection.

Forty years earlier, the creek had been "restored" to a natural condition along its eight-mile length from the beach to the hatchery to facilitate salmon migration. Fishing was not allowed, and the right of way on both banks belonged to the county. Fish ladders were not needed. This was a wild waterway. Several culverts crossing the unpaved logging road up the valley had been modified to avoid the accumulation of silt, and many "NCV" trees and shrubs with no commercial value had been planted strategically to provide cover and keep the water cool. The creek bed had been reconfigured, deepened or cleared, in a number of places. Drafted by his father during school holidays, James had done some of the heavy lifting himself, learning to use a bulldozer and drive a logging rig. He wondered how much of that monumental effort engineered and led by a manic, authoritarian Purple Heart major had been lost in the interim, after the defunding and shutdown of Wildlife & Fish. Judging by the first section of the creek, the prospects were good.

Their first objective that morning was to blaze a trail east under the crumbling concrete viaduct as far as the riverside beach, where the gravel road came down the incline in dusty switchbacks from the Old Coast Highway. The spot was easy to find. The dust always left seemingly indelible white tire marks on the asphalt above, once upon a time inviting the mammoth logging trucks to turn in. But the trucks and the swerving marks of their giant tires were things of the past, like so many features of the green, marshy, pleasant valley.

It was at this beachhead that the locals used to swim and fish illegally, James recalled, the place where settlers a century and a half earlier had built rustic wooden piers and shacks, and where around 1880 the narrow-gauge logging trains had come down on sturdy rough-hewn trestles from Big Mountain, appearing under black clouds of soot and steam from the thick fir woods on the north side of the creek. From there they banked north again along the shoulder of the old highway before entering the mill on the headlands two miles away. The settlers, the train, the mill, the trees were gone, even the local children who swam and fished at the beach were gone, by the looks of it, like the trucks and the dusty tracks on the tarmac.

Parked on the shoulder of the gravel road by the steep rocky beach, Maggie awaited them with a thermos and, at Taz's request, a bag of cinnamon rolls. She had declined the honor of trekking on the abandoned trail. Unlike James and Taz, who shared a natural resistance to poison oak, Maggie was virulently sensitive to the noxious oil on the plant's shiny, oak-like leaves. More than once after coming in contact with it, she had been hospitalized with suppurating boils, an alarming purple-and-red rash, conjunctivitis that swelled her eyelids into elephantine flaps, and severe respiratory difficulty. Injected and coated with cortisone, then wrapped head to foot in bandages, she had looked like a burn victim or a mummy. That was why she ran each morning on the beach, never inland. No inducement short of imminent peril could persuade her to venture anywhere poison oak might grow.

"So far so good," James reported, rinsing his face and hands in the cold creek water before approaching. Maggie set the coffee and rolls on the hood of the car and backed off, retracting her hands into the sleeves of her winter coat.

"Even if I just brush your clothes with my skin I'll get it," she said, seemingly faced by bearers of the plague.

"It looks like fish could still swim up," Taz remarked, brimming with instant expertise and unusual brio. "We might have to haul those old truck tires out of the creek," he added, echoing the comments James had made along the way, "and who knows what lies ahead, right?"

"Right," said James, amused. "We still have five miles to go."

The ocean wind had died down and the sun was struggling through the river mist. James had forgotten how radically the weather could change just a few miles inland from the beach.

Pumped full of coffee, their bloodstreams rushing with sugar, they set off again, the trail seemingly easier to follow along this second section of the creek, thanks to the proximity of the old logging road. Jogging parallel to the south bank, it was still used by the handful of longtime locals homesteading the ragged edges of the lower Five Mile Valley in what had once been primeval forestlands. Traffic was negligible but when a car or truck did pass by, volutes of dust rose, coating the vegetation and suffocating anyone nearby. Farther northeast, the road petered out at a crest on Big Mountain near the fountainhead of Five Mile Creek, but they would not be walking that far.

For several miles after the beachhead, the creek ran in a gentle curve over a rocky bed protected by stands of birch, aspen, and cotton willow, their quaking leaves a mesmerizing yellow, russet, and pistachio blur, the only touches of color in a universe of stubby green firs and barren brown clear-cuts. Reeds grew along the edges of the creek. Perched here and there on branches overcasting the water or hidden in the overhanging vegetation were kingfishers and egrets. Taz spotted a brace of quail seconds before the birds burst out of the riverside tangle, blowing past with extravagant trailing feathers. Ducks bobbed and quacked midstream, taking flight at the approach of the explorers, then circling and landing noisily moments later, spraying water to both sides as they landed.

"What's the word?" James shouted back over his shoulder.

"Bird brain," Taz said. "Those ducks are, like, pretty stupid." Before James could answer, Taz added, "I smell a skunk. Maybe we should go up and walk on the road for a while."

"Nah." James laughed. "It'll run away once it smells us. I'd rather walk in the water anyway. Best way to escape a skunk—or a dog." He veered down to the bank and clambered into the stream, feeling the iciness of the water through the rubber waders and boots. "Come on down, I don't think the salmon will bite you."

It wasn't just the weather that changed radically the farther away from the ocean you went. The human fauna also morphed from mildly obnoxious hick, hayseed, and hip-neck on the coastal strip, to potentially lethal hillbilly and Appalachian-style throwback a few miles upstream. Supplementing the usual NO TRESPASSING signs, James spotted several variations on the theme. Taz took photos from the middle of the creek, zooming in as they walked swiftly along, more amused than frightened. *We Shoot 2 Kill* promised one, *God Bless Semiautomatics* announced another, *The Second Amendment Starts Here!* shouted a third. Taz's favorites were the farthest inland, marking the razor wire and recycled box spring border fence of a colorful, stinking, hound-filled rural slum. *Thou Shalt Not Enter Without Being Shot Full of Holes* said one, *Trespassers Will Be Shot. Survivors Will Be Shot Again!* read the other, echoing the sign James had seen on the fence around the mill property.

By 11:30 A.M. they had covered about five miles of picturesque waterway and had found few impediments to fish migration. The incline increased slowly but steadily, the creek narrowing with the valley as the confluents became smaller, clearer, colder, faster, and fluty. James was feeling upbeat. "We have half an hour to cover the last mile," he announced.

"Picnic lunch here we come!" Taz yelled.

Splashing and sliding as they ran up the creek, laughing out loud, shouting and quacking like loons, they suddenly slackened their pace when they clambered up the banks near the former hatchery and saw Maggie was not there.

"Think she had a flat tire?" Taz asked, digging for his smartphone in the bottomless pockets of his overalls. Striding and searching as if divining for water, he ranged far and wide, trying but failing to find connectivity. "No service," he announced, "no Grandma."

"She probably bumped into Beverley at the supermarket," James remarked, "you know how Beverley talks."

"Right," Taz said, unconvinced.

Surveying the site, James could not repress a moan. In disbelief he walked the periphery of the parking lot and the old Wildlife & Fish headquarters, avoiding the paper and plastic bags, the dirty Styrofoam containers and balled up fast food wrappers, the broken beer bottles, used condoms in a kaleidoscope of black, red, white, yellow, and green, and the mounds of filthy tissue paper and human excrement. There were piles of discarded household appliances—a stove, a water heater, a tangle of cast-iron radiators—mountains of rubble, worn-out car and truck tires, used syringes, crumpled cigarette packs, and other waste he could not identify. Some of it was sealed in large gray plastic bags. Nudging cautiously with his rubber waders, he rolled one of the bags over and saw it was marked with a radioactivity symbol, a skull and crossbones, and the words HOSPITAL WASTE.

Beyond the slumping, broken-down chain-link fence stood the charred remains of what had been his father's office, a long one-story building with a slanting shingle roof now shot full of holes. The lab buildings, huts, sheds, garages, and dormitories once used by Wildlife & Fish employees for their various tasks were likewise charred ruins, their walls sprayed with swastikas and incomprehensible slogans or tags. The vandalism was so virulent and thorough that James found himself gloomily thinking the only thing to do would be to bulldoze what remained and start afresh.

The heart of the hatchery lay in back, in the woods by the creek. Pushing through another collapsed fence and following a rutted logging road across the compound, he found the parallel channels and deep millraces built of concrete, with gates and locks, flow-through tanks, pens and pools of various size and depth where the fertilized eggs of the fish were deposited and the fry hatched and grown, spending the crucial early phases of their development. This was where the mysterious instinctive programming occurred, the scent and peculiar qualities of the waters of Five Mile Creek somehow embedding themselves into the primitive brains and navigational systems of the fish. When mature enough, they would be released to swim downstream to the sea, where they disappeared for a number of years. Later in their life spans, when the time came to spawn, the salmon would somehow retrace their way, sensing the creek's waters in the vastness of the ocean, then struggling upstream until they found the spot to lay eggs or deposit sperm. Worn out from their efforts, their bodies torn and ulcer-ated, they would wait passively in the shallows until going belly up and rotting, or being seized in beak or claw by hawks, ravens, raccoons, coyotes, foxes, or bears.

Ignoring the blistered and bent NO TRESPASSING signs lying on the litter-covered ground, James climbed through a third ring of broken fencing and inspected the channels and pools. Nearly all were choked with the giant gray hospital refuse bags, plus leaves, dirt, and dead branches. The water barely trickled through. The largest pool, in effect a holding pond with a dam, had become a cesspit filled with thick, black, foul-smelling sludge. Glancing into it, James caught sight of an oblong animal trap seemingly dumped there. Above it, looped around the branch of an overhanging beech tree, swung a winch and tackle. "Stay back," he shouted at Taz, "get back out into the parking lot." Looking as if he'd been slapped across the face, Taz retreated on tiptoe.

Immobilized, James stared at the pit. The vision of Jack Murphy in his bamboo cage in the Mekong Delta welled up, Jack's chin barely above water level as he whimpered and screamed and thrashed in madness. A single word revolved in James's mind like a vulture swirling overhead. *Why? Why? Why?*

With a hunted, hangdog look, Taz waited by a downed fence, peering around at the wreckage. "So, like, where's the hatchery?"

Muttering, James waved at the system of water channels they'd seen then turned suddenly, hearing a mechanical sound, a strange yet familiar sound of a car approaching and something else. He and Taz looked up simultaneously to see a large octopus-like drone hovering over the treetops down the road in the direction they had come from. In the silence of the valley, the swirling rotors sounded like hornets swarming around an electric lawn mower. Striding back through the last ring of fences and standing in the pocked, garbage-strewn parking lot, they shaded their eyes and watched the drone zip suddenly toward the gravel road, then fly directly above a compact car that was bumping slowly toward them over the ruts, raising convolutions of grayish-white dust. Before the dust could settle, the drone shot straight up at lightning speed, spun around and flew back down the valley, a mutant dragonfly from hell.

Waiting a full minute for the dust to settle before stepping out of her car, Maggie leaned on the jamb and stared up at the sky. "You didn't order anything else with my credit card did you, Alex?" The ironic tone made her sound like Mae West asking about pistols in pockets.

"Pizza," he said. No one laughed.

"Somehow, I don't think we'll be having our picnic here," James added before Maggie could finish apologizing for being late, or comment on the strange sensation she had had while driving. She knew she was being followed and observed, she said, but could not see or hear her pursuer.

Swapping their expeditionary outfits for normal clothes and hiking boots, then wiping their hands, arms, and faces with an oil-removing gel, the two men piled glumly into the car with Maggie at the wheel.

"Road" was an imperfect description of the trashed, rutted, potholed dirt squiggle that wormed its way up through tatty second- and third-growth fir forests clinging to steep ravines on the flanks of Big Mountain. The average running speed of the low-slung rear-wheel-drive compact was five miles per hour. By the time they emerged from the scruffy woods and neared the end of the road, about three miles upstream from the hatchery, they had been driving for about forty minutes. It was one P.M. Despite the drone and the scene at the hatchery, all three had worked up a more than healthy appetite and, at least superficially, their good spirits had returned.

Rounding a final bend and parking on the edge of a clearing, they were surprised to see a vintage Carverville School District bus pulled up across the way under a stand of mature Douglas firs, the only full-grown trees left for as far as the eye could see. James peered at the windows of the bus and wondered why they were covered with thick iron grillwork.

"School excursion," Taz said, "I remember when we came up here, like, four years ago. But I think there were more trees."

Maggie and James exchanged doubtful glances and made evasive remarks, each sketchily recalling their own excursions to this hallowed spot, where, in their day, teens had flocked at night to drink, smoke, listen to music on their eight-track car stereos, and have sex. Neither had been back in nearly forty years, but both vaguely remembered the well-worn hiking trail to Narrow Rocks and the source of Five Mile Creek, where, in theory, they would find picnic tables and bathrooms and a "sacred forest" in memory of the Yono tribe, whose land this once had been.

"I have a better idea," Maggie said, rummaging in the trunk and producing a worn, faded old blanket. "The picnic area will be full of those schoolkids, so let's go into the woods over there instead."

James and Taz grabbed the picnic bags and thermos and rushed ahead, checking for poison oak and giving the all clear—the terrain had been bulldozed during a recent clear-cut, then charred by wildfires. Nothing green had survived.

The air was cooler here at nearly two thousand feet above sea level, almost cold, and there was more wind than in the valley. Pockets of fog clung to the canyons and hollows below. Vultures and red-tailed hawks hung on thermals in the powder-blue sky. Far out to sea, a wall of black clouds closed off the western horizon.

"Weather is on the way," James remarked.

"Nah," said Taz, "that happens all the time then it, like, never rains."

Maggie agreed. "We've seen those very same black clouds appear every few months for the last five years," she said. "It's a standing joke."

"If I could get up to a Doppler radar website I could, like, check on the thunderheads," Taz added, trying his smartphone again. There was no connectivity here, either.

James shook his head skeptically but was too ravenous, his mind packed with gruesome images from the hatchery, to worry about the weather.

They found a sunny spot on a lichen-etched granite boulder and laid out their feast from the Farmstead Market at the Seaside Mall—potato salad, cold cuts, a sourdough baguette, and fresh-squeezed apple juice. "I'll bring out the coffee and chocolate chip cookies later," Maggie promised.

A quarter hour of silent contentment followed, while each of them sank into thoughtful contemplation of the view and enjoyment of the simple pleasures of food.

As the crow flies, their boulder stood approximately seven miles inland, James calculated, gazing back down the winding road but unable to see either the hatchery or the viaduct on the Old Coast Highway. Carverville lay to the south, hidden by another, lower mountain and several ridges.

"How come they cut down all the trees?" Taz asked, his eyes moving from stump to blackened stump across what appeared to be a scene of endless devastation.

James stifled a snort and let Maggie answer. "You took Econ 101 last year, Alex," she teased. "And we watched those old movies, *Wall Street* and *China-town*, remember?"

Taz nodded. "Greed is good," he said histrionically.

"Someone wants this water," Maggie added. "The whole valley will be developed before long. I didn't have the heart to tell you, JP."

James had difficulty swallowing. "You've seen the permit applications?" he asked. Maggie nodded.

"I guess what I mean," Taz cut in, "is, how come they, like, didn't replant or something, or use the land for something else? Isn't it bad economics to wreck everything?"

"Greed isn't good, ever," James said far too seriously, "and don't let anyone convince you of the contrary."

Taz eyed him, clearly struggling not to challenge the statement. "When the settlers came out here and, like, killed the Native Americans and chopped down the trees and got rich and took over the country, did they, like, replant things?"

Maggie shook her head and let out an unexpected ironic laugh. "They were even more ignorant back then. They wanted to clear out the trees and make farmland and pastures, like the ones they knew back home in Europe."

"Is this what Europe looks like?" Taz asked incredulously. He pronounced the word "Yerp." "No wonder they left."

"They thought the forests were inexhaustible," Maggie continued. "By the time they cut one area another had grown back. There were few people around back then, and it took time to do things like chop down forests."

"Not anymore," James said. "And they had God on their side."

"Some still do," Maggie added.

With unspoken consent they silently finished their coffee and cookies, packed the leftovers and supplies back in the car, and walked toward Narrow Rocks to see the fountainhead of Five Mile Creek, Taz speculating loquaciously on the future role of artificial intelligence. High on caffeine, he bounced along, saying he was of the opinion smart drones and robots could be used for almost anything, from giving massages or physiotherapy to operating fishing boats and public transit, cooking and cleaning or logging and reforesting land and babysitting the young or the aged.

"The drone that followed you out," he said enthusiastically to Maggie, "it was, like, equipped with multiple spy cameras, super high-definition, the kind they had in Boston where they could see the faces of the guys who blew up those bombs at the marathon, remember? Those were first generation. They're a lot better now and a lot lighter so you can put them on a small drone and see everything for miles around, even at night. Sometimes they have heat sensors, so you could find someone who had, like, climbed up a tree to hide, it's really cool."

"Very cool." James grunted. "You could even say chilling."

"You could even arm that drone if you wanted and, like, use it for hunting."

"Or for tracking down wanted fugitives?" Maggie asked.

"Sure."

"And people in the resistance trying to overthrow an illegitimate totalitarian government?"

"Yep," Taz said brightly. "Counterterrorism is already using them. The price has come down so local police departments can buy them. They're almost as good as the military models, but the range is, like, still limited and the payload, too. But it's really cool, it's totally, like, awesome what you can do. I could become a professional pilot. That would be cooler than writing code. We do that in the computer lab, I mean, we, like, have simulators, and we got to pilot a real long-range BVLOS police drone on the football field yesterday. They use the radio station broadcast tower and fly forty miles, Beyond Visual Line of Sight . . ."

"We get it," said Maggie. "I know. It's cool."

"Very cool," James muttered bleakly. "Can you hack into that system, too, and crash the drones if you want?"

"Probably," Taz said, his eyes widening, "that would be even cooler, I'll see if I can figure that out, I'd have to override the Failsafe Return to Home function or crash it within, like, the two-second time limit . . . maybe they're wired into the security video system. We already hacked that, it was easy."

"We?"

"Yeah, three of us, in the computer lab, but don't ask me to tell you who they are, we swore we would keep it a secret."

"Great," James said, "that's sure to remain a secret, all right, three teenagers . . ."

"Sometimes teenagers are good at keeping secrets," Maggie said enigmatically. Taking James by the hand she slowed his pace. "Alex, run ahead and see how far it is to the waterfall, okay? I'm tired." When Taz had disappeared around a kink in the trail, Maggie stopped and pulled James toward her. They hugged. "This thing with the drone is just the beginning, I know it," she whispered. "When we get back to the house we have to talk. I need to share some things with you."

"Of course," he said, trying to sound unconcerned. "We need to compare notes."

They released each other as Taz came trotting back, breathless. "The waterfall is around the corner but it's so weird." He slumped like a tired child on Maggie's shoulder.

"What's weird?"

"It's, like, all these people in pink uniforms are walking in the forest around the stumps, with shovels, and they're planting things, I think they're trees. It's, like, so weird, we were just talking about it."

"A reforestation crew." James smiled. "Better late than never."

"Yeah, except there's, like, a woman and a man in some kind of green uniform, with machine guns and they're, like, watching everyone. I think I've seen some of them before . . ."

Rounding the corner, they paused by the picnic tables. The "sacred forest" of the long-gone Yono tribe was no longer. Scattered across the crest above were fifteen or twenty male convicts in striped prison outfits—the stripes were pink and black, not white and black. They were shackled by twos. Half carried shovels or picks, the other half cardboard boxes bristling with foot-high fir seedlings. On the hiking trail below, the guards had set up two sandwich boards warning DO NOT APPROACH CONVICTS. WE SHOOT AT 50 YARDS.

James and Maggie each raised a hand to signal their presence. The guards signaled back without taking their eyes off the prisoners.

"Politicals," James asked, "or run-of-the-mill felons?"

Maggie dipped and shook her head meaninglessly, her usual tic, as she looked at the convicts one by one. "They could be anyone nowadays."

"I thought they'd stopped using the chain gangs," James remarked.

"Not in this county. It's a local jurisdiction issue as of last summer. You remember the 287(g) Program. Those are probably illegal immigrants. Harvey came up with the pink and black stripes and the female guards to humiliate the male prisoners. I hear the men also have pink underwear—"

"Now I know," Taz blurted out, interrupting, "some of those guys were in the emergency ward, remember?"

James shaded his eyes, stared, emitted a grunt and looked away, his mind filled with images of prisons, courtrooms, crime scenes, and the DA's offices he had occupied when a young prosecutor. "Not good," he muttered, "not good."

Taz had already lost interest. He raced to the waterfall, where he stood leaning precariously over a boulder, gazing into the thundering precipice where the giant ferns and carpets of moss glowed bright green in the watery sun. "Slippery!" he shouted through cupped hands as Maggie and James joined him. She stood back and grabbed James's arm.

"I'm not usually afraid of heights, but this is pretty bad."

"Awesome," said Taz. "It's, like, a hundred yards at least and look at all the water. This must be trickle-down . . ." His goofy face was met by blank stares. "Econ 101," he added.

James peered over the edge at the spring bubbling up and gushing from the side of the mountain, then spilling liquid silver into the void. The wind whisked the droplets into a mesmerizing mist that rose and fell before their eyes, following the gusts of wind. He glanced seaward and saw that the black wall of weather had almost reached the coast. "Let's hustle," he said. "I think the five-year joke is about to end."

James sensed something was wrong as they approached the car. It leaned off-kilter on one side, and as they neared, they could see the two driver's-side tires had been slashed. Inspecting them, James also saw the valve on the front passenger-side tire had been unscrewed partway and most of the air had escaped. So, they had three flats, one spare, and one instant repair bottle to reinflate and patch leaks, not slashes. The equation did not add up.

Glancing around, they saw no one and no trace of lingering dust. Should they risk getting shot and ask the guards for a ride down the hill?

Maggie put her hands on her hips and cursed under her breath. "Now I'm mad," she said, "somebody's going to pay for this."

"Who did it, Grandma?"

Maggie stared through Taz to the serpentine road back down the hill. "You know who did it, Alex, don't be naïve."

"I can't believe there's no connectivity up here," Taz said, divining for water again with his phone. "We could call Beverley or Triple A."

"Surely the prison guards could call someone or give us a ride . . ." James began but fell silent as Maggie stared him down, shaking her head. Checking his watch then rummaging through the glove compartment, he found a flashlight. "We'd better start walking, then," he said. "We've got two hours of daylight and eight miles to cover. Let's grab the water and the rest of the picnic in case we get hungry, and bundle up. We'll come back tomorrow with Beverley's truck and change the tires."

"And then what?" Maggie asked.

James glanced away, unwilling to meet her stare. "Maybe we can figure that out before we reach home," he said. "There's nothing like a little hike to clear the mind."

TWENTY-THREE

They felt the first drops strike about a mile downhill from the parking lot. Pattering like clumsy fingers on a keyboard, knocking the dust off the leaves and brittle branches of the scrub and contorted fir saplings along the road, within minutes the rain turned to hail, then snow, then sleet, then hail, then heavy rain again. The black sky swallowed the woods and road, the wind tossing and breaking its way across the landscape, whipping up windmills of dust and returning them as mud. Leaning forward into the gale, the three walked as fast as the gusts and stinging raindrops or sleet would permit.

Zigzagging like drunkards, they slipped into potholes newly changed into mud puddles. Shouting into the gusts and grabbing at each other's sleeves or hoods trying to stay upright, they each in turn cursed the man who had slashed the car tires and the gods who had unleashed this storm at this moment after years of parched, choking drought. Exploding like a hail of bomblets, the sleety squall ripped the picnic bags out of their hands and scattered potato salad, bread, and napkins into the maelstrom. Vainly trying to order chaos, James switched on the flashlight and waved it, leading the way. Rarely had he been wetter or colder, the chill penetrating until his teeth began to chatter and his limbs to shake as if palsied. Glancing back for the umpteenth time, he barely made out the silhouettes of Maggie and Taz, though they were staggering along only a few yards behind.

At the point where the road widened and the grade began to relent, they heard a rumbling and turned one after the other. Six powerful headlights and roof lights swinging wildly to left and right lunged toward them, raking first one side then the other of the road. Jumping clear, they watched the bus loaded with convicts bucking, heaving, and rocking past, barely missing them. James shouted, waving his flashlight and pounding on the corrugated yellow side of the bus. Jerking to a halt, its single folding side door sprang open. "Thank god," James gasped as he stepped forward. An armed guard, the woman from the ridge, raised her machine gun and ordered him to stop and back away.

"You can't ride in here," she yelled, the veins bulging in her neck. "It's against the law. We will radio for help. Keep walking."

The door slammed shut and the bus rocked away, its dual rear wheels sinking into the mud then spinning and spraying a brown wake of slush.

There was no choice but to keep moving. Gray in the face as he had been at the hospital, Taz seemed about to collapse. Maggie swayed, trying to keep her balance. Clasping them in his widespread arms, James shouted, "Move! Or we'll die. They're sending help."

Another half hour of paralyzing numbness ensued as the hurricane raged and the dark, muddy, icy waters and punch-drunk winds pushed then dragged them staggering downhill. James lost sensation in his toes and fingers. His lips would not move. Trying to shout, his voice died into a hoarse croaking. Four words thumped with the blood in his temples, keeping pace with his shallow, erratic breathing and stumbling steps. "Let it come down," he heard himself chanting, "let it come down."

They had nearly reached the hatchery when another set of headlights swung into view on the road below. Seen through the downpour, the twinkling, swirling orange and yellow lights on the lumbering vehicle's roof made it look like a funfair attraction. Only when a hundred yards off did the keening, pealing siren tear through the sodden darkness before going silent as the SUV skidded to a stop. They flung themselves at the doors, Taz and Maggie piling into the back and James into the front passenger seat. The locks clicked shut.

"Hell of a storm," said Harvey, shouting over the noise of the heater fan, windshield wipers, defogger, and crackling police radio. "Hell of a time to be hiking through the woods." He stared straight ahead through the windshield, his wolfish smile filling the rearview mirror. James could see Maggie's and Taz's electrified eyes watching it through the metal grid dividing the passenger compartment from the front. An automatic assault weapon attached to the grid on his side reminded James he should not be sitting where he was.

"I can't talk," James stuttered at the sheriff's jutting profile, his lips still numb.

"Chilly, isn't it?" Harvey nodded to himself, pleased. "Good thing I came along, I guess." He paused, seemingly expecting them to signal or say something. "Now, I've got to turn this turkey around and get us out before you need a boat instead of a car." Reaching for the transceiver, he barked out his ID and reported he had found the "lost hikers." James still shivered too violently to speak. Swiveling in his seat, he saw Maggie and Taz collapsed into each other's arms. "I'll bet that heat feels good," Harvey said, turning it to full blast front and rear. "We're down to freezing. Hell of a storm, never seen one like it . . . already dumped something like six inches in an hour."

"Someone . . . slashed . . . my tires," Maggie croaked, leaning forward and clinging to the wire mesh.

"Say that again?"

"They slashed the tires of my car," she shouted and fell back as the SUV bucked and slid along.

Harvey's smile was the portrait of demonic beauty, James decided, admiring the way the puckered mouth and fleshy lips were at one and the same time twisted downward, back and to the side. Somehow without changing his expression, Harvey executed a quick three-point U-turn and headed the SUV due west at high speed, no longer fully in control. The four-wheel-drive vehicle bucked and banged over the ruts and holes and hydroplaned forward into the gale, touching down then squirming and wriggling through the mud and rain.

James spoke loudly and clearly. "She said they slashed two tires and let the air out of a third."

"Now, who would go and do a thing like that?" Harvey asked. "Probably the same folks who put those bones in that old cage, I'm guessing, some kind of pranksters who wish you people would up and leave the neighborhood, maybe." He swiveled his head with the studied theatricality James had noticed at Beverley's, then added, "Too bad the drone didn't fly on up the road to where you were, we might've seen the perpetuators at work. We tested that drone today and it does fly like magic, by God, we could see everything up and down the coast, we saw Bev's place and the beach, and we got up to the old mansion and thought, well, why not take a look and see how old Maddie and Alex and JP are doing? But you all were not in, so we thought let's just fly up the valley and have a look at that scenic river before it gets turned into a lake with condos on it and, by God, there you were, Maddie, driving that jalopy, and there were Alex and JP trampling all over those 'no trespassing' signs as if they didn't see them. I'll bet you didn't see them, did you?"

James glowered, speechless, but Taz leaned forward lashing and nodding his head and in a choked voice bellowed, "What signs?"

"Smart kid." Harvey laughed.

"There's n-no c-connectivity in the v-valley," Taz added, stuttering now, "s-so you c-couldn't control the d-drone unless you have a s-satellite s-system."

"Got your drone flying lesson yesterday at the football field, did you, Alex?" Harvey laughed. "Better learn fast, so you can become a pilot. We're buying a whole fleet. No place is going to be unsafe." Pausing and swiveling his head, he added, "I am so glad you are thawing out enough to speak. We can go straight to the station and take a statement if you like, get my boys on this right away. Once the storm lets up, we'll find those vandals imperiling the lives of upstanding citizens out for a picnic."

"How did you know we were having a picnic?" James asked.

"Oh, we know lots of things, JP."

As if in split-screen mode, James watched Maggie and Taz in the rearview mirror, while Harvey, his face contorted with deep pleasure, drove, leaning forward then suddenly frowning at the windshield and jerking the car to the right then the left.

"We'll lodge a complaint later," James said evenly, sensation slowly returning to his lips and limbs. Hanging on to the armrest with one hand and propping himself away from the dashboard with the other, he was about to ask Harvey to slow down when the sheriff started up again.

"Yeah, you all need to get home and have some hot cocoa or herbal tea." Harvey laughed. "It's the herbal stuff you and Sally slurp up, isn't it, Maddie? See, JP, they play cards together with Bev and a bunch of other fine gals. What I wouldn't give to be a fly on the wall. Must be some hellified conversations they have." The radio crackled and Harvey snatched up the transceiver and spoke into it. "We're approaching the highway, at the bottom of the hill by the beach, it's good and flooded out here, I'd say a foot deep in some places, we're going to have to run it and hope we don't stall. I'm signing off." Harvey went back to smiling maliciously and barked, "Hold on, we're going for a swim."

Flooring it, he let out a "Yee-hah" as the heavy-duty Interceptor SUV leaped across the knee-high deluge of water churning down the gravel road to the creek. Momentarily blinded by the wave of mud flying onto the windshield and side windows, they felt the vehicle's tires biting into the gravel and dirt on the other side of the flood. "I don't believe you would have made it out in your little old car," Harvey said, glowing with satisfaction. "I don't believe you would be alive if I hadn't driven up to get you."

"You sound like you regret it," Maggie scoffed.

"Oh, I have no regrets, Maddie." Harvey laughed. "The best is yet to come."

James was too stunned to speak. The radio crackled again and Harvey talked into it, driving up the switchbacks with one hand like a rodeo champion on his bucking bronco. Speaking at James in a hectoring voice, he said, "Now, if you weren't frozen like halibut you could come out and help us, like Pete and Gus are doing with the volunteer fire department. We got a trailer floating away and some other fine people stranded or lost in town, and half a dozen trees and poles down, but something tells me you're going to have plenty to do at the old mansion. Not sure how anyone's going to keep her up on the cliff much longer. I do hope you have a dinghy." Chortling and coughing and choking on his own saliva, he let down the window to spit. "One way or another, she's coming down, the whole district is about to be condemned and reconfigured, ask Maddie, she's seen the plans at city hall." He paused to wink at her, then went on. "We'll have direct access for boating to Lake Five Mile and the condos and casino, a new viaduct, a new highway, and we might even put in a little steam train up to the Headlands, like once upon a time."

While Harvey cackled, they hit the Old Coast Highway and bucked north through ankle-deep water, the storm showing no sign of abating. Crossing the pitted viaduct and following the slippery black asphalt west for another half mile, Harvey swerved to avoid a fallen telephone pole, its top sparking with broken live electricity cables. Then he yanked the SUV into the parking lot at the mansion next to the RV. The water was up to the axles. "You two wade on in and take hot baths while you still have some hot water and a bathtub," he ordered. "It's the best way to warm up. Now that he's all thawed out, JP's going to sit with me another minute, aren't you, JP?"

After waiting a beat, James nodded and indicated that Maggie and Taz should go. "Get warm," he said, "I'll be right in."

"Harvey," Maggie growled, staring him down. Harvey stared back then flinched and glanced away. She slammed the door and, leaning on Taz, limped up the stairs.

The porch and staircase had become cascades, the water tumbling down them like a fish ladder. James watched the two disappear through the front door, momentarily thankful for the howling darkness. It kept him from seeing how deep the water was in the parking lot and on the lawn. He tried to imagine what must be happening to the foundations and the cliff. The gusts striking the SUV from the ocean made it rock.

"This is the big one," Harvey said gleefully, "the one we've been expecting."

"Can't this wait?"

"I don't think so, JP, otherwise I wouldn't be wasting my time and maybe letting some decent folks drown so I can talk to you in private. So, listen up, because I'm not saying it again." His malicious smile reappeared as he fiddled with the heater and windshield wipers, toning down the decibels. "It's like this, your DNA is a matter of public record," he began, throwing James off guard, "and since this is a free country, any law enforcement agency has the right to access it."

"Now wait a minute," James objected, but Harvey cut him off.

"Just let me say my piece. We found scraps of skin and clothing on that razor wire around the trap and we analyzed them. Since the results seemed so strange and everything was so out of character and so unlikely, we decided to double check using the stuff the people at Carverville Hospital collected in a specimen bag, just in case the suspicious individuals who barged in and disrupted emergency relief there should be sought by the authorities." Harvey held up his hand to keep James from interrupting. "We did not know those two hysterical persons were you and Alex, remember?" He paused again to squelch the radio. "Strange, strange, strange, JP, the match up was one hundred per-cent across the board. There you were—it's undeniable who *you* are—making a perfect match with the samples from the trap, and from Beverley's garden and the shack, too, and the motel kitchen and the bathroom and the RV and the hospital.

"Now listen to this, JP, because it's the best yet and I guess at first, I couldn't believe it myself, so that's why I had the tests redone, and that's why I'm telling you now, instead of rescuing people at the trailer park like I should be. The material from the cappuccino kid matches yours, not a hundred percent but high enough to prove in any court of law that you are the father or maybe the grandfather or uncle of that smart-ass mulatto."

James began trembling, more from outrage than cold. "Beyond the offensive rhetoric," he blurted out in his deepest, darkest voice, "the trouble with your theory is I don't have children, and if I don't have children how can I have grandchildren? I don't have brothers or sisters, so how can I be an uncle? This is beyond ridiculous, Harvey, this is grotesque. Give it up and go out and rescue those people, will you?" He unbuckled his seat belt and tried to unlock his door. The latch would not respond.

"Oh, it's ridiculous, is it? Just listen, JP, because I love this part. I say to myself, okay, we have all these half-baked stories about the kid and Maddie and her possibly fictitious son who up and disappeared, and here comes JP back to town all of a sudden. Maybe this is what really happened. Listen up. JP and Maddie have been in touch over the years, no one knows it. They've communicated in secret, JP being a judge and married has to keep it quiet. Like so many good men we all know, he has needs, and maybe he has a lady friend he keeps somewhere, and she's from south of the border, an illegal immigrant or a black lady and he doesn't want people to know she's expecting. Out comes the cappuccino kid, and what do they do with him to hide him away? They bring him up to old Maddie and pretend it's her grandson."

"Ridiculous," James scoffed, laughing out loud. "Absurd. The timing is all wrong. Taz is seventeen for chrissake. I never had an extramarital relationship first of all, and second I wasn't in touch with Maggie, and third the theory is totally false and unfounded and frankly idiotic. Here's what I think, there's some simple mistake being made. Someone mixed up the DNA samples. It's as simple as that, unless someone involved is acting maliciously for some cockeyed reason."

"Yeah, you may be right about the cockeyed stuff, JP," Harvey said, enjoying himself. "You may just be right about that part of it. That's the thing. You're awful good at half-truths and fake news–type stuff, Your Honor. Thing is, we also have Maddie's DNA on record for reasons you don't need to know, and we got some fresh material to sample from her desk at city hall anyway, and guess what? I'll be damned if that boy isn't her son or grandson, just like she's been saying. He's at least part made up of you, and part of old Maddie, with some ethnic stuff tossed in." Harvey let the shrapnel from this bombshell fly in silence. It struck, mangling James's soul.

"It can't be," James muttered.

"Oh, it not only *can* be, JP, it *is*. Now listen here. One of you is going to have to fess up and straighten things out for that boy, and I think it better be you, because Maddie, she's even more pigheaded than you, and she's liable to be hysterical sometimes and tell all kinds of tall tales."

James had lost his voice again. Swinging his head menacingly he summoned a growling scoff, "I don't believe you," he said, "I don't know what you're up to, but I don't believe a thing you've said."

Harvey sucked his teeth, let down his window and spat into the wind and rain. "It don't matter, JP, whether you do or you don't, it happens to be true and I mean true-true, this ain't no fake news bullshit, but I figured you might react this way. I think you ought to go on in and have a little powwow with Mrs. Hansen, and we pick up our conversation down the road. I've got work to do. But I'll be happy to help you all to pack when the time is right."

The radio screamed and Harvey, gloating, lifted the handset and said, "Yeah, I'm heading up to the Headlands, see if I can pull that trailer out of the highway." He clicked a switch unlocking the passenger door. "You better let them know down south we need help," he continued, talking to the dispatcher, "this is the goddamn worst thing ever. Electricity is out most places, and there's some live lines in the highway where it ain't. I know it's already a state of emergency, damn it, call it a natural catastrophe, or tell them it's a hurricane or whatever. Call the National Guard. And send some body bags, too, sandbags and body bags."

James got out and stood on the porch, shivering, watching the downpour, watching Harvey's SUV kick up mud and gravel from the lot then fly north on a highway that had become a black river choked with fallen trees and utility poles. The phrase "sandbags and body bags" lodged in his mind as he walked to the end of the porch and leaned into the gusting wind, watching the floodwaters shoot off the bluff into Five Mile Creek. It had climbed a third of the way up the gully, meaning over ten feet. Its brown waters were fanning wide across the beach, then being pulverized into gray-green spray and mist by thunderous twenty-foot breakers.

Opening the front door and feeling the wind blow past him, whisking magazines and piano music to the floor, he shouted, "Maggie, I'm checking around the outside." He slammed the door shut, cutting off the rush of horizontal rain, then stalked back down the porch. From it he could not see beneath the house, so he ventured farther, unlatching the gate and climbing down the rickety stairway to the first landing. Barely able to stand straight, he clung to the quaking railings and peered up. The visibility was only a few yards, but he could see and hear the rainwater gushing like a geyser down the storm drain and out a corrugated steel drainpipe suspended from heavy wires. *If the drain gets blocked,* he told himself, *we're going down.*

Wading across the garden in shin-deep freezing water, James sloshed to the roadside culvert and began pulling branches and dirt away from it. With a sudden chill, he felt a hand on his shoulder and started upright, spinning around, catching his breath, prepared to fight.

"I brought the rake," Taz shouted.

Catching his breath again, James couldn't help laughing out loud, partly because Taz looked so ridiculous in a wet suit too short and too tight for him. His off-kilter goggles were bright yellow. A yellow snorkel dangled by his cheek.

Together they cleared the drain, then dragged over sandbags and an uprooted tree to channel the water away from the parking area. By the time they had finished, James was shaking and numb again. His limbs felt as if they had been sawed off and the stumps stuck full of pins. He stumbled and fell into the cascading water when climbing the front steps.

The house was dark except for the light projected by the roaring fires in the wood-burning stove and fireplace and two candles in lanterns on the piano. "You all right?" James asked Taz as they squelched into the living room.

"Sure, I'm nice and hot in here." Seized by hilarity, Taz began hooting and piping through the snorkel, doing a rain dance. "I might keep this on," he said.

Slogging into the bathroom, James found Maggie wrapped in a terry-cloth robe drying her hair with a towel by candlelight. Nodding at the bathtub she said, "It's dirty but it's hot." Shivering he climbed into the claw-foot tub and sank down as far as his length would allow him.

"I hope it was you who took the first bath," he said through chattering teeth.

"Oh yes," Maggie said. "You two probably have poison oak oil on you somewhere, so scrub yourself clean and wash your hair twice, or I won't be able to touch you. After you dry off, you can come out and tell me what that bastard said."

But before James could finish rinsing he felt the house shake and heard a booming roar. Taz rushed in shouting, telling them both to get dressed. Either there had been an earthquake or the cliff had given way.

TWENTY-FOUR

Only partly dressed, still wet from his bath, and crazed from cold and fear, with Maggie in a bathrobe and Taz in his wet suit rushing to and fro in the darkness, James raced through the house, trying to put out the fires in the fireplace and stove, turning off the propane valve in the kitchen, then grabbing essentials. He snatched up and struggled into clean clothes, stuffed underwear and a sweater into his duffel bag, stuffed the laptop into a backpack and, dragging his hooded windbreaker behind, caught up with Taz and Maggie already standing on the porch, bundled into mismatched everything and laden with suitcases, purses, and high-tech equipment.

"We're getting faster," Taz yelled in triumph, "last time we were slow like you."

Seeing the perplexity on James's features, Maggie shouted, "We've had to evacuate twice already."

As they stood panting, frozen by fear, reluctance, and cold, the banister on the creek side of the porch gave way, the house started to lean, and the far edge of the garden tilted and slipped into a yawning brown crevice that tore open before their eyes, a ravenous gurgling mouth. Fumbling in his pockets and trying to stay calm, James suddenly knew he did not have the keys to the RV.

"Shit," Maggie screamed, "I washed your pants . . . they're in that bowl on the dresser upstairs . . ."

Glancing into the slanting, splintering house, James dumped his bags on the threshold then ran inside feeling drunk and dizzy. The staircase leaned crazily. Navigating the tilting hallway and forcing his way into the spare bedroom, he found the dresser no longer against the wall. Everything on it including the porcelain bowl with the keys had fallen to the floor, skittering, shattering, and sliding under the bed. On his hands and knees, crawling in the dark, he heard the window behind fly open, broken glass exploding in the wind. Feeling under the bed, he cut himself on the edge of the broken bowl but kept groping and finally found the key fob. Pocketing it, he raced back downstairs shouting as if momentarily insane, snagged his bags off the porch and rushed to the RV where Maggie and Taz waited, hopping from foot to foot in drenched, freezing terror.

The RV had not been started in days. The extreme damp had penetrated the ignition system and the engine would not start. Turning and turning but not catching, with a belch and a roar it finally bucked to life. Revving wildly James backed out blind, swinging the tail of the heavy vehicle onto the highway. He watched aghast through the fogged windshield as part of the side garden and the parking area fell away into the widening dark crevice, a scoop of pudding sliding off a plate. Slamming hard into something behind, James hit the brakes and checked his mirrors but could see nothing. He lurched forward into the shin-high water on the highway and began rolling south.

"What was it," Maggie demanded. Crammed with Taz into the front passenger seat, she could not see out. She thrashed, trying to turn around. "What was that?"

James shook his head, hesitating, full of foreboding. "Probably a tree . . ." he blurted out. Hitting the brakes again, he stopped the RV, reversed, jumped out and ran back in time to see the rest of the side garden slide away, taking most of the porch with it over the melting cliff. On the road ahead, lying on its side writhing and squealing and sounding hauntingly like the howling gale, lay a wounded feral hog, its neck or back broken. It wriggled and squealed, beseeching with human eyes. "My god," James shouted, unsure what to do. *If only I had a gun*, he thought, *I could put it out of its misery.* "My god, my god, my god, why are you doing this, goddamn it?" he cursed.

Sprinting back to the RV, he tore open the passenger-side door and barked at Maggie. "Give me that revolver, I know you have one, I saw it."

"What's going on?" she began to ask, but James grabbed her purse, flipped open the leather flap and found the small .32-caliber handgun. Before she could stop him, he disappeared again up the highway. A shot sounded, then another. Seconds later James jumped back into the RV muttering and cursing, tossed the gun onto the dashboard, and began driving south, his headlights picking out an obstacle course of fallen branches and utility poles, rocks wrenched down from the sloping shoulder of the road, and mud banks a foot high. He blurted out a single, gasping, airless word, "Hog," caught his breath, and wiped his face, only then feeling the blood from his cut fingers in his eyes.

"Roadkill," Taz said in a burlesque baritone, his goofy nervous laugh welling up seemingly from nowhere. "Radioactive and riddled with parasites."

James swiveled his head and stared at him menacingly. "What are you saying?"

"Everyone knows the hogs wallow in the radioactive pits and drink contaminated water and they're full of parasites, too, otherwise people would, like, eat them."

James's face contorted into a pained grimace the shape of a question mark. He was unable to process this latest display of Taz's strangeness. "Beverley's is three miles from here," he said, aware now of the cold seizing his hands, arms, and shoulders.

"I hope she's okay," Maggie said, removing the gun from the dashboard, wiping it clean of James's blood, and slipping it back into her purse without a word.

"I hope the road hasn't washed out," Taz added, his face a sickly gray out of which a pair of bulging luminous blue eyes stared into the darkness. "What if the motel slid, too?"

Twice they were forced to get out and dislodge small fallen trees and mangled outdoor advertising panels, and once they used the RV to nudge a downed cypress to the side before rolling onward. Halfway to the Eden Resort, the right side of the highway had collapsed into a ditch. James detoured onto the soft, squishy inland shoulder of the road, the RV nearly tipping over. Seconds after they had rolled back onto the pavement, they braked and looked into the rearview mirrors. Slowly, ineluctably, the shoulder they had just used subsided, silently slipping into the surf with the rest of the highway.

Flashing his headlights as he pulled into the flooded lot fronting the motel, James honked several times then grabbed his backpack and duffel bag and watched as Maggie and Taz slid out into the rain. The lights were on inside Beverley's office. The distant droning of an emergency generator explained the acrid diesel fumes whipping around them in the gusty wind.

Mummified in a purple raincoat with the collar flipped up, Beverley was wearing phosphorescent yellow rubber boots and standing at the threshold with an enormous pink umbrella at the ready. Pointing it toward them, she popped it open and watched as they dashed forward. "Armageddon," she said with surprising relish, "the Deluge, at last." She bustled in once they had gone past and continued, "Let me guess, you were so concerned about my safety that you risked your lives and drove down to check, seeing as the telephone and Internet are down, or maybe it's just that you, too, enjoy schadenfreude."

Before anyone could speak, Beverley held up a soft, pink-tipped hand and said, "I know you think this is no time to be facetious, but you're wrong, if not now, when? Either you're too scared to sleep in the house, or the house is no longer where it's supposed to be and, judging by your accoutrements and shattered state, that's the probable winner. One way or the other, Maddie's car broke down or maybe you couldn't get through with it on the highway, otherwise why drive the RV?"

Taz goggled at Beverley and bleated with astonishment, "How did you know?"

"Welcome back to Baker Street," James said, relieved to feel the tension draining out of him. "We almost died coming down the mountainside after our picnic, then we got back and the house started to slip off the bluff—"

"Want me to tell you exactly what happened?" Taz interrupted, poking Beverley with his eerily long index finger. She seemed as taken aback by the sudden change in his tone as by his wet suit, snorkel, and goggles. "Because it's a real cliff-hanger," Taz added, then laughed his goofy, spastic Alfred E. Neuman laugh.

It was contagious. Guffawing and snorting, they roared until tears filled their eyes and their ribs ached. "We're lucky to be alive," Maggie said at last. "That's what counts."

"You said it," Beverley chortled, "Just think, if the house was all right and you three were Dundee instead, that might be slightly worse." They laughed again until she raised a finger at Taz. "Now, don't just stand there dripping on the carpet," she ordered, "take this key and get yourself into number eight, take a hot shower and put on some normal clothes or else you'll get a rash from that rubber suit. You smell like an old tennis shoe."

Still snickering, Taz glanced at Maggie and James then took the key and began to slink away. "But," he said, "but where . . . ?"

"But, but what? They're staying in their own room, in a cottage, not Sea Breeze, not yet. Ocean View is just as nice, and you can create *new* memories there." Beverley paused to enjoy the look of embarrassment spreading on Maggie's tired face. "You all get warm and dry and then come back up in half an hour. I'll thaw out another batch of minestrone and put the garlic bread in the oven. Now git!"

Handing James the umbrella and a flashlight, and Maggie a set of keys, she said, "I think you know where Ocean View is. We completely rebuilt it, so it's guaranteed free of ghosts and goblins. Not likely that one's going to slide tonight, and now it really does have an ocean view. Those pesky eucalyptus trees came down at two P.M. on the dot. It was uncanny, like dominoes from left to right, south to north. I'm glad they fell toward the beach and not on me. Maybe they'll prop up the cliff some, but I think they may have taken out the staircase. Go on ahead. You must be more dead than alive by now. When you get back, I'll uncork a good bottle. None of this screw-top plonk tonight. We're going to celebrate. You're safe and I'm safe, and that damn Harvey can't spy on us because the mains are out and the telephones and Internet and surveillance cameras are out, too, hallelujah! Tonight, it's a speakeasy. If only we could get the rest of the cell to come down."

Pleased to see Beverley back to form, James peered at Maggie as they stepped toward the door. He asked, "The cell?"

"Don't tell me he still doesn't know," Beverley said, her fingers going automatically to her pearl necklace.

"Well, he's going to find out," Maggie said, suppressing a yawn. "Sorry. I was going to lay it all out this afternoon, but the storm got in the way."

"Storms will do that," Beverley said, sliding the pearl worry beads back and forth. "Looks like it's about to give up trying to wipe us off the map," she added cheerfully.

"There's no time like the present," James said, not letting them off the hook.

"Well," Beverley said, buying time and glancing at Maggie, waiting for a nod. "You see, Your Honor, in the beginning we were worried because you were the perfect plant . . ."

"A plant? Me?"

"Poison oak," Taz blurted out, leaning back in through the doorjamb where he had been lurking.

James smiled despite himself. Beverley and Maggie laughed out loud, and Taz put on his goofiest face.

"Git!" Beverley shouted at him, watching this time until he really was gone. She crossed her thick upper arms and rocked from side to side. "How could we trust you?" she asked James when Taz was out of earshot. "Here we are, fighting it out in the sandy trenches, and along comes the mystery man, Mr. Perfect, Mr. Perry Mason, the old flame, the avenger, the sharpshooting lumberjack with a heart of gold and a brain of platinum, all wrapped in one tall, good-looking package. Wouldn't it seem a little too good to you, Your Honor?" She paused to take a breath and James tried to speak, but she overruled him with a wave of a pudgy hand. "I showed you the eight and nine of clubs more than once and gave you a hundred hints about the number seventeen. I figured someone trustworthy might have sent you. But you never gave the countersigns. That letter I found in my parking lot was a little too good. Then I discovered you were Harvey's best friend . . ."

James batted his eyes in exhausted incomprehension. "You thought I was one of them?" he asked incredulously.

"No, I didn't," Maggie protested, taking him by the hand. "I'm just too tired to do this right now, we've got to rest and regroup."

"Hurry up your business, please," Beverley said with wicked glee. "I'm thirsty and dying to talk this through."

TWENTY-FIVE

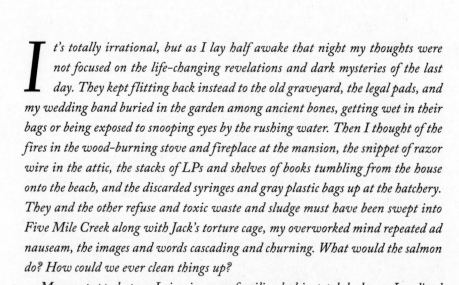

*I*t's totally irrational, but as I lay half awake that night my thoughts were not focused on the life-changing revelations and dark mysteries of the last day. They kept flitting back instead to the old graveyard, the legal pads, and my wedding band buried in the garden among ancient bones, getting wet in their bags or being exposed to snooping eyes by the rushing water. Then I thought of the fires in the wood-burning stove and fireplace at the mansion, the snippet of razor wire in the attic, the stacks of LPs and shelves of books tumbling from the house onto the beach, and the discarded syringes and gray plastic bags up at the hatchery. They and the other refuse and toxic waste and sludge must have been swept into Five Mile Creek along with Jack's torture cage, my overworked mind repeated ad nauseam, the images and words cascading and churning. What would the salmon do? How could we ever clean things up?

My eyes popped open. Lying in an unfamiliar bed in total darkness, I realized I was hyperventilating like one of Harvey's upside-down squirrels, taking shallow panicky breaths. Unable to force myself to relax and get back to sleep, at around four A.M., without waking Maggie, I got up, still unsure where I was. Putting on my clammy pants and a sweater, I stepped onto the small porch of the Ocean View cottage and immediately felt better. The rain had stopped, but the wind was blowing hard from the west. As Beverley had said, you could now see the ocean, a black, seething, *foaming, thundering mass daubed with whitecaps above a jagged, waving horizon line of fallen eucalyptus trees.*

I'd left my sodden boots on the porch hoping the wind would dry them. It hadn't. Struggling into them, I squelched down into the garden on the wood chip trail. Most of the chips had been washed away or had piled up with a scalloping effect. Stumbling, I found my way to the rose garden and the hole where I had hidden the legal pads, but there was no hole to be seen; on the contrary mud and leaves were piled high. There were no bones or gravestones exposed, either, and it seemed there was little risk for the time being that anyone, including me, would find my buried treasure.

Backtracking and heading west to where the shack and potting shed had been, I discovered, to my dismay, that they were no longer upright. Many trees and shrubs in the thicket above them had fallen over, and here, too, the floodwaters had carried down mud and branches, burying everything—the shack, the shed, and the piles of crab pots and old traps. Squinting into the night, I could just make out one of the tattered old blue tarps caught and flapping in the upper branches of a bay tree standing near the bluff. Nearby were a number of sizable white plastic tankards I had never seen before. They looked like empty Clorox bottles. The McCulloch must be buried under there somewhere, I reasoned, saddened beyond all proportion that the chainsaw had been lost just when I had rebuilt it.

Picking up a long branch, I stripped the leaves off and snapped it to make a walking stick. Feeling and poking my way tentatively, I clambered over the heaped-up vegetation and detritus and reached the rickety stairway to the beach. One of the eucalyptus trees had fallen in front of it, and that's probably what had kept the stairway from washing away, I guessed. The night was too dark for me to see the bottom treads, but it seemed as if it might still reach down to the sand.

Standing there looking out to sea, my mind began to clear and the practicalities to crowd back in. The video camera in my head rewound and reviewed the events of the last hours. The telephone system and Internet had still been down at dinnertime, but as we swallowed bowlfuls of Beverley's delicious minestrone and garlicky homemade bread, she picked up on her cheap little AM radio the police and fire and weather reports. The highways into and out of Carverville were unpassable, the reports claimed. Flash flooding had wrecked bridges and culverts, shoulders had collapsed, people were stranded in cars and houses in low-lying areas, the trailer parks were underwater, three condo complexes had skated with the mud into the Yono River by the cannery, several first responders were missing, and so on and so forth.

It sounded like a West Coast version of Hurricane Sandy—Hurricane Harvey, I corrected myself. Luckily, only a few people were reported dead, though in addition to the lost first responders, a dozen residents were still missing, and the toll was sure to rise. I thought of the emergency room staff at the hospital and wondered if any of them were among the dead.

Then the gravity of our own situation struck me. How could we get back to the house and salvage what was left, if anything? How could we help other survivors in town? Like everyone else, we were stranded. If the old dirt roads and footpaths were passable, we could walk from the Eden Resort into Carverville and volunteer our services. And I assumed, without any basis for my optimism, that my bike was still strapped to the roof of the RV and could be ridden almost anywhere.

Then I began replaying in my head the brief conversation Maggie and I had before dinner, and the second part of it we had lying in bed before we fell asleep. We were both too exhausted to make much sense of what either of us was saying, and the many glasses of Oregon Pinot Noir we consumed with our meal certainly helped relax us and enliven the conversation. But it also made us comatose by nine P.M.

"Tell me what Harvey said to you in the car," Maggie had demanded in an unfamiliar, quarrelsome tone once we had unpacked our things in the cottage and collapsed onto a couch before dinner.

"Okay," I said, "we definitely need to talk about that and his craziness, but I think it requires more time and energy than we have right now. So, how about you tell me about the cell instead?"

Maggie sucked her lower lip then yawned, and I realized, with a pang of guilt, that she wasn't being quarrelsome, she was simply too exhausted and traumatized to speak. "Same thing, there's too much to explain, plus I'm famished," she said. "I hardly ate any of the picnic food and that was a long time ago." She yawned so wide that her jaw made a popping sound. I yawned, too, and felt a deep, irresistible weariness.

"If I close my eyes," I started to say.

"Don't. We have to go to dinner in five minutes or Beverley will kill us." She yawned again and shook her head and started to settle into my arms, shivering. "I'll talk, to stay awake," she said. "I'll tell you about the cell. . . . So, it started out as a joke. It was a card club, and since some of us read spy novels and thrillers we called it a cell. No men allowed, women's secrets, our own uninterrupted conversations, you know." She suppressed another yawn. "Beverley and I are the only unattached ones, but since we both have baggage, that didn't matter when the others griped about a

current husband or child, we were good at evoking fond memories." She smiled up at me, then yawned again. "And, of course, there's Taz, he's a handful, and boy do I have colorful stories."

"So, the cell is just a regular hen party?"

Maggie feigned disapproval. "They were hen parties until things changed and the roundups started, and then Harvey was appointed sheriff a couple years ago, and life became unpleasant for a lot of people in the county, including me. He and some of his men are deputized immigration agents. They don't even need to deal with ICE. And then he went and created his own citizen posse of good white boys, like Gus and Pete and Clem, saying everyone was doing it, just look at Maricopa County and how it had worked great down there. That's when the cell became a way for us to share our concerns and organize a local women's resistance movement. We called it The Seventeen Club—that was Beverley's idea." She paused and watched me raise a skeptical eyebrow.

"Go on," I said.

"The password phrase for members was 'What's your favorite number and your favorite suit of cards?' and the right answer was 'The nine and eight of clubs make seventeen.' Since none of us is exactly a radical, we moved slowly and had the benefit of seeing what happened to other groups around the country that organized openly. I couldn't afford to wind up in a chain gang—I had Taz to take care of. So, we decided to keep ours secret, a clandestine cell in what must be the dirtiest, most reactionary, dangerous county in the state and maybe the country, and that's saying a lot, JP. When I moved back ten years ago, I had no idea Harvey would create a reign of terror. And then you rolled in, disguised like a troll . . ."

"I have no regrets," I said.

"You may yet live long enough to have them." She stopped and yawned and I yawned back and looked at my watch. It was past time for dinner.

"To be continued," I said. She nodded and we kissed, then crossed the windswept garden hand in hand.

Where is the pause button? This isn't a memo I'm dictating to my assistant. I'm merely trying to keep things in order in my mind, and it is not easy. I mustn't forget that during dinner we talked mostly about practical problems needing quick solutions, like getting a moving truck over to the cliff-hanger, as we'd all started to call the mansion, before the vandals and looters could get at it. Or fixing Beverley's leaking roof and repairing the washed-out highway and bridge so we could escape, plus dealing with the Greenwood Gulch side of Beverley's property where another section of cliff slid out. Has that mass grave of the obliterated Yono nation been exposed at last, I wonder, or are those animal bones jutting from the sandy loam? To be confirmed, as Harvey would say. The time has come to build a jetty where Egmont's pier was or kiss the Eden Resort goodbye like the mansion on Five Mile Creek.

Then Beverley surprised us all by announcing that despite the storm, for the first time since the cage had washed up on the beach, she was feeling physically and psychologically well, and that the fear of Harvey eavesdropping on her and the voices she was hearing had been driving her crazy. Now they had stopped. That's when Taz perked up and asked what she meant. He hadn't heard about the voices. "There are plenty of things you haven't heard about that you're going to be hearing about now," she quipped. Then she winked at Maggie and repeated to the two of them what she had already told me in the garden, about Number Three visiting her in the night and telling her to sell and move out of town.

Taz listened and suddenly seemed very adult.

But I have gotten ahead of myself and behind myself all at once in the telling. Let's go back to me at about 4:30 A.M. While I was standing alone in the dark garden trying to clear my head, Beverley appeared at the top of the hill and came tearing down toward the Ocean View cottage as I was walking up to it. "Come with me," she whispered in that choked voice of hers, "Number Three is talking again, I swear, I'm not crazy. Come up and get a gun!"

"I will not use a gun."

Without arguing the point or bothering to ask why I was out before dawn, she grabbed me by the sleeve and hustled me up the hill and into her bedroom. "Shhh," she hissed, creeping and tiptoeing as if she might scare a spirit away. "Listen . . ."

Suspended somewhere between incipient, punch-drunk hilarity from extreme fatigue, and genuine alarm, I perched on the edge of her unmade bed and closed my eyes, listening. And I'll be damned if I didn't hear a whispering voice. I broke into a cold sweat, bolted to my feet and began tracking around the room on tiptoe, trying to find where the sound was coming from. Then I stood by the intercom near the door, my heart thumping like the distant surf, and I signaled her over. "Here," I whispered conspiratorially. The ghostly otherworldly voice beckoned, saying, "Beverley? Beverley? Can you hear me, Beverley?" It repeated itself a little louder and sounded suspiciously familiar, though I could not place it. Beverley was quaking with fear. Then the voice went silent and a few seconds later a knock came at the door. We both gasped then froze. I felt my hair rise into a hogback of bristles. Beverley pulled out her derringer and pointed it, her hand shaking violently. The door swung open and there stood Taz, that goofy look on his face.

Beverley slumped and I barely had time to catch her and the gun before they hit the floor.

"What in god's name," I started to say.

"What are you doing here?" Taz asked me. "It's so cool, I figured it out. Did you guys hear me?"

Beverley had revived by then. "Hear you?"

"Through the intercom," he said as if we were dense. Holding up a modular clip-like device, he said, "Bluetooth retrofit to your old system. I guessed that was what they'd done. You can, like, take over anything. A friend at the computer lab hacked into his parents' nursery intercom through the Wi-Fi and scared his little sister a bunch of times, it was pretty neat. I've heard of people, like, taking over those talking dolls and teddy bears you can buy . . ."

Beverley and I stared at each other, then looked at Taz with a blend of ire and admiration. "Awesome," I said. "That's the first time I've ever used that word and I hope it's the last."

Taz's theory sounded like science fiction to me, but I have learned since that this kind of spying and psychological manipulation are not only possible, they have become common practice. The ingeniousness and sheer nastiness of humans never cease to amaze me. Telephone tapping has gone on for decades and everyone knows you can remotely control a smartphone or PC or other "smart device" including household appliances. But who could have imagined some hacker would devise ways to retrofit old TV sets and antiquated intercom systems, not to mention toys or alarm clocks, into Bluetooth devices not only for listening, but also for whispering or speaking to victims in the middle of the night?

Taz said that when things went back to normal and the "backhaul" for the cell network was working, he would let himself into the county sheriff's surveillance system again and figure out what they've been up to. "Then maybe I can, like, take the whole system down . . ."

"Awesomely cool," Beverley said with steely irony. "Somebody just got a death sentence from yours truly. You can't torture the Tater with impunity."

So, Beverley was not having aural hallucinations. Someone was trying to spook her and get her to leave. I could tell she was boiling. Her face flushed mauve, the color of her bath towels and curtains, and she began to wheeze and cough. The only way to calm her was to remind her that the connection had been disabled for the time being. They would not be talking to her in the dead of night anymore, and we could always unplug the old telephones and turn off the Wi-Fi in future if we needed to talk confidentially. "Or step into the rose garden," she said, "with the raccoons."

We decided to get back to our respective beds and grab another hour or two of sleep, if we could. I paddled Taz on the shoulder and told him he was amazing and there was hope for humanity after all. That seemed to go down well.

On the way back to the cottage, while trying to puzzle out why Harvey was persecuting and intimidating Beverley, I suddenly recalled our bizarre conversation in the SUV about genetics, and his absurd claim that I was Taz's grandfather. If true, Taz must have inherited his geek genes from Maggie's side of the family, unless my mother, the straight-laced historian, was a computer or math whizz without anyone knowing it.

The thought of my mother made me think next of the buddleia, and on an irrational impulse, I decided to go back down to see if it had survived the storm. As I picked my way there I somehow remembered the plastic tankards I'd seen earlier and detoured to them. Kicking one free of the branches and tangled muddy mess, I punted it out to where I could inspect it. Down on my hands and knees, I got my eyes to the proper focal distance and was able to read the beginning of the word "Glyph—." Puzzled, I found a stick and slid it through the handle, hoisted the tankard and brought it up to Ocean View. Leaving the thing on the porch, I took off my boots and snuck inside to get the flashlight and my reading glasses. By then it must have been nearly five A.M.

"Who's there?" I heard Maggie bark in the same kind of choked, hoarse voice Beverley had used. I told her it was me and she sighed. I heard her fumbling around, putting something back in her purse. "I might have shot you," she said. The Virginian drawl of her youth resurfaced, as it often did in moments of tension or passion. I was too startled to summon repartee. "Maybe now's the time to talk," she added, "seeing that you're awake and you woke me, too."

"All right," I said, "I'm sorry, I couldn't sleep. Just give me a second." I got the flashlight and my reading glasses and went back out on the porch and read the label off the tankard. "Glyphosate" was the word. Herbicide. Domestic Agent Orange. "Well," I said with weary irony, stepping inside and stripping off my clothes, then climbing back into bed, "at least I know why there's no poison oak on the property. Another big mystery solved."

Maggie stared at me, blinking her eyes in the flashlight beam. "Who told you?"

"Told me what?"

"Told you they killed the poison oak so they could use the property without getting a rash."

"I don't understand."

Maggie stared hard then relented. "No, you don't. So, now I'm going to tell you. Let's make some of that drip coffee first," she said, getting up and climbing into several layers of mismatched pants, sweaters, and a coat. "It's freezing and damp . . ."

"I was about to try to get some sleep," I protested.

"Who can sleep?"

"Beverley can sleep easy now," I said, yawning. "We figured out what those voices were. I mean Taz did."

"Alex? What did he do?"

I explained what had happened and Maggie listened so attentively that she kept spooning out the coffee and filled the whole filter. I watched her spoon half of it back into the can. "Okay," she said, putting the machine in motion. "Now this is starting to make sense. Let's try to join some dots."

The first dot, she suggested, as the coffee spluttered and dripped, was the convenient existence of an isolated, abandoned motel with various outbuildings, direct beach access, and a pier or dock.

We grabbed our mugs of coffee and went out onto the porch, watching the sky begin to lighten. "So, you remember how there used to be a ramp and a dock?" Maggie asked. I said I did, that I'd often gone fishing with Egmont. "Well, the ramp was washed out about three and a half years ago, and the dock went right afterward. Then the county put the place up for auction. In other words, Beverley and Ron Rossi got the motel once there was no more ramp or dock, and it was of no use anymore."

"Of no use for what and to whom?" I asked, letting her do the explaining.

That's when Maggie said here was dot number two. If you wanted to do something like smuggle drugs or people in and out, it was the ideal place to own. She repeated in her own words the outlandish theory about the disappearances Beverley had propounded to me as we stood in the rose garden. It was sounding less and less outlandish, but I still could not see why Harvey and his patriot posse of white-bread cowboys would run the risk of forcing undesirables into old feral hog traps, drag

233

them down a ramp, load them on a boat, and dump them overboard once out to sea. Why not just shoot them in the woods and bury them in a mass grave? Why not fill a bus with them and drive them off a cliff and make it look like an accident? Why not expose them to lethal doses of carfentanil or another opioid or alpha-PVP? And why were they knocking off so many people in the first place? All they had to do was arrest and incarcerate or deport them.

Maggie listened, nodding, shaking her head, frowning, and sucking her lower lip. "That's lots of other dots," she said. The sky was pinking and I could see the property and her face clearly now. "What if," she said, "you aren't taking into account several items you don't have information about?" I asked what she meant and she asked rhetorically, "What if the undesirables, as you call them, came individually or in small batches, and what if they were people Harvey knew and had worked with? What if you were interested in making money by milking the dealers and growers and the human traffickers before getting rid of them? There are only so many drug deaths you can explain or justify, and large numbers of deaths don't look good on the books. And what if you wanted to make sure the bodies would never be found? Shooting people in the forest and digging graves is harder than you think, JP, and so is staging an accident. You know that better than I do. There's always evidence. Dogs smell the graves. Investigators spot them from the air."

"Well," I said, "a cage or trap can always wash up and one has."

"True," she countered, "but who can identify the remains? Who can prove who the perpetrators were?"

"The perpetuators, you mean?"

Maggie laughed despite herself. "He is a sick, dangerous man," she said, "a malign narcissist and worse, a mass murderer, sadist, and serial rapist. He's also greedy and he's gotten very rich. Have you seen his house?"

I shook my head. Taken aback by the vehemence in her voice, I had to wonder out loud, "Why haven't they just bumped off Beverley or us?"

"Who says they haven't tried?" Maggie finished her coffee and added, "It's easier to scare people like us away than jail or kill us. You know that, too. It's messy disposing of bodies and lives. Bev and I know too many people, and people can talk. You can bump off iffy outsiders who have no business being here, but you can't kill everyone in Carverville. Harvey may be the FBI and ICE's point man up here, and they like it when he gets rid of 'undesirables.' But I'm not sure how many good white folks he can kill without being canned or killed himself."

I am not a natural conspiracy theorist and everything Maggie had said sounded so improbable that I couldn't help frowning and grunting with incredulity. I swallowed the rest of my coffee and, without meaning to seem impatient, stretched my arms and legs, feeling stiff in the chill wind. "All right," I said. "Here's another dot for you, since we're playing this game. Assuming your theory is correct, they abandon this place when the ramp and dock are out of commission and where do they go to continue their nefarious activities?"

"It isn't a game, JP."

"I know, I know but . . ." I paused. "Look, what scares me is I think you and Beverley might be right. Have you been to the Headlands?" Maggie shook her head and said she hadn't gone inside since we had, together, in the good old days. I told her what I thought, what I had tried not to believe. "They moved operations up there and used a helicopter instead of a boat. It was even neater. You build or repair the cages out in an abandoned hangar, you trap your hogs and force your victims inside, the helicopter hovers overhead and lifts the cage, and you're right on the beach in a spot no one goes to, and who could possibly know what was in the cage other than the pig, even if they saw it heading out to sea swinging under the helicopter? They might be delivering something to one of the offshore rigs or just dumping a feral hog in the ocean to get rid of it."

Maggie's smile was bitter. "I knew there was a reason I kept on loving you all these years," she said. "I'm glad you figured it out for yourself, so I don't have to convince you. Why else would they put up a surveillance camera on the highway by the old mill entrance? Alex showed you, didn't he?"

Thinking of Taz and how he had hacked the surveillance camera system, I realized now he was deeply involved in the cell. They could easily call it treason and, given his looks and possible birthplace, invent some link to radical Islamic terrorism. "Look, this is seriously dangerous stuff for professionals and it's suicidal for amateur sleuths," I said. "We've got to get out of here while we can."

"And abandon everyone else? And let Harvey and his posse get away with this? I don't think so."

"Where's the proof, where's the body, where's the smoking gun, the DNA left on the chainsaw, the fingerprints, the evidence of corruption, malfeasance, the photos or video footage, where are the eyewitnesses—other than Beverley, whose testimony wouldn't stand up for more than two seconds?" I paused to catch my breath and realized I now knew why the dirty old McCulloch chain had disappeared. Could

tiny filaments of human flesh remain lodged in a chainsaw chain even after many trees had been sawed by that chain? The thought sent a convulsion through my body.

"*And what if we had all those proofs and pieces of evidence, then what?*" *Maggie asked, flushed. She watched me pacing, wringing my hands like Lady Macbeth and making pained faces.*

"*That's the tragedy,*" *I said at last. Without thinking, I began drumming my fingers on the railing and this brought my mind back to Beverley and her summons last night and the interrupted conversation I was trying to have with Maggie before dinner.* "*Somehow we've strayed from the conversation we needed to have. Let's take a walk. It's stopped raining.*"

Maggie assented and said she was about to propose the same thing. We needed to get to South Carverville, she insisted, so she could show me and tell me the rest of her tale—an "object lesson."

TWENTY-SIX

T he "object lesson," as Maggie put it, consisted of marching me into the breaking dawn, down the rickety staircase from the Eden Resort to Graveyard Beach, then south for two meandering miles, over the Yono River embankment on the footbridge and up a looping bike lane-cum-hiking trail to a retirement home in South Carverville. It was a depressing place of sour smells and sorrowful lamentations, with views not of the ocean but of the bypass to the east. Maggie said she had to make sure a certain Jackie was all right, and check that the home hadn't been damaged by the storm. I would understand why soon enough.

On the way, as we walked and talked battered by gusts of salty wind, she told me what she knew about the disappearances, and I gathered she had gleaned her information not only from Beverley but from other sources she still would not reveal. Her sources were either members of The Seventeen Club cell or people in officialdom who were too scared to act but whose unclean consciences required them to confess or confide in someone and come clean.

"Clean" is not a word I would use to describe the condition of the beach or the paths and trails we used. Flash flooding is a notoriously bad housekeeper. It was as if the ocean had finally had enough of us and vomited back the vileness we have been pouring down its gullet for generations. The sand was littered and piled not only with driftwood and the usual algae-tinted plastic or Styrofoam but also with dead *dogs and cats, a hog and a horse already partly decomposed, a dozen or more rusted oil drums, the corroded bent frames of old cars and stolen shopping carts, crumpled refrigerators without doors, coils of cable, car batteries, electrical transformers, an entire chicken coop, smashed crab and lobster pots, and too many tires to count, most of them encrusted with barnacles and tangled in seaweed. We both scanned the beach for animal traps and human bones and were relieved not to find any.*

Though it had stopped raining hours earlier, the floodwater was still running like a stream down the hills we climbed to get from the beach up and under the bypass. The highway looked like a swimming pool dotted with floating cars and trucks. The road surface of the viaduct was too high up for us to see clearly, but I assumed the water level was still too deep for the stranded vehicles to move. We saw no sign of life. "Shoddy" was the word that came to mind, shoddily, hastily built infrastructure, jerry-rigged by the modern mafiosi who have taken over our government.

When we finally reached the retirement home, I was drenched in sweat from the climb. Maggie was obviously relieved to find that the facility had not been seriously damaged. Some windowpanes were broken, and I saw a number of shingles on the ground, but compared with the devastation we'd encountered on the way, this was nothing. We stepped inside at about seven A.M. I was surprised to see the lights on and the staff at work that early until I remembered that retirement homes and hospitals operate 24/7. Presumably they, too, had an emergency power source. The bright lights and forced cheer did nothing to hide the stench of institutional food and soiled underclothes.

Maggie introduced me to a flustered admin woman of middle years who had been forced to spend the night in the facility, she said, unable to drive home. Then we spoke to an affable orderly named Mike, with a tiny ace-of-spades tattoo on his neck, and he asked after Alex. Eventually, we arrived at the fluorescent-lit room on the third floor occupied by Jackie. She is a large, pale woman in her late thirties or early forties, I would guess. Maggie said Jackie has been in the home for the last decade and was a client of hers. Jackie seemed thrilled to see Maggie but also pleased to meet me.

Jackie is mentally retarded, with severe birth defects I find difficult to describe. Parts of her are misshapen and others appear to be missing—most of her right ear, for example, and several fingers. We spoke with her as if speaking to a child of four or five, staying for only a quarter of an hour, walking down the hallway with her, and leaving her back in her room sitting contentedly in front of the television, her faithful companion. I was surprised the TV worked, then realized the programs might be on a sanitized closed-circuit system.

"Inbreeding," Maggie said quietly as we exited, "incest."

The word smacked me in the face, waking me from the other urgent thoughts I admit I was having.

On the way back to the bike path to the beach, I was about to ask what this visit had been about when Maggie fixed me in the eye and said in that low calm professional voice of hers, "Jackie is the eldest child of Sally Murphy, Tom's mother, Harvey's sister, you remember Sally from high school?" She paused. "Need I say more?"

Waiting a beat, I shook my head, then I took Maggie by the hand and led her to a bench overlooking the ocean. Drying off the damp wooden surface with my handkerchief, I sat and pulled Maggie next to me, huddling close in the wind.

"You're not going to enjoy this," I said, cupping a hand over her ear to avoid shouting, "but since you are aware of what went on, I must share what I know." I instantly regretted my lawyerly tone and scansion. Without further ado, I told her in the clearest way possible about the closet and the air mattress and Harvey's boast. Maggie listened with practiced patience and disinterested calm, as I always had when interviewing clients or interrogating suspects and expert witnesses.

"That certainly confirms what we knew," she said. Her face seemed to grow paler than before. "It was not an isolated incident," she added, "it was repeated incestuous rape." Maggie then explained that Sally was not only her friend of longest standing but was or had been a client and had brought Jackie to see her nearly a decade ago at her short-lived private practice.

"Did Sally consider pressing charges?"

A wry look took hold of Maggie's handsome, haggard face. "Sometimes your ingenuousness surprises me," she said gently. She leaned her head on my shoulder. "I think that's another reason I always loved you. For a man who has seen what you've seen, to be able to ask such a question shows fundamental decency." She stopped and laughed at herself for sounding so serious. "The Italians have a word for why Sally never reported him," she continued. "I'm sure you know it: omertà. Don't ask, don't tell, don't ever tell the authorities, and above all, don't ever betray family or friends. The older I get, the more I think families are the same everywhere. It's the Mafia's modus operandi."

Pondering this before reacting, I bent and kissed her lips, then I said, "The Mafia dream is the American dream."

"The American nightmare, you mean?"

"The dream is just greed dressed in frilly clothes. Harvey Murphy is the nightmare incarnate. He's the mirror image of what this country has become."

"What it always was."

"Yes, but only in part, and that part was kept in check by counterweights. Now it's in control."

We walked slowly over to the mall hoping to find breakfast, but nothing was open—the parking lot was still shin-deep in water. So, we headed back to the beach and strode north, eager to get back to Beverley and Taz, though uncertain about what course of action to take.

"What about Tom?" I asked, thinking back to our encounter with Jackie.

"No, he's Pete's," Maggie confirmed, *"so is Annie, the younger sister, though sometimes I wonder if they're short a chromosome or two."*

"So, Harvey got Pete to marry Sally to cover what he'd been doing?"

Maggie nodded and shook her head simultaneously. *"Apparently, he and Pete were sharing her. It's worse than inexcusable, even among adolescents, and it makes me furious all these years later."*

"Don't get angry," I said. *"Anger just makes you sick."*

"Yes," she said, squeezing my hand, *"I'm glad you agree, because I've got something else to tell you, and it's even more important. It explains a lot of things, including the reason Alex hasn't been confined or deported."* She went silent as we detoured around the obstacles on the beach. Glancing up, I was amazed at the ability of dive-bombing seagulls to stay airborne in the gusting wind, and I admired the way they stayed on balance no matter what nature threw at them. *"Cool heads always prevail, don't they?"* Maggie asked a moment later. Again, I agreed, bracing myself for some unpleasant revelation. Sangfroid was essential for survival, I commented. *"Promise me you will keep a cool head and not seek revenge,"* she said quickly, *"that you will not use violence, and that you will tell no one about this, not Alex or Beverley or anyone else?"*

"Tell them about what?" The impatience in my voice was hard to disguise.

"Promise first."

"All right, I promise," I said, increasingly anxious, my sangfroid already strained. The wind was another irritant making the conversation difficult. It blew us off course, catching my hooded windbreaker and turning it into a sail. As we rounded the giant trunk of a washed-up tree, bleached by the sun and worn smooth by the sand

and waves, Maggie pulled me by the hands and made me sit. It was in this precarious posture, with the gale gusting and the waves crashing, that she told me about Harvey and how he had cornered and raped her in his parents' house one day, decades ago, when she had gone over to visit Sally. It was way back when, she added, exactly two days after I had left for college, at the end of a semester break and our last encounter.

I felt the blood rushing to my face, and tears of outrage and frustration filling my wind-stung eyes.

With studied, clinical detachment, but in an unnaturally low, slow voice, she recounted how she hadn't wanted to tell me at the time. She feared I might come back and spoil my semester and never get into law school and possibly do something rash. When she discovered six weeks later that she was pregnant, she wasn't sure if the baby was Harvey's or mine.

"Or Professor Johnson's, you mean?" I couldn't help asking.

She stifled a bitter laugh, covering her mouth then leaning over and hugging me. "Haven't you figured it out yet? I gave you plenty of hints. Professor Johnson was gay. If he loved anyone it was you. He married me as a favor to both of us, so my parents wouldn't force me to have an abortion or make me give up the baby for adoption. Actually, he was glad to have me as a cover—don't you remember how hard it was to be homosexual back then? He was from Little Rock, for goodness' sakes."

I was too stunned to speak. The enormity of it weighed me down. The only thing I could do was hold Maggie and rock back and forth. My head burned with apocalyptic thoughts. Harvey was not only a sadistic swine who abused his own sister, he had also raped Maggie and god knew how many others. And the child, Paul, whose child was he really, Harvey's or mine? Before I could find a way to formulate the question, Maggie said, "Yes, he was yours, I felt he was from the start, but I couldn't be sure and I couldn't bring myself to get rid of him. You never wanted children, JP, you made that clear, and I didn't want children, either, but it was stronger than me, do you understand?" She struggled to maintain a dignified facade. "I was not going to make you go against your convictions and spoil your career by having you marry a teenage girl, a ball and chain when you were up and running into a wonderful new life."

The wind helped cover my sobs. I could not find the words to express the thousand conflicting emotions tearing through me, burning holes in my stomach and setting my clothes and hair on fire. The monster Harvey had been right, Taz was my grandson. All I could do was chant her name, "Maggie, Maggie, Maggie," and bawl, "What a fool I was not to track you down, an egotistic weak fool with bruised pride . . ." I kissed the tears running down her cheeks.

"Maybe I shouldn't have kept him," she said, "I made a mess of motherhood, and he came out so wrong, so unlike you or me, except he was like you physically, and he had so many of your mannerisms, it was uncanny. But he was angry and cruel like Harvey, and something kept nagging at me saying he had part of Harvey in him. I wondered if it was possible my twins could have two fathers, and Harvey was his." She paused and blew her nose. "You must think I'm crazy. For a long time I thought it was an idiotic notion. I'm not a cat, even though he always called me Kitten Caboodle. It was only years later that I learned fraternal twins can each have a different father. It's called bipaternalism. There was no genetic testing then and besides, I had nowhere to turn, I'd left Carverville. I was in a place where the Confederacy lives on, who was I supposed to confide in or get advice from? I was just a kid."

As if in a trance, I listened and could not stop shaking my head. "All I know is, I love you more than ever," I said and meant it. "And all I can do is apologize for failing you then and thinking the worst, but we were so young, I thought you'd jilted me, I thought you loved Professor Johnson. Your pain is filling me now. You've lived a life of pain because of me and my stupid pride." I thought of the long scar on her flat, white belly, and the stillborn boy choked by Paul's umbilical cord, and I shivered.

"No," she said, pulling away and searching my eyes. "It was my decision, I took responsibility then and I take it now for what happened. I should have let you know. But when I did track you down you were married." She paused again then added, "In the end what's important is we have Alex and we have each other again. Harvey knows that if anything happens to Alex or me, Sally will turn on him and turn him in."

We rocked each other back and forth, letting ourselves be buffeted by the wind. Her words played in my head. "We have Alex and we have each other." But I could not help adding a coda, a poisonous sting in the tail. We also have Harvey. His name and the image it summoned made me sick with rage. Who could she report him to, who could arrest or restrain him? Whatever happened, someone high up would pardon him, he would get away scot-free. My hands and voice trembling, I began to formulate some way to express my bewilderment and anger when Maggie stopped me and said, "Remember your promise. I know what you're thinking. Don't let Harvey get between us again. If you try to get revenge, he'll kill us this time. I know him better than you do."

Her words cut deep. They made me feel like a powerless cuckold. I couldn't help thinking, He won't best me again, never again. I choked the words back. "Why in god's name did you come back?"

Maggie kept her cool. "Harvey was just a little sheriff's deputy no one took seriously, JP," she said. "We didn't know he had friends in the bureau, and who could have dreamed up the turn things would take in Washington. I told him if he ever came near me I'd report him and he might wind up with a paternity suit on top of it. That fixed him good. Then Paul showed up with Alex, and Harvey started going after him, and that forced me to prove Alex was my grandson, don't you see? Harvey knew he could check the results against his own DNA, and when he found out he was clear, I had to come up with another way to keep him off. Even when we were in high school together I knew about him and Sally, but I had no proof, and Sally swore me to silence. So, I used the DNA trick on him, I got his from Sally. She hates him as much as I do. Then we got Jackie's DNA and it is incontrovertible evidence of incest. Dr. Dewey has it and so does my lawyer in the city, and Harvey knows it."

"We're not dealing with a rational person," I blurted out, my words sucked away by the wind. "We're not dealing with functional courts of law." Taking deep breaths and trying to regain my composure, I said, "Look, we both agree we can't stay in Carverville. It's suicidal. He'll assume you've told me by now. He'll hunt us down and grab Taz. He might even kill Sally."

"We've got to get out with Alex," she said, her voice hoarse again, her head slumping on my chest as her facade of composure slid into the waves. "I can't believe it's come to this. I can't believe our world has changed like this."

There must be a way, I told myself, to get Harvey. There must be a way to keep him from ever doing damage again. Silently I stroked Maggie's fine translucent hair, the pinkness of her scalp showing through like baby's skin. Cradling her, I stood up, my knees aching, and carried her to the tide line. When I set her down on her feet and bent to kiss her, we both heard the swooshing of the rotors and looked up. The drone slowed and paused and hovered overhead. Then it jerked up as if vacuumed from above, spun counterclockwise like a dog chasing its tail, and plunged into the breakers. We gaped with open mouths at the spot, then sprinted north on the tide line, our footprints scarring the soft wet sand.

TWENTY-SEVEN

They had not expected to find a lavish breakfast awaiting them in Beverley's kitchen. Out of breath and soaked with sweat from their two-mile run on the beach, Maggie and James discovered Beverley humming and smiling as she poured the buttermilk batter into the waffle iron. Taz, seated at the table, fiddled with the twin joysticks on his drone remote controller unit. The smell of fresh coffee wafted up.

"Sit down," Beverley commanded before anyone else could speak. "What's the panic? Taz just got rid of one of those darn insects and no one can get at us from any side." She twisted the volume knob on her AM radio and the 24/7 emergency report flowed out, a sober male basso with a rural twang, intoning names and numbers, damage estimates and warnings. The highways were still out, the voice said. The ocean was too rough for ships to land. The winds were too strong for helicopters to fly. The landing strip at Carverville's tiny airport was underwater . . . Beverley lowered the volume and chortled. "Have you ever seen a sheriff more than one hundred yards from his SUV? I haven't. No one's going to hike in here. We're safe and I have a week's worth of frozen food and fuel, and a month's worth of dry supplies, and the water comes from my well, so to hell with all of them!"

Beaming, she turned the volume back up. Looting would not be tolerated, said the radio voice. Sheriff's deputies would shoot to kill for any infraction of the public order. The state of emergency was now officially martial law. Mobile cellphone units with hydraulic masts would soon be installed in and around Carverville to reestablish Wi-Fi. Crews were working around the clock to get the telephone and power lines back up. If the weather held, the situation would begin to return to normal in three to four days. In the meantime, residents were requested to stay at home, stay calm and carry on—and help when and where they could. Beverley switched off the radio and seemed surprised that no one was cheering along with her.

James shuffled silently in wet stocking feet to the bathroom and washed his face and hands before returning to the kitchen. Seemingly dazed by the surreal quality of the scene, Maggie had plopped down opposite Taz. He was too engrossed in his smartphone and controller to speak or look up. "Just a sec," he said. "I, like, didn't mean to crash it," he added, smiling guiltily. "Next time I'll be more careful."

James began to ask, "It was you—"

"I thought . . ." Maggie started to say, interrupting him.

"We were much more careful about disconnecting that darn camera on the highway." Beverley overrode them with glee. "Taz is a young man of many talents."

"It was easy," Taz enthused. "We, like, pulled the wiring out from below and sabotaged it and then covered things up so that, like, they'll think it was water damage."

As they sat blinking in a state of shock, Maggie and James seemed to be watching a tennis match, their eyes and heads moving back and forth between Taz and Beverley.

Sensing impending chaos and a culinary flop, Beverley ordered them to clear the table and make room for the waffles, butter, and hot syrup, the fried eggs and strips of bacon she was carrying across the kitchen on two immense platters. "Now stop wrecking the sheriff's hardware, Taz, and make yourself useful," she barked. "Can't you see your grandparents are about to die from caffeine deprivation? We have plenty to celebrate . . ."

Taz pushed the controller away and stared into space as if he had been slapped across his goofy face. "My *grandparents*?"

"Yes, your *grandparents*, plural, how can you be surprised?" Beverley asked rhetorically, serving up the food while the others sat speechless. She pointed at the eggs and waffles and bacon and made shoveling motions with her hands while raising her eyebrows like Groucho Marx. "After careful observation and study of your testimony, I've come to the following conclusion." She waved the spatula at Taz. "You've got his hands and feet and eyes and height," she said, pointing to James, who sat with his eyebrows arched, "and you're about as distracted and ingenuous as he is, too. In a couple years, you'll have his same voice, I wager. On top of that, neither of you gets poison oak and believe me that is as rare as an honest judge, apologies, Your Honor, but you know what I mean. You have the same queer mannerisms and Martian intensity, too, not to mention a peculiar brand of pigheadedness. Shall I go on while you let the food get cold? Now come on and eat, all of you!" She plunged in her fork, began eating heartily, and spoke before anyone else could get a word in.

"I'll tell you how I figured it out," she volunteered, watching Maggie then James then Taz lift their forks wordlessly. "Look at the timing. When granddad here left town to go back to college after being here on vacation, conveniently your grannie there pretends to get hooked up with a gay English teacher so she can lay her egg in a comfortable nest where no one will snatch it from her. The fledgling boy resulting from this heavenly union of love birds can only be the son of Judge James Paul Adams, because as I know from Madeleine Simpson's mysterious, nameless depositions over the years, he was her only and true love, though she did have a sticky run-in with some depraved blackguard whose name we're all too familiar with."

"What are you talking about?" Taz blurted out.

"What I'm saying is clear. Harvey could not possibly be your grandfather. Harvey is short and fat and mean and vicious, and there's nothing of him in you, and man are you lucky there isn't. Besides, your grandma always knew your grandad would show up one day, sooner or later, or am I mistaken?"

Maggie swung her head and swallowed her coffee, almost gagging on it. "She's right," she said a moment later to Taz. "I don't know how she figured it out, but she's right."

"It had to happen," Beverley said, smiling her crocodile smile and pointing to Taz. "He's seventeen, it's the seventeenth day since I figured out who the mystery man really is, and when I put all the elements together yesterday afternoon the clock had just struck five P.M.—seventeen hundred hours, ROTC time."

"We were going to tell you, but now she's done it for us," said Maggie, watching Taz.

"I am stunned," James spluttered, sucking down his coffee like a man dying of thirst on the edge of a watering hole. "This isn't going to change our relationship, Taz," he added hastily, "I won't even stop calling you Taz, unless you want me to be like Grandma and call you Alex."

With kaleidoscope eyes the size of LPs, now it was Taz's turn to play ping-pong. Glancing back and forth from Maggie to James to Beverley, he nodded and swung his head in his trademark meaningless way, and smiled his goofy smile, turning his attention simultaneously to the waffles, eggs, and bacon, and fiddling with his smartphone. "It's, like, whatever you want," he said softly, "but I don't think I can start calling you Grandpa or anything."

"God forbid," James said, his face flushing and twitching at the word.

"God's got nothing to do with it," Maggie quipped, stifling a laugh.

"You three can work all of this family stuff out later," Beverley interrupted with mirth, her teeth and pearls shining, "in the privacy of your RV, or wherever you wind up living. In the meanwhile, what's the plan, Sherlock?" She turned to face James, raising her fork and digging back into her breakfast, then striking her patented reptilian smile. "You heard those first responders who died last night were Gus and Pete?" James grimaced and nodded. "Swept away by the Yono, serves them right."

Thinking of Gus's young son, James was about to object out of a sense of judicial propriety and former friendship when he decided against it. "If they did what we think they did," he started to say.

"They did," Maggie added.

"They sure did," Beverley echoed her, "and worse. Remember the hogs! And what about that cage at the hatchery?"

Maggie nodded. "I told him everything."

"Everything?" Beverley sounded skeptical. She snorted while she ate. "Well, you told him enough for the time being, I'm sure. No one knows everything about The Seventeen Club." She finished her waffle in two heroic bites, downed half a cup of coffee in one swallow, and drummed her fingers on the table. Then she served herself another egg and two slices of bacon. "So, I repeat my question, what's the plan?"

The four of them ate in silence for a full minute, and when the eggs and bacon and waffles had disappeared into their mouths, and the coffeepot was empty, James leaned on his elbows, propped up his aching head, and said he proposed to do the following, though if anyone had a better idea he was all ears.

What if, he asked, they were to hike along the beach to the mansion, get two or three backpacks and warm winter gear and a tent if there was one, grab as much lightweight packaged food as they could, remove any important documents and precious objects they could find, then hike back to the resort and hide the precious items here. Provided, he added, that the house hasn't already collapsed into the waves.

"The next step," he said, "is, I drive the RV as far south on the highway as I can get and leave it on the shoulder of the road. I walk back up the highway on the asphalt, then I get down to the beach, probably on the Yono embankment, and walk back up here on the tide line."

"No footprints." Beverley nodded, raising a finger for emphasis. "That's good, Your Honor, that's clever. But so far you haven't gotten very far, as far as I can see," she added.

"Let me finish," James protested. "Meanwhile, you three have packed the food and filled some plastic bottles with water, as much as we can carry. Taz should print out maps of the hiking trails and back roads, from Carverville to the north and east. The RV is a decoy so they think we went south."

"We get that."

"Once I'm back up here, we put on the packs and head north, or we go east first then north till we hit a town where I can rent a car."

Maggie and Taz eyed each other skeptically. "How far do we have to hike?" he asked. James shook his head and said he didn't know.

"What happens when it starts to rain again?" Beverley asked.

"We get wet," said Maggie. She paused. "Where will we go afterward?"

James opened his hands wide, studying his palms and fingers. "I have cousins in British Columbia," he said. "I'm sure they'd welcome us as refugees, they've taken in thousands. We say Taz's papers were lost in the flash floods, and we hope for the best."

The seriousness of the proposition seemed to hit home with the mention of the "r" word. Maggie swung her head and nodded and wondered out loud what Beverley would do and added that they couldn't abandon her. But Beverley waved Maggie's words away with a broad gesture. "I'll take care of myself." She snorted. "I'd rather die than hike in the rain, and I've got more guns and ammo than the whole county sheriff's department." No one laughed, so she added gingerly, "Jokes aside, you three should get while the getting's good. Harvey and the Tom Cat aren't going to mess with me, and if they do, I'll go down biting and scratching. You'll hear about it in the land of maple leaves, or is it maple syrup? Speaking of which, does anyone want another waffle?"

Taz raised his eyes from his smartphone and grinned. "I can, like, run interference with the drones while you drive the RV south," he said. "Then we could rig up a stretcher and carry Beverley with us."

Before Maggie or James could speak, Beverley broke out in uncontrollable laughter, got up and embraced the boy for the first time. Mopping tears of hilarity from her eyes, she coughed out the words, "Do you have any idea what the Tater weighs?" She slapped her thighs and laughed until she was purple in the face. "You'd need a packhorse."

TWENTY-EIGHT

T his time the RV started up right away. I backed out carefully, the three of them watching me. Then I swung south and drove through mud and ankle-deep water at the proverbial snail's pace. For some reason, until that moment, I hadn't thought of the RV as a snail, but now as I crossed Greenwood Gulch and bumped through sludgy potholes toward the Yono River, I realized it had been my mobile shell for the better part of a year. I would be naked without it, naked and defenseless.

My plan had been adopted as tabled, though we had decided unanimously to delay our departure until the following morning. That was because of the complications we encountered walking to and from Eden to Five Mile Creek after our breakfast. It took us the rest of that morning and most of the afternoon. For one thing, we hadn't counted on the continuing violence of the surf. It forced us up the beach onto loose sand. The number of obstacles was daunting, and the filth and stench nauseating. How had a small, isolated community faced by a seemingly boundless ocean managed to befoul the waters to this extent? I couldn't help wondering what the coastline must look like down south, closer to the city. The fumes had a corrosive effect on my eyes and lungs. Though it was no longer raining, the sky was still dark and the breakers so high we could not see the offshore rigs. Had they been destroyed by the storm? If so, that might explain the oily quality of the noxious stench.

The second problem arose in the form of another beached hog trap, then another, and a third. The first was empty, thank god. The second contained green and black lumps of matter covered with seaweed. In the third were the largely decomposed remains of two or more human beings and a large feral hog. I will not describe the horror of the scene—the hair-matted skulls and broken bones jutting from shredded heavy-duty garbage bags, the rotting tatters of clothing and sacking, the jutting pig tusks trailing kelp, and the miasmic, revolting stench. In the state we were in, it seemed miraculous that we managed to continue walking north. A troubling thought resurfaced and swam to mind. I could not help wondering again if the missing Paul had fallen afoul of Harvey and Tom without Maggie knowing it and wound up in one of those cages.

Yet the sudden apparition of the wrecked old mansion hanging off the cliff welling up through the river mist, held aloft by the cables run through the foundations and balanced precariously on the concrete buttresses, filled me with even greater dread than the battered cages. The creek was still raging, the waters so high above the level of the beach that it was impossible to contemplate crossing. Reconnoitering, we decided Taz and I would have to backtrack and scramble up the bluffs to the highway—no easy task. Maggie would remain on the beach where she could see the house. The bluffs were covered with poison oak, and the last thing anyone wanted was for her to have an allergic reaction just as we were setting out to trek across country.

The suddenness of the change in the weather also threw us off balance. Just as we made it through the dense vegetation and up onto the paved road, the wind dropped and the clouds seemed to tear asunder, revealing a milky blue sky. This was great on the one hand—we could now see clearly, and the sunshine improved our mood. On the other hand, we all must have realized simultaneously that the drones and helicopters would soon be out again, patrolling. Part of that would be legitimate: The search-and-rescue missions would be checking the beaches and outlying areas for victims, and probably also checking the offshore facilities.

The other part of their mission might be more sinister. They would be on the lookout for cages, and fishing for them with cable and hook, trying to drag and dump them back out to sea before anyone could report them. This made me worry about Maggie, standing alone on the beach near the last cage and the mouth of Five Mile Creek. I hoped she would have similar thoughts and find shelter behind the driftwood, if an airborne vehicle approached. With the Internet still down, there was no way to reach her by cellphone, and in any case, it was legitimate to assume our calls and texts were being intercepted.

The anxiety increased as Taz and I neared the house and heard the heavy thrumming beat of rotors. Diving behind shrubbery along the highway, we watched the helicopter streak by above us, circle the house several times, reverse direction, then prowl slowly south over the beach from the direction it had come.

Once it had flown south a quarter mile, Taz ran in a stoop to the far edge of the highway and began filming the scene with his phone. I couldn't help remembering those funfair arcade games of decades past where you used a tethered helicopter to fish for prizes in a big Plexiglas tank. Here the helicopter swung around chasing its tail slowly as it dropped the familiar cable and hook and grappled with one of the cages, the one full of decomposing body parts. After several minutes of trying unsuccessfully to hook the cage, the 'copter slowly sank and hovered ten feet or so above the level of the beach. Seconds later, a small man in blue overalls wearing a harness and yellow reflective vest lowered himself from the cockpit, ran to the cage and looped the cable and hook through it. Then he ran back and was pulled up, clambering into the hovering machine.

From where we stood, I could see Maggie behind a tree trunk only twenty or thirty feet from the cage. In her right hand she held her tiny pistol. Would they spot her as the helicopter rose? We held our breath and watched. The rotors and engine roared, the cage was yanked up and swung around like a yo-yo out of control, then disappeared into the blinding glare on the western horizon. Maggie looked up at us and waved. I cupped my hands and shouted, but there was no way she could hear me saying, "Stay down, stay there!" The roar of the creek and the pounding of the waves were deafening. We would soon see if the 'copter circled back to get her. If she moved they would spot her. I waved madly, trying to get her to sit and hide, and then I thought how stupid and arrogant and male could I be? Maggie was at least as smart as I am. She had hidden in time just minutes before. If we stood here waving and jumping up and down, we would be spotted and probably be shot and killed like feral hogs.

With the terrible deafening eggbeater sound of the helicopter already coming at us again, we dove into the luxuriant, glossy tangle of poison oak and coyote bush and waited for the infernal thrumming to let up. As I lay there, my heart beating in time with the rotors, I wondered if they were hunting Maggie, if they would land and scoop her up, or shoot her from above. Judging by the size of his eyes and the terror-stricken look on his face, Taz was thinking similar thoughts.

So, it was with more than mere relief that we emerged from cover a few minutes later and, glancing down, saw Maggie wedged under the tree trunk, only her head and shoulders emerging and visible from our cliff-top angle.

Sprinting to the teetering house, we didn't bother to test if our weight and move-ments were likely to break the camel's back and send the slumping mansion sliding onto the beach. Another, wider crevice had opened between the grassy area and the porch. I nosed the air and smelled decomposition and a smoldering fire. Two twin-faced images sprang to mind: rotting road-killed feral hog and gas leak, plus fireplace and wood-burning stove. A curl of smoke rose from the collapsed chimney corresponding to the stove, and I knew then what I'd feared all along, that I'd failed to extinguish the fire. The stove was an airtight model, and Maggie had loaded it to the gills. Did it matter now? As these thoughts raced through my head, I could see the house shake and slip an inch or more. It was insanity to go inside. We should leave or it would be too late. Then before I knew it, both of us had jumped over the crevice and were standing in the entrance by the broken bow window.

We had talked through our plan beforehand, dividing up the tasks. Taz was to get the hiking and camping gear from the closet in the rumpus room, then go into the kitchen and start stuffing lightweight dried food into the backpacks. Meantime, I rushed into the master bedroom, grabbed a handbag full of documents Maggie had forgotten, then took two stairs at a time until I was on the second floor in Taz's room. The walk-in closet ladder had fallen over and jammed against the wall. I wrestled it up, feeling the house shudder. Climbing at an angle, I pushed upward on the trapdoor above, but it would not budge. Cursing and pounding at it, I finally forced the door to give, and I scrambled on hands and knees into the attic. The dormer window had blown open. I smelled sulfur and burning wood in the air. Tearing up the floorboards, I grabbed the scrapbook and my Kropotkin, the piece of bone and snippet of razor wire and the burned-out end of a welding rod, and started climbing down the ladder, when suddenly everything went black.

When I opened my eyes, Taz was standing over me, shaking me and shouting. I'd never seen him so scared or so scary looking. Looming above my face, the curl seemed to have gone out of his green hair, and the stud in his tongue flashed in the sunlight streaming down from above. His totem pole head seemed twice its normal size. The trapdoor had fallen and knocked me out, he shouted.

As we picked up the scattered scrapbook, bones, razor wire, and welding rod, the house lurched westward. We froze. The air was filled with smoke. Then we both leaped to our feet and tore downstairs. Taz had found the tent and clothing and packs. We rushed past the wood-burning stove into the kitchen, flung open the cupboards and began stuffing crackers and packages of instant soup and roasted cashews and bags of raisins into our packs and pockets, when the west side of the house buckled and the porch broke free and slid. Through the kitchen's broken windowpanes, we could see splintered glass and wood raining from the upper stories, and we snatched up what we could and ran out onto the highway. This time the mansion was going down, I knew it.

"The door of the stove was open," Taz said, his teeth chattering with fear. "I should go back. . . ." Shaking my head in answer, I grabbed him by the sleeve and pulled him along. We backed away and started running down the highway. That's when I spotted Maggie on the beach below and heard the helicopter again. We dove to the side of the road and turned in time to see the house implode, catch fire, and slide toward Five Mile Creek, the 'copter chasing its tail directly above the burning roof.

Then the real spectacle began. With sparks flying from the roof, the propane gas tank next to the house was dragged by its pipes into the flaming wreckage and exploded with such force it knocked me on my back into the bushes. Bursting flames shot into the sky, the blaze scorching the low-flying helicopter, setting its tail and engine on fire. Roaring westward out to sea with tongues of fire pouring out of its back, the helicopter went orange and black as if struck by lightning, and a thunderous blast followed as a thousand jagged pieces of Plexiglas and twisted steel spun and sizzled through the air. I watched, fascinated, while the shredded blue overalls and smoking, mangled bodies of the two-man crew drifted like parachute troopers down and around and around again, splashing into the raging creek.

His mouth gaping and lungs gasping for air, Taz had been filming the scene and only now seemed to realize what he had witnessed. Waving wildly at Maggie emerging from her hiding place on the beach, we tore down the bluff and stood side by side, staring dumbly at the smoldering wreckage of the helicopter and the house. With a creaking, bellowing animal wail, the remnants of the old mansion subsided into Five Mile Creek and were ripped apart and carried board by board across the beach and into the ocean waves.

My first impulse was to hug Maggie, but Taz and I were covered with poison oak oil and she was still clutching her pistol tight in her right hand. So, we stood apart, looking on helplessly as our lives and our memories disappeared.

The above may explain why we had to postpone our departure. By the time we made it to the Eden Resort, cleaned ourselves up, repacked, and hid our precious documents and hardware, it was dusk. We were beyond exhausted and dropping with hunger. Despite the fatigue, getting to sleep proved a challenge, and I for one woke up feeling more tired than I ever have.

So, when at dawn we breakfasted quickly and silently then parted, and I piloted the RV south toward the Yono embankment, I was in no condition to put up another fight. My hope was I would encounter no one and be back at the Eden Resort by eight A.M. That would give us a full day to hike, and if the rain stayed away and no one came after us, we could cover anywhere from ten to fifteen miles before looking for a place to camp.

The thought of the hike—I preferred to think of it in those terms instead of as an exodus—buoyed me. Somehow, I found the energy to navigate the RV down the highway, park it and leave enough tracks in the mud heading south to throw them off for a while, I hoped. I doubled back north, tramping through puddles on the paved surface so as not to leave muddy footprints, then jumped from the last puddle into the shrubbery, and slid down to the bike lane leading to the banks of the Yono River and from there to the beach.

It must have been my state of deep preoccupation and anxious exhaustion, and the noise of the rushing river, that prevented me from sensing the flashing roof lights and hearing the SUV as it approached from behind. We were almost at the point where the low concrete seawall of the embankment meets the sand, with a drop of six feet or so into the Yono's raging waters. Why would I expect anyone to drive down a bike lane at dawn without sounding a horn?

Jumping clear at the last second, I turned and saw the SUV a couple feet behind, then I rolled to the side and watched the vehicle brake and skid, jerking over at an angle. The driver's door swung open and a cane appeared, followed by Harvey's legs. I could hear the police radio squawking. Swiveling his bulk and stepping heavily out of the car, Harvey smiled and glowered at me in one spine-tingling glance painted yellow and red by the spinning rooftop lights.

"Fancy meeting you here, JP," he chortled. I could see his coat was drawn back and his holster open. "Out for some early-morning exercise while the world goes to hell?" He snorted and cackled for emphasis and added, "Where's Maddie? Gone up in flames along with that goddamn house of yours?" Using his cane for a pointer, Harvey signaled me over to the seawall above the river. "Sit down my friend," he said with false bonhomie. "We've still got some catching up to do, and I think this may be our last opportunity."

I did as he ordered, my eyes unconsciously glued to the outsized handgun in his holster. "Over there," he barked, poking at me with the cane. "Let's get comfortable. I've been looking forward to this."

"I heard about Gus and Pete," I said.

"Yeah, I'll bet you did, who didn't? It was on the radio. We stretched nets out down here but all we caught were some waterlogged trees and a couple dead sea otters." Raising his cane, he indicated the seawalls on both sides of the river. That's when I noticed the nets. They looked like badminton or volleyball nets that somehow had been stretched across the embankment and anchored on each side.

"Yeah," he started up again, "I came down to see if we'd caught anything this morning and look who I find come down to help. Thank you, JP, thank you in advance for your kindness and your concern. Maybe you thought we'd find Sam and Clem in there, too? Nah, you know better." Laughing with sinister relish, Harvey spit into the river and lumbered forward, perching on the seawall and then facing me, the gun now in his hand. "Come on down where I can see you, JP. The water's pretty loud. I don't like to shout."

Again, I obeyed, wracking my brain, trying to figure out what to say and how to escape. "Maggie is fine," I blurted out, "but the house is gone."

"Fuck the house," Harvey raged. "Sam is dead, too, he was in that 'copter and so was Clem, goddamn it."

Nodding lamely, I forced myself to take a deep breath through my nose and try to appear calm. I opened my mouth, but Harvey cut me off.

"So, Maddie's all right, is she," he said flatly, tapping the wall with his cane and swiveling his head back and forth, back and forth, as if his neck was sore. His eyes never left mine. "It's a funny thing, JP. Everyone else called her Maddie, but you always called her Maggie and you still call her Maggie. People are glad to call me Harv, but for you it's always Harvey. That's how it is across the board, except for Gus and Pete and Clem because those are their God-given names, goddamn it. Maddie or Maggie, which is it? You always were different, and difficult, and diffident, and now you're some kind of dissident, aren't you?"

I couldn't help smiling ironically. "I never knew you to play with words, Harvey," I said, and took another deep breath, "congratulations."

"Oh, I know, you always thought I was a dumb fuck, but I've done all right for myself." He spoke in what passed for an affable tone. "I'm not so sure you're in for a happy ending, after all your shining brilliance." Pausing, he rapped the cane on the ground, moving it up and down, up and down in his massive left hand. The folksy tone had gone out of his voice. "Let's cut the crap, JP, I'm getting tired of this."

"That makes two of us."

"Good, we finally agree. So, tell me, have you ever been in a helicopter?"

I hesitated, but seeing we were in an endgame, I said, "Only inside, never dangling underneath."

Grunting, Harvey sucked his teeth, spit again and said, "Good, so you do know. That saves us time."

"I'm all for it. We're both busy men. One of us has to get back to it." I paused. "Tell me something," I said in my earnest, lawyerly voice. "Was it you who came up with the idea or was it Clem or Pete or Gus or someone in the bureau?"

Harvey thundered out a belly laugh and struck at my legs with the cane. I moved in time to save my knees but felt the wooden tip smack painfully into my lower left thigh. Wincing, I repressed a shout and glared at him. "That's a heap of questions in one, JP," he said as if nothing had happened. "But since you won't likely be sharing the answers with anyone except the Lord or Charlie the Tuna, I'll tell you. Pete and Gus didn't have ideas. They never owned an idea in their lifetimes, bless their souls. Clem was smart, he was as sharp as you. He thought I was his flunky, but he had no flair, if you see what I mean. He was an editor, he fixed things other people wrote, and told stories about other people's lives, so maybe he tweaked the plan I came up with, the master plan, and made it better, but it was mine, all mine. My friends in the bureau said they'd be sure they never knew. 'We have no knowledge and no recollection,'" Harvey mimicked in a theatrical voice, and laughed sardonically.

"I'll tell you why I'm going to lay it out now, JP. Either you're dead this morning and, in that case, it don't matter a tinker's damn, or I am, and then it sure don't matter to me. Either way, I have the pleasure of sharing with a true connoisseur, a real sophisticate from the city."

"If it wasn't for that gun, you know I would thrash you."

"Yeah, maybe, but the gun is here where it should be, and I suspect you've seen what a body looks like once a .45 has been at it. So, relax and enjoy, JP, it's going to get worse." Pausing to snicker and spit, he hefted the cane trying to get me to cringe. Then he laughed a hyena laugh. "I just want you to know how much fun your grandson is going to have in the county jail before he has his tragic accident. And I also want to reassure you that our dear Maddie, our old Kitten sweetheart, won't be alone. She'll always have Harv to take care of her."

Before I knew it, I'd scoffed and jumped up and was laughing at him savagely. "You think you can go back to screwing your sister and Maggie? Wait and see, Harvey. They'll cut your little dick off. Jackie will live to spit on your grave."

"But you won't." He grinned. "I'm glad to see you've still got the fighting spirit, JP. There's one last thing you need to know. Those bones in that ugly old cage of yours? I almost told you the other day, but I decided to save it for dessert. Well I'll be damned if those bones didn't still have some meat on them, a chunk of stuff up on the gums between the teeth. Imagine that, after all these years. And now, who do you think that lucky piece of dead meat was, JP? I'll give you a hint. He was the son of a bitch and a bastard, and he screwed a nigger squaw, and I'll be damned if he wasn't your kith and kin, your very own son. Now you go and put that in a movie and people will complain and want their money back, but that's the damnedest thing about life, JP, it's stranger than any movie I've seen. I've done the world a big favor. I've gotten rid of a whole tribe of treacherous, subversive terrorists." He stopped smiling and waved the gun, grunting at me threateningly.

"Go on and get up on the end of that wall, JP, so I can kill you clean in one shot. Otherwise I'll have to shoot off one piece at a time and make you crawl, because I ain't going to drag you. Go on, over there, so you don't wind up in the nets."

Buying time, I said, "They know I'm here, everyone knows."

"Oh, everyone, now," he snarled. "Who's that and who cares? Go on, right over there to the edge . . ."

The seawall was only a foot higher than the bike lane, and as I stepped up and turned I heard a thrumming, whirring sound nearby and so did Harvey. He looked up and smiled wide. "Isn't that beautiful," he blurted out, getting to his feet and beaming like an angel. "Isn't that great? Tom gets to watch, and it'll be on video, just like a snuff movie. I think I'll show it to Taz and Maddie, show them how JP got blown away by stupid old Harvey Murphy." He waved at the drone and said, "Do salmon eat dead things, JP?" The drone hovered closer, its lenses moving in and out.

"Crabs do," I said, "bottom-feeders and shit-eaters like you." I bellowed at him, about to spring. Harvey raised his pistol and shot at the ground between my legs. He raised it higher, smiling beatifically, but the drone dove at his arm and knocked him off balance. The shot grazed my windbreaker. I jumped down from the wall and ran toward him. Stunned and still off balance, Harvey struck out with his cane, waving it in the air and batting at the drone. But it rose vertically out of reach, then dove again and rammed him in the face. Stumbling backward over the seawall and pitching into the Yono River, Harvey shouted and grappled to stop his fall. A shot rang out. I dove and grabbed at his ankles, catching his left boot near *the heel. Struggling to pull him back up, his screams sounding like the keening of a stuck pig, I heard the gun go off again and felt a bullet fly past, grazing my shoulder. With a slippery, sickening twist of tendon and flesh, his boot came off in my hands, and I watched as he fell screaming into the current.*

Chasing its tail around and around above me, the drone flew up then dove into the river after him, leaving me alone on the seawall with the SUV, its driver's door still open and roof lights swirling to the squawking and crackling of the police radio.

POSTSCRIPT

Y ou will want to know what I did with the boot. I threw it in the Yono, put the SUV in drive, wiped off my prints, and watched the vehicle roll down the bike path, bump its way across the beach, and disappear into the surf.

Back at the Eden Resort, the trekkers were ready for anything. They had watched the showdown live on Taz's smartphone screen. I told them I was going to unpack and asked Beverley if we could do a swap: hard labor for the use of the Ocean View and Sea Breeze cottages for six months. We'd have fun fixing them and digging out the garden. There was a breakwater to build. We might even figure out how to re-create a ramp and a dock on Greenwood Gulch and do some archeological excavations. Now that Beverley was going to be the mayor pro tem, she'd have no trouble with permits.

I pulled the McCulloch out of the mud and cleaned it inside and out. It never worked better. I haven't told anyone what it was used for by Harvey, and I haven't mentioned that the skull and thighbone are Paul's. The blissful ignorance won't last.

Taz is finishing community college a year early and could already teach his courses. He got that driver's license after all. It's amazing what you can find in an archive if you look hard enough, a birth certificate, for instance, not to mention what can be lost, like a developer's construction permit. Meanwhile, Maggie has revived her private practice. The Tom Cat is her latest client. She has special permission to see him behind bars at the county jail, before he's shipped to a federal penitentiary.

Oh, and The Seventeen Club has gone out of county, with cells multiplying, clusters of unkillable, resilient resistance cells that one day will grow into a renascent democracy.

Of course, there is no Carverville and never has been. But if you paint some redwoods into the picture, knock together several real places I know on the Northern California coast, in the Sierra Nevada and the Pacific Northwest, then change the names not to protect the innocent but to satisfy curious readers, I think you'll figure out where and what the place is.

As to me, I still don't know why Holmes was obsessed by the number seventeen or what crime Mark Twain committed in the eyes of Ronald Rossi, Beverley's Number Three. One day I'll find out. In the meantime, I am pruning roses, making cuttings from them and the buddleia, and trying to figure out how to get those fish back up our rivers. I'm too old to spawn, but I'll be damned if I don't drop dead happy one day in the middle of Five Mile Creek.

ACKNOWLEDGMENTS

With thanks and love to A. M. H. for her encouragement and unflagging aid, to E. M. for her early readings and exquisite words, to J. S., A. J. B., P. A. T. and B. M. for their perceptive, helpful comments, and to J. R. S. for being such a fine friend for over fifty years.

I would also like to thank my enthusiastic editor Jessica Case-Hancock and my wonderful agent Alice Fried-Martell for their wisdom, patience and generosity. The affable Donald Bordenave of OPC Drone Services of California provided the essential information on drones and cellular telephony.